## NAZI STRIKE FORCE

Colonel Ed Gripper dropped to the ground behind the boulder when he heard the men's voices. He hoped he hadn't been spotted. He crawled to the far side of the boulder and lifted himself up.

There were three of them and they were wearing German uniforms—the kind worn by soldiers of Rommel's Afrika Korp.

"But what the hell are they doing here?" Gripper asked himself.

And suddenly there wasn't any doubt in his mind that the men were part of a German strike force heading north to the Texas border. How the force had gotten to the middle of the Mexican desert didn't interest him. All he knew was they were here to invade the United States and that he had to get back to Fort Bliss and warn General Hanahan that the General's war games were ov[illegible] the *real* war had already started!

# OPERATION ZIMMERMANN

BY FRANK GERON

ZEBRA BOOKS
KENSINGTON PUBLISHING CORP.

ZEBRA BOOKS

are published by

Kensington Publishing Corp.
475 Park Avenue South
New York, NY 10016



First printing: May 1986

Printed in the United States of America

*"There are few die well that die in a battle."*
*Henry V*
William Shakespeare

# Prologue

*August, 1985*

Douglas Turk put the phone down and shook his head. "I sure as hell don't understand this," he muttered; then, looking at his wife, he said in a louder voice, "Some joker just told me the number I dialed wasn't John Pike's."

"You could have made a mistake," Lauren suggested from the bed where she was resting, propped up by two pillows.

"I dialed the same damn number I dialed last night in New York," Turk growled. "Pike is supposed to meet us for cocktails this evening, at about four."

"Do you want me to try?" she asked.

"No."

"Something could be wrong with the telephone lines," Lauren said.

Turk rubbed his right hand across his chin. "That's probably it," he agreed and picking up the phone again, he dialed the operator.

"How many years has it been since we've been back here?" Lauren asked.

"Too many to remember," Turk answered.

"Were we ever that young?" she asked.

"Must have been," he said. "We sure as hell must have been."

The operator came on the line. "May I help you," she asked with a distinctive southwestern drawl.

"I hope so," Turk answered. "I've been dialing six two four three eight five nine and I was told—"

"That number has been disconnected," the operator said.

"It couldn't be. I just spoke—"

"That number has been disconnected," the operator repeated.

"When?" Turk asked.

"I have no record of that," the woman replied.

"But I spoke to Mr. Pike at that number last night," Turk said, trying hard not to become angry.

"Perhaps a supervisor might be able to help you?" the operator suggested.

"Yes, let me speak to your supervisor."

"Please hold . . ." the operator said.

Turk put his hand over the mouthpiece. "I was just told that the phone was disconnected."

"I gathered as much," Lauren responded.

Turk frowned. "I didn't come all the way down here to El Paso from New York—"

"I'm Mrs. Williams," the voice on the other end said. "May I help you?"

Turk explained the problem.

"That number is disconnected," Mrs. Williams said.

"But I spoke to Mr. Pike last night from New York," Turk told her. "It was in service then."

"I'm sorry, sir, but that phone is no longer in service."

"Since when?" Turk exploded angrily. "I want to know when that damn number was disconnected."

"I'm sorry, sir, but I don't have that information."

"Is there anyone who can tell me when the phone was disconnected?" he shouted.

"You'll have to write to our central office for that information," the supervisor said.

"I don't have time to write to any damn central office," Turk stormed. "I want to know now!"

Lauren left the bed and gently wrested the phone from Turk's hand. "Thank you," she said to the woman on the other end, then placed the phone back into its cradle. "Now why were you yelling at that woman?" she asked.

Turk didn't answer. He moved away from the desk, where the phone was, and crossing the room to the window, looked down on the busy sunlit street, fourteen floors below.

Turk was a rangy man of seventy, with a full head of white hair, a neatly trimmed white beard, and steel-gray eyes. "I don't like it when I'm being given the run-around," he said crankily. "And furthermore," he continued, facing her, "I came down here to do two things: one is to meet with Pike, and other is to—"

"You never did tell me why you have to meet with Mr. Pike," Lauren said. "Maybe it's time you should."

Turk shook his head. "I'll tell you when the time is right," he said. "And now is not the right time."

Lauren sighed. She knew he wouldn't tell her anything until he was ready. "You're just as stubborn as a mule," she told him.

"I will tell you," he said. "I promise."

"As for the woman on the phone," Lauren said, "she

was only telling you what she tells other people who ask about other disconnected phones."

"I know that."

"Then you shouldn't have yelled at her."

"I'm sorry," Turk said.

"Don't tell me."

"Well, I sure as hell can't tell her," Turk answered.

Lauren smiled. Five years younger than Turk, she was still a very attractive woman. Her hair, like his, was white; she wore it piled up in a bun on the back of her head. Her eyes were blue and full of laughter.

"Okay," Turk said, "okay. I promise to control myself."

"A real promise?"

"A real one," he responded.

"My suggestion," Lauren said, "is to wait until after four o'clock. If your Mr. Pike doesn't show, we'll decide then what to do. . . . In the meantime we'll do whatever that other thing is you want to do."

"Put flowers on Manuel's grave," Turk said.

Turk bought two dozen roses for himself and a large bouquet for Lauren in the hotel florist shop; then he rented a car to drive out to the cemetery, which was located three miles to the southwest of Juárez.

"Aren't you going straight to the bridge?" Lauren asked, as Turk turned off Santa Fe Street, away from the bridge that would have taken them into Mexico.

"Estaban!" Turk answered. "I'm sure he'd want to come with us."

Lauren leaned over and kissed him on the cheek. "You're really an incredible man," she said softly. "And I love you."

"Even if I bark at telephone supervisors?" he asked, grinning at her.

"Yes," she answered. "And even if you still haven't told me why you have to meet with Mr. Pike."

Turk turned into a street that ran parallel to the railroad yards. "I remember Estaban's luncheonette was somewhere along here," he said.

"Your memory is better than mine," Lauren commented.

"This part of the city hasn't changed—it's still as dirty as when I first saw it more than forty years ago."

"Up ahead on the right . . . That looks like a place to eat," Lauren said. "Could that be it?"

Turk slowed down and came to a stop directly across from a shabby looking diner. "Must be the place," he said. "You wait here and—"

"I'm not going to sit in the car by myself," Lauren told him.

"Okay, c'mon," Turk responded as he closed his door and stretched. He went around to the other side of the car to help her out. "I don't remember it being so hot," he commented.

"We were here in December and now it's mid-July," Lauren said.

Holding hands they crossed the street, and paused in front of the diner.

"My God, it's shabby looking," Turk said.

"Not even a name," Lauren commented. "And the windows look as if they haven't been washed for years."

"They probably haven't," Turk said, moving forward again.

"Do you think he'll remember? . . ."

"Estaban will remember—if he's here," Turk said confidently, as he opened the door and stepped across the threshold.

The air inside was filled with the pungent odor of garlic and chili. The labored whirring of an old air-conditioner was the only sound in the place. Two dark-complexioned men sat at the counter. They turned to look at Turk and Lauren.

"This might be a mistake," Lauren whispered.

Turk didn't answer.

The men at the counter continued to stare at them.

"Just follow me," Turk said in a low voice to Lauren.

"The only other choice I have is to run, and I'm too old to that."

Turk stopped a smile that was beginning to form, and walking to the counter, he said in Spanish, "Excuse me, could you tell me where Señor Estaban is?"

The men looked surprised.

"We're old friends," Turk continued in Spanish, pleased he could still speak the language even though he hadn't spoken it for many years.

One of the men pointed to the door separating the kitchen from the eating area.

Turk nodded, thanked them, and going behind the counter, he pushed the door open. "José, you have visitors," he called in Spanish. "Better get your ass out here."

The men at the counter chortled and poked each other in the ribs.

"Son of whore," Estaban yelled, "can't a man even take a crap without being bothered?"

Turk grinned and retreated to the other side of the counter. "Estaban," he yelled, Have your balls shrunk so much that you forgot when you were a man and knew other men?"

The two men at the counter laughed so hard they

began to cough.

"Now," Estaban said, charging through the swinging door, "who's braying like donkey?"

"Me," Turk answered.

Estaban stopped. His black eyes went from Turk to Lauren and back to Turk again. He was a heavyset man, with a bald pate and a deeply wrinkled face. He wore a dirty apron around his middle. "Turk? . . . Lauren? . . ." he asked.

"Yes," Turk answered.

Estaban stepped forward and wrapped his arms around Turk, kissing him on both cheeks. "You came back. . . . After all these years, you came back."

"We never forgot you, José," Lauren said, finding herself in Estaban's embrace.

Suddenly Estaban turned to the men at the counter. "These are my friends," he said, "—so what the fuck are you staring at?"

The men turned away.

"We're going to put flowers on Manuel's grave," Turk explained. "And I thought you'd like to go with us."

Estaban nodded. "It'll take a few minutes for me to close up."

"We're in no hurry," Turk answered.

Fifteen minutes later, Turk, Lauren, and Estaban crossed the street to the car.

"José," Lauren said, "sit up front with Doug."

"No . . . No, you—"

"It's all right," Lauren said. "I can stretch my poor old legs in the back."

As soon as the three of them were settled in the car, Turk switched on the ignition and pulled away from the curb. A few minutes later they were in one of the many lines of traffic converging on the Santa Fe bridge.

The conversation between the three of them moved easily between Spanish and English.

Turk learned that Estaban's son had been killed in Nam and that his wife had died the previous year.

"Now," Estaban said, "I have three graves to visit on the feast days."

"Thank you for visiting Manuel's," Lauren said.

Estaban nodded. "Thank you for remembering me."

The lines at customs were short—only ten minutes—and they were soon cleared and on the Mexican side.

"It won't be so fast coming back," Estaban commented.

The stop-and-go traffic in Juárez gave Turk the opportunity to look around. The street was a tawdry as he remembered, with its clubs, restaurants, and souvenir stands. Even though it was early Saturday afternoon, it was crowded with people from the States. Most of them, though they weren't wearing uniforms, were soldiers from Fort Bliss.

Turk glanced up into the rearview mirror. A black limo was behind him. He had seen the same car while waiting on the line to cross the bridge. At the next street, he turned right. "Don't ask questions," he said, before either Lauren or Estaban should speak.

He checked the mirror again. The limo was turning. "We're being followed," he said calmly.

Lauren shifted her position and looked out the rear window. "You mean the black car is following us?"

"That's exactly what I mean," Turk answered.

"But why would anyone want to follow us?" she asked.

Turk shrugged, but he didn't answer.

"Doug . . ."

"Later," Turk said, "we'll talk about it later, when we're back in the hotel."

Lauren sighed and said to Estaban, "He hasn't changed. He still thinks he's a young man and can do the things a young man can."

Turk grinned. "I'm not the one who's following me," he said, looking back at her. "Besides, as long as I can do those things that make you think you're a young woman, you have no reason to complain."

Lauren made a *moue.*

Turk chuckled and turned again. "I'll go back to the main drag and pick up the highway."

"Juárez has grown," Estaban said. "There are houses all the way out to the cemetery . . . It's not used anymore, even by the very poor people . . . There's a bigger one on the other side of town."

Turk didn't answer and Lauren began talking to Estaban, leaving Turk with his own thoughts. He didn't like the idea of houses crowding down on Manuel's grave. It was all the boy had ever really had. He pursed his lips. Even the dead needed space. . . .

"Doug, you never told me you sent José money," she said.

"What?" Turk responded.

"You never told me that you sent money to José," she said.

"You never asked," he answered.

"Difficult," Lauren said, "that's what you are . . . difficult. And what is worse, is that you take pride in it. . . . I know you're smirking—well, don't. Being difficult is nothing to smirk about."

"Me, I never smirk," Turk responded. "I might

laugh, even chuckle . . . but smirking is not my style. . . . I don't even giggle."

"The car is still with us," Estaban said, looking back.

Turk nodded.

"It could be coincidence," Lauren offered.

"If it is," Turk said, "it's a hell of a lot of coincidence."

A few minutes later they were on the highway.

"Where do I make the turn onto the side road?" Turk asked.

"In a few miles," Estaban answered. "There's a McDonalds On the right. . . . The turn is there."

But isn't that almost—"

"*Si* . . . *si* . . . It's next to the cemetery," Estaban said.

"I always knew there was a good reason why I could never eat in one of those places," Turk growled. "Imagine, building a place like that next to—

"There it is . . . on the right—slow down."

Turk slowed. "I don't see the goddamn wall!" he exclaimed. "They didn't take the wall down, did they?"

"It's there."

Turk made the turn. The roadway was blacktopped for a few yards; then it became the rutted dirt road Turk remembered. A cloud of yellow dust rose up behind the car.

"There's the wall," Estaban said, pointing to it.

Turk nodded. He had forgotten how low it was. Over the years it had become more imposing and had even acquired an iron gate; but in reality it was perhaps three feet high, if that. And it was made of rough gray fieldstones.

"Better slow down some more," Estaban advised. "Make the left coming up."

Turk eased the wheel over.

"It's by the wall, at the very end of the roadway," Estaban said.

"I don't think I'd have been able to find it without you," Turk told him.

"Wasn't there a church nearby?" Lauren asked.

"*Si* . . . Yes . . . It burned down about twenty years ago on Christmas Eve and was never rebuilt," Estaban said, looking back at Lauren. "The priest who was at Manuel's funeral was killed in the fire."

"He was a good man," Lauren said.

Estaban nodded. "He was my cousin, on my mother's side," he said quietly.

"I didn't know that," Lauren responded. "Doug, did you—"

"No . . . you never told me he was your cousin," Turk said.

Estaban shrugged.

Turk saw the wall in front of him, stopped, and switched off the ignition. "We'll put the roses on the grave," he said to Estaban.

"Doug, the car isn't behind us!" Lauren exclaimed, peering through the settling dust. "Maybe it was just a coincidence after all?"

"Maybe," Turk acknowledged with a nod. "But I don't really think so. There's only one way into this place and one way out, and it's the same way. . . . Whoever they are, they're probably pulled into McDonalds."

Turk opened the door and the heat slammed down on him. He waited until Lauren and Estaban were out of the car before he started to walk slowly toward the grave. The three of them moved together. The sun was very bright and the sky very blue.

Turk looked down. Swirls of brown dust rose with

every step he took. "It's like being in a goddamn oven," he commented.

"Worse this summer because of the spring drought," Estaban said. "Even in the mountains there wasn't any rain this spring."

Suddenly Turk saw the simple stone that marked Manuel's grave. "There it is," he said, looking at Lauren.

"Yes, I see it," she answered, putting her hand on his arm.

The three of them stopped. Turk opened the paper wrapping around the roses and gave half of them to Estaban.

Lauren was the first to approach the grave; she gently placed her bouquet at its foot. Then, moving back, she said in a low voice, "I have always been sorry that I never knew him." Looking at Turk, she asked, "Are you all right?"

"I'm all right," he answered.

Then Estaban stepped forward and laid his roses next to Lauren's flowers. "He was a wild one, but he had the heart of an angel," Estaban said.

Turk waited until Lauren and Estaban moved back before he went to the grave. He knelt down close to the gray slate headstone and put his free hand on its coarse-textured surface. He had fought in two wars and had seen many of his friends die, but he relived this boy's death almost every day of his life. This Mexican waif had become over the years the son he and Lauren never had. This son had died for him. . . . Turk pursed his lips and placed the roses on the grave against the headstone. Then he stood up and said, "I made arrangements for us to be buried next to him."

"If that's what you want," Lauren said.

"It's what I want," Turk answered. He looked around and said, "It's not the place I would have chosen for us, but he's here, and I wouldn't want to be anywhere else. Besides, we couldn't be in better company, could we?"

"No, we couldn't," Lauren answered.

Turk bent down and picked up three smooth rocks and placed them on the headstone. "Had he lived," Turk commented, "he would have been old enough to have children of his own."

Lauren extended her hand. "Come," she said, "let's go back to the car."

Turk nodded and took hold of her hand.

Without speaking, the three of them walked away from the grave and settled in the car.

Turk turned on the ignition and the air-conditioning, and putting the car in motion, he said, "I guess I should have spoken to you about our burial arrangements before I made them. But I figured you'd want to be where I am—and I want to be where Manuel is."

"It's all right," Lauren said.

"You sure?" Turk asked, glancing at her over his shoulder.

"Absolutely."

"Good," he exclaimed. "Very good!"

As soon as Turk came out of the cemetery, he looked for the black limo in the McDonalds parking lot. "Our coincidence is waiting for us," he said.

"Who could they be?" Lauren asked.

"No one I know," Turk answered. "But you can bet they're not friends."

"I wish you wouldn't say things like that," Lauren told him.

"But it's true."

"I don't know how you could know that," she said.

"Friendly folks don't do what they're doing," Turk responded.

Lauren remained silent.

"José, why don't you come back to the hotel with us and have a drink," Turk asked.

"I'd like that," Estaban said.

Turk left the highway and turned onto the main street in Juárez. Traffic going north into the United States was heavy, and it took almost forty minutes for them to reach the front of the line.

Rolling down the window, Turk said, "I have nothing to declare."

"And the others with you?" the customs agent asked.

"Nothing," Estaban answered.

"Nothing," Lauren said.

The agent looked at Estaban. "Are you a citizen of the United States?" he asked.

Estaban fished his wallet out of his back pocket and took out a photostat of his citizenship papers.

Turk passed the document to the customs agent and glanced up into the rearview mirror. The limo was two cars back.

"Okay, you're okay," the agent said, waving them forward. "Go ahead."

Within moments they were rolling across the bridge.

"That car is still behind us, Estaban said.

"And it's going to stay there," Turk commented. "If I were younger, I'd give them a run for it the way we did forty years ago."

"You had someplace to go then," Lauren said. "Now the only place we have is the hotel. . . . Besides, we don't even know who they are."

Turk didn't answer. He wove through the traffic in El

Paso and finally pulled up in front of the hotel. "The two of you go in. I'll park the car and—"

"No," Lauren said. "I know you too well to fall for that. The hotel has valet parking—give the keys to the doorman. The three of us will go into the hotel together."

Turk was going to object; then, with a shrug, he changed his mind. "Okay, the three of us will go together."

Lauren nodded.

A moment later the three of them were walking into the lobby.

"Let's go into the bar," Turk said. "Pike, if he shows, will meet us there. I told him last night to ask for me in the bar."

"It's ten of four now," Lauren told him, looking at her watch.

The three of them entered the dimly lit bar that could have been used for a western film set.

Turk stopped just inside the room and scanned the tables, then the bar.

"Anything wrong?" Lauren asked.

"See that man sitting toward this side of the bar," Turk said.

"Which man?"

"The one who's picking up his glass and drinking."

"What about—It's Ed . . . It's Ed Gripper!" she exclaimed.

Turk smiled broadly and nodded.

"That's the surprise?" Lauren asked.

"That's it," Turk answered; then to Estaban he said, "We were in the army together . . . he was best man at my wedding."

"If he's your friend," Estaban answered, "he is my

friend."

Turk led the way to his friend. "Hello, General," he said.

Gripper turned. Still chunkily built, he was in his mid-eighties, with iron-gray hair and sad eyes. He smiled at them and leaned forward to kiss Lauren on the cheek.

Turk introduced Estaban.

Gripper shook his hand. "Glad to know you, José," he said in a gravelly voice that had become even rougher over the years.

"We better sit down at a table, Ed," Turk said.

"If that's your pleasure," Ed answered.

Turk found an empty table for them and they sat down.

"You're looking good, Doug," Gripper said. "And you, Lauren, are as beautiful as I remembered."

"Why thank you, Ed," Lauren said. "It's good to hear, even though it's not true."

Turk filled his pipe, lit it, and then, signaling to one of the barmaids, he said, "Let's have a drink—I'm as dry as the damn desert."

"I'll have another one," Gripper said, finishing the drink he had brought with him from the bar. "I can't make up my mind whether this place should be a whorehouse or set for a grade z western."

"I was thinking just about the same thing," Turk said with a smile. "It just tries too hard to be a western bar."

The barmaid came to the table. She wore a white leather miniskirt, a western-type brown blouse opened down to the third button, and no bra. On her right side was a leather holster and a .45 made of wood. A pair of brown leather boots matched the ten-gallon hat that rested on the back of her neck.

Turk ordered scotch on the rocks for himself, a pink lady for Lauren, bourbon-and-branch-waters for Gripper and Estaban. When the barmaid left the table, Turk said, "We're waiting for Mr. John Pike—he's the man I told you about, Ed."

Gripper nodded. "You sure he has what he says he has?" he asked.

"And I"d like to know exactly what it is," Lauren said. "Doug, are you going to tell me?" she asked.

"You mean you haven't told her why you're here?" Gripper exclaimed in amazement.

Turk shook his head. "It wasn't the right time." He looked at Lauren. "But now—"

The barmaid returned with the drinks and a bowl of bar nuts. "We have just great chili and ribs," she told them.

"Maybe later," Turk told her. He waited until she was gone before he said, "Mr. Pike found a German helmet out in the desert."

Lauren's eyes widened.

"In his letter to me," Turk said, "he intimated that he had found other things, too."

"But no one was ever supposed to go there," Lauren whispered.

Turk nodded. "But that was over forty years ago."

Lauren looked at Ed. "Doug wrote to you about it and—"

"I asked if I could meet him down here and have a look-see at what this Mr. Pike has," Gripper said.

"If I could get the incident cleared," Turk said, "just think of the article I could write. I was there, Ed was there, and now . . ."

"And just how do you expect to get it cleared?" Lauren asked.

"The Freedom of Information Act," Turk answered. "I still have enough pull in the government to give it a try."

Lauren shook her head. "I think you're on a wild-goose chase. But I know anything I say won't stop you."

Turk grinned and picking up his drink, he toasted, "To all of us—good health and good luck."

They touched each other's glass, then drank.

"It's exactly four," Gripper said, looking at his watch.

Turk didn't answer.

"José, did you ever hear anything about a battle taking place not too far from here during the big war?" Gripper asked.

"Only about a train that was shot up," Estaban answered. "But that was a long time ago. People said that banditos did it."

"They were some banditos," Gripper said with a smile. "Some banditos."

"How long are you going to wait for your Mr. Pike?" Lauren asked.

"Give him until a quarter after, Doug; then phone him," Gripper said.

"Something is wrong with his phone," Turk replied, and he explained what had happened earlier when he had phoned Pike.

Gripper rubbed his hand over his chin. "Is that what you meant by something strange going on?"

"That's part of it," Turk said.

"When you first wrote to me about the helmet, you said you read about it in an advertisement in one of those tin soldier magazines."

"It was *Mercenaries in Action.*"

"Like I said, a tin soldier magazine," Gripper responded. "That means other people must have read it. . . . Maybe someone in the government picked up on it, too."

Turk shrugged. "I wouldn't doubt it."

"You know where this Mr. Pike lives?" Gripper asked.

"Yes."

"Then let's pay him a visit," Gripper said.

Turk looked at Lauren. "You stay here. If Pike comes, he'll ask for me at the bar. José, stay with her."

Estaban nodded.

"We'll be back as soon as we can," Turk said. "If anything comes up, I'll call you."

"I don't like this," Lauren complained. "I don't like phone numbers that suddenly don't exist, and I don't like being followed by a black limo."

"That the other part of what's strange?" Gripper asked.

Turk nodded.

"When did that happen?" Gripper asked.

"Earlier, when we drove over the border to put flowers on Manuel's grave," Turk said, emptying his pipe into an ashtray.

"There might be a connection between—"

"Probably is," Turk said. He looked at his watch. "Four twenty. I think we better pay Mr. Pike a visit," he said. He stood up and went around to where Lauren was seated. "Don't worry about us—we'll be fine." Bending over her, he kissed the top of her head. "See you in a little while."

"I don't like this, Doug," she said, looking up at him.

"Neither do I," Turk answered. "I don't like being given a run-around over a phone number I know exists, and I don't like being followed by a black limo." He put his hand on her shoulders and gave them a gentle squeeze. "Don't worry, I'll be fine," he assured her.

Turk was at the wheel; Gripper sat beside him. Neither man had much need to speak. Nothing was said until they were on the highway going north; then Turk said, "The garage attendant said that it's out toward the Franklin Mountains."

"Who the hell would want to live there?" Gripper asked.

Turk shrugged. "Obviously somebody does," he said.

Gripper looked through the rear window. "Black limo on our tail," he said.

Turk checked the rearview mirror and nodded.

"Are you armed?" Gripper asked.

"No. It's been years since I carried a piece. Do you—?"

"I don't have one, either," Gripper said.

Turk pursed his lips. "It must be the government. . . Who else would be able to monkey around with the phones?"

Gripper lit a cigarette, blew smoke into the rear of the car, and looking at the limo, he said, "We could give it up."

"I want to write that story," Turk said. "It probably will be my last one—and it's the one I've always wanted to write."

"Then I guess we'll just have to visit Mr. Pike," Gripper responded.

The two didn't speak again until Turk said, "Pike lives on Oakland Street and that's off the golf course."

"Golf course!" Gripper exclaimed. "I don't remember one way out here."

"This whole area is new," Turk said. "In '41, only the mountains and the desert were here."

After a few moments' silence, Gripper said, "I liked it better that way."

"So did I," Turk told him.

The two men looked at one another and laughed.

"Comes to a point in one's life," Turk said, gesturing toward the neat rows of identical houses, "where progress doesn't mean diddly squat and isn't nearly as good as what it replaces."

"Too bad you have to become old to understand that," Gripper commented.

Turk slowed down when he came in sight of the golf course. "The streets go off to the left . . . There's Oakland." He signaled and made the turn. "Forty-four," he said.

"Should be on the right, about halfway up the hill," Gripper said.

Turk spotted the number and pulled up to the curb in front of a small tan-colored ranch.

"The limo just turned into the street," Gripper said, glancing down the hill through the rear window.

Turk nodded. "Let's go find out what this is all about," he said, and opened the door.

The two men walked toward the house.

"The limo stopped," Turk said.

"I can see that," Gripper answered.

They reached the front door.

Turk rang the bell.

No one answered.

Gripper tried the knob. It turned and the door opened. "What do we do?" he asked.

Turk looked at the black limo. It was still there.

"What do we do?" Gripper asked again.

Turk's heart began to race. Despite the dryness, he was sweating. "Go in," he said.

"Is there a Mrs. Pike?" Gripper asked.

"He's divorced," Turk said. "Now go in."

Gripper stepped across the threshold and Turk followed. They were in a small foyer. The living room was directly in front of them. It was furnished with two red-leather club chairs and a zebra-striped, three-piece sectional sofa. A fireplace was cut out of one wall and a gray-tinted sliding door led out into a yard, where there was a barbecue pit.

"Don't like it," Turk whispered.

Gripper nodded. "Let's get the fuck out of here," he said.

Turk swallowed hard. "Pike," he called. "John Pike?"

After a few moments', Gripper said, "He's not here. . . . Maybe he's at the hotel."

Turk took a few steps into the living room and turned toward the kitchen. "Pike's here," he said pointing. "He's sprawled out on the floor."

Gripper joined Turk. "Dead?" he asked.

"Looks that way," Turk said. He went to where Pike lay and bent over him. "Two bullet holes—"

"Freeze!" a man ordered.

Turk remained motionless.

"You there at the body, stand up slowly," the man ordered.

"Slowly," Turk repeated. He could hear the thumping of his heart.

"Now the two of you turn around."

Turk and Gripper faced the man. He was solidly built, with a square face and hard black eyes. He wore a dark-blue business suit and a gray Stetson on his head. And he held a .357 in his right hand. There was a man on either side of him. One was slightly taller and other was thinner. But they were dressed the same and each held a .357 in his hand.

"I'm National Security Agent Thomas Drew. The man on my right is Agent Williams and the agent on my left is Paul Quick. Now turn around slowly." Then he told one of the other men to cuff them. "The two of you are being charged with the murder of Federal Agent John Pike."

"The *what*?" Turk said.

Drew ignored him, gave their rights under the Miranda Act. Then he said to the men with him, "Get them into the car and we'll take them down to the Federal Building."

Turk and Gripper were shoved into the back of the limo. Quick sat on a jump seat in the back with them. Drew took the wheel, and the third agent followed in the car that Turk had rented.

"I hope your chief likes long stories," Turk said, with a weary sigh, "because this one is very long."

Neither of the agents answered.

# 1

*December 5, 1941*

*Northern Mexico.* . . . A tawny-colored mongrel bitch, belonging to no one in the village, slept just inside the door of the blacksmith's shop, where some of the heat spilled out of the forge and spread along the dirt floor to where the animal lay. The late afternoon was cold. A biting wind blowing from the north brought with it gray clouds that alternately hid the sun completely, or made it seem to be no more than a pallid white disk.

The wind raised curtains of beige sand from the surrounding desert. It thrummed the overhead telephone wires and wailed as it rushed over the corrugated-iron roof of the blacksmith's shop. The dog listened to the familiar sound of the wind and to the rhythmic clang of the smithy's hammer as he fashioned the iron rim for a wagon wheel.

The dog stretched, got to her feet, walked around in a tight circle several times and settled down again in the same place it had occupied a few moments before, though now her head was where her tail had been. She lay with her brown eyes half closed. Suddenly she was on her feet again. Her ears were up and her head was cocked to the right. She was listening to a third sound. A completely unfamiliar one. A high-pitched whine that was coming from the low hills, to the south of the village.

The dog began to bark.

"Quiet," the blacksmith shouted. "Quiet, bitch!"

But the dog continued to bark.

"Daughter of a whore!" the blacksmith yelled, flinging a piece of red-hot coal at the dog.

Used to the blacksmith's anger, the dog ran into the deserted street, where she looked toward the hills and continued to bark.

The blacksmith, curious about what the dog was barking at, came to the door and looked out. Because of the blowing sand, he could see nothing beyond the last house. His clapboarded shop stood at one end of the village and a small store, owned by his brother-in-law, was at the other end. In between them were ten houses made of mud, stones, and pieces of wood. Only his shop had a metal roof. The cold and the wind kept everyone indoors.

The dog was still barking.

"Your mother's shame," the blacksmith shouted. "You're barking at nothing." He turned and was just about to retreat into the warmth of his shop when the first shell exploded in the street, sending up a dense column of smoke. The next explosion threw him back into the shop. He was dead before his body struck the anvil.

Within minutes everything in the village was burning. All of its inhabitants were either dead or dying. Only the mongrel bitch survived, and as she cowered against the smashed wall of the blacksmith shop, she watched the soldiers pass through the village.

# 2

A large situation topographical map of southwest Texas, eastern New Mexico, and northern Mexico dominated the wall opposite the two windows overlooking the main quadrangle of Fort Bliss, Texas. The grass was still green, though it was the fifth of December. The map was shaded: light tan to indicate flat terrain; dark brown for the mountainous regions. All rivers were colored in blue. Cities, towns, and villages were red if they had populations of more than ten thousand people, or black if their population was below that figure. Most towns and villages were black.

Lieutenant General Patrick Hanahan's attention was focused on the map. In command of the Blue Army, he was responsible for defending the city of El Paso from attack and capture by the Gray Army, commanded by Lieutenant General Harry Alt. The disposition of Hanahan's troops was indicated by pins topped with blue flags, while known positions of the Gray Army were shown by pins topped with gray flags. The type of each unit and the number of its men and weaponry were printed in black ink on each flag.

For the purposes of the war games, each army had sixty thousand men, along with several hundred trucks with signs painted on them to indicate whether they were heavy, medium, or light tanks. Three Piper Cub aircraft had been supposed to simulate strafing, by flying low over the troops, or bombing, by dropping five-pound bags of flour on selected targets. But two of the aircraft were down for mechanical repairs and wouldn't be available until the games were over, and the third aircraft was on reconnaissance flight.

The exercise had begun at 0600 hours on the previous day, the fourth of December, 1941, and was scheduled to last until 2400 hours on the tenth of December. It had been conceived by the war department to test the effectiveness of the army's training program, and to allow the generals and their staffs to acquire field experience in realistic situations.

Hanahan moved his swagger stick in a ninety-degree arc east and south of El Paso on the map. "They're going to come at us from somewhere along that line," he spoke with a decided Southern accent, "—and I'm going to pounce on them like the proverbial wolf on the fold." Turning from the map, he faced his deputy, Major General Charles Fitzhugh, Commanding General of Fort Bliss. Each man wore a campaign hat, a light tan shirt and a dark brown tie, light tan breeches, highly polished jack boots, and a web belt with holstered .45-caliber automatic.

"You agree that Harry will come at us from somewhere along that arc?" Hanahan asked.

"They might," Fitzhugh said, moving his hand over

the map. "But until we know where Harry's main armor force is, we can't be sure. He could just as easily feint toward us along that arc, and then run south into Mexico and come around from the west." The broad *a*'s of his voice betrayed his Boston background.

"It would take him another twenty-four hours to do that," Hanahan commented. "Suppose I pulled back two, maybe three battalions along the east-southeast line. He'll think we're giving way to pressure and throw more of his men into the corridor we prepare. Then when we spot his armor, we can move in and pinch it off."

"That'll put his advance force within twenty miles of the city," Fitzhugh said, "and on flat terrain. Now he's got those mountains to cross on our eastern flank."

Hanahan pushed his right hand against the rim of his campaign hat, moving it back on his head. "Hell, Charley, how am I going to sucker Harry in if I don't give him something to go after?" He moved over to the desk, took a cigar out of a humidor, and went through the ritual of smelling and twirling it in his fingers before snipping off the end and lighting it. He sent a column of smoke toward the ceiling. "If I know Harry, he won't do anything spectacular."

"I wouldn't give him a chance to get his armor out on that flat terrain," Fitzhugh commented. He walked to the window. At the far side of the quadrangle, several prisoners from the stockade were working under the watchful eyes of two armed guards. "We've got to know where his armor is before we make our move."

"Who's looking for it?" Hanahan asked, blowing another column of smoke. He was impatient to make a spectacular move—one that would prove to the people in Washington that he was capable of field command.

"Colonel Gripper. He's in an observation plane some fifty miles south of here. I also told him to be on the lookout for those Mexican units assigned to Harry's force."

Hanahan rolled the cigar from the right side of his mouth to the left. "I'm damn glad he got saddled with them," he said, meaning the two Mexican units taking part in the war games. "They won't be worth a shit and they'll just foul things up."

Fitzhugh didn't answer. He was sure Harry Alt would use the Mexican units to their fullest.

Hanahan went back to the map. "I could destroy half of Harry's army if I could get him to move—" A knock at the door made him turn from the map. "Come in," he said.

A captain entered the room. "Beggin' your pardon, sir," he said. "But this came in over the radio a few minutes ago and I thought you should see it."

"Is it from Colonel Gripper," Hanahan asked, stepping toward the captain.

"No sir," the captain responded, "it's from our observation post, Two Eyes South."

Hanahan read the message aloud: "*Under heavy bombardment. Advise.*" He looked at Fitzhugh. "What the fuck does that mean?" he asked, his face suddenly flushing.

Fitzhugh crossed the room to look at the map. "Two Eyes South is assigned to the village of Charo. It's exactly one hundred miles from the border."

Hanahan came alongside of Fitzhugh. "Who the hell put an OP down there?"

"I did," Fitzhugh said, "just in case Harry decided to swing around us from the south. I thought we'd want to know about it before he made contact with our outer defense perimeter. We've got a second louie, a sergeant, and two enlisted men there."

Hanahan waved the message toward the map. "I still don't know what the fuck this means."

"None of the units are authorized to use live ammo anywhere south of the border," Fitzhugh explained.

"Someone is either shooting or having fun," Hanahan growled. "Either way I'm going to have their goddamn ass." He turned to the captain. "Get those guys in Two Eyes South on the radio now!"

"Yes, sir," the captain answered. He saluted, did an about-face, and hurried out of the office.

"Let's see what this is all about," Hanahan said. "If there's one thing I won't tolerate it's some junior officer trying to be a smart ass. These damn war games are too important to allow any shit like that."

Fitzhugh agreed with a nod. They left the office and walked down the hallway to the communications center, where the post's central switchboard, its main radio receiver and transmitter, and its teletype machines were located.

The communications officer on duty was a Major Robert Driscol. He saluted the two generals and reported, "We can't raise Two Eyes South."

"What time was their previous transmission before the last one?" Fitzhugh asked.

Driscol checked his log book. "Eleven hundred hours," he answered. "Just a routine check."

"Try them again, Major," Hanahan said.

"Go ahead, Sergeant," Driscol told the man at the radio set.

The sergeant flipped a switch and said, "This is Blue Chief. . . . This is Blue Chief callin' Two Eyes South. Do you read me?" He repeated the call three times;

then, shaking his head, he looked toward Major Driscol. "Nothing, sir."

"Some of the Mex units assigned to Harry might be operating there," Fitzhugh offered.

"They might," Hanahan agreed. "But why the hell would they start shooting, especially with artillery?"

Fitzhugh shrugged.

"Those damn spics shoot the way we sneeze," Hanahan commented. "I knew they'd be trouble the moment I was told they'd be included in these games." Then to Driscol he said, "Get General Alt on the phone. I'll be in my office." And he stomped out of the communications room.

During the five minutes it took for Alt to come on the line, Hanahan drummed the fingers of his right hand on the top of the desk. He didn't like surprises of any kind.

Fitzhugh returned to the window. The work detail of prisoners was gone. Men from the post's headquarters detachment were heading across the quadrangle. He recognized a few of them.

Suddenly the phone rang.

Hanahan picked it up. "Harry, this is Patrick," he said. "Have you authorized the use of live ammo in any area within the last two hours?"

"Only in Sector Two-A," Alt answered.

Hanahan stood up and faced the situation map. Harry was putting more pressure on his front.

"East-southwest of El Paso," Alt told him. "What's the problem?"

Hanahan ignored the question. "Have you any Mex units operating in the vicinity of El Charo?" he asked.

"Patrick, I'm you enemy, remember?"

"Harry, I just got a report from my OP down there

that they're being shelled with live stuff."

"Did you confirm it?"

"I can't raise them on the radio."

"Okay, Patrick. I don't have any Mexican units within twenty-five miles of El Charo."

"Thanks," Hanahan said. "I'll do you a favor, if the opportunity comes along."

"Lose the war," Alt responded.

Hanahan managed a laugh. "Thanks again," he said, then he put the phone down and looked at Fitzhugh. "There are no Mexican units near El Charo."

Before Fitzhugh could speak, Hanahan had Driscol on the phone. "Major, have we a phone in there?"

"No, sir," Driscol answered. "But the store down there has a phone. Lieutenant Wheatly—the officer in charge of the OP—mentioned it to me yesterday."

"Try it," Hanahan said. "I'll hang on."

Speaking in Spanish to the Mexican operator, Driscol put the call through himself. "Sorry, sir," he said after a minute or two, "but the operator says something is wrong with the lines."

"Does he know what's wrong?" Hanahan asked.

"No, sir."

Hanahan thanked him, put the phone down, and began to pace. His cigar had gone out and he chewed on it. "Harry could be pulling a fast one," he said, suddenly stopping. "He authorized the use of live ammo in the area just in front of the units I intended to pull back. He might be playing with us."

"Have Ed Gripper check it out," Fitzhugh suggested. "He'll be able to fly over El Charo and tell us whether or not Harry is trying to swing around us. You know, it just might be one of those bandit groups."

"With field pieces?"

"Some of them are well-armed. Why not with an old cannon or two?"

"All right, I'll speak to Ed," Hanahan said. "If it's bandits, then the Federales will go in and take care of them."

"I don't see how it can be anything else," Fitzhugh replied. "It's either bandits or a couple of our guys clowning around."

"If it's a few dogfaces clowning around," Hanahan growled, "I'll throw the fucking book at them. They'll spend the rest of their lives breaking rocks in Leavenworth. I swear to Christ they will!"

# 3

The late morning sun was so bright it made Douglas Turk squint. He stood in a shallow valley alongside a young second lieutenant.

Turk had come out to the field from Mexico City to see what was going on for himself. The day before, he had phoned his best friend, Colonel Ed Gripper, and asked him whether it would be worthwhile to visit the field before he checked into headquarters at Fort Bliss. In his characteristically gravel voice Ed had told him, "Go out to the field first; then you'll know when you're being given bullshit by the command's information officer."

The lieutenant gestured with his swagger stick toward two small hills to the east, and in a slow, midwestern drawl he said, "My men are goin' to knock out the machine gun on the hill to the right. I'm goin' to use two squads in a leapfrog action to do it."

Turk didn't even bother to nod. He stuck a cigarette into his mouth, lit it, and let the smoke rush out of his nostrils. He was a tall, lean man with large strong hands, a square jaw, brown hair with a touch of gray on the sideburns, and restless green eyes tinged with sadness.

"The observers," the lieutenant said, "are goin' to be right behind us. That machine gun guards a crossroads directly behind it. You can't see it from here, but it's on the map. It's one of the main supply roads for the Grays."

This time Turk nodded.

The lieutenant looked at his watch. "Time to join my men."

"Good luck," Turk said. But he knew what the outcome of the action would be. The lieutenant was green and so were the men he led. Still, Turk decided to wait until the attack was over before he drove to Blue Army headquarters at Fort Bliss.

Turk ordinarily covered Mexico City for the International News Service. But because of his service with the United States Army and with the Republican Army during the Spanish Civil War, the New York office had felt he was the best man to cover these war games, the biggest ever held by the United States during peacetime.

Turk hadn't wanted the assignment. He'd have much preferred to stay in Mexico City, where he could be close to Lauren Zwig.

Halfway through the cigarette, Turk dropped it to the ground and crushed it under his heel. He watched the lieutenant move his two squads toward their objective.

Half the men were armed with wooden rifles and all

of them were still wearing World War I helmets and puttees.

The lieutenant blew his whistle.

The first squad dropped on their stomachs and began to shout: "*Bang* . . . *Bang* . . . *Bang*. . . ."

The men in the machine-gun emplacement held their fire.

The two squads of Blue infantry leapfrogged toward the hill. Then the lieutenant blew three short blasts on his whistle. Four men ran forward to lob make-believe hand grenades at the emplacement.

Suddenly coming over the hill was a truck, carrying a sign: THIS IS A TANK.

Within moments the lieutenant's two squads were in the crossfire from the machine-gun emplacement and the tank.

The Gray Army men were shouting, "Rat a tat tat. . . . Rat tat tat. . . . You bastards are dead. Rat tat tat. . . . You fuckers are gone!"

Disgusted by what he saw, Turk dug his hands into his coat pockets, turned, and went to his car. The war in Europe had been going on for two years now. Spain had fallen to Franco; Germany controlled all of Western Europe. Japan had a good-sized chunk of China. And the United States was still using wooden guns to train its men. Yet Turk was convinced the war couldn't be avoided—not if the United States wanted to remain free.

Turk lit another cigarette, took a deep drag on it, and eased himself behind the wheel of his rented green De Soto.

After a few minutes, Turk's thoughts shifted from the world situation to his own. Because Lauren's husband Walther was on a business trip to Tampico, Turk had been able to spend his last night in Mexico City with her. He had brought her back to his apartment. He remembered everything, even the wavering light coming from the fireplace, which was mostly yellow and it remained fused to the gray stones immediately in front of the hearth. There was just enough heat in the room to keep the night chill from entering. . . .

He removed the dark wool rebozo from Lauren's shoulders, dropped it on a nearby chair, and turned her to him. The top of her head fit neatly under his chin and her hair smelled of jasmine. He tilted up her face and kissed her.

After a few moments, Lauren eased herself out of his arms. She walked to the hearth and looked into the fire. "Now and then I look into the mirror and find myself saying, 'You're a married woman. You're married to a man who has given you everything. He has even made it possible for you to mature as an artist—' "

Interrupting her, Turk said, "He also told you that if you were discreet, he wouldn't mind if you took a lover. After all, he's a very understanding man." Turk had never told her that he had had a check run on Zwig by some of his friends at the American embassy and had found that the man had a penchant for young men.

"Walther doesn't think of me in a sexual way," Lauren responded. "We have an arrangement: I'm there to act as his hostess, to be his beautiful decoration, and in return—"

He crossed the distance between them and took hold of her arms. "Divorce him," he said. "You don't have anything with him. Can't you see that? Divorce him and marry me!"

She asked for time to think.

"I'll be gone a few days," he said. "I'll probably be back by the middle of the month. That should give you enough time to make up your mind."

There was nothing more to discuss. He took her in his arms and led her to his bed. They made love slowly, yet passionately. Afterwards, just before they went to sleep, Turk remembered something. "When Walther comes back from Tampico, will you ask him if he has ever heard of a ship called the *City of Cadiz*?"

"Why?" she asked. "What's so important about that ship?" She moved even closer, placing one of her bare legs over his.

"I'm thinking of buying it," he replied, aware of the pressure of her body against his.

She began to giggle. "That's funny."

"It's a funny ship," he said. "A friend of mine at the British embassy thinks so too."

"That it's a funny ship?"

"Yes," he answered. A moment later he was asleep.

Turk smiled. It had been a dumb thing to think of after having made love, and even dumber to ask Lauren to question Walther about a ship. In fact, he suddenly found himself thinking that asking Lauren to marry him might have been the most selfish thing he had ever done. After all, he couldn't even offer her security. He'd soon be back in the army, albeit as a brevet lieutenant colonel, but that rank wouldn't guarantee they'd have much time together. And when war did come, Turk knew himself well enough to know that he'd want to be where the fighting was.

He flicked the cigarette butt into the desert and

pushed himself back into the seat. "I'm sure as hell not offering her much," Turk said aloud. After a few moments he added, "But at least with me, she'd be a woman." He pursed his lips and wondered how a man could live in the same house with a woman as beautiful as Lauren and not want her.

Turk left the secondary road and turned west on 62, toward El Paso. He passed several convoys of trucks marked TANKS, heading toward the area he had just left. Ten minutes later he came on a battalion of infantry, strung out along the shoulder of the road. Most of them were armed with wooden guns. The men waved to him and he waved back. They were tired-looking and covered with desert sand. Most of them were draftees, but when the war came, they'd be the ones who'd do most of the fighting, most of the dying. But it would take professionals like him to train and lead them, which was why he wanted to go back into the army. But there was another reason, a more personal one: It was a debt he owed to the men he knew who had been killed or imprisoned in Spain.

It was the price for his continued self-respect. Before Turk knew it he was on Pershing Drive, tailing behind a long convoy going into Fort Bliss. He looked forward to his dinner with Ed Gripper. If there was going to be a wedding, Turk wanted Ed to be his best man.

Turk stepped out of the press room, made a left turn, and walked to the water cooler, located just across from the base communications center. The cold water relieved the parched, scratchy feeling in his throat that came from smoking too many cigarettes while he had waited with two dozen other reporters for something interesting to happen, something really newsworthy instead of the pap that had been fed to the press at 1130 and 1700 hours by Captain Steven Jennings, General Hanahan's aide and the public information officer for the duration of the war games. He had missed the 1130 briefing. But he had gathered enough material for a blistering article on the combat readiness of the troops he had seen.

Turk stood erect and wiped his mouth with a handkerchief. He wished he was back in Mexico City with Lauren.

Suddenly the door to the communications center opened, a sergeant started out, stopped, turned halfway around and said to someone inside the room, "If any more of our units get shot at, I don't want to know about it until I come back on duty tomorrow. Got that?"

The sergeant laughed, closed the door, and started down the hall.

Turk was about to go after him when he saw Generals Hanahan and Fitzhugh come rushing out of the post commander's office.

"Gentlemen," Turk said, stepping in front of them.

They stopped. The two were completely dissimilar. Hanahan was a tall, distinguished-looking man with iron-gray hair, piercing blue eyes, a strong cleft chin, and narrow lips. At age sixy he was still a handsome, vigorous man who womanized, much to the chagrin of his oft-forgiving wife, Lou-Ann. Yet it was thanks to the ten million dollars of Lou-Ann's inheritance from the Newgate tobacco fortune that Hanahan was the wealthiest officer in the army.

Fitzhugh was short and wiry, with a craggy face, gray eyes, and red hair that gave him the appearance of a bantam cock. He had been two years behind Hanahan at West Point, where he had graduated first in his class. He was fifty-eight years old. His wife Sally had died from pneumonia three years before and he still felt her loss keenly.

Both men had seen action in the Argonne, during World War I. But until Hanahan was given command of the Blue Army, most of his assignments had been either on the General Staff, or at some other high level of administration. Fitzhugh, on the other hand, had much more field experience, including the command of troops in China in the late thirties.

Turk shook hands with Hanahan and then with Fitzhugh. He knew the two of them from his army days. He had taken Hanahan's course in geo-political history at West Point and had found him a dull instructor. And he had served under Fitzhugh in Tientsin, China, in 1929. Fitzhugh was not only an excellent commander, he was also a fair man.

"I didn't expect to see you here," Hanahan said. "I heard you were down in Mexico City living the life of ease with those beautiful señoritas."

"Come on, Hanahan, when did you live anything else but a life of ease?" Turk shot back.

Hanahan glared at him.

"I can tell you from experience," Turk said, "that these games you're playing out here won't prepare you for the real thing."

"Ed mentioned you're coming back in," Fitzhugh said, interrupting the conversation before the exchange became ugly.

"The first of January, as a brevet, lieutenant colonel," Turk answered, looking straight at Hanahan as he spoke. "I was told the army needs officers with field experience more than they need paper jockeys."

"Still the smart-ass?" Hanahan challenged. Without waiting for a response, he started to walk away.

"I hear someone was smart enough to let a unit get shot up."

Hanahan stopped, wheeled around. "You heard wrong, Mister. General Fitzhugh, we have something to do, don't we?"

"You push hard," Fitzhugh whispered to Turk.

"Not as hard as I'd like to," Turk answered.

"General Fitzhugh!" Hanahan called. This time the order to join him was implicit in the tone of his voice.

"See you," Turk said.

"Even when I taught at the Point I didn't like Turk," Hanahan commented once they were inside the communications center. "I don't trust him. Any man who'd resign his commission to fight in the Lincoln Brigade has to be a commie. I mean, Franco wasn't the worst thing that could happen to Spain. It might have gone to the commies."

"Turk was a first lieutenant with me in Tientsin," Fitzhugh responded. "I'll tell you this about him: he's steady man under fire."

"I still don't like the son of a bitch," Hanahan growled.

Major Driscol came forward and saluted.

"Get me Colonel Gripper," Hanahan barked.

"Sergeant, get Colonel Gripper for General Hanahan," Driscol ordered the radioman on duty.

"This is Blue Chief calling Blue Eagle," the sergeant said. "Blue Chief calling Blue Eagle. Do you read me?"

"Loud and clear."

"What's your position now?" Hanahan asked.

"Best estimate—"

Ed's transmission was interrupted by static:

"Say again," Hanahan told him. "Say again, Where are you now?"

"One hundred miles southeast of El Paso," Ed said.

"I want you to fly over El Charo and report back to me when you're over the village. Tell me what you see down there."

"That's thirty or forty miles due west from where I am. What am I supposed to be looking for?"

"Just tell me what you see down there, Blue Eagle. Over."

"Roger, I'll take a look," Ed responded.

Hanahan turned to Fitzhugh. "Better put a lid on this until we know what we're dealing with. I'll stay here just in case some other transmissions come in about . . ."—he was at a loss to define it—". . . Transmissions that I should be aware of," he finally said. "With any luck, Ed will give us the kind of information we need."

"I'll clue Captain Jennings in to what has been happening," Fitzhugh said.

Hanahan nodded. "I don't want anything released to the press until I approve it." He was worried about just how much Turk knew. "Have an orderly bring me a couple of my cigars."

"Sure," Fitzhugh answered and left the communications center.

Hanahan turned his attention back to the radio. The sergeant had picked something up.

"We've been getting a lot of that," Driscol said, coming alongside of Hanahan.

Hanahan listened. "Sounds like spics talking, doesn't

it?"

"It's Spanish all right," Driscol answered. "But stiffer."

"Stiffer?" Hanahan questioned.

Driscol turned to the sergeant. "You said that, didn't you?"

"Yes, sir. It's stiffer."

"Stiffer, shit!" Hanahan exclaimed and began to pace.

# 4

The small, high-winged monoplane cast a long shadow on the dun-colored landscape below it. Now and then the plane would drop several dozen feet into an air pocket or be lifted by a sudden updraft. The throbbing sound of its engine and the smell of gasoline filled the cabin.

Colonel Edward Gripper sat forward of the pilot, Second Lieutenant Paul Allway. Ed scanned the land to the south and west of the plane with field glasses. He saw nothing unusual. He checked the map spread out on his lap. According to his reckoning, El Charo was ten, maybe twelve minutes away.

To get his attention, Allway poked Ed on his right shoulder. "Operations at Biggs says the barometer has started to drop," he shouted above the drone of the plane's engine. "A snowstorm is coming in from the north. We've been advised to return to base."

Ed shook his head. "Orders are to take a look at El Charo," he answered firmly—though he himself couldn't understand why Hanahan was in a stew over it, unless the Grays had captured the town.

Allway pointed north. "Just look at that weather roll off the mountains!"

Ed nodded. "I've seen worse," he answered and faced front.

"Goddamn!" Allway exclaimed under his breath. It was just his bad luck to be assigned to iron-ass Ed. A mustang, if there ever was one. He had come up through the ranks, and the army was the man's mother, father, wife, and children.

Ed was a compactly built, broad-shouldered man, with intense black eyes, a leathery complexion, and a square face, accentuated by a crew cut. On either side of his nose there was a tracery of blue veins.

"Just fifty miles south of here," he said, pointing in that direction, "are huge *estancias*, ranches. Each one is several hundred square miles, and each has tens of thousands of heads of cattle. When I was just a boy I spent some time in El Charo. I went back there two years ago, while I was a military attaché in Mexico. It was the way I remembered it: a general store at one end and the blacksmith shop at the other."

Ed had started his army career when he was sixteen. Now he had twenty-five years of service behind him. He had joined up to ride with General Black Jack Pershing against Pancho Villa. By the time he had reached his twentieth birthday, Gripper was a veteran of the First World War, with a wound in his right leg and several medals to prove it, including three Silver Stars for bravery.

"Colonel, I think we should head back," Allway

responded. He was becoming more and more concerned by the rapid deterioration of the weather.

"Not till we get a look-see at El Charo," Ed answered, picking up the field glasses again.

Allway silently mimicked him, but he had no choice other than to hold the plane on its present course.

Ed watched the plane's shadow fold against a low hill. Only a short time ago, so it seemed, he had been a private in a cavalry troop slowly moving south over that same terrain. In another month, by act of Congress, he'd be promoted to the rank of brigadier general, and he was still young enough to be given one or two more stars.

Allway pressed one earphone against his head.

"This is Blue Chief. Put me through to Blue Eagle."

Allway tapped Ed on the shoulder. "General Hanahan," he said. Ed picked up the headset and mike, pushed a toggle switch on the instrument panel in front of him, and said, "Blue Eagle here."

"Say again," Hanahan responded.

"Blue Eagle here."

"What's your position?" Hanahan asked.

"El Charo should be coming into view within the next few minutes," Ed answered.

"Say again."

Ed repeated his last transmission.

"I'm standing by for your report," Hanahan said. "Over."

"Roger," Ed responded and flicked the toggle switch into its off position. He turned to Allway as he took the headset off his ears and said, "Got a helluva lot of static coming over. Can't we get it clearer?"

Allway pointed to the storm. "We're lucky to get anything with that coming down on us."

The clouds were almost black.

"It's going to be a bumpy ride home," Ed said, and faced front again. He was beginning to feel cramped in the narrow space of the cabin.

Suddenly he leaned forward. There was a smudge of dark gray smoke directly in front of him. He lifted the field glasses and focused them on the source of the smoke.

"My God," Ed shouted, "El Charo is burning. . . . Get Hanahan on the air."

A moment later Hanahan responded to Allway's call.

"El Charo is burning!" Ed reported. He no longer needed the field glasses to see where the smoke was coming from.

"Blue Eagle, you should be over the target area by now," Hanahan responded.

Ed checked the altimeter. The plane was flying at three thousand feet. He swiveled around and shouted to Allway, "Take her down to two hundred."

"Blue Eagle, do you read me?" Hanahan shouted.

"El Charo is burning," Ed answered.

Allway thrust the control stick to the right and forward. He'd give that mustang a ride he'd never forget. The plane slipped to the right and hurtled down.

The wind screamed past the diving plane.

With one hand Ed braced himself against the instrument panel, and with the other he held the mike close to his mouth. "El Charo is burning. Repeat, El Charo is burning."

"Say again!" Hanahan shouted.

"The goddamn place is burning." Ed realized Hanahan wasn't receiving him.

"Burning," Hanahan shouted. "What the hell is

burning?"

Allway watched the altimeter needle spin counter-clockwise. He began counting. Eight hundred . . . seven hundred. Six hundred. Six hundred and fifty. He eased back on the control stick.

The plane began to shudder.

"I hope the fucking wings stay on," Allway shouted above the shriek of the tortured plane.

Ed was forced to use two hands to brace himself against the g-forces exerted on him as the plane fought its way out of the dive.

"Five hundred feet," Allway yelled.

Ed looked down. They were flying directly over the burning town. "Blue Chief, there are tire marks—I'll be a son of a bitch!"

"Blue Eagle, can't read you," Hanahan said.

"There are armored cars down there. Trucks and armored cars. Blue Chief, there's a fucking armored battalion down here."

"Blue Eagle, I can't hear you."

Suddenly Ed heard a tearing sound. He glanced at the starboard wing. A large rent scarred the doped surface. Another rent appeared, and then one of the wooden sections splintered.

"Machine guns!" he shouted to Allway. "Get us the fuck out of here!"

Allway eased on the control stick and pushed the throttle forward.

The plane responded.

Another burst of machine-gun fire put holes in the port wing.

"We better haul ass!" Ed yelled.

"Can't do any better," Allway answered. "I don't want to stall her."

"What's going on out there?" Hanahan yelled. "I can't hear you. Say again."

Suddenly a puff of black smoke erupted from the engine.

"Holy shit!" Allway exclaimed. "We caught one."

Ed looked at the altimeter. They had reached fifteen hundred feet and were still climbing.

The engine was smoking heavily.

"I'm going to have to level her out," Allway shouted.

"Blue Chief, we've got bandits," Ed yelled. "There's an armored unit at El Charo."

"Blue Eagle, I can't read you," Hanahan complained.

"I'm going to try and make it into the storm," Allway said.

Ed nodded. Already yellow tongues of flame were visible behind the dark gray smoke.

Suddenly the plane was caught in an updraft.

A stream of yellow and red flames shot back from the engine. An instant later the plane went into a nose-dive.

Allway fought to level the ship out. "We're going to crash, Colonel," he shouted above the screaming of the wind. "We're going to crash." He managed to lessen the steep dive at two hundred feet.

"Can you put her down?" Ed yelled.

"No way! We're going in for the count."

Using his two hands, Ed braced himself against the side of the cabin. He watched the earth rush up at them. He took a deep breath and waited for the crash to wrench him from this life and hurt him into eternity.

The plane slammed into the hardpan flats. Its landing gear buckled. It skidded along the ground, tearing its wings off and raising a curtain of dust on either side of it. A tremendous explosion lifted Ed out of his seat and threw him into the blackness of complete oblivion. . . .

Turk poured himself a cup of coffee from the large urn set up in the rear of the makeshift press room. He walked to the window and looked out on the quadrangle steeped in the early twilight. The lights in the barracks were on as the men prepared for the final formation of the day.

Suddenly the press room door opened and Rick Nathan, a reporter for the *New York Herald Tribune*, came in, looked around, and spotting Turk, headed straight for him. "Doug, Colonel Gripper went down somewhere south of here."

Turk winced. He clenched his teeth and tried to steady his suddenly trembling hands.

"I know you guys were friends," Nathan said.

Turk nodded. He put his cup of coffee down on the table. "You sure he's down?" he asked in a choked voice.

"I was over at Biggs in the control tower. We couldn't hear all of the transmission because of the storm, but we heard the pilot say they were 'goin' in for the count.' I'm sorry."

Turk took several ragged breaths before he could speak. "Thanks for telling me."

"They might have been able to crash-land," Nathan offered.

"They might have," Turk agreed. Though his hands still trembled, he managed to light a cigarette. "We were going to have dinner tonight. I was going to ask Ed to be my best man."

Nathan shook his head.

Turk ran his hand through his hair. Suddenly he had a great need to be alone.

"Are you goin' to be all right?" Nathan asked.

"Yeah," Turk answered. "I'll be all right."

Again the door of the press room opened and the *Los Angeles Times* man, Hank Owens, stepped inside and announced, "Something is going on. I went out for a breath of fresh air and—"

"Fresh air would kill you," one of the other reporters quipped. "If it didn't have cigarette smoke in it, you wouldn't know how to breath it."

"Up yours!" Owen answered. "I'm telling you guys something is going on."

Nathan called out to Owens, "Okay, tell us what's going on."

"I counted some fifteen officers going in and out of Fitzhugh's office and I was only out in the hall for five minutes at the very most." Owens rolled his froglike eyes. "Usually, about this time Hanahan and the rest of his team move over to the officer's club for a few drinks."

"Maybe they have a night exercise going on," one of the reporters offered.

"Might be about Ed," Nathan offered in a voice just low enough for Turk to hear. "Hanahan might be deciding to send out a rescue team."

"Maybe," Turk answered, wondering if there was any connection between Ed going down and the shooting he had heard about. As yet, he hadn't mentioned what he had overheard to anyone. Before he did any digging on his own, he was waiting to see how much information Hanahan would release.

"Whatever is happening," one of the men at the window said, "it's not changing the routine. The evening formation is taking place as usual."

"Poor bastards!" another reporter exclaimed. "Imagine having to go through that shit every time you want to eat."

The man at the window agreed.

"I'm going out into the hallway for a few minutes," Turk said. "Maybe I can buttonhole one of the officers and get some answers."

"It's worth a try," Nathan agreed.

Unobtrusively, Turk made his way to the door, stepped out into the hallway, and went to the water cooler. Within the space of three minutes four officers came out of Fitzhugh's office. Finally Fitzhugh himself came out.

Turk didn't hesitate. He went straight to Fitzhugh and said, "I know Ed went down."

"I'm sorry," Fitzhugh said. "I know the two of you were good friends."

Turk nodded. "I've known him about as long as I've known you."

"We think he went down because of the storm," Fitzhugh explained.

"Then there's no connection between the shooting and him going down?" Turk asked.

"I just told you what we think caused it," Fitzhugh answered.

"If a rescue team is going out for Ed, I'd like to go along," Turk said.

"It's Hanahan's decision," Fitzhugh told him. "And I don't think he'd give you the right time in a clock shop."

Turk managed a smile. "I'd give *him* the right time—but then I'd count the clocks. . . . Anything more about that shooting business?" Turk asked.

"You know I can't comment on it," Fitzhugh said.

"Then it did happen?"

"No comment," Fitzhugh said, turned, and walked away.

Turk went back into the press room.

"Find out anything?" Owens asked.

Turk shook his head. "I suppose we'll get the word from Captain Jennings when he comes to brief us."

Several of the reporters started to laugh and one of them said, "Don't you know Hanahan winds Jennings up just enough to let him give us his spiel and then get back to wherever he's stored when he's not here? Jennings wouldn't know a good story if he fell over it. And if he did know it, he wouldn't give it to us. He'd sell it himself."

Turk shrugged, filled another cup with black coffee, and sat down at his assigned desk. He knew damn well that Hanahan wouldn't let him go out with any rescue mission. There was nothing he could do, except wait until he knew whether Ed was alive or dead. And if he was dead—well, at least if they brought the body back for burial, he'd be at the funeral. He knew it would have meant something to Ed to have a friend there at the end.

Turk knocked a cigarette out from a pack and lit it. If Ed could survive, Turk knew he would. Ed was the kind of man who wouldn't die easily.

The door opened and Captain Jennings entered carrying a manila folder in his right hand. He was a tall man, with a weak chin, dark-brown eyes behind horn-rimmed glasses, and thinning brown hair. He went directly to the lectern, removed his campaign hat, placed it in the upper right-hand corner of the lectern, and set the folder down directly in front of him.

"Gentlemen," he siad in a dry voice, "may I have

your attention?"

"Not really," one of the men answered.

"Gentlemen, General Hanahan wishes me to inform you that as of 1600 the Blue Army is still in command of all its key defensive positions. If you gentlemen will look at your mimeographed maps, page three of General Hanahan's explanation of—"

"Goddamn it, Jennings," the man from the *New York Daily News* exclaimed, "we don't want bullshit! We want to know what the hell is going on."

"Gentlemen, nothing extraordinary has occurred in any sector."

"Then why all the traffic in and out of Fitzhugh's office?" Owens asked.

"Gentlemen, General Fitzhugh's office is the command headquarters for the Blue Army. Naturally there would be traffic—"

"Captain," Nathan interrupted, "would you care to comment on Colonel Gripper?"

Jennings shifted uneasily and took a few moments to move a handkerchief across his forehead before he opened the manila folder. "Because we do not have a great deal of information at the present time, we can only tell you that Colonel Edward Gripper and Second Lieutenant Paul Allway are overdue from a routine reconnaissance mission."

The hubbub exploded before Jennings finished his statement.

"Where was he flying?" the *New York Times* man shouted.

"Has he crashed?" another reporter demanded to know.

"What time was he last heard from?" the man from the *Washington Post* called out.

Jennings held his hand up for silence.

To Turk he looked like a gospel minister, getting ready either to ask God for His blessing, or ask the congregation to make a generous donation when the basket was passed around.

"Gentlemen," Jennings said, "we are not able to answer any of your questions."

Suddenly Nathan was on his feet. "Come on, Jennings, I was in the control tower at Briggs. I heard Lieutenant Allway shout they were going down for the count."

The other reporters turned toward him.

"Now what the hell does 'going down for the count' mean in your book?" Nathan asked.

Jennings turned beet-red. He licked his thin lips. "We have nothing more to say. Thank you, gentlemen." He gathered up his manila folder and replaced his campaign hat on his head. He was about to move away from the lectern, when several of the reporters surrounded him to demand more information.

"They're not going to get anything else out of him," Turk said to Nathan. He stood up. "I'm going back to the hotel."

"See you later?" Nathan asked.

Turk nodded. "The Tivoli in Juárez."

"Unless you know a better place," Nathan responded.

"I don't."

Nathan smiled. "For my money, the food and the women are the best in Juárez."

Turk didn't comment. He wasn't on the prowl, looking for a woman to spend the night with. He had never been much for one-night stands, though over the years he had had his share of them.

In the corridor there were four flyboys from Biggs

waiting for news about Lieutenant Allway. Their young faces were grave with concern. They spoke in low voices.

As Turk passed them one said to another, "Just the other day Paul put in his request for a transfer to a fighter squadron."

And the other pilot answered. "Yeah, I know. I did the same thing. . . ."

Turk quickened his pace, left the building, and went straight to the green De Soto. Before he slid behind he wheel, Turk looked off to the west, toward the bare rock-face of the Franklin Mountains. The sky beyond them was covered with clouds, but overhead and to the east the stars were very bright, and the new gibbous moon was just rising.

Turk drove out of the base, turned south on Pershing Drive, and headed into El Paso, the twin beams from his headlights now and again momentarily transfixing a rabbit. To the left, a long freight train slowly moved north. The mournful wail of its whistle flowed over the flat terrain until it was lost in the vast emptiness of the land.

Turk forced himself not to think about Ed. It wasn't easy. The only way he could do it was to focus his thoughts on Lauren. He desperately needed her to comfort him.

But he realized that Lauren not marrying him was a very real possibility. After all, he was going back into the army and if the United States—but there was no *if*. War was coming; it was only a matter of when. He was not, by any standard, a good risk. But then again, what man was during a war?

He reached the outskirts of the city and passed several squatter's shacks with windows yellowed by light coming from coal-oil lanterns.

Within minutes, Turk was in the city. He drove halfway around San Jacinto Plaza, which was directly across the street from the Hotel Cortés, and pulled into an empty parking place. The plaza was really a small park in which there was an enclosed area for alligators. Several of the reporters had dubbed the place Alligator Park.

He entered the hotel and hurried straight to the desk clerk. "Have there been any messages for Douglas Turk?" he asked.

The clerk turned around and scanned the pigeonholes behind him. "Nothing, señor," he said, facing Turk.

"Thanks," Turk said, dropping a quarter on the counter. "If anyone should want me, I'll be in my room."

The clerk nodded.

Turk crossed the lobby and stepped into the elevator. "Five," he told the operator. A few minutes later he stood at his window drinking a neat scotch. A sudden gust of wind rattled sand against the glass pane and bent the trees in the plaza. "I hope you make it, old friend," Turk said, gesturing with his glass toward the vast desert that stretched into the night. "I hope you make it." He downed the rest of the scotch, turned away from the window, and went to the dresser to pour another drink for himself.

Lauren entered the dining room, went directly to where Walther was seated at the head of the candlelit table, and kissed him on the forehead. "Thank you for the lovely gown." She moved two paces back and turned completely around for his benefit. She was a petite woman, with shoulder-length hair the color of dark honey. Gray eyes. A sensual mouth. And a firm, slender body with full high breasts and wide hips.

"I'm glad you like it," Walther said with a pleased smile. "I was sure royal blue would become you, and it does. It comes from Paris. I was told it's pure silk." He spoke Spanish, rather than English, which he didn't like, or German, which Lauren had difficulty with.

Lauren hugged herself and played her fingers over the soft material. "Yes, it most certainly is silk." She had hoped he wouldn't bring her a gift. But he always brought her one whenever he returned from a trip. She knew it was his way of telling her that she meant something to him, though he was unable to express his feelings the way another man might. But now this gift was getting in the way of what she had to say to him. She didn't want to hurt him. He had been gentle, kind, and considerate. He had even made it possible for her to develop as a painter.

Walther puffed up his lips and nodded. He was a tall thin man of fifty-eight years, with a leonine head of gray hair, accentuating his black eyes. Because he was a handsome and Lauren was a beautiful woman, they made a striking couple.

"Did you have a good trip?" she asked, taking her place across the candlelit table.

"Very!" he answered enthusiastically. "I won't have to go to Tampico for a while. Picking up a small silver bell, Walther rang for the servants to commence dinner. "I even managed to get some excellent French wine and, believe it or not, several cases of German beer. I didn't believe my eyes when I saw them. But there they were in the warehouse, next to several pieces of farm machinery I had ordered."

Julio, the butler, offered Lauren an appetizer of grilled prawns.

"No, thank you," she said. She was too nervous to eat.

"They're very good," Julio told her.

Rather than risking calling Walther's attention to her tenseness, she smiled up at Julio and said, "On your recommendation, I'll take two."

"You know," Walther said, "I was thinking of having a Christmas party."

Lauren suppressed a smile. He had given a Christmas party every year during the five years of their marriage, and his statement wasn't much of a surprise.

"Something around a hundred to a hundred and fifty people," Walther continued. "I think it would be very nice, don't you?"

Lauren wasn't really listening to him. She was trying to find the courage she needed to tell him she wanted a divorce.

"Lauren?" Walther called.

"Yes."

"Did you hear what I just asked?" he asked.

"I'm sorry," she admitted. "My mind was somewhere else. You were talking about having a Christmas party."

"Yes. Well, what do you think about it?"

She was about to answer when Delores, one of the young servants, entered the room to remove the fish plates and silverware.

"A hundred and fifty people would be about all that I'd care to entertain," Walther said.

"Did we have as many last year?" Lauren asked, using the question to buy her a few more minutes' time. Her heart was racing and her stomach gathered into a large knot of apprehension.

Julio returned with a silver tureen of bean and sherry soup.

"You were right about the prawns," she told him.

He smiled broadly and ladled the soup into her dish.

"I took the liberty of inviting several of my rancher friends from the north," Walther said. "They have been good customers, and I did not think you would mind if they were our guests for a few days."

"How many is several?"

Walther laughed. "Now that's a question a woman should ask."

"But I am a woman," she answered with more harshness then she had intended.

Walther stopped the spoon midway between the soup dish and his mouth. "Is anything wrong?" he asked.

From the expression on his face, Lauren knew she had hurt him. "Nothing is wrong," she lied, purposefully keeping her voice soft. "I'm just a bit more tired than usual."

Walther swallowed the soup from the spoon before he said, "I thought you looked a bit peaked before I left for Tampico. You're working too hard at your painting. I know the signs. I think you need a vacation."

Julio served the main course of roast lamb and mint jelly, baked yams, and broccoli.

"If the weather is nice," Walther said, "we could hold the party out in the garden. We have enough room for twice the number of people that will be invited."

"I'd rather like a garden party," Lauren answered.

Walther smiled. "Then you shall have a garden party. If the weather is not warm enough, I'll have a large tent set up and make my own weather."

She took a deep breath. It was difficult to go through the charade of talking about a Christmas party when she knew that by Christmas, she'd be with Doug. . . . Suddenly she remembered the name of the ship Doug had asked her to inquire about. At least, she hoped, the question would change the subject and get the conversation into another area.

"By the way," she began, to get Walther's attention, "did you ever hear of a ship named the *City of Cadiz*?"

Walther stopped eating. His face went white. He reached for a glass of wine, tried to speak, but immediately began to cough.

"Are you all right?" Lauren asked, frowning. His reaction to the question surprised her.

He nodded and croaked, "A piece of meat went down the wrong way." It took him a few more minutes to gain his voice. "Where did you hear the name of that ship?" His face was becoming very red and there was suppressed anger in his voice.

Lauren shrugged. "I don't remember. At some luncheon or other."

Walther suddenly turned to Julio. "Leave us!" he ordered. "I'll ring when I want you." He stood up, moved behind his chair, and rested his hands on the back of it. "I must know where you heard the name of the ship." His voice was strident with urgency. "Lauren, this is very important!"

"I don't remember," she said petulantly. She had never seen him so angry. He disdained anger in himself and others. "Anger," he'd often said, "is a less than satisfactory way of expressing displeasure."

Walther began to pace. Several times he went as far as the french doors that opened out to the garden, then stopped and turned to look at her. He finally returned to the back of his chair. "We have had a good life together and I thought we had made a good adjustment to our different sexual needs. In all other respects we've been very compatible, even, I'd say, happy. Am I wrong to—" Walther stopped and smacked his forehead. "Turk . . . Mister Douglas Turk, that's who!"

Before Lauren realized it, Walther was in front of her.

"Does he know about the ship?" he shouted, grabbing hold of her arms and shaking her. "Tell me, did he ask you to ask me about the ship?"

"Let go of me," she cried. "You're hurting me." She struggled to her feet.

"Did Turk ask—?"

The words burst out of her. "I'm leaving you, Walther. I'm leaving you for good!"

"*Hure!*" he bellowed, reverting to German. "Slut!" He struck her in the face.

The blow knocked Lauren to the floor. Blood poured out of her nose and tears filled her eyes.

"Of all the men you had to take to your bed," Walther said venomously, "you had to take a man who fought in Spain. A lousy communist!" He looked down at her, spat, and turning on his heel, he walked swiftly out of the dining room.

Lauren pulled herself up on her feet. She wasn't going to remain in the house one more minute than was necessary. She was halfway up the steps when Walther was coming out of his room.

"You are not to leave this house," he said, standing at the head of the steps.

She didn't answer.

"Leave this house and I can't be responsible for what happens to you," Walther shouted, starting down the steps.

"Your responsibility to me is over," Lauren told him. "Over! I will do what I please and go where I want. And don't try to stop me."

He glared at her, then rushed down the remainder of the steps and out of the door.

Lauren shook her head. She had hoped to tell Walther she was leaving him in a different way. She would have taken the blame for breaking up the marriage and completely absolved him from any responsibility. She had no desire to hurt him or to be in the least bit vindictive. . . . But that the mere mention of a ship's name could have completely wrecked her plans—indeed, might have wrecked the marriage even if she had still wanted to keep it intact—seemed absolutely incredible. That ship had to be very important to Walther for him to react the way he had. Suddenly Lauren realized the ship was so important to him that he had actually threatened her. And for the first time that night she became frightened.

# 5

Turk stepped outside the hotel lobby. A cold, grainy wind was blowing from the north and the sky was black with clouds. He looked for a cab to take him across the Santa Fe bridge into Juárez, on the other side of the Rio Grande River.

"Where are all the cabs?" Turk asked the wizened doorman.

"Not many around after eight o'clock even when it's a good night," the man answered.

Turk accepted the answer with a silent nod. Cities like El Paso, as the saying went, pulled in their sidewalks after six. He raised the collar of his trench coat, set his hat more securely on his head, and started to walk toward the Santa Fe bridge. Few people were on the streets.

Turk passed a large drugstore and stopped to buy a pack of cigarettes. The soda counter and white marble-topped tables were crowded with young people. Two GI's were seated on stools at the counter. A radio was playing "Deep In The Heart of Texas."

The young people were local couples out for a Friday night date. They were laughing, holding hands and either looking at one another with sheep's eyes or, with hot eyes that betrayed their true interest.

One of the soldiers was a sandy-haired, freckle-faced boy of nineteen or twenty. The other was about the same age, dark-haired and square-faced. The two looked lonely, almost forlorn. Their uniforms were too big for them. They drank their coffee and ate their sandwiches without speaking.

Turk was tempted to go over to the soldiers and speak to them. But he decided against it. Nothing he could say would change their loneliness or their feeling of isolation. He walked back into the street and continued toward the bridge.

It cost two cents for Turk to cross it. Below him the Rio Grande was a narrow stream perhaps no more than three yards wide. On the Mexican side there were several large bonfires. Around them were dozens of men, women, and children. They were shoeless. Despite the cold, few wore any sort of outer covering.

As soon as Turk was across the bridge, he was on a street bright with flashing lights and neon signs. People were everywhere. Juárez offered cheap food, booze, and women. Native El Pasoans took advantage of what it had to offer, and ranchers for hundreds of miles around El Paso also made the trip to Juárez for the pleasures it offered.

Turk hadn't progressed more than a dozen feet along Juárez Avenue when a street urchin began to walk alongside of him. He expected the boy to beg for money and was ready to hand him a few coins.

"Bad night," the boy said in English.

"Yes, it is," Turk answered.

The boy was probably ten or eleven years old, but because of his small size, he might have been mistakenly judged younger. He was thin. His black eyes were very alert. He had black straight hair and the high cheekbones of an Indian. But he had enough Spanish blood to make him a mestizo.

The boy kept pace with Turk and said, "My name is Manuel Ortega."

"That's a good name," Turk responded, impressed by the child's aplomb.

"Everyone knows me," Manuel said.

"I don't doubt that," Turk replied, wondering if he should switch to Spanish.

"I am the man in my family," Manuel told him.

Turk didn't have to ask about Manuel's father. He doubted if the boy had ever known him.

"You have somewhere special to go?" the boy asked.

Turk ignored the question and looked down at him. He was dressed better than most of the other urchins. He had shoes and was wearing a brown, heavy woolen sweater.

"I tell you, mister," the boy said, "I have a special deal for you because you are my friend."

With a suppressed smile, Turk asked, "What's the deal?"

The boy stopped. "You can fuck my sister for five dollars. She's a virgin."

"Is that what you're selling?" Turk asked, neither shocked nor amused. He had had similar propositions in Spain during the war there, and in China before that.

"She's fifteen, a real woman," the boy continued. "I tell you what—because you're my friend you can do it for four, I mean three, dollars."

"Three dollars," Turk repeated.

"Amigo, you are my good friend. Two dollars. What do you say? Just two dollars. I give one to my sister and I keep one."

Turk shook his head.

"You can't get a woman for less, even in the cribs near the railroad tracks."

"I don't want a woman," Turk said.

With his head cocked to one side, the boy raised his heavy black eyebrows. Then suddenly the expression on his face changed. He smiled and said, "To fuck me it will cost you five dollars."

Turk stopped. "I don't want either you or your sister," he said. He was becoming angry and was annoyed with himself for allowing the boy to walk with him. He should have told him to get lost, but he had been taken with the boy's smooth manner and had been curious about what would be offered to him eventually. He should have known it would be sex, in one form or another.

"Listen, if you want a sheep—"

Turk grabbed at the boy, but he nimbly darted out of reach and tauntingly shouted, "Amigo, I don't think you have a prick at all!"

Passers-by were stopping to look at them.

"Amigo," the boy yelled, obviously enjoying the audience, "maybe you just got a slit like my sister and want somebody to fuck you?"

Turk hurried away.

The boy came after him, shouting insults.

Finally Turk reached his destination, the Club Tivoli. He stopped and turned around. The boy was there, but far enough away to be safe. "If you're here when I come out," Turk said, "I'm going to beat the crap out of you."

"Amigo," the boy answered, "you can bet on your mother's cunt I'll be here."

Turk glared at him and went inside. He gave the scantily dressed hat-check girl his coat and hat. The Tivoli was decorated like a grotto, complete with waterfalls, real trees and shrubs and rocky enclosures that provided complete privacy for anyone who wanted it. The room was filled with a dim greenish light. Upstairs was a brothel where a woman cost ten dollars for an hour, or twenty-five from midnight to six the next morning. A four-piece combo and a female singer were doing a fair rendition of "Dolores." It was a popular place for ranchers out for a night of sex and booze.

Turk went straight to the horseshoe-shaped bar. In the center of it was a huge tank of water where two completely nude women were swimming.

Nathan was already there. So was Owens and the *New York Times* man, whose name he didn't know.

"I was wondering if you were going to come," Nathan said.

"Better here than in the hotel room," Turk answered. His encounter with Manuel had left him feeling foolish.

Owens introduced him to the *Times* man, saying "Douglas Turk, meet Charles Browning."

"Your friend tells me," Browning said, shaking Turk's hand, "that you're an old army man."

"That's right," Turk replied. He hadn't told either Nathan or Owens that he would be back in the army by the first of the year.

What do you think is going on out there in the desert?" Browning asked.

"You know as much about it as I do," Turk answered. He summoned the barkeeper and asked for a beer. "Make it a *Negro Morella*," he told him in Spanish.

Two more reporters—Sam Jones from the *San Francisco Chronicle* and Bill Green from the *New York Daily News*—drifted in and came over to where Turk and his friends were.

"I could name about ten other places I'd rather be

than El Paso," Browning said, holding his glass in front of him.

"Why?" Jones laughed. "There's nothing wrong with El Paso, if you don't mind being in the ass-end of the States."

"Make that the ass-end of the world," Green said. "Thank God for Juárez. At least there's booze and broads here."

"But just think of those poor bastards who are down somewhere in the desert south of here," Jones commented. "They're really in shit up to their eyeballs. Some old mustang colonel named Gripper and a young pilot. If they're not dead from the crash, those Mex bandits will finish them off."

"That old mustang," Turk said in a low flat voice, "just happens to be a good friend of mine. I wouldn't count him out so quickly."

"I didn't mean—"

"It's okay," Turk said. "You were calling the shot as you see it." He finished off his beer and ordered another one. "We're going to need Ed Gripper when the war comes."

"I don't think it will come," Green said. "The Japs will see things our way, and as for Hitler, we don't have any reason to fight him and he doesn't want to fight us."

Turk drank some of the beer before he said, "We should have stopped the fascists in Spain. But we didn't. But now we're going to have to stop them."

"Excuse me, señors," said a tall handsome man with mustachios, "my name is Luis Garcia."

"What can we do for you, Señor Garcia?" Nathan asked.

"You gentlemen are Americans, no?"

"Yes. We're reporters."

Garcia nodded. "Covering the maneuvers of the American Army?"

"That's right."

"I couldn't help overhearing your conversation," Garcia said. He looked at Turk and smiled. "There was no reason for the United States or any other nation to stop Hitler in Spain. The German and Italian forces were there by invitation of General Franco. They were needed to help defeat the communists who were trying to take over the country."

"Señor," Turk responded, "it isn't polite to listen to other people's conversations."

The man stiffened.

"Go easy," Nathan whispered. "Down here they shoot first and ask questions later."

"And what do you know about Spain?" the man challenged.

"I was there," Turk answered straightforwardly.

The man moved closer. He spoke in Spanish to his two friends, who were on the other side of him.

"What was all that about?" Owens asked.

Turk smiled. "He told his friends he has found himself an American pig to stick."

"Why don't we just pay and leave," Green suggested.

"He and his friends wouldn't let us," Turk answered.

"So you were in Spain," the man said. He was grinning broadly.

"I said I was," Turk replied, speaking in Spanish to let the man know he understood the language.

"And what were you doing in Spain?"

"Fighting against Franco and his butchers."

The man nodded. "Then you must be a lousy communist!" he exclaimed loudly. A knife blade flashed through the air. "I stick you now, gringo, and put a big hole in your gut."

A few of the nearby women screamed.

Turk side-stepped the knife stroke. He smashed a beer bottle against the bar and pushed the jagged end directly against the man's neck. "Drop the knife," he ordered calmly, speaking in English again. "Drop it or I'll put another set of lips on your neck."

The man glared at him but dropped the knife. Turk could feel the tension in the room. Owens picked up the knife and put it on the bar.

"Go back to your friends!" Turk exclaimed.

"You come back here," the man threatened, "and your life won't be worth shit."

"Go back to your friends," Turk said, "before I really become angry." He lowered the broken bottle and heard an audible sigh of relief.

The man backed away.

"I'm going to have another beer," Turk said, "and then leave."

"We'll go with you," Jones offered.

"No need to," Turk responded. "Stay and enjoy yourselves. I don't feel much like having steak dinner." He apologized to the barkeep for breaking the bottle. Instead of another beer, he asked for Chivas, neat, as he pocketed the knife.

The moment Turk stepped out of the Tivoli, he expected Manuel to come flying at him with a barrage of insults. But the boy didn't. He was nowhere in sight. After what had happened at the bar, Turk was grateful to be left alone. He wanted to get back to the Texas side as soon as possible.

He started to walk toward the bridge. The street was not nearly as crowded as it had been earlier. But the lights were as bright and the shills for the various brothels were as busy as ever.

He paused and looked back over his shoulder just as a man was leaving the Tivoli. Turk thought it might be one of Garcia's friends, or that maybe Garcia himself might want to prove to them that he still had a pair of balls. The way it now stood, Garcia had lost face, and Turk expected the man to follow him. But the man went off in the opposite direction. Relieved, Turk continued to walk.

The experience at the bar played itself over in his brain. Had it really gone to a push-comes-to-shove situation, he would have opened the man's throat. Prickles raced down his back. Luckily it hadn't happened that way.

He passed a doorway and saw a boy sleeping Indian-fashion—legs drawn up, arms resting on the knees, and the head face down on the arms. It was Manuel. Turk continued to walk, but then stopped and went back to where Manuel was. He shook him by his shoulder and asked, "Is this where you usually sleep?"

Manuel blinked, rubbed his eyes, and said, "I was waiting for you." He got to his feet.

The two of them walked side by side.

"I didn't mean the things I said," Manuel told him. "But you can still have my sister—"

Turk gave him a quick look.

"Okay, okay—you don't want her or me."

Turk dug into back pocket and fished out his wallet. He handed Manuel a five-dollar bill. "Buy yourself something to eat and give the rest to your sister."

"I don't take money unless I do something for it," Manuel said proudly.

"Take it and give part of it to your sister."

"She's not my sister. Carmen is just a girl who lets me peddle her ass."

"No mother?" Turk asked.

"I don't know where she is."

"Who taught you English?"

"Carmen."

Turked returned the five-dollar bill to the wallet.

"I tell you what," Manuel said, "I can take care of you. Do things like shine your shoes. Run errands. You look like you need someone to do those things for you."

"What about Carmen?"

"She's got a couple of other boys to peddle her ass. One of them is even old enough to fuck her himself. Do we have a deal?"

Turk realized it would be a crazy thing to do. But he had done crazier things. Anyway, it would only be for a few days. And it would give the boy a chance to earn a few dollars. He admired Manuel for not taking his money without doing something for it. Besides, the boy had suddenly made him remember André, a boy about Manuel's age, who had led him and four other men through the passes of the Pyrenees to France. A ten-year-old soldier complete with rifle and bandolier, as brave as any man. Turk had tried to find out what happened to him but no one knew. He had probably been killed like so many other soldiers who fought for the Republican cause.

"Okay," Turk said, "we have a deal. But how are you going to cross the bridge into El Paso?"

"I'm not going to use the same bridge you do," Manuel told him. "I'll come across on the railroad bridge. I know El Paso. You tell me where to meet you and I'll be there."

"Do you know the big drugstore across from the park where the alligators are?"

"Sure."

"You meet me in the drugstore and we'll have a sandwich together."

"Okay."

"By the way, where will you sleep?" Turk asked.

"I'll find a place," Manuel answered with a smile.

Turk didn't answer. He knew the boy would probably end up sleeping on a makeshift bed in his room.

"See you at the drugstore," Manuel said; he scampered down a side street.

A few minutes later Turk was back across the bridge. He chuckled when he thought about how Lauren would take the news that he had acquired a ten-year-old "man friday."

Thinking about Lauren made him aware of just how very much he missed her. He wondered if he'd ever see her again—and if she'd had the courage to leave Walther.

Walther went directly to the house at 142 Donata Guera and was led to the study by the butler. As he stepped into the book-lined room, he saw Colonel Stephan Krieger move out from behind the highly polished oak-wood desk to greet him. The colonel's Alsatian shepherd, Dimitri, moved with him.

"I am sorry to disturb you," Walther said. "But something has happened. . . ." He kept his eyes on the dog, who made low throaty sounds and whose fangs were bared.

Krieger put his arm around Walther's shoulders. He was a tall, broad-shouldered man with a bald head and bull neck. He was an acknowledged expert on Mexican pottery and a successful owner of a chemical manufacturing plant. He was also the chief of the German intelligence operation in Mexico and Central America.

Krieger gestured to the large, dark leather chair in front of the desk and said, "Please, you sit down and we will talk." He returned to the desk and settled into the high-back swivel chair. The dog stretched out next to the chair.

Walther couldn't remain seated. He stood up.

"If it makes it any easier for you," Krieger said, "feel

free to pace."

"Thank you," Walther replied. He took a deep breath and when he exhaled, he said, "At dinner, not more than an hour ago, my wife asked me if I knew of a ship named the *City of Cadiz*."

Kreiger rubbed his temples. "Where do you suppose she heard that name, or more importantly, why did she ask the question?"

Walther walked to the fireplace, and resting one hand on the mantle he looked at the low fire. "She has been sleeping with that American reporter Douglas Turk."

"Turk, eh!" Krieger exclaimed, and using a small key on the end of a gold chain he unlocked a drawer. "I have a dossier on him here," he said, moving his fingers along the index tabs of the manila folders within until he found the one with "Turk, Douglas" printed on it in block letters. He opened it and read silently for several minutes. Now and then he reached down and patted the dog's head.

Walther said nothing. He was aware of the silence in the room and the thumping sound of his own heart."

"A very interesting man, this Douglas Turk," Krieger said, closing the folder. He took time to light a cigar before he said, "Now tell me exactly what happened between you and your charming wife."

"We had words," Walther told him.

"Was that before or after she asked about the ship?"

"After. . . . We had words about Turk. I knew he had—"

Krieger held up his hand. "We might have a problem," he said. "One of our agents followed an officer from the *City of Cadiz* to a meeting he had with Richard Harris."

"Isn't Harris a member of the British embassy staff?"

"Was. He had to be killed. So did the ship's officer,

who we were later able to identify as a member of MI6, as was Harris."

"But how did your Mr. Turk know about the ship?"

"That doesn't matter now," Krieger answered. "We must deal with the fact that he knows and must be silenced. Do you know where he is?"

"Before I left for Tampico, Lauren mentioned the fact that he was going to cover the American war games in the southwest."

"Then he'll probably be in El Paso," Krieger said. "There are not too many hotels where he would stay, and I'd venture to guess that he'd be the only man with the name Douglas Turk at whatever hotel he would be staying at. I'll arrange to have him killed."

"I don't understand how Lauren could have chosen him. Of all the men. . . ."

"Walther, if you recall, I warned you about marrying her," Krieger said. "I warned you. . . . But we will discuss that in a few minutes. Now I must send word to Berlin about the developments involving the *City of Cadiz*. The entire Zimmermann Operation could be compromised by these developments. Admiral Canaris must be apprised of the situation. Will you excuse me?"

Walther nodded.

"If you like, I'll have some food sent to you," Krieger offered.

"No, thank you; I have lost my appetite."

"Understandable," Krieger said, walking toward the door.

The moment Walther was alone, he began to pace.

Krieger returned much sooner than Walther had expected him to. "I told the cook to prepare a few sandwiches for us," he said, going straight back to his desk. "I also issued the necessary instructions to silence Turk."

"Now what do we do?" Walther asked, sitting down

again in the leather chair in front of the desk.

"We wait for an answer from the Abwehr," Krieger answered. "But in the meantime we must decide what to do about your wife."

Walther moved forward on the chair. "I do not think she knows anything more than the name of a ship."

Krieger relit his cigar. "Can you be absolutely certain of that?"

"No."

Krieger nodded and puffed at his cigar, sending a cloud of grayish white smoke across the desk. "Let me put this question to you: Can you be absolutely certain that within the next few days she will not mention the *City of Cadiz* to anyone else?"

"No."

"Then you understand what must be done," Krieger said.

Walther stood up slowly.

"I understand how difficult this is for you," Krieger said sympathetically. "I realize that in your own way you care for her."

"She has left me," Walther told him.

"What do you mean, she has left you?"

Walther began to pace again. Krieger was not an easy man to talk to, especially about sexual relationships.

"You were warned about the marriage," Krieger reminded him after allowing a moment to pass. "But you were sure you would be able to handle the situation. "You handled it, all right. You literally put your wife into bed with an American, a former—"

"I didn't think sex would be so important to her."

"The men who are your lovers are important to you," aren't they?" Krieger challenged.

Walther nodded. He had always felt that Krieger hated him because he was a homosexual, and now that hate was surfacing.

"Has she ever had access to your private papers?"

"Lauren never took an interest in what I was doing," Walther said. "She's an artist, not a spy."

"That's not a very clever statement, Walther. If she *were* a spy, would you know?"

Walther shook his head.

"I will send one of my men with you," Krieger said, rubbing his temples. "She must be brought here, interrogated, and then killed. It will be made to look like an accident. Is she at home?"

"I don't know."

"Find out," Krieger said, handing Walther the phone and then dialing his number. "Tell her you're sorry for what happened. The blame is yours and you will be home shortly."

Walther held the phone to his ear. "It's ringing," he said, and after a few moments he added, "She's either not answering or she isn't there."

"She must be found," Krieger said. "I will go with you myself."

Walther nodded. In a tight voice he said, "I understand."

"I hope you do!"

"All I wanted of her was that she be discreet," Walther said, barely managing to speak.

"It was a foolish thing to ask," Krieger answered.

"Very foolish," Walther agreed.

"Major, why the fuck can't we get through to Este Grande?" Hanahan asked in a growl. "According to my status board we have an OP and a four-man medic detachment there." He rolled the dead cigar to the other side of his mouth. Because of the unusual situation, he had made the communications room his temporary headquarters and was now unhappy about it. He was on a short fuse.

Major Redding, the four-to-midnight communications officer, was a short man with thin brown hair and green eyes. "Sir," he began, "Sergeant Cross says the storm—"

Hanahan crossed the distance between himself and the major with three long strides. "You go on telling me about the fucking storm and I'm going to make sure that you wind up in some fucking supply depot. I *know* there's a goddamn storm. I have a goddamn plane down because of it, and I have a goddamn town that has taken fire."

"Yes, sir," Redding answered, working hard to keep the tremor out of his voice.

Hanahan stared at him. "You got a goddamn tick on the left side of your face, Major?"

"Yes, sir."

Hanahan spun around to one of his aides. "You get Major Driscol back here. How the hell am I supposed to think looking at the left side of a man's face jump up and down."

He walked back to the opposite wall, where a large map of the southwestern United States and northern Mexico was hung and studied it. He was forced to acknowledge there was a remote possibility that the bandits who shot up El Charo had also shot Gripper down. Hell, a couple of well-placed slugs from a .38 could have done the job, let alone a few rounds from a rifle, or even a machine gun. Why not a machine gun? The bastards obviously had some cannons with them!

Suddenly a voice came over the loudspeaker. "Blue Chief, this is Blue Grass. We're experiencing heavy pressure on our right flank. Estimate two, possibly three infantry battalions."

Hanahan had a clear picture of where Blue Grass

was positioned and what was happening. He took the mike from the sergeant and said, "This is Blue Chief. Notify team observers you have arty support as of this time 1850 hours. Support fire directed from field units thirteen, twenty, and twenty-two."

". . . Support fire reported, Blue Chief. Pressure still heavy."

The door opened and General Fitzhugh and Major Driscol entered.

"Harry is involved in a night action against my right flank." Hanahan told Fitzhugh. "I called in three units of arty fire. But Blue Grass says the pressure is still heavy."

Fitzhugh went to the map. Blue Grass was stretched out along a group of low ridges to the southwest of the city.

"Blue Chief, we've been given a loss of twenty percent," the voice said.

"Can you hold?" Hanahan asked.

"Yeah, they're falling back."

"Notify observers that artillery firing has ceased as of 1900." Hanahan turned to Fitzhugh. Shaking his head, he told him, "If this was a real fight, Harry's men would have been cut to pieces by my artillery."

Before Fitzhugh could answer, another voice came over the PA. "Blue Chief, this is Blue Indian. Gray Armor is coming this way."

"The bastard is trying to flank me!" Hanahan shouted. "He's coming at me from the west."

"Blue Chief, this is Blue Indian. Spotted four tanks."

Fitzhugh turned back to the map. Harry was attacking the way he thought he would, from the southwest.

"I hadn't figured Harry to flank me, especially at night," Hanahan said.

"He hasn't done it yet," Fitzhugh answered.

Hanahan went to the map. "Suppose we split our

force," he said. "We put enough on the high ground to hold Harry, and the rest we send against the flank of his column. We cut off its supplies and we have it."

"We might even be able to chew up that column," Fitzhugh responded. "But even if we don't, we'll keep Alt's guns away from the city."

Hanahan put the coffee down and went to the humidor on a nearby desk. When his cigar was well lit, he said, "Now what the hell are we going to do about El Charo and Ed? We still haven't been able to raise Este Grande." Hanahan puffed vigorously on the cigar. "This damn business has caught me by the short hairs."

"Maybe we should contact Washington," Fitzhugh suggested. "After all—"

"And what the hell am I going to tell them?" Hanahan asked. "They're going to want to know the facts and I don't have any, except that there's been some shooting around a Mex village and one of my planes is down." He flicked the cigar's ash into an ashtray. "Okay, we'll send out a scout team. An armored car and two . . . jeeps, I think the men call them. Something has gone haywire out there. If it's bandits, I'm going to send my own men after them. To hell with waiting for the Federales to move their asses." He turned to one of his aides. "I want a scout team ready to move within fifteen minutes. They're to be fully armed and carry live ammo. Is that understood?"

"Yes, sir," the officer answered.

"As soon as the team is ready, report to me by phone," Hanahan said, returning the officer's salute.

"How do you want the press handled?" Fitzhugh asked.

"We've got to keep the lid on it until we know more."

"Turk is going to want to know more about Ed," Fitzhugh told him.

"Yeah, that fucker will push," Hanahan commented.

"Okay, at tomorrow's noon press briefing, you tell the gentlemen from the Fourth Estate that Ed did go down as a result of the storm, and that a Mexican unit is on the way to the crash site."

"Turk won't buy it," Fitzhugh said. "Besides, we already told them that Ed was overdue."

"Then—"

"General Hanahan," the switchboard operator said, "your aide is on line ten."

"Hanahan here."

"General, Captain George Barth is standing by. He's in command of the team."

"Put him on." Hanahan waited a moment, then spoke briskly into the handset. "Captain, you're to take no chances. I want to know what the hell is going on at Este Grande. Keep your men in radio communication and I want you to check in with me every fifteen minutes. Oh yes, I don't want your men to know they'll be operating in Mexico."

"Yes, sir. Is there anything else?"

"No, Captain. Just be damn careful—and good luck."

Hanahan put the phone down. The last time he had sent a group of men out on a real reconnaissance mission was during the Battle of the Argonne, twenty-three years before. That these men might have to shoot their way out of some situation with Mexican bandits made him pause and puff hard on his cigar, supremely confident that he had made the right decision.

"What do you think happened out there?" Fitzhugh asked.

"Beats the shit out of me," Hanahan answered. "If the weather was any good, I'd send up another plane to look around. It would be a hell of a lot safer than sending a scout team."

"Couldn't do that, whatever the weather. Not counting Gripper's plane, I have only two, and those are both down because I can't get spare parts."

Hanahan shook his head. "If we had to fight the Krauts now, we'd lose hands-down. They outclass us in every department of men and materiel."

Fitzhugh didn't answer. He poured himself a cup of coffee and drank it black.

"Better settle down," Hanahan said. "It's going to be a long fucking night, unless Harry decides to pull another action."

"I don't think he will."

"I don't either," Hanahan said with a grin, "because he thinks he has it knocked up. But the son of a bitch hadn't."

# 6

Turk arrived at the drugstore before Manuel, but it was too cold and windy for him to wait outside for the boy. He walked into the store and looked for an empty table. There were none. Some of the faces from his previous visit were familiar, but there were a few new ones and the two sad-looking GI's were gone. A Nat King Cole rendition of "Chattanooga Choo-Choo" was on the radio.

Turk opened his trench coat and pushed back his hat before sitting down at the counter.

The door opened.

Turk glanced at it, saw it was another couple, and turned away.

"What will ya have?" the counterman asked. He was a tall, horse-faced man with freckles on his forearms.

"Coffee, to start with," Turk answered.

"A java coming up!" the man resounded, handing Turk a menu. "The special of the day is a cup of rice and tomato soup, chicken-fried steak, hashbrowns, and bread and butter for one dollar and twenty-five cents."

Turk looked over the grill. Two hamburgers were sizzling on it. "The burgers look good," Turk said, when the counterman put the coffee down in front of him.

"Best in El Paso," the man responded.

The door opened.

Turk turned toward it and saw Manuel. "I'm over here," he called out.

The boy smiled and made his way over to the stool next to Turk. "I couldn't get here sooner because a freight train was crossing the bridge," Manuel explained. "I had to hang over the side until it was gone. Lucky it wasn't a very long one. I counted fifty cars. But some of them are more than a hundred. . . ."

"I figured there was a good reason why you weren't here."

"Okay if I have coffee?" Manuel asked.

"Sure. You can have anything you want to eat."

"We don't serve Mex kids here," the man behind the counter said.

Turk took a deep breath, nodded, and slowly faced the counterman. "Tell me that again," he said, his eyes going to slits.

"We don't serve none of them here," the man said. "This place is fer us. White people. There are places down by the railroad station that serve them."

Manuel put his hand on Turk's arm. "Hey, amigo, let's go."

"You'll serve me, won't you?" Turk asked.

The counterman nodded. "Never said I wouldn't."

"Good. Get me another cup of coffee," Turk said.

"Can't do that," the counterman responded.

"You can and you will," Turk said, flatly. "There's no rule about serving whites, right? And I'm white."

"You're only going to give it to the kid."

Turk turned around for a few moments, then faced the counterman again. "I count twenty people here, twenty-one including yourself. I want twenty-one cups of coffee—one for every person here—and twenty-one orders of burgers."

"You're joking!"

Turk shook his head. "Some of those boys sitting at the tables are going to be damn angry if I tell them you wouldn't allow me to buy coffee and a burger for them. . . . They might be so angry that they'll decide to, say, throw a chair or two through your plate-glass windows."

The counterman was very pale. "I'll have to talk to Mr. Byrnes about it. It's his place. He makes the rules."

"Talk to him," Turk said.

The counterman disappeared behind a door at the far end of the counter. Within a minute another man came out. He was short and stocky, with a cherubic face and white metal-rim glasses perched low on the bridge of his nose.

"Lenny tells me you're giving him trouble," he said, looking at Manuel while he spoke. "We don't want trouble, mister."

"I don't want any trouble either," Turk answered.

"You take that boy across the border with you?" Byrnes asked.

"He's my son," Turk said.

"He's a Mex, mister, and you're no Mex. He's got Indian blood in him. More than likely his mother is a prostitute and only God knows who his father is. . . . But what I'd like to know, mister, is why you brought him across the border? What's your game?"

Turk suddenly realized the background chatter coming from the tables had stopped. The only sound came from the announcer on the radio. Turk turned his head toward the tables. The young men and women were staring at him with open hostility. He realized that he wasn't going to be able to sway them to his side with a cup of coffee and a burger.

"Why don't you leave, mister," Byrnes said. "You don't even have to pay for your coffee."

"You're a sport, a real sport!" Turk answered. He slid off the stool. "Come on, Manuel, we'll find another place."

"You won't have any trouble near the railroad station," Byrnes said.

Suddenly Turk's hand shot out. He grabbed hold of Byrne's tie and pulled him across the marble-top counter, upsetting the coffee cup. "The only thing you did, mister, was stop a kid from eating. You think of that when you go to sleep tonight. Better still, think about it when you go to church on Sunday."

Byrne's face turned a deep red. To free himself, he tried pushing against the counter with his hands.

Turked jerked hard on the tie. "If God had rules about who not to feed and who to feed, they would have been in the Ten Commandments," he said; then he let go of the tie and walked slowly to the door. When he reached it, he turned toward the couples at the tables. "If any of you jocks think you can take me, come and try it."

No one moved.

"Let's go, Manuel," Turk said, "the air in here stinks." He opened the door and walked outside.

"Hey, amigo," Manuel said, "you sure told that fuck off."

"Yeah," Turk agreed, "I sure did. But now let's go and find a place to eat."

"I know where there's one."

"Don't tell me where it is. Let me guess—it's down by the railroad station, right?"

"Right," Manuel laughed, digging his hand into his

pocket. "You follow me. I take you there."

They walked quickly with their heads bent against the wind.

"Cold as a witch's twat," Manuel commented.

"Colder," Turk answered.

Manuel led Turk to a storefront luncheonette run by a gray-haired man named José Estaban, who was surprised to see Turk walk in and sit down at the wooden counter, and even more surprised when Manuel, who he seemed to know, announced that Turk was his *amigo*.

They ate well. Turk had chicken tacos, guacamole and frijoles, followed by two cups of strong black coffee, while Manuel devoured a bowl of chili and order of frijoles and a Coke, which was followed by a second bowl of chili and another Coke. The boy was obviously very hungry.

On the way back to the hotel, Turk said, "Tomorrow, I'll give you money for an American-style haircut and to buy some decent clothes. Later I'll arrange for you to have your own room at the hotel while I'm there."

"Anything you say," Manuel answered.

"Aren't you going to ask me how long I'll be here?"

With a shrug, Manuel said, "Listen, amigo, good things don't last. I learned that a long time ago."

Turk didn't continue the conversation. If he knew that at ten or eleven, the boy was already wiser than most adults.

When they reached the hotel, Turk gave the night desk clerk five dollars. "Send up a cot for my kid brother," he said, gesturing toward Manuel.

The clerk gave him a contemptuous look; the expression on the elevator operator's face a minute later was even more disdainful.

"You're giving me a bad reputation," Turk said, as he opened the door to the room, and with his left hand reached inside along the wall for the light switch.

As soon as the light was on Manuel ran into the room, went to the window, and exclaimed, "Hey, amigo, I can see down into the park, where the alligators are." He turned around and saw the portable typewriter on the desk. "Amigo, are you a . . ." He paused to think of the word.

"I'm a reporter," Turk said. "I write for the International News Service."

"I know all about reporters," Manuel responded. "I see them in the movies. What are you reporting on here in El Paso? A murder, or something like that?"

"The American Army. . . . Now you hop into the shower and get yourself cleaned up."

"I'm clean," Manuel said. "I don't have any lice and—"

"In the shower or—"

A knock at the door stopped Turk. He opened it. A porter delivered the cot and extra bedding. Turk gave him a tip; then he turned to Manuel. "In the shower."

"Okay, okay."

Turk loosened his tie, opened his collar, and removed his jacket. He poured himself a drink and lighting a cigarette, sat down in a ranch-style easy chair. Turk admired anyone with courage, and Manuel surely had it. The boy wasn't afraid to fight for what he wanted. He was the kind of kid to lift himself out of the gutter. Turk took a long drag on the cigarette. He was surprised at his reaction to the boy. It was more intense than he would have expected.

The sudden knifelike ring of the phone sliced off his train of thinking. It was either a call from headquarters, or from Lauren. Maybe it was someone with news of Ed.

"Turk," he said, picking up the phone.

"Doug, I've been trying to get through to you for

hours," Lauren said. "But the lines were busy."

Her voice was faint.

"Speak louder," he told her.

"I'm coming to El Paso," she said.

He heard that. "I love you," he replied loudly. "I love you!"

"And I love you," she answered.

"What made you change your mind?" Turk asked, smiling broadly.

"Walther became wild when I asked if he knew anything about the *City of Cadiz*. But I decided to leave him before that."

"You're not making much sense," Turk told her. "The connection is bad."

"I was trying to find a way to tell him at dinner," she said. "Then I asked him about the ship. He went wild. Never saw him like that. He blamed you. He guessed you asked me to ask him. He threatened me, Turk. Not in so many words, but the threat was there. I don't understand why he became so angry."

"Are you all right?"

"Yes . . . yes. I left the house just after he did. He told me that if I left the house he couldn't be responsible for my safety."

Turk stubbed out his cigarette and asked, "Where are you now?" He managed to keep the concern he felt out of his voice.

"The Hotel Geneve."

That was the worst place for her to be. Walther's Kraut buddies often frequented it. She was bound to be seen and her whereabouts reported to Walther. . . . And if he was angry enough to make threats, he might also be angry enough to carry them out.

"Doug, I can't hear you," Lauren said.

"I was thinking," he answered. He was frightened for her.

"Hey, amigo, are you talking to yourself," Manuel asked. He was standing in the open doorway to the bathroom with a towel wrapped around his middle.

"Hit the sack," Doug said. "Go to bed."

"Who are you talking to?" Lauren asked. "If you have another woman there. . . ."

"A kid I picked up," Turk told her.

"Who's there with you?"

"I told you. You'll meet him when you come up here.

"Now listen to me,' 'he continued. "Do exactly what I tell you. I want you to call a friend of mine, Louis Dijon. He's a Frenchman, but he has Mexican citizenship. He'll fly you to El Paso. You tell him I need you here to help me. He'll understand. You should be here sometime early tomorrow morning, at least before dawn. Leave everything in the hotel."

"You want him to fly me up tonight?" Lauren asked.

"Don't worry about it," Turk assured her. "Louis flew in Spain. He's good, very good. Take this number down. Two-two-nine-four-nineteen-nine-twelve. I'm in the Hotel Cortés, room number three-oh-four. If I'm not here, just ask the room clerk for the key. Tell him you're Mrs. Turk—that should give him something to think about."

"What does that mean?"

"Nothing. . . . Call Louis as soon as I hang up."

"I love you," Lauren said.

"See you soon," he answered, and put the phone down.

"She your woman?" Manuel asked. He was stretched out on the cot with his head propped up between his hands.

"Yes," Turk answered, lighting another cigarette and picking up his drink. He went to the windows and looked down at the park. It was deserted.

"As soon as I'm old enough to fuck," Manuel said,

"I'm going to have a woman."

Turk looked back at him. "I'm going to marry her," Turk said.

"Lots of men marry the women they fuck," Manuel responded. "I guess it's okay either way." He yawned and put his head down on the pillow. "Thanks for being okay, amigo." A moment later he was asleep.

Turk returned to the easy chair. Walther's reaction confused him. That he and Lauren were lovers was something Walther knew about and had chosen to ignore for the last six months. Why should his attitude suddenly change? Why should a question about a particular ship make him so angry?"

Turk wondered if he should phone Peter Harris and ask him what the hell was so special about the *City of Cadiz* that it put Walther in a rage?

Harris had called him a few days before and had asked him to find out if the *City of Cadiz* had docked in Tampico within the last few days. Harris had explained it would be damn awkward if he asked around about the ship, since it was Spanish and the relations between Spain and England were anything but friendly.

If Turk hadn't remembered about Walther's trip to Tampico, he'd never have thought of asking Lauren to mention the ship to Walther. At any rate, it obviously had been the wrong thing to do.

Turk finished off his whiskey. After he spoke to Lauren and got a better picture of what happened between her and Walther, he'd call Harris and find out more about the *City of Cadiz*. Maybe there was a good story there.

He looked at his watch. It was not yet midnight, and he decided to drive out to Bliss. Turk ground out his cigarette in an ashtray and stood up. He was too worked up to sleep, and maybe there'd be some additional information about Ed.

Turk glanced down at Manuel. Asleep, the boy looked like the child he was. Turk smiled, slipped into his jacket, took his coat and hat, and silently left the room, locking the door behind him.

A few minutes later he was in his car, tooling his way along Pershing Drive toward Fort Bliss.

# 7

Walther and Krieger sat in the rear of a black, chauffeur-driven Mercedes.

"It's really very kind of you to come," Walther said, hoping to break the silence between them.

"Let us hope she can be found," Krieger answered.

"There is no possible way she'd be able to leave Mexico City," Walther commented, more to reassure himself than to convince Krieger. "After all, it's not like Berlin, or even New York, with trains leaving at all hours of the night."

Krieger didn't answer and Walther retreated into his own silence, behind which he cowered in fear. Krieger was not the only one who had warned him against the marriage. His own brother, Otto, had cautioned him in a letter about taking an American wife, if for no other reason than the difference between their politics. "In the long run," Otto had written, "you will either convert her to National Socialism, or she will destroy you."

Walther uttered a rugged sigh. His generosity had

been abused by the only woman he had ever trusted.

"I blame Turk," Walther said. "If he had not—"

"Blame yourself," Krieger shot back.

Walther made no effort to continue the conversation. He closed his eyes and listened to the pounding of his own heart. . . . Twenty minutes later, he unlocked the front door of his house and stepped aside to allow Krieger to enter.

"I'll wait in the library," Krieger said. "Now remember: Tell Lauren I'm here on a social call. When she comes down, you make an excuse to leave the room. The rest I will handle."

Walther nodded. "Yes, I know. I may have made a mistake, but I'm not a fool," he said in a sudden surge of anger.

"That's a point I don't wish to discuss," Krieger answered. He turned and went directly toward the study.

Walther hurried up the steps. He entered Lauren's room, calling her name. She wasn't there. He went to the studio. She wasn't there, either. Perspiring, he ran back to the bedroom and opened the closet. Some of her clothing was missing.

Walther sat down on the bed. He hadn't really expected her to be there. But it would have eased his situation with Krieger if she had. He took time to light a cigarette, then stood up and walked slowly down the steps. He entered the library. "She's gone."

Krieger lifted himself out of the easy chair he had occupied. He was still wearing his coat and hat.

"She might have gone to one of her friends," Walther suggested.

"Do you know any of them?"

"Yes."

"Call them," Krieger said. "If Lauren is there. . . ."

"I doubt if I could convince her to return here," Walther told him.

"Ask her to meet you somewhere," Krieger said. "Tell her you just want to speak to her. You must convince her to meet you."

Walther went to the desk, picked up the phone, and dialed. "Hello, Alyce, this is Walther. Is Lauren there? . . . I came home late and I thought she might be visiting you. If she drops by, would you tell her I called. . . . Thank you." Zwig pressed the circuit breaker, then dialed another number. After a half-dozen rings, he put the phone down. "No answer."

"Call some of her other friends," Krieger said.

"There aren't any other friends to whom she would go," Walther answered.

Krieger rubbed his temples. "She must be found, Walther. I'm sure Berlin will insist that she be found. Did you ask the servants? She might have told one of them where she was going."

"It would be a waste of time. They're completely loyal to her."

"Hotels!" Krieger exclaimed. "If she's not with her friends, she must be at a hotel. Of course, if she went to one of her friends with a suitcase, she'd have to give some sort of an explanation. . . . What hotel would she choose?"

"Probably the Geneve," Walther answered. "It's the one we frequented most."

Krieger smiled. He came to the desk, picked up the phone, and dialed the Geneve's number. "This is Señor Zwig calling," he said, speaking in Spanish. "Is Mrs. Zwig there? . . . Yes. . . . Very good. . . . No, I don't want to be connected. Thank you very much." He put the phone down. "Let's go, Walther. She's in room five sixteen." He hurried out of the study.

"I didn't think she'd actually do it," Walther said, once he and Krieger were seated in the rear of the car.

Krieger looked askance at him. "What did you expect her to do after you flew into such a rage?"

"That she knew the name of the ship took me by complete surprise. . . ."

"Even if she only knew the name, she now knows it has a significance beyond itself, so much so that the mere mention of it sends you into a tirade."

"She did more than mention it," Walther said defensively. "She asked about it. She wanted to know if I had ever heard of it."

"You might have said *no* and that would have been the end of it, or you could have told her you had heard something about the ship, but you didn't remember what you had heard. . . . There were several things you could have said, all of which would have given us the time we need."

"Lauren would not have asked the question on her own. The question had to come from Turk."

"And who asked Turk about the *City of Cadiz*?" Krieger asked. "That's the real question. My guess is that Harris asked Turk to find out what he could about the ship. If I'm right, then Turk is the only one—besides Lauren—whose suspicions about the ship might be aroused."

"I am very fond of her," Walther said in a low voice. "There have been times during our marriage when I actually thought I could bring myself to her bed."

"And do what?" Krieger asked scornfully. He lit a cigar and the rear of the car quickly filled with smoke.

Walther flushed with embarrassment. He had foolishly revealed something intimate about himself.

He should have known better than to expect anything but scorn from a man like Krieger.

"Did you know that they would be together while you were in Tampico?" Krieger asked, lowering the window alongside him to allow the smoke to escape.

What could he answer? Walther thought. "Yes, I knew it," he said after a few moments' hesitation.

Krieger puffed at his cigar but refrained from making any comment.

"I knew she was in love with him," Walther said softly.

"If you knew that, you were remiss in not reporting it to me," Krieger responded. "There might have been the possibility of convincing Lauren to work for us."

"She never would—"

"My dear Walther," Krieger interrupted, "there are so many ways of making a person do what they don't want to do, especially when love and sex are involved."

They entered the city on the Avenue Insurgentes Norte. Traffic was very light. Fifteen minutes later they were in front of the Hotel Geneve on Londres. A uniformed doorman stepped forward and opened the rear door on Krieger's side.

Walther followed Krieger out of the car.

The lobby was done in white marble and, except for the potted palms, it had an Italianate look about it. Dance music floated out of the dining room.

"You go to the desk and get a key for the room," Krieger told Walther. "Tell the clerk that something has gone wrong with the plumbing in your house and you and your wife will be spending the next few days here. Try to make a joke of it."

"I'll do the best I can," Walther answered, going off to

the desk.

The clerk greeted him with a warm smile and without a moment's hesitation gave him the key, saying, "It's always a pleasure to have you with us, Señor Zwig."

Walther rejoined Krieger and together they rode the elevator up to the fifth floor.

"It might be necessary to use force," Krieger said.

Walther swallowed hard. His heart was beating very fast. He moved his tongue over his dry lips.

"I don't enjoy this any more than you do," Krieger said.

Walther didn't answer.

The elevator came to a slow stop. The operator opened the door and Krieger stepped out into the hallway, Walther following.

"Give me the key," Krieger said.

Walther gave it to him.

"If she has the chain on," Krieger said, "I'll have to throw my shoulder against the door to open it." He slipped the key into the lock and turned it. A moment later he pushed the door open. "Her clothes're on the bed but she's not here."

Walther entered the room and went straight to the phone. As soon as the desk clerk came on the line, he said, "Excuse me, but did you happen to see Mrs. Zwig within the last hour or so? I told her to wait in the room for me and she's not here."

The man laughed good-naturedly. "Just as you went up in one elevator, she stepped out of the other. I told her you were on the way up, and she said she would be back in a few minutes."

Walther thanked him, put the phone down, and repeated what the clerk had just told him.

Krieger dropped down into a chair and rubbed his temples.

"There are several phone numbers here," Walther said, looking down at a pad of paper next to the phone.

"Check them with the operator," Krieger said. "Maybe we'll be able to find out if she's really coming back."

After a few minutes of speaking to the operator, Walther said, "The first number is for the Hotel Cortés in El Paso and the second is for a man named Louis Dijon here in Mexico City."

"Dijon!" Krieger exclaimed. "I know that name. . . . I know it!" He was out of the chair and began walking back and forth. "She obviously spoke to Turk. Probably to tell him what happened between the two of you and to make arrangements to join him."

"You can't be certain about those things," Walther protested.

Krieger stopped, and taking the cigar out of his mouth, he pointed it at him. "I've been with enough women to have some ideas about how they think. But where does Dijon come into this? Where?" He began pacing again, then suddenly stopped. "Dijon flew in Spain; I have a dossier on him. Turk told her to call Dijon and he would fly her to El Paso. Lauren was on her way to meet Dijon." He rushed to the telephone and dialed his home number. "Paul," he said to the man who answered the phone, "meet me at the airport. Bring two men with you. Come armed. Yes, as soon as possible." He dropped the phone down in its cradle. "We've got to stop Dijon from taking off." He was out of the room before he finished the sentence.

Walther hurried after him.

Lauren walked quickly along the Niza. Her high heels made a sharp, staccato sound against the concrete sidewalk.

Dijon had agreed to meet her in front of the Café Valencia. If she could have run, she would have. She was frightened, very frightened, now that she knew Walther and his friend had gone to the hotel for her. Any moment she expected them to come charging after her. She had never liked Krieger; whenever he saw her, he undressed her with his eyes. Several times over the past few years, she sensed he had been on the verge of propositioning her.

Lauren started to cross a street. The Valencia was in the next block, close to the far corner. Dijon had told her he would be driving a green Ford. She didn't see any car parked in front of the cafe.

Lauren glanced at her watch. It was eleven-thirty. Dijon had said he'd be at the cafe within fifteen minutes. At least ten minutes had passed since she had left the hotel.

She passed two men. They were walking in the opposite direction. One of them turned and fell in alongside her. She was in no mood for a display of machismo.

The man put his hand on her arm. "If you come with us, you'll find us very generous."

Lauren glanced over her shoulder. The friend was a few paces behind. No one else was on the street.

"I tell you what," the man said, his hand going to her breast, "you come with us—"

She pushed his hand away. "You're making a mistake!"

The other man came up behind her. Suddenly she

found herself between the two of them. That they intended to rape her flashed through her mind. She tried to move forward but was stopped.

"Come with us," the man who had accosted her said, "and we'll show you—"

With a squeal of brakes a car came to an abrupt halt. The swung door opened and a short, compact man came loping toward them.

"Dijon?" Lauren called.

"Yes. Are you all right?"

Before Lauren could answer, Dijon had dropped the man standing in front of her with a punch in the right kidney. The other man ran.

"Scum!" Dijon hissed, and drove his foot into the man's chest. He took hold of Lauren's hand and led her to the car.

She was shaking. "They tried to force me to go with them."

"Bastards!" Dijon muttered. He removed a pack of cigarettes from his pocket; lit one of her, and one for himself. "The plane will be ready to take off as soon as we arrive. I phoned ahead to have it fueled and warmed up. We should be in El Paso by eight o'clock in the morning."

Lauren took a deep drag on the cigarette. In a matter of hours her nicely ordered world was disintegrating, dissolving the way a child's sand castle at the beach did once the waves got at it. She let the smoke loose and said, "Thank God you came along when you did."

Dijon nodded. "Feeling better?"

"I'm not shaking anymore." She held out her hand. "Steady as a rock."

"Like Turk," Dijon answered.

"You know him from Spain," she said. "He told me that on the phone."

"Did he tell you how we met?"

"No."

"I was shot down by an Italian fighter plane," Dijon said. "It was in the closing days of the battle for Barcelona. . . . I went down and I couldn't jump free of the plane. I crashed with the ship—Turk saw me get hit. He came after me and pulled me free of the wreckage. . . . I doubt if one man in ten thousand would have jumped into those flames to pull a stranger free. I tell you this—he's the bravest man I've ever known."

Lauren realized there were tears in her eyes. She was almost ashamed to wipe them away. "I know it's silly, but—"

"No," Dijon said, "it's not silly. Not silly at all. To save me, he came with a hair's breath of getting himself killed."

"I'm sorry I didn't meet you before," she told him.

"Turk told me about you."

"Oh!" She didn't like the idea that she might have been the topic of discussion between Doug and his friends.

Dijon glanced at her. "Only that he was in love with you," he said.

"I wonder if he told you before he told me," she said with a nervous laugh.

"The second time he saw you," Dijon said.

She flushed, remembering that was the first time they had made love. She had gone back to his apartment with him, expecting to have sex; indeed, wanting to have it with him, since he was an attractive, virile-looking man. "He told you," she admitted, "before he told me."

"Just let me tell you one more thing about Turk," Dijon said.

"I'm listening," Lauren responded.

"When he escaped from the internment camp—"

"I never knew he was in one," she said softly. "He never said much about the war, or about what happened afterward."

"His friend Colonel Gripper helped to arrange the escape. But Turk wouldn't go alone. He took six men with him. I know the six. . . . Any one of them would be willing to die for him."

"I know he's a very special man,' she said.

"Unique," Dijon replied. "Unique."

Directly ahead of them they could see the large searchlight on top of the airport control tower, making its slow circle. The tip of its beam dissolved in the vastness of the star-filled night sky.

"We're being followed," Dijon commented matter-of-factly.

Lauren realized he was looking up into the rearview mirror. Her heart skipped a beat, then began to race. She turned around. "There are two cars," she said, having to clear her throat before she could get the words out.

"Hold on," Dijon told her. "We're going to have to do some ground flying." He floored the accelerator and the car leaped forward.

Lauren looked into the rearview mirror. "They picked up speed," she said.

Dijon didn't answer.

They came alongside the airport fence.

"Open the glove compartment," Dijon said, "and take out the gun."

Lauren did as she was told. She held the revolver in the palm of her hand and looked questioningly at Dijon.

"Have you ever used one of those before?" he asked.

She shook her head; then, realizing that he wasn't looking at her, she answered in a low, strained voice, "No, I never have."

Dijon glanced up in the rearview mirror again. "If they gain on us, I want to throw a few shots at them. It will make them think twice about coming too close."

"Has it got bullets? . . ."

"It's loaded and it doesn't have a safety. Roll down the window; point the gun at the cars in back of us. Hold it with your two hands, and when I tell you to, squeeze the trigger."

Lauren cranked down the window. The wind whistled past them.

"Get the gun outside," Dijon said.

Lauren twisted around. She could see the two cars. They were coming up very fast.

"Okay," Dijon said. "Squeeze the trigger twice."

Two explosions merged into one. The force of the first almost ripped the gun out of Lauren's hands but she held on to it.

"That slowed them down!" Dijon explained, looking up at the rearview mirror. "The bastards didn't expect that. . . . Okay, the gate to the airport will be coming up fast," he said. "Pull the gun back inside. And hold tight—we're going to make a very sharp turn."

When Dijon hit the brake to make the turn, the car did a three-hundred-and-sixty-degree spin. It took him a few seconds to regain control. They raced toward the area between two hangars where his plane was waiting.

The two cars following them made the same spin

when they tried to brake for the turn.

"As soon as we reach the plane," Dijon said, "I'll stop. You get out and run for it. I'll swing around the ship and come into the cockpit from the other side."

Lauren was too frightened to answer.

"Take the gun with you," Dijon told her.

Even as they sped toward the hangars, a battery of searchlights on the control tower went on and fixed all three cars in their beams.

"We're going to have the Federales out here any minute," Dijon said. "Nothing gets them moving better than a good chase."

They went over a bump. Lauren jounced up and struck her head on the roof of the car. The pain knifing through her skull flooded her eyes with tears.

Dijon slowed and turned into the hangar bay. "There's the plane," he said. "Get ready to run for it."

The wail of sirens pierced the air.

"The Federales," Dijon exclaimed. He brought the car to a screeching halt alongside the right wing of the monoplane.

Lauren flung open the door and ran for the plane.

Dijon pulled away and quickly drove around to the other side of the ship.

Lauren suddenly realized his car was rolling away from the plane. The other two cars were now inside the bay.

The door on the other side of the cabin opened and Dijon lifted himself into the pilot's seat.

"The car—" Lauren managed to say.

The same instant later, Dijon's car crashed into one of the other cars. The two of them burst into flame and came to a halt.

"That changes the odds a bit," Dijon said, pushing

the throttle forward. They began to move.

The remaining car was still coming toward them.

Lauren looked out the window. She could see Walther; Krieger was seated next to him.

"They're going to try to crash into us," Dijon told her.

The car came alongside.

"Use the gun," Dijon shouted above the roar of the engine. "*Use the gun.*"

Lauren pushed the muzzle out the window and squeezed off three shots.

Suddenly the car swerved away from them.

The next instant the plane's tail was off the ground. A few moments later they were airborne, flying over the red flashing lights of the Federales' car.

"You're okay," Dijon laughed. "You're okay!"

Lauren rolled up the window and for a few moments closed her eyes. She was too frightened to acknowledge Dijon's compliment. All she wanted to do was take several deep breaths and wait until she stopped trembling and her heart stopped racing.

# 8

Gustav Winkler stood at the right side of the dance floor where the buffet supper was quietly being set up while the last speaker of the evening, Dr. Herman Linge, a gray-haired man with horn-rimmed glasses, was telling the members of the German-American Bund that Germany and the United States were friends.

"Look around you," the doctor said, "and what do you see? . . . Here on my right is a photograph of Germany's beloved Führer and on the left is the President of this great country. Here on my right is Germany's flag and on my left is the Stars and Stripes. . . . The walls and ceiling are decorated with"—the roar of a passing train on the nearby Third Avenue el forced him to stop—"The walls and ceilings are decorated with swastikas and American flags. We are friends. You," he told them, pointing a thick forefinger at the upturned faces, "you here now, on this Friday night, December fifth, nineteen hundred and forty-one, are living proof of the friendship between

Germany and this country."

The audience shouted its approval.

"I can tell you that I have it on the highest authority," Dr. Linge said, "that there will be no war between Germany and the United States, and when you go to your churches on Sunday morning, you can thank God for the peace that exists between the Fatherland of your parents and this great country of ours."

An explosion of applause filled the room. Several men went up on the speaker's platform and shook Dr. Linge's hand.

"Ladies and gentlemen," a man shouted from the speaker's platform, "our midnight buffet has been set up for your pleasure. Eat, drink, and be merry!" Like many of the men at the dinner dance, he wore the tan uniform of the National Socialist Party, complete with a black-swastika armband.

Gustav Winkler eased his way over to where the beer was. There were three wooden kegs set on a large table and twice that number on the floor behind it. He filled a large paper cup and moved away. The beer was flat but he drank it anyway. With a roar, another train passed. Though the building shook, the people around Winkler were totally oblivious to the movement and sound.

Winkler had a nodding acquaintance with several of the other guests of both sexes. He had attended four other dinner-dances sponsored by the German-American Bund in the predominantly German Yorkville section of Manhattan.

The dances were held on the first Friday night of every month. The entrance fee was five dollars per couple and three dollars for a single ticket.

Winkler had come alone, hoping he'd be able to pick

up one of the many young women, who also were alone, and spend the rest of the weekend fucking her. Winkler was just six feet tall, blond, with dark blue eyes and a boyish face that made him look younger than his twenty-four years. The women he had met in the past were eager to dance, even to become involved in kissing and some hot petting during which he might be able to put his hand into their bra, or manage to caress their vagina. But so far, he hadn't been able to convince any of them to do anything more than masturbate him.

Despite the lack of success, Winkler clung to the fantasy of having one of them in bed for the weekend. He had returned after an absence of three weeks, during which he had been in Tampico, waiting for the arrival of the *City of Cadiz*.

What was supposed to have been a simple escort assignment for him had turned out to be something more. After having trailed one of the ship's officers to the British consulate in Mexico City, he had been ordered by Colonel Krieger to kill the man. As soon as that had been accomplished, he had immediately returned to New York. There was no doubt in Winkler's mind that Krieger had also sent someone to kill the British cultural attaché, whose name was Peter Harris. Winkler did not want to think about the ship's officer, or the Britisher, and turned his attention to the women at the dance. He saw one that held his interest.

"Ah, Gustav, I thought I saw you," a man said, coming toward Winkler from the right.

Winkler made a half-turn. The man was Alfred Side, one of the top aides to Fritz Kuhn, head of the German-American Bund.

Side's hand shot and grasped Winkler's. "I missed

you the last couple of Fridays." For a short, rotund man, he had a surprisingly strong grip.

"I had to go to Milwaukee on business," Winkler lied, pumping Side's hand good-naturedly.

"What did you think of Dr. Linge's speech?"

"Excellent. The man seems to be very well informed," Winkler said, though he knew that Linge was just mouthing words.

"Come, join me at the tables," Side said. "I've spoken to a few people about you and they'd like to meet you, especially since you run your own tool-and-die shop."

"I'm getting out of that business," Winkler responded easily. "As a matter of fact, that is why I went to Milwaukee. A man there wants to buy me out." When he had first met Side, he had pretended to be a mechanical engineer, who owned a small tool-and-die shop in Brooklyn. It wasn't too far from the truth. Before he had become a member of the Abwehr he had obtained a degree in mechanical engineering from the Berlin Technical Institute.

"Never mind," Side laughed. "Let's get something to eat."

They queued up on the end of the line, which moved very slowly.

"All this food," Side said proudly, "was donated by various people here in Yorkville and other German communities in the city."

There was an enormous amount of food. Platters of hot and cold potato salad. Coleslaw. Sauerkraut. Sliced hams. Wursts. Roast beef. Sauerbraten. Several different kinds of breads. Fruit salad. Cakes and cookies . . . All of it was spread out on three very long tables. As a platter was emptied, another took its place. Everything was decorated with small swastikas.

"I recommend the hot potato salad and the bratwurst," Side said. "But everything is top quality."

They found a smaller table off to the side and sat down.

A train passed.

The sudden roar caught Winkler by surprise. It was the first one he had heard in at least fifteen minutes, though he was sure several others had passed.

"Now Gustav," Side said, before taking another mouthful, "we should talk about the future. Your future with the Bund. I know your sympathies are with us. . . . I know you're a good German. Why not join us? Become a member of the Bund. I would gladly sponsor your membership."

"I would be proud to belong," Winkler said, offering his hand across the table and smiling broadly. "You honor me by offering to sponsor me."

"Nonsense. I'm always willing to sponsor someone who'll be a credit to the organization."

By now the members of the band were beginning to tune up. The five musicians were dressed in lederhosen, complete with colorful red and green suspenders, high brown socks, and white peasant shirts, over which they wore small leather vests with brass buttons. A feathered Alpine hat was perched on each of their heads.

"They play good," Side said. "We've had them here several times."

Winkler only half-heard him. He watched the same young woman he had seen before move nearby. She had long auburn hair done up in a bun on the top of her head. She was lovely. Perhaps even beautiful. Tall, though not as tall as he. A simple V-neck black dress accentuated the fullness of her breasts and flare of her hips. She was standing with two other women. One of them said something to her and she turned to look at him.

He gave her a big smile.

She immediately frowned and turned away.

"Who is she?" Winkler asked, drawing Side's attention to the woman.

Side nodded appreciatively. "Hilda Schmidt. She's the daughter of Martin Schmidt, one of our staunchest supporters and a very wealthy man. Made his money is construction."

"Introduce me," Winkler said.

Side nodded.

"Someday I'll do you a favor," Winkler told him as they crossed the floor together.

"Miss Schmidt," Side immediately began, "I would like to introduce my good friend, Mr. Gustav Winkler."

She nodded and held out her hand. "It's a pleasure to meet you, Mr. Winkler," she said, in a mellow voice.

He lifted her hand and kissing the back of it, he answered, "The pleasure is entirely mine." He held her hand a few moments longer than the situation called for.

The band struck up a lively polka.

"Dance?" Winkler asked.

She scanned the faces of her two companions; then with a nod said, "Why not, Mr. Winkler?"

He led her out on the floor. "I'd much prefer it if you called me Gustav," he said, circling her waist with his arm.

She smiled at him.

The dance was vigorous. The polka was followed by a waltz, then by a slow foxtrot. Holding her very close, he could feel the press of her breasts on his chest and the movement of her hips against his.

Winkler realized she wasn't making the slightest bit of effort to avoid body contact, and after the dance he drew her off to one side. "Why don't we leave and go someplace where we can sit down and talk?" he suggested.

"I don't even know you," Hilda said with a smile, "and you're asking me to leave my friends and go with you."

"You're not going to know me, if we stay here." He took her hand and again pressed his lips to the back of it. "And I want you to know me."

"I should tell you that I'm engaged."

"If I were your financé," Winkler said in a low passionate voice, "I'd never leave your side."

She glowered at him.

"I'll drive you home," he offered.

"You have a car?"

"I must if I am going to drive you home," he said with a smile. "I assure you there is no other way."

Hilda's glower changed to a smile and she nodded.

"Does that mean you'll go with me?"

"Yes. But I don't want to hear any more disparaging remarks about my financé," she said.

Winkler placed his forefinger across his lips. "Not another word about the fool—I'm sorry, I mean the man."

"I must say good-night to my friends," Hilda told him.

Winkler nodded. He watched the sensual gyration of her hips as she walked across the room.

Hilda returned. "I live in the Richmond Hill section of Brooklyn," she said.

"Will you be able to tell me how to get there?"

Winkler asked.

She nodded.

Winkler helped Hilda with her coat and then put his own on. He took hold of her gloved hand and held it as they walked under the trestle of the Third Avenue el. A train thundered overhead, creating its own lightning and sending down a shower of sparks.

"Have you any special place in mind?" Hilda asked.

"None. I really don't know too much about the city," he admitted.

When they reached the car, Winkler opened her door for her and closed it when she was seated. A few moments later he slipped behind the wheel.

"You must do very well to own such a lovely car," Hilda commented.

"Well enough," Winkler answered, slowly turning away from the curb. "Tell me about yourself?"

"Not much to tell," she laughed. "I graduated from Richmond Hill High School, where I took a commercial course, and now I help my father's business. I keep his books, answer the phone, and type his letters."

Winkler feigned interest. But he couldn't have cared less what she did. What mattered was that she was in the car with him. Her perfume brought visions of her sprawled naked on a bed, with her thighs open to him.

"And what do you do?" Hilda asked. "Besides pick up women?"

Winkler laughed. "I'm a mechanical engineer," he answered, sticking with the story he had told Side. "I have my own business. . . . A machine shop. But I'm going to sell it and go into something else."

"What?"

"I haven't made up my mind," he answered, bringing the car to a stop for a red light. He removed the bottle of schnapps from his hip pocket and took a swallow. "Have a drink," he said, handing the bottle to Hilda as they started to move again. "It will warm you up."

She drank, but not as much as he had. "You're right," she giggled, "it warms you up."

"Tell me where you want to go," Winkler said.

"Are you hungry?" she asked.

"Not really. I ate quite a bit at the dance," he answered. "Besides, I'd rather just stay here in the car, drive, and talk to you."

"I'm not hungry either," she said.

Winkler helped himself to another drink of schnapps and held the bottle out to her.

"Just one more," Hilda said. "I can already feel the first one going to my head."

Winkler laughed and patted her knee. "Where do you want to drive?"

"Better go into Brooklyn," she said, handing the bottle back to him. "We can take the Williamsburg Bridge and then go up Metropolitan Avenue."

"If we want the Williamsburg Bridge, we're going in the wrong direction," Winkler said.

"I thought you didn't know?"

"Things like the bridges I know," Winkler said. "But special places I don't." He turned down a side street and onto Second Avenue. He put his arm around her shoulder and started to ease her closer to him.

"No," she protested. "No."

"Give me one good reason why not."

"I'm engaged."

"Not good enough," he laughed. "Besides, it will be much warmer if we are closer together." And he applied a gentle pressure to her shoulder.

She moved closer. "That whiskey has made me light-headed," Hilda complained.

"Not much left in the bottle," Winkler said, holding it out for her to see. "Some for me and a little bit for you." He drank and handed the bottle to her.

She finished it.

"You smell so good," Winkler said. "What kind of perfume is that?"

"I don't remember its name. But it's supposed to have a floral scent," she answered, facing him.

They stopped for a red light. Winkler shifted into neutral, kept his foot on the brake, and, clasping her in his arms, kissed her hard on the lips. At first, he thought she'd pull away and tell him to take her home immediately. But to his delight, he felt her arms move around his neck and her body strain against his. Though the light had changed, he still held her to him. His hand found her breasts and gently caressed them.

The light changed. Winkler moved away from Hilda. He shifted into first, second, then third. "You feel the same thing I do," he said in a low, urgent voice.

"I shouldn't have had that last drink of schnapps. My head is going around and around."

Winkler lit a cigarette. He tried to think of something that would impress her, something that would help convince her to go into the back seat with him. He figured that if she did it with him once, she would do it whenever she saw him—and he needed a steady woman, especially since he expected to remain in the United States.

"What are you thinking about?" Hilda asked.

Winkler smiled. "How lucky I am to have met you." He put his arm around her again.

"I feel the same way," Hilda said, looking up at him.

Winkler turned onto Delancey Street. "A place of

Jews," he muttered. "Street after street of filthy Jews. . . . But someday soon, they'll be wiped off the face of the earth for good." While he was still in Germany, a friend of his in the SS had told him of the Führer's secret plan for the final solution of the Jewish problem.

"What I don't understand," Hilda said, "is why they were allowed to come to this country to begin with. Everyone knows what they are. . . . You know, I heard that there're places in these streets where Christian babies are sacrificed and their blood is drunk by rabbis."

"We had that in Germany, too—" He stopped. He had made a slip and had to cover himself quickly. "What I meant, is that I had heard of similar things happening in Germany until the Fürher put a stop to it."

She gave him a quizzical look and said in a low voice, "Tell me the truth, Gustav—you're from Germany, aren't you?"

They were on the Williamsburg Bridge and the whirring sound made by the tires on the steel gratings was too loud to allow either of them to be heard. The few minutes it took for them to cross the bridge gave him time to think. Hilda was smarter than he had thought, and even if he denied it, she wouldn't believe him. Yet if he owned up to it, he could jeopardize his own future safety. The best way to cope with the situation, he decided, was to neither affirm or deny. That way he'd cloak himself with a air of mystery, which might help to seduce her.

"Turn left onto Roebling Street," Hilda said, as soon as they were off the bridge. "That will take you into Metropolitan Avenue."

Winkler followed her instructions.

"Do you come from Germany?" she asked again.

"I'll let you decide that," Winkler answered, now enjoying the game he had accidentally started.

After several moments, Hilda said, "I think you do."

He did not respond.

"At the next traffic light you make a right turn onto Metropolitan Avenue," she told him.

The light turned red before Winkler could make the turn. He took the opportunity to kiss her again. And this time he unbuttoned the front of her coat and gently squeezed her breasts. Even through her clothing he could feel the thrust of her nipples.

She moaned softly.

He was about to place his hand inside her bra, when someone behind them began blowing his horn.

Hilda pulled away from him. "The light changed to green," she gasped.

Winkler threw the shift into first. "Idiots," he grumbled, slowly making the turn. He had almost had an erection.

"Now you look angry," Hilda said.

"I sometimes wonder why Americans are so stupid!" he exclaimed.

"If they hadn't seen us kissing, they probably would have driven around us. I'm sure they thought they were being very funny."

"They weren't being funny," he said sullenly. "They were just being a horse's ass."

She linked her arm with his. "They're not worth becoming angry over," she said. "Come now, let me see you smile. You know, you have a very nice smile."

"Only for you," Winkler said, smiling broadly. He put his arm around her again and let his hand rest just above her breasts.

Hilda glanced at him but said nothing.

Winkler played his fingers along the side and front of her neck. Twice he made her tremble.

She moved closer to him.

Extending his fingers, Winkler touched the top of her right breast.

She uttered a low gasp, but didn't make any effort to remove his hand.

"I can feel you breathing," he said to her. "You're breathing very rapidly."

Winkler realized they were passing a wooded area. "Where are we?" he asked.

"Forest Park," she answered.

He saw more than one car with a couple in it parked at the curb. He eased over to the side and slowly came to a stop. Before Hilda could ask what he was doing, he began kissing her again. His hand went into her bra and closed over her warm breast. Her nipple was hard.

She responded passionately, opening her mouth to let his tongue meet hers.

Winkler managed to free her breasts and greedily sucked on the nipple. He moved his hand under the hem of her dress until it was between her thighs. "Let's go into the back of the car," he said, pausing to take several breaths between words.

She shook her head.

He kissed her again, this time his fingers on her sex.

Hilda eased away. "No . . . No, you mustn't do that."

"I want you," he told her.

She reached over and put her hand over his erect penis. "I will do for you what I do for my financé." She began to unbutton his fly.

Winkler took hold of her hand and pulled it away. "I

want you," he said.

"I can make you feel better," Hilda told him soothingly. "But I won't let you go inside of me. I'm still a virgin and I'll be one until I marry." She moved her hand back to his fly.

"I'm not a boy," Winkler growled. "I don't want to play games." He switched on the ignition and sped away from the curb. "And most of all," he said, "I don't enjoy being cheated." He glanced at her.

"I'm not a whore," she answered, drawing away from him.

"Whore, you're a tease!"

"You're going too fast," she complained.

"Not fast enough!" he answered, reaching over to pull her close to him again.

Hilda pushed him away. Then suddenly she grabbed the wheel as she shouted, "Oh, my God!"

Winkler wrenched it away from her. "What are you trying to do?" he shouted.

"*The truck!*"

He faced front. A truck was bearing down on them, coming straight for them. He didn't have time to think before he heard the terrible sound of metal smashing into metal.

The car jumped up; the doors sprung open. He could hear Hilda scream. The steering wheel came back and struck him in the chest. His head was jounced backward. The next instant, the car rolled over and there was the din of metal striking metal. The pain that rushed through his body threw him into a black pit. . . .

When he regained consciousness, Winkler smelled smoke before he saw the flames. The front of the car and truck were burning.

Then he heard someone say, "He's alive. . . . Hurry, we've got to get him out before the car explodes."

Several pairs of hands took hold of his shoulders and began to pull.

Winkler screamed.

They pulled again.

The pain sucked him into a raging, inky blackness.

When he opened his eyes again, Winkler found himself looking up at the tops of trees and the sky beyond. He realized he was lying on the ground. He felt very cold, and the salty taste of blood was in his mouth.

A man bent over him and said to someone else, "He's in bad shape."

Moments afterward, he was lifted onto a stretcher and carried into an ambulance. He tried to raise his head and ask about Hilda. But instead he vomited blood.

# 9

Ed sprawled against a boulder. He was very cold. Every part of his body ached, especially his neck and head. There was dried blood on his chin and on the torn sleeve of his jacket.

He was having great difficulty remaining conscious. He lacked the strength to stop himself from being sucked into the swirling black vortex of nausea that welled up intermittently inside him.

Each time, just before he sank back into unconsciousness, he feared that he wouldn't eventually come to. But he always had. And now there were fewer periods of unconsciousness, and longer periods of time between them.

Eventually Ed was able to force himself to think about what had happened: The plane had been shot down by machine-gun fire. From where he was, he could just about see the wreckage through the wind-blown sand. By sheer luck, he had been thrown clear of the aircraft on impact. He had no idea whether Lieutenant Allway, his pilot, had survived the crash.

Ed suddenly remembered he had made an appointment with Douglas Turk to go into Juárez to do some serious drinking—and here he was down somewhere in the desert south of the border. Doug had said that he had something important to talk to him about. He was sure it was either about Doug's return to the army or about a woman. Doug had mentioned a woman to him—someone he had met in Mexico City. He couldn't remember her name because another wave of nausea was starting to build up inside of him. . . .

Ed wondered if he had sustained internal injuries and was experiencing bleeding. That would mean, given where he was, that he was going to die—probably a long, slow death. If he *was* going to die he would much prefer to have it happen quickly, with a bullet in his head.

Once again Ed fought to remain conscious. But the blackness swept over him, dragging him into its swirl. This time he continued to struggle, even after he was whirling around and around. . . .

Ed felt as if he were using his arms and feet to fight his way out. Then, suddenly, he was conscious once again. And aware of the cold, the wind, the blowing sand.

Ed slowly ran his hands over his arms and legs. Nothing was broken, but every part of him had been badly jarred. Through the blowing sand he could see the plane's wreckage. He realized that after he had been thrown clear, he must have crawled to where he now lay.

He was just about to call out to Allway when he heard the sound of voices coming from the other side of the plane. His heart began to pound. If they belonged to the bandits who had shot him down, he had no chance of staying alive. They'd think as much about killing him as they would about spitting.

Ed strained to hear what they were saying. They moved closer, but he still couldn't make out their Spanish.

Ed shook his head. The sudden movement brought

the nausea roaring up out of his stomach again. He struggled to remain above it. He wanted to hold on to reality. Despite the cold, he was sweating profusely.

The men were talking again.

"But it's German," Ed whispered to himself. "Mexican bandits speaking German!" That was crazy. He was sure something was wrong with his hearing, or maybe he was hallucinating. Possibly—

Two shots suddenly were fired in rapid succession.

The explosions pounded against Ed's ears, causing a surge of pain in his skull. Afraid there would be more shots, he pressed his hands against his ears. But a few moments later the hard, white light of magnesium flares burst over the wrecked aircraft.

Reflexively, Ed threw himself on his stomach. As he watched the slow, parachute descent of the flares, he had the peculiar feeling that he was back in no-man's land on the Western Front. He hugged the ground, hoping he wouldn't be spotted.

The two men were obviously looking for the downed plane and having found it, they stopped to examine it.

Still using German, they started to speak again.

The flare drifted off to the right and went out.

Ed forced himself to start crawling to the far side of the boulder. The effort was excruciatingly painful. He stopped twice, afraid that he was going to lose consciousness. When he reached the other side of the huge rock, Ed lifted himself up and looked toward the wreck. Though he couldn't see the men, he could still hear them.

He picked up the word *todt* and knew they had found Allway's body. His command of German was very rusty. Most of what he knew he had learned while he was on occupation duty after the Great War.

But Ed was able to understand more of what he was listening to than he realized. One of the men was explaining that in the morning other troops would either move the wreckage and the body in it closer to the border, which was about a hundred kilometers to the north, or camouflage it, to prevent any search planes from finding it.

And another man commented, *"Colonel Becker wind bestimmen was zu turn ware."*

A Colonel Becker would decide what to do with the wreck? Ed thought confusedly. He took several deep breaths. These weren't Mexican bandits! He dropped down on all fours and made his way back to where he had been. His movements were less painful than they had been.

As soon as he reached the side of the boulder, he was able to see the men. There were three of them and they were wearing German uniforms, the kind worn by the members of the Africa Korps.

"But what the hell are they doing here?" Ed asked himself. The answer made his heart race again. He remembered seeing the tire and treadmarks just before the machine guns had opened up. "A Kraut strike force, that's what hit El Charo. . . . A goddamn Kraut strike force!" There wasn't any doubt in Gripper's mind that it was heading toward the States. How it had gotten to El Charo didn't interest him. He knew it was there to invade the United States, and he had to get back to Bliss to warn Hanahan that the war games were over—that the real war had already started.

Ed was sweating again. Those Krauts were obviously going to spend the night close to the wreckage.

Suddenly he realized one of the Germans was coming straight toward him. Probably looking for a place to shit. Ed slipped his trench knife free of its sheath and dropped into a low crouch. When the man was close enough, Gripper lunged up to him, driving the knife into his heart.

The man dropped to his knees; then pitched forward.

Ed quickly took the gunman's rifle, ammunition, and potato-masher grenades. Then he slipped back behind the boulder. And waited.

After a few minutes one of the other men called, "*Willie, wo bist du*?"

Ed picked up one of the potato mashers.

The man who had called to Willie told his companion, "*Etwas ist schief gegangen. Ich shau'nach.*" He advanced with his rifle held at low port, ready to be snapped up to his shoulder in an instant. He shouted back to the other man that he was having difficulty seeing because of the windblown sand.

An instant later two shots were fired. Two flares began drifting down.

"Willie!" the man shouted. Running to where the body was, he bent over it.

The second man came at a jog to where his companion was.

Ed pulled the tape from the potato masher and threw it at the kneeling figures. The explosion occurred just as one of the flares went out. The second flare died.

Without waiting to see the effects of the first grenade, Ed threw another one. Then he ran from his place behind the boulder. He had no idea which direction he was going in, and he wouldn't know until morning, when he'd be able to see the portion of the sky that became light first. Once he knew which way was east, he'd be able to track north and head for the town of Este Guzman. There he'd be able to get a vehicle to take him the rest of the way into the United States.

He moved as swiftly as he could. But now and then, because his body and head ached so much, he had to slow down and sometimes even stop, at least until his heart was no longer racing.

Ed knew that in the morning, when the other Krauts came to the wreckage and found their three dead companions, they'd turn over every damn boulder in the desert between the wreckage and the border looking for him. If he made it to the States before they crossed the border, they would have lost the element of surprise. And they needed that. . . .

A strong wind was blowing, and large, round clumps of dead tumbleweed bounced in front of Turk's car, making him slow down. Now and then he moved through a cloud of dust that, when first touched by the headlight beams, looked like a white wall, but as he entered it changed into a cloak that obliterated everything else. He kept the window on his side cracked about an inch, which was just enough of an opening to let the smoke from his cigarette escape.

Turk was looking forward to being with Lauren again. Then, remembering that Manuel was in the room, he laughed and said aloud, "Is she going to be surprised when she sees the boy!"

Turk had no idea what Lauren's feelings were toward children, especially a gutter rat like Manuel. Neither did he have any clear plan for what he intended to do with Manuel. But he was certain that he would try to do something to provide the boy with food and shelter—no, more than that: a home.

He turned into Pershing Circle and headed for the post headquarters building. All the windows were illuminated. He drove into one of the slots in the parking area and stopped. Before leaving the car, he took time to light another cigarette. Then he headed up the steps and the corridor, which was deserted except for the newly posted guard at the door of the communications center. He went into the empty press room and helped himself to a cup of coffee. He drank half of it, and walked out into the hallway. He went up to the guard. "Is General Fitzhugh inside?" Turk asked.

"No, sir," the young man answered. "He left a few minutes ago."

Turk nodded and said, "Will you tell him Douglas Turk is in the press room when he returns?"

"Yes, sir."

"Thanks, soldier," Turk said and walked back to the press room. The guard at the door to the communications center was enough to confirm his suspicions that something more than just the war games was going on. And he intended to find out exactly what it was. . . .

Hanahan was red-eyed and had a heartburn that just wouldn't go away no matter how many bicarbonate of sodas he drank. He paced back and forth, listening to the Spanish chatter coming over the loudspeaker.

"They seem to be having a goddamn ball out there," he commented to Major Driscol, the communications officer. "If they're part of this operation. . . ."

Another voice came over the second loudspeaker: "This is Blue Scout . . . Blue Chief, this is Blue Scout . . . Do you read me?"

Hanahan went over to the radio desk and took the mike from the sergeant. "Go ahead, Blue Scout, this is Blue Chief . . . I read you loud and clear." He signaled the sergeant to turn down the volume on the other speaker.

"Approaching Este Grande," Captain Barth announced.

"See anything?"

"Negative . . . We still have a lot of blowing dust and sand."

"Over," Hanahan said and handed the mike back to the radio sergeant. He went to the desk at the far side of the room and dropped down into the chair behind it. He was just about to close his eyes, when Fitzhugh entered.

"Barth reported in," Hanahan said. "He doesn't see anything. But he's closing on Este Grande."

Fitzhugh nodded. He too was red-eyed from lack of sleep, and though he wasn't suffering from heartburn, he had a throbbing headache. "Turk is back in the press room," he said.

"What the fuck is he doing here at this time of night?" Hanahan growled. "Tell him to get his ass back to the hotel and—"

"He smells something," Fitzhugh said. "Besides, he probably wants to know if we have any information on Gripper."

Hanahan rubbed the sides of his head and looked bellicosely up at the first loudspeaker. "Doesn't that son of a bitch understand Spanish?"

"What?"

"Turk. Doesn't the bastard understand the spics?"

"Yes."

"Get him in here," Hanahan said. "Maybe he can tell us what the hell the spics are chattering about."

Fitzhugh left the room, and Hanahan went up to the radio sergeant and told him to raise Blue Scout. As soon as Barth came on, Hanahan asked, "Are you getting a lot of spic talk on the radio?"

"Negative . . . I'm holding to our preassigned frequency."

"See anything yet?"

"No, sir."

"Over," Hanahan said.

The door opened and Fitzhugh entered with Turk in tow.

Hanahan crossed the room. "How much Spanish do you understand?" he asked, standing directly in front of Turk with his hands on his hips. He wasn't in any mood to pussyfoot around and he wanted Turk to know it.

"Fluently," Turk answered succinctly.

Hanahan took a step back. "Sergeant, turn the volume up." He pointed to the loudspeaker. "Can you tell me what that's all about? . . . Sergeant, turn it up louder."

"It's fine as it is," Turk said, moving closer to the speaker. "Too much volume distorts the sound."

"I want to know if it's one of the Mex units assigned to—"

"Quiet!" Turk snapped.

Hanahan's jaw dropped. No one had spoken to him that way in years.

"The commanding officer is a Colonel Becker . . . He's leading a column north—"

"What the hell are you talking about," Hanahan shouted. "Are you telling me that's not coming from one of the Mex units assigned to us?"

"I'm not telling you anything," Turk shot back. "I'm translating . . . They spotted an enemy scout patrol—"

Suddenly Barth's voice came over the loudspeaker. "Holy Christ," he shouted, "we're being attacked!"

Hanahan picked up the mike. "What the hell are you talking about?"

Barth saw the orange-red gun flashed directly in front of him. "Turn," he shouted to the drivers of the other two scout cars. "*Turn!*"

There were explosions all around the three vehicles. The scout car to his right suddenly became an orange ball and fell behind.

"Blue Chief," Barth yelled, "we're taking heavy fire!"

"Make a run for it," Hanahan shouted.

There was more cannon fire.

"Negative . . . Negative . . . Blue Chief, we're on fire—"

"Blue Scout," Hanahan shouted. "Blue Scout, do you read me?"

There was nothing but static on the loud speaker.

"It's over," Hanahan shouted. "In less than two minutes they got the three of them." He wiped the sweat from his brow with his sleeve.

Suddenly a burst of Spanish came out of the loud-speaker.

Hanahan looked at Turk.

"They're reporting that they just destroyed an enemy mobile unit and killed all personnel. You're not going to believe this one . . . But General Rommel is congratulating them."

"What the hell did you say?" Hanahan bellowed.

"Rommel," Turk answered stubbornly. "General Irwin Rommel, the Desert Fox. He seems to be the overall commander for the operation."

"Are you trying to wise-ass me? Because if you are. . . ."

"Hanahan, you asked me to translate, and that's just what I'm doing," Turk said angrily. "I don't give a fuck if you don't like what you hear. Besides, I know the way the Krauts speak Spanish. I heard them in Spain."

Hanahan glared at him, and then turning to Fitzhugh he said, "Can't we get one plane in the air?"

Fitzhugh shook his head.

"Ed was shot down, wasn't he?" Turk asked.

"Maybe," Fitzhugh answered. "But there was a storm blowing out there."

"Before we jump to any conclusions, let's find out what's really going on," Hanahan shouted. He was thinking about how the loss of one plane and several scout cars would be taken in Washington.

"I'll tell you what's going on," Turk answered. "There are goddamn Germans just below the border and they're heading this way. Ed must have spotted them, gone down to get a better look, and got himself blasted out of the sky. I saw it happen a good many times in Spain."

"This isn't Spain!" Hanahan responded. "If you're so fucking smart, you tell me how the Krauts got there."

"That's not the problem. They're there. Sergeant, turn up the loudspeaker."

The sergeant looked questioningly at Hanahan.

"Turn it up!" Hanahan ordered.

"Nothing but static," Turk commented disgustedly. "They're not transmitting."

"Fitzhugh," Hanahan said, "call General Alt. Have him here as soon as possible. Make the call from your office."

"I'll get on it," Fitzhugh answered, and he left the room.

Hanahan turned to Turk. "I want you to keep all of this under wraps until—"

"Don't take too long, General," Turk said. "Something is happening, something that might turn into a catastrophe."

Hanahan turned white with rage. "You were never one to mince words, not even at the Point."

"You didn't send a scout patrol just to look for Ed," Turk answered. "There's more that you're not telling me. That's okay with me, but—"

"I could put you under arrest."

"Try it, General, and see just how long I.N.S. would stand for it."

"You're coming back into the Army. I have friends—"

"General," Turk said in a flat voice, "I couldn't care less about your friends. You tell me what's happening out there. Tell me, and then do something about it. Because if Rommel is in command, he wasn't sent to play games in the Mexican desert. He was brought here to strike into the United States."

"That's really pushing it!"

"No, General," Turk answered, "I'm just remembering the German dream during World War One. Remember, the Krauts wanted to invade the United States though Mexico—only they were hoping the Mexicans and the Japanese would do it for them. But now they aren't asking anyone else to do it. They seem to be doing it themselves."

"Are you finished?"

"No. I'm going to be at my hotel," Turk said. "If any word about Ed comes in, have me called."

"Is that an order?"

"Take it any way you want, General," Turk answered, going to the door and opening it. "But have someone call me at the Hotel Cortés."

Hanahan strode into Fitzhugh's office, slamming the door behind him. He was red with anger. "Goddamn commie bastard!" he exclaimed. "Once that son of a bitch is back in service, he'll sing a different tune." He picked up a cigar, bit off the end, and spat it into a nearby wastepaper basket. "Just who the fuck does Turk think he is?"

"Alt says he'll be here in three, maybe four hours at the very latest," Fitzhugh answered, ignoring Hanahan's anger.

Hanahan lit the cigar and blew a cloud of smoke. "What the hell do you think is out there?"

Fitzhugh stood up and walked to the window. The

barracks across the quadrangle were totally dark, except for the glimmer of red lights at the fire exits. "I don't think there are Germans out there," he said. "I think Barth was hit by bandits, maybe even Federales. There could be some sort of an uprising going on, and we wouldn't know about it until it was all over."

Hanahan grunted his agreement. "That makes sense. But guys like Turk see Krauts coming out of the woodwork. I mean, common sense would have to tell you that there is no way for them to get here, much less move an armored column here."

Fitzhugh turned from the window. "That's why I think Turk was translating something that happened just after Barth was taken out by—"

Hanahan pointed the cigar at him. "Okay, that's the way I see it. A kind of coincidence—that's what it really was. When Alt gets here we'll fill him in, and then we'll figure out how to handle the situation."

"Washington—"

"I tell you, Fitzhugh, we have more to worry about from those idiots in Washington than we do from the bandits, or whatever the fuck they are." He took a long drag on the cigar and sent a cloud of smoke halfway across the room before he said, "When Alt gets here we'll go over the various ways this situation could be handled so that Washington's involvement is held to a minimum."

"Perhaps it would be a good idea," Fitzhugh suggested, "to contact some of our friends in the State Department. They might be able to tell us if anything is happening in Mexico."

"Do it later in the morning," Hanahan said.

Fitzhugh looked at his watch. "Alt won't be here for awhile. I think I'm going to sack out for about an hour."

"Good idea," Hanahan said. "We're going to have to be sharp as a tack when Alt gets here."

"There are a few cots set up in the room down the hall. You're welcome to one of them."

"Thanks," Hanahan said. "I'll make myself comfortable here."

"See you in about an hour," Fitzhugh said from the door.

Hanahan sat down behind the desk, glad to be alone. He put the cigar down in an ashtray, leaned back into the chair, and closed his eyes. He had his career to think about and something like this, if it was mishandled, could have disastrous effects. After all, there was a war coming and he wanted a field command. Only by proving himself in the field could he ever hope to get upped for a much bigger job. He should have never asked Turk to translate. Never. "Bandits," he said aloud.

"That's what they are. . . . Fucking bandits!"

# 10

*December 6, 1941*

Turk floored the accelerator. He was furious with Hanahan and said aloud, "That stupid son of a bitch. Right in front of his face and he can't see it. . . ."

Easing his foot off the gas pedal, Turk held the wheel with one hand and with the other lit a cigarette. His anger with Hanahan had begun to be replaced by an enormous feeling of weariness coupled with a growing doubt about his own interpretation of what he had heard. He was absolutely certain that Barth's scout patrol had been destroyed. But by whom? Now he wasn't at all sure that the Germans he had heard were not involved in an action against the British in North Africa. The heavyside phenomenon could have made it possible to pick up the German transmission. And Turk had to admit overreacting when he heard Rommel congratulate his men. Rommel, as everyone knew, was in the Western Desert, taking a mauling from Auckenleck's newly formed Eighth Army.

Turk stubbed out the cigarette against the side of the car and flipped the butt into the desert. Germany lacked the means of putting troops into Mexico, much less supplying them, even though a great number of wealthy Mexicans, especially the owners of *estancias* in the north, openly favored Nazi Germany.

The odds, Turk thought, of hearing Germans talk about having destroyed three scout cars at the same time Barth's patrol was being knocked out were probably on the order of a million to one, if not ten million to one.

"Bandits," Turk exclaimed. "Just goddamn lousy bandits!" He decided he'd been too hard on Hanahan and that he owed the man an apology, though it would be difficult to give.

Turk swung around Alligator Park and eased into the same parking spot he had previously occupied in front of the hotel. To his surprise, Manuel was sitting on the hotel step.

"I couldn't sleep, amigo," Manuel said, coming up to the car and opening the door.

Turk slid out from behind the wheel.

"I'm not happy alone," Manual told him.

"You mean, you're not used to the bed and room," Turk said.

"Si, si. I sleep in a doorway. . . . Sometimes on the floor in Carmen's room."

"Not much to do around here at this hour," Turk said. "But maybe we could walk across the street and look at the 'gators."

"You think they're awake?" Manuel asked.

Turk shrugged. "Let's go see."

They crossed the street and walked into the park. Turk lit a cigarette and took several deep drags on it.

"You tired, amigo?" Manuel asked.

"Yes. So damn tired, I probably won't be able to sleep."

"I'm tired too," Manuel said. "But not that tired."

The two of them walked up to the iron fence in front of the alligator pit. Two large streetlamps poured their yellow light over the rocks, but the small pool of water directly beneath them was pitch black.

"I don't see them," Manuel said, hanging over the fence.

"They're probably in the water."

Manuel pulled himself back. "You like being a reporter?" he asked.

"It's been good," Turk said. "But after the first of the year I'll be back in the army. Covering the war games is my last assignment."

Manuel spit. "I don't like soldiers. They walk around as if they own the world. . . . Sometimes they come to Carmen and make her fuck for nothing. They say 'Fuck or we'll stick a bayonet up your cunt.' "

Turk put his hand on Manuel's shoulder.

"When I'm a man," Manuel said, "I'm going to be a reporter. Reporters are a lot better than soldiers."

"Sometimes," Turk said gently, "there is a need for soldiers."

"Is that why you're going into the army?" Manuel asked.

"Yes," Turk answered. "There's a big war going on."

"I know all about that. Germany is fighting England and Russia."

"That's right, and soon the United States will become involved."

Suddenly Manuel reached up and took hold of his hand. "You're not going to fight, are you? You'll be safe, won't you?"

"When the war comes," Turk said, "I'll have to fight."

"But you could be killed!" Manuel cried.

"If I'm lucky, I won't be."

"I'll pray for you," Manuel said. "Yes, I'll go to church every day and pray for you, amigo. The Holy Mother will hear my prayers and protect you."

Once again Turk put his hand on Manuel's shoulder.

"Come," he said, "let's go up to the room and go to sleep." The boy's concern for his well-being touched him more than he cared to show.

They walked out of the park, crossed the street, and went into the lobby of the hotel.

Turk stopped at the desk and asked, "Are there any messages for room five-oh-four?"

The clerk checked the mail slot and shook his head.

A few minutes later Turk luxuriated under a hot shower. When he returned to the bedroom in clean shorts and a T-shirt, he helped himself to a drink of scotch straight from the bottle and then settled down on the bed.

Manuel was asleep.

Turk listened to the boy's slow, regular breathing and found himself thinking about his own boyhood, which was so very different from Manuel's. Born into a moderately wealthy New York family, he had lived in a large, brick, two-story house on Glenwood Road in the Midwood section of Brooklyn. Though located in the city, in many ways it had been like living in the country. There were still working farms within walking distance of the house. And where Glenwood Road intersected Ocean Avenue there was a running stream and a very large strand of woods. His father, John Turk, a printer by trade, had eventually become the owner of the second largest printing house in New York, and had a summer home in Port Jefferson overlooking the small, picturesque harbor.

Since Turk was the only child, nothing in the way of education had been spared him. He was sent to private schools from the day he had become of age to go to school. But oddly enough, he wasn't spoiled either by Helen, his mother, a lovely-looking woman with a soft voice, long black hair, and sloe eyes, or by his father, who was a tall man, with red hair and a freckled face.

Turk took another pull on the bottle, put it down, and helped himself to a cigarette. Despite the family's affluence, John Turk had been an extremely liberal man believing more in his fellow men, with all their faults, than in God. His mother had sometimes gone to Mass. "Just to hear the Latin," she would say. But she would never go to confession or communion. "I'm not about to tell any man, especially a priest," she had once told him when he was home on leave, "what I do in bed with my husband." Then with a mischievous laugh she'd added, "I wouldn't want to be responsible for giving him a heart attack, now would I?"

He could almost hear those words and the soft laugh that followed. He had grown up knowing that his parents loved one another and that love had filled his life was well as theirs.

Turk stubbed out the cigarette and took another drink. When it had come time for him to choose a college, he had the grades to apply to any Ivy League school. But he had chosen the Point, to the complete surprise of his parents and friends.

"I never knew you had any inclination toward the military," his father had said, after Turk had announced his intention.

And his mother had added, "I had hoped you would become a doctor. A surgeon, perhaps?"

He couldn't really explain the reason for his choice then, other than to say, "There is nothing else I'd rather be than an officer."

His parents hadn't tried to argue him out of his decision. Perhaps they'd hoped he would change his mind. But he hadn't. He'd become the first captain and an honor student, taking honors in English, history, and military science.

Turk smiled, pleased with the memory of his own achievement. Then looking at Manuel he said aloud,

"But what the hell am I going to do for you?" He was about to reach for the bottle again when the phone rang. He looked at it. Despite the amount of scotch he had drunk, Turk knew it was well past two in the morning.

The phone rang again.

Manuel raised his head. "You want me to answer it, amigo?" the boy asked.

Turk picked up the phone. "Hello!" The next instant he heard the click on the other end. The line went dead.

"No one," Turk said, still holding the phone.

Manuel shrugged.

Turk dropped the phone back into its cradle and lit another cigarette. "Go back to sleep."

"I'm not sleepy anymore," Manuel answered. He sat up in bed and pointed to the bottle of scotch. "Amigo, you drink too much."

"You're absolutely right," Turk said.

"I knew a man—His name was Juan Gonzogo. . . . He drank so much he got something wrong with his stomach and one day he began to vomit blood. He died."

"Go to sleep!"

"I swear on my mother's grave that I—"

"Shush!" Turk exclaimed, putting his fingers across his lips. "The door," he whispered, switching off the lamp.

Manuel turned toward it.

Turk slipped his shoes off and padded to the door. Someone was trying to work the lock open with a flat piece of metal. He beckoned to Manuel.

"We goin' to fight him?" Manuel asked in an excited whisper. "I have a knife."

"Go into the bathroom," Turk said. "Wet a towel and bring it to me. Close the bathroom door. I don't want our friend out there to guess we're on to him."

Manuel flashed him a bright smile and scampered off.

Turk moved to the right side of the door, in position to strike at the intruder the moment he stepped across the threshold. Turk had had a similar experience in Lisbon, just after the fall of Paris. One of Admiral Canaris's Abwehr goons had tried to get into his room and he had handled the situation the same way he intended to now.

Manuel came back with the wet towel.

Turk knotted one end of the towel. He motioned Manuel to the far side of the door, where the boy would be completely hidden. As he hefted the wet towel, Turk heard the lock click open. He took a deep breath and slowly exhaled. His heart was racing.

Turk watched the knob slowly turn. He swallowed and licked his lips.

The knob stopped moving and the door began to open. Slowly.

The man on the other side was taking his time. He wasn't going to risk having a single squeak.

Turk realized he was perspiring.

Manuel moved.

The door stopped.

Several moments passed before the man resumed his gentle pressure on the door.

Turk flattened himself against the wall. He glanced toward the window. The light from the street lamp just touched the bottom of it.

The door was slightly less than half open. There was another pause.

A knife blade clicked open.

Turk hoped it wasn't Manuel's.

The door started to move again, somewhat more rapidly.

The opening was wide enough for the man to step through it. And he did, pushing the door completely open. The light from the hallway jumped into the room ahead of him.

Manuel leaped from behind the door.

The man heard him, whirled at the boy. There were two popping sounds.

Manuel slumped to the floor as Turk struck the side of the man's head with the knotted end of the towel. The blow staggered him. He tried to turn toward Turk. There were two more pops. The acrid smell of burnt powder filled the room.

Turk threw the towel over the man's face, then drove his fist into the man's stomach.

The man staggered as he pulled the towel off. He still held the gun.

Turk tossed him against the wall. He went after him, grabbed hold of his right hand and bent it back.

The man struck Turk with the balled fist of his free hand; then he tried to claw his eyes out.

Turk forced the man's right hand even further back.

With a groan of pain the man dropped the gun.

Turk pushed on the man's hand until the bones snapped.

The man fainted.

Breathing hard, Turk picked up the gun and cracked it over the man's head. A sudden gush of blood welled up from the wound.

Turk went to the phone, called the switchboard, and said, "Call an ambulance and the police. Send them to my room." Then he went to Manuel; lifting the boy in his arms, he set him down on the cot.

"Bad fire in my stomach," Manuel said in Spanish.

"You're going to be okay," Turk said, answering in the same language.

"Through the crack in the door, I saw the gun,"

Manuel told him.

"Don't talk."

Manuel took several deep breaths. "It hurts," he whispered, fighting back the tears.

"Squeeze on my hand," Turk said, extending it to Manuel. "Squeeze as hard as you can."

"Amigo, you think I will go heaven?" Manuel answered.

Turk was going to say *not for a long time,* but instead he nodded and said, "Sure you will."

"I did lots of bad things. I stole. I was a pimp and I even tried to fuck one of the girls."

"You'll go to heaven, amigo," Turk said, having to swallow hard after he spoke.

Manuel smiled, then uttered a ragged sigh and died.

Turk closed Manuel's eyes, sat down in the chair, and reached for the bottle. But with a shake of his head, he put it down. He stood up and went to the window. Tears blurred his vision. He looked back at Manuel's body.

The man began to groan.

Turk went to him. He reached down and pulled him to his feet.

The man opened his eyes. Fear made his lower lip tremble.

"You killed the boy," Turk said, backhanding him across the face. "You killed him."

The man staggered and dropped to his knees.

"That's it, mister. . . . Freeze right there!"

Turk looked toward the door. A cop was standing there. He was holding a gun.

"Special Agent Kiern Crowly," the man said, flashing his FBI identification. "I'm looking for Lieutenant Arthur Fioredeliso." He spoke with a decided Western drawl. He wasn't at all pleased that he wouldn't be home early enough to have a romp in the sack with his wife, Mary Jean. Lately he had been too tired to do much sack romping. But since it was a weekend, he'd been looking forward to it.

"He's at the patient's bed," the nurse answered. "Fourth from the end with the screen around it, on the right-hand side."

Crowly thanked her and started toward the screen. He was a lean man of middling height, thirty-five years old, with gray eyes and crew-cut hair. He wore a dark-blue business suit, while shirt, and blue tie. He carried his loose-fitting winter coat on his arm.

This was Crowly's first visit to the King's County Hospital in the east Flatbush section of Brooklyn since his assignment to the New York field office from Houston, three months before.

The ward smelled strongly of iodoform. Some of the patients moaned in their sleep, but there were a few whc were awake and Crowly felt them following him with their eyes. Even before he reached the screen a short man in a police uniform came out from behind it. Crowly identified himself. He guessed Fioredeliso to be somewhere in his early fifties.

Fioredeliso offered his hand and said, "Sorry that I had to call you down here on a Friday night. But we've got something that might interest your people." He motioned to Crowly to follow him to the end of the ward. "No one will be able to hear us here," he explained.

Crowly saw that the beds on either side of the aisle were empty.

"The man behind the screen is named Gustav Winkler. Earlier, he was in a head-on collision with a truck on Metropolitan Avenue, in the Richmond Hill section. Fioredeliso paused for a moment. "According to two of the eyewitnesses he was in the wrong lane. He was with a young woman, a Hilda Schmidt. She was thrown clear on impact and suffered a few fractured ribs. From what she told me, she met Winkler at a dinner and dance in Yorkville."

"The usual Thursday-night Bund dance?" Crowley asked, knowing that Yorkville and Richmond Hill were German neighborhoods.

"You hit it on the head," Fioredeliso answered. "She said Winkler was angry with her because she refused to go into the back seat of the car with him."

"So far I don't see anything for the Bureau," Crowly told him.

"Winkler was carrying a German passport under his own name—that is, if it is his own name. And we also found in his apartment an Argentinian diplomatic passport under the name of Raul Sanchez, with Winkler's picture in it."

"That's something my people would be interested in," Crowly said.

"He shares the apartment with a man named Otto Ziegler. Actually, the apartment is leased to Ziegler."

"Where is it located?"

"Forty-four West Eighteenth Street," Fioredeliso answered. "The superintendent there said that they were good tenants and kept to themselves. I left word to have Ziegler call me as soon as he gets in."

"Find anything interesting on Ziegler?"

"No. My guess is that he's either native-born or a naturalized citizen. Maybe even an illegal alien?"

"My people can check that out," Crowly said. "You've been damn thorough, Lieutenant."

Fioredeliso smiled. "There's more. Winkler must have been in Mexico City recently and in Dallas. He had a book of matches from the Hotel Geneve in Mexico City and one from the Char Pit, a restaurant in Dallas."

"He could have picked them up somewhere."

Fioredeliso shook his head. "Don't think so."

"I can check the hotel for either of his names," Crowly said. "Have you taken a set of prints?"

"Yes," Fioredeliso answered, "but they won't turn up anything. This guy is a German, which was why I asked for someone from the Bureau who speaks German. Do you?"

"Fluently."

"Then Mister Winkler is all yours," Crowly said. "Whatever he's saying, he's repeating over and over again. It doesn't sound like the name of the woman he was with."

"We'll see," Crowly said, dropping his coat over the foot of one of the empty beds. He slipped behind the screen. The man in the bed was swathed in bandages. His eyes were glazed and his face was badly bruised.

"Chest was crushed," Fioredeliso whispered. "Bad internal injuries."

Crowly glanced at him. "Any chance?"

"Fifty-fifty. But the doc says he'll never be the same again."

Crowly bent close to Winkler. Speaking in German, he asked. "Do you know where you are, Winkler?"

Winkler's eyes shifted slowly toward Crowly.

"You're in a hospital. You were in an accident," Crowly told him.

Winkler moved his lips.

Crowly moved closer to him.

*"Der Fuchs war an der Stelle,"* Winkler whispered.

"Can you make out what he said?" Fioredeliso asked.

" 'The fox is in place,' whatever that means," Crowly answered.

*"Der Fuchs war an der Stelle!"* Winkler repeated, even more urgently.

"I don't think he's going to say anything else until the sedation wears off." Crowly stood up. "Is there anything else you think I should know?"

"Nothing."

The two of them moved to the outside of the screen.

"Is Miss Schmidt in the hospital?" Crowly asked.

"Her father came and took her home. But I have her address."

Crowly took out a small leather bound pad and a fountain pen.

"Fifty Decatur Street," Fioredeliso said. "That's off Metropolitan Avenue. A good forty minutes from here."

"What do you think about Winkler?" Fioredeliso asked, when they were near the empty beds again.

"Same as yourself," Crowly answered evasively. "How many other people know about the two passports and the matchbooks?"

"Just my captain."

"Better tell him to keep it quiet," Crowly said. "We don't want the newspapers or anyone interested in Winkler or his friend."

"I'll see to it."

"Can you arrange to have Winkler moved into a private room and a twenty-four-hour guard put on him?"

"We have a prison section here. . . ."

"No. Just a room."

"I'll take care of it," Fioredeliso said.

Crowly picked up his coat, and with Fioredeliso at his side walked out of the ward.

"I'm going to want to speak to Ziegler too," Crowly said, pushing the button for the elevator. "Call me at my office tomorrow."

Fioredeliso nodded.

The elevator came and the door slid open.

"You did one hell of a job," Crowly said, shaking Fioredeliso's hand. "Thanks." He stepped into the elevator, faced front, and said, "See you around." When the doors closed, Crowly looked at his watch. It was one-thirty in the morning. Saturday, December sixth. He sighed. He'd be lucky if he got to sleep by noon, and by that time, Crowly knew, he'd be just too plumb tuckered out to do anything worthwhile with his wife, Mary Jean.

It took Crowly forty-five minutes to drive out to the Schmidt house, which was located on a tree-lined street. The two-story house had a fieldstone front and a gable over the door. There were bushes and trees in the front and a large open expanse in the back. The house was completely dark.

Crowly eased himself out from behind the wheel, walked up to the door, and rang the bell. After a long wait, the door opened and he found himself looking at a jowly, heavyset, bald-headed man with porcine eyes. "What do you want?"

"I'm Special Agent Kiern Crowly," Crowly said, at the same time showing an identification card. "I would like to speak to your— Are you Mister Schmidt?" he purposely didn't speak German, figuring to use it only if it gave him some advantage.

"Yeah," the man answered.

"Your daughter was in an automobile accident earlier," Crowly said. "I want to ask her some questions about the man she was with."

"Who is it, Papa?" a woman called from the head of the steps.

"Go back to sleep, Clara," he ordered. "Go back to sleep!"

"It will only take a few minutes," Crowly said.

Schmidt opened the water. "Wait in the parlor," he said. "I go upstairs and fetch Hilda."

Crowly walked into the house. The light in the parlor was already on. He took off his coat and hat, and sat down on a large, overstuffed green-upholstered chair. The room was spotless. The furniture was European style. Many of the pieces, especially the oak endtables and cabinet, looked as if they had been made in the nineteenth century. A highly polished, concert grand Bosendefer was alongside the heavy dark-brown drapes covering the two front windows. Despite the fact that the room was very warm and airless, it was, as the Germans would say, gemültich. Comfortable.

Crowly heard Schmidt tell Hilda in German, "You are nothing but a tramp, not much better than a whore, who's going to bring disgrace and ruin to the family."

"It wasn't my fault," Hilda answered. "Why don't you believe me?"

"If I can't trust you, how can I believe you!" Schmidt answered. "Now we go downstairs and you answer the man's questions."

Crowly stood up the moment he heard them start down the steps. By any man's standards, Hilda was a looker. Despite the heavy woolen pink bathrobe she wore, the thrust of her breasts and flare of her hips were pronounced. Her eyes were red and puffy from crying. There were bruises on the right side of her face. He could see that she was in pain.

"I'm sorry to disturb you," Crowly said, "but I have some questions about Mr. Winkler."

"I just met him tonight," Hilda offered.

Crowly nodded and suggested they sit down.

She chose the chair he had sat in. Her father stood alongside her.

"Had you ever seen him before?"

"No."

"You met him tonight at the weekly Bund dinner and dance?"

She glanced up at her father and then nodded. "Yes."

"Did he tell you anything about himself?"

"He said he was a mechanical engineer, and that he had a small business which he was soon going to sell."

"How did the crash happen, Miss Schmidt?" Crowly asked, settling on the couch opposite her.

She hesitated, then said in a low voice. "He tried to pull me to him and lost control of the wheel."

"If I tell her once, I tell her a hundred times, not to go with strange men," Mr. Schmidt said. His face was flushed.

"Did Winkler say anything unusual? Let me put it a different way: Did he say anything that might lead you to suspect he wasn't telling you the truth?"

Hilda shook her head.

"Did he say anything about taking a trip to Mexico?"

"He went to Milwaukee to sell his machine shop."

"When?"

"Within the last three weeks," Hilda answered.

Suddenly the phone rang.

Schmidt raised his eyebrows, walked to the endtable in the foyer where the phone was, and answered. "It's a police Lieutenant Fioredeliso," he said. "He wants to speak with you, Mr. Crowly."

Crowly thanked him, and taking hold of the phone he said, "Crowly here."

"Winkler's roommate Ziegler called," Fioredeliso said. "He was very upset. Said he'd drop by the precinct to talk with me tomorrow. But when I told him you wanted to talk to him also, the line went dead. I sent some men over to the apartment to take a look. Ziegler had skipped, bag and baggage."

"Thanks," Crowly said.

"Anything about the fräulein?"

Crowly glanced at her.

She was looking at him. Her eyes were wide with anxiety.

"Nothing worth commenting on," he said.

"Winkler has already been moved to a private room and a guard posted."

"Thanks. I'll be in touch. Good night." He put the phone down and walked slowly back into the living room. "Winkler's friend ran away," he said. "I wonder why he did that?"

"I knew nothing about his friend," Hilda responded.

"I believe you," Crowly said. "But I want to know what else you know about Winkler."

"Nothing. . . . I told you. Nothing."

"You spent three, maybe four hours with him, isn't that right?"

"Yes."

"He must have said something to you."

"Just small talk, but . . ."

"But what?"

"When we passed through the East Side of Manhattan near the Williamsburg Bridge, he said a lot about the Jews."

"What did he say about the Jews?" Crowly asked, switching to German.

Her hand flew to her mouth. She was too surprised to speak.

"Better tell me what he said," Crowly told her, still speaking German. "I think I know what he said," he lied. "But I want to hear it from you."

"He said that in German the Führer put a stop to the killing of Christian babies by the Jews."

"Did Winkler say that he had come from Germany?"

She shook her head.

"But you're sure that he did, aren't you?" Crowly

asked.

"Yes," she answered with a sob. "I'm sure that he came from Germany."

"Thank you, Hilda," he said switching back to English and taking hold of her hands. "Thank you so very much."

A short time later Crowly was in his car, on the way back to Manhattan. Despite the cold, he drove with the window down and puffed contentedly on his pipe. After he checked out whether Sanchez or Winkler stayed at the Geneve in Mexico City during the last two weeks, he'd call the Bureau in Washington and give them what he had. They in turn would pass the information on to M.I. 6. But no matter what M.I. 6 did with it, there was no doubt in Crowly's mind that Winkler and his friend Ziegler were German agents. And thanks to an automobile accident, or more precisely Winkler's sex drive, he had him. . . .

# 11

Detective Lieutenant John Hicks was a short, compact man. He wore a Western-style suit, a shoulder holster, a Stetson hat, and tooled brown-leather cowboy boots. He smoked a large, almost-black Cuban cigar. Looking across his desk at Turk, he said in a slow Texas drawl, "I know ya didn't kill the Mex kid. But what I want to know is, What were ya doin' with him in the first place?"

Turk was seated alongside Detective Hick's desk. The clock on the wall behind the detective was going on ten of four. "I already told you half a dozen times," Turk said, reaching over to an ashtray to squash a cigarette.

"Ya sure did," Hicks laughed. "But I think it's a crock of shit."

"That's your right," Turk answered.

"Now let me tell ya what ya told me. . . . Ya go into Juárez. This Mex kid comes up to ya, offers ya a piece of ass. Y' say no and go to meet yar buddies in the Tivoli. After ya're finished there ya come out. This kid is sleepin' in a doorway. Ya feel sorry for him and take him back to yar hotel room."

"Essentially that's right," Turk said, moving his shoulders to ease the cramp in them. He wondered idly why all police stations had the same down-at-the-heels quality about them. They all had the same urinal-smell, too, no matter where they were. Hick's office was not much more than a cubicle with a door in it and a barred window in one wall.

"Now you know why ya wanted that kid, Mr. Turk, and so do I," Hicks said. "Like I told ya, we know ya didn't kill him. But ya did want him for yourself, now didn't you?" There was a wide grin on Hick's face. "All ya gotta do to make this easy is 'fess up."

Turk felt the color rise to his cheeks. He clenched his teeth together.

"Now even if the kid was a Mex, we still got laws against—"

"Okay," Turk said, "you arrest me now on whatever charge you think I'm guilty of, and see how fucking fast your ass will be in the fire." He leaned slightly forward. "Come on, Detective Hicks, stop trying to play the smart cop."

Hicks chomped down on his cigar.

"I told you who I am, what I'm doing here, and why Manuel was in my room." Turk stood up. "I'm going back to the hotel. If you have any more questions, come see me there."

"I'll tell you when you can go," Hicks said leaping out of his seat.

"You can't tell me anything unless you arrest me," Turk answered.

"You're a goddamn wise-ass, aren't you?" Hicks growled.

Turk didn't answer.

"Sit down!" Hicks ordered.

"You can't hold me—"

"I'm not holding ya," Hicks said. "I brought ya in for questionin' and I'm not done yet. . . . Now are ya goin' to sit down, or do I have to call a couple of my men to make ya sit down?"

Turk returned to his chair.

"That's a lot better," Hicks said, sitting down again. He leaned back in his swivel chair. "I'm goin' to run a check on ya, Mr. Turk, with the FBI. How does that grab ya?"

Turk lit another cigarette. "You'll find I was an army officer and that I fought in Spain and now I'm a newspaper reporter."

"Ya have all the answers, even when I didn't ask the questions."

"I thought I'd save you the trouble," Turk said.

Suddenly the phone rang. Hicks answered it. He listened for a few moments; then he said, "Keep me posted." And he hung up. "The guy was hired to kill ya."

"Before or after he robbed me?" Turk asked flippantly, though he immediately thought that Walther might have bought the gun. He had the money and the motive. But the idea was too absurd. Walther was several things—most of them distasteful to Turk—but he wasn't a killer, even by proxy.

"He was sent to kill ya," Hicks said. "Now why would anyone want to do that to a nice guy like you? Maybe it has something to do with the kid, eh? Maybe he's family, and he didn't like the idea of ya playin' around with his kid brother?"

"You're going to have to have a lot better maybes than that," Turk answered.

"Okay, wise-ass, tell me why he was sent to kill ya."

"Did he happen to say who sent him?"

The phone rang again.

Hicks picked it up and listened. "Thanks, Bill," he said, and put the phone down. "That was the coroner. There was no evidence of sexual molestation on the kid."

"So that's what you wanted to know?"

"Yeah, that's what I wanted to know. Ya can go now," Hicks said.

Turk stubbed out his cigarette. "If you find out why someone was sent to kill me, let me know."

"Ya'll be the first one I'll call," Hicks said.

Turk stood up and without either offering his hand or saying another word, he turned around and started to leave. Then he stopped and faced Hicks. "Who do I see about claiming Manuel's body? I want to give him a proper burial."

"Fought in Spain, eh!" Hicks said, puffing on his cigar. "What was it really like there?"

"Look, Hicks. . . ."

"Hey, I'm really interested."

Turk took a deep breath, and after a few moments he said in a softer tone, "There were a lot of children like Manuel there."

"Ya're not a commie, are ya?"

Turk gave a slight laugh. "No, I'm not a communist."

"Didn't think ya were," Hicks said, blowing smoke.

"Do I get Manuel's body?"

"I'll take care of it," Hicks said.

"Thanks."

"Glad to be of service," Hicks answered. His right hand went to the brim of his Stetson in a mock salute.

Turk nodded, turned toward the door, and left. A few minutes later he was back in the hotel moving to a different room. He wasn't going to make love to Lauren where Manuel had been killed.

Josef Klemp fitted a second cigarette into the black onyx cigarette holder he was holding. He was a wiry-built man of middling height, with a dark brown mustache, graying slightly; his hair, the same color, was also graying, especially in the area just above his sideburns. He had been a young, ambitious colonel in the German Army when, in 1916, he was a victim of a French gas attack and was retired from field duty.

Klemp was ensconced in a large club chair, his hazel eyes fixed on the far wall several feet behind, where Ziegler sat nervously on the edge of a small couch.

"I told Winkler to keep away from the Bund," Ziegler complained. "But he said it was the best place to find a woman, and now, because he found a woman . . ." He stopped and shook his head.

Klemp asked, "Are you sure that Mister Crowly is an FBI agent?"

"Yes. The police lieutenant I spoke to said he was."

Klemp stood up and went to the window on the west side of the sitting room. The corner suite he occupied was on the eighteenth floor of the Hotel St. George, on Clark Street in Brooklyn. From it he could see north across Manhattan to that part of the Hudson known as the North River, where the huge ocean liners had docked before the war. But now it was occupied by freighters and the enormous bulk of the French liner *Normandie*, seized by the United States to prevent it from going to Germany when France surrendered.

The windows on the south side gave Klemp an excellent view of the shipbuilding activity in the Brooklyn Navy Yard and the upper New York Bay, where ships gathered for the convoys that supplied England with everything from planes to food.

Klemp said, without turning to face Ziegler, "We do indeed have a problem."

Ziegler stood up. "I can't go back to the apartment now."

"You can spend a few nights here. We'll find you another place to live," Klemp told him. "Now we have a greater concern."

Ziegler agreed.

"Winkler must not be able to tell him anything," Klemp said.

"Well, I don't know how we're going to stop him from talking," Ziegler answered.

"You can stretch out on the couch while I'm gone," Klemp said. "I'll be back in a while."

"Where are you going?"

"To make sure Winkler doesn't say anything that would terminate our mission here," Klemp said. "But before I go, I'll send word to Berlin about what happened. The admiral will want to know about it and the measures we've taken to minimize the danger to the rest of our mission here in New York. . . . Now, if you will excuse me, I will dress." He went into the bedroom and closed the door behind him.

Klemp picked up the copy of the Gideon Bible, leafed through several pages, and stopped at Judges, chapter 15, verse 4. Using a cipher book, he quickly encoded a message informing Admiral Canaris that the Fox might have been freed. Then he dialed a phone number in Brooklyn.

After six rings a man answered, "Fred isn't here."

Klemp acknowledged the sign with the countersign: "I want the preacher."

"Ready," the man answered.

"Can the gospel be given tonight?" Klemp asked, after he finished giving him the coded message.

"Yes," the man answered.

The click informed Klemp that the man had hung up. He put the phone down, tore the message up into small bits of paper and flushed them down the toilet. Then he started to dress.

A few minutes later, when Klemp came out of the room, Ziegler asked, "Do you want me to drive?"

"No. A car waiting around just might attract attention. I'll either go by subway or by cab. But thank you anyway for the offer."

Klemp left his suite, rode the elevator to the lobby, and nodded to the desk clerk.

Klemp knew that the clerk would not think it at all unusual that he was leaving the hotel at three in the morning. For the five years that he had occupied the suite he had acted the part of a very wealthy retired eccentric, going in and out of the hotel at odd hours.

Rather than use one of the cabs immediately outside the St. George, Klemp walked a few blocks to the Hotel Somerset and hailed a cab there. He sat back and relaxed during the twenty-minute ride to the hospital. He enjoyed the quiet of the early morning hours.

When he arrived at the hospital, Klemp went straight to the emergency room. It was very busy. The doctors and nurses were having difficulty coping with several accident victims, two men suffering with knife wounds, and a middle-aged man who was having a heart attack.

The confusion suited Klemp's purpose. Spying a stethoscope on a desk he picked it up and quickly placed it around his neck. Then, pointing to the man with the heart condition, he said to a nurse, "Better get him upstairs."

"Yes, Doctor. . . . Right away!" she answered.

Klemp nodded. So far so good. He made his way to the information desk outside the emergency room and said to the man at the desk, "I'm Dr. Strauss. You have a Mr. Winkler here. . . ."

The man thumbed through the cards. "Room sixteen; tenth floor, east wing."

Klemp nodded and headed for the elevator bank. A few minutes later, he approached the room where Winkler was and found it guarded by a cop. Klemp made a quick decision, and going up to the officer, he said, "I'm Special Agent Crowly." He began to reach for his wallet.

"It's okay," the officer said. "I was told you might come back."

Klemp nodded and walked into the room. The cop started to follow. "I need a few minutes alone with him," he said.

"Sure," the cop said. "Want the door closed?"

"If you don't mind."

Klemp went to the bed. Winkler was asleep. His breathing was labored.

Klemp put his right hand over Winkler's mouth and with his left hand, he held Winkler's nose shut.

Winkler's eyes opened.

"It's better this way," Klemp said in German. "Don't fight. . . . Relax and it will be over quickly."

Winkler's eyes went wide with terror. He tried to free his head. He was sweating profusely. But Klemp held it fast. "Not much longer," he said softly, still speaking in German. Despite his small frame, he had surprisingly strong hands.

Winkler's body arched; then fell back.

Klemp counted to fifty before releasing his hold. Then he placed the stethoscope over Winkler's heart and listened for a beat. There was none. Replacing the stethoscope in his pocket, he opened the door and said to the cop, "Thank you. He's asleep now."

The cop looked into the room and nodded.

"Thanks again," Klemp said; he walked down the hall to the elevator.

Lauren and Dijon were bathed in a greenish glow coming from the lights in the plane's instrument panel. She found it very difficult to speak to Dijon above the loud throb of the engine. Now and then Dijon was in radio communication with someone on the ground; otherwise he seemed perfectly content to remain silent and fly the plane.

Lauren was very much aware of the enormity of the sky, the brightness of the stars, and the red and green navigation lights on the wing tips. From time to time she glimpsed down at the earth. It was totally dark, making it seem as if she and Dijon were the only living beings in the universe.

Dijon leaned closer to her and said, "The Mexican Air Force wants to know what the hell is going on. . . . I told them that some people tried to stop me from taking off. They asked me where I was heading and I pretended not to be able to hear."

Lauren nodded and asked, "Do you think they'll try to stop us?"

Dijon shook his head and moved away from her, resuming his former position. She resumed looking out the window.

"Getting a lot of German," Dijon said, leaning close to her again.

"From where?"

He pointed past her, to the right. "From the u-boats in the Gulf of Mexico or farther out in the Caribbean. They surface at night to recharge their batteries and give the crews a chance to breathe fresh air."

She was about to ask him if he knew anything about the ship, *City of Cadiz,* when he said, "I'm picking up stuff from North Africa."

"That's thousands of miles away!"

"Has to do with atmospheric conditions," he said. "You understand German, don't you?"

She nodded. "Some."

Dijon removed the headpiece from his head and handed it to her. "Just hold one of the earphones close to your ear."

"Something about a Colonel Becker." She listened a while longer. "Too much static to hear anything clearly." She handed the headset back to Dijon.

He nodded.

Within a matter of moments Lauren was again conscious of the engine's monotonous throbbing. The sound was beginning to have a soporific effect. She closed her eyes, took several deep breaths, and rested her head against the back of the seat. That she was flying through the night to be with Doug seemed unreal. But everything that had happened to her during the past few hours had the same unreal quality.

A sudden, sharp drop made Lauren open her eyes and sit upright.

"Air pocket," Dijon explained. Pointing off to the left, he said, "There's a storm out there. We'll probably see it in a couple of hours. I'm getting reports on it from the weather station at Biggs, the army airfield adjacent to Fort Bliss."

She nodded.

"Better tighten your safety belt," he warned, "so that you don't go bouncing all over the cabin."

Lauren did as she was told. She wanted to ask him if they were in any danger, but decided not to. There was nothing she could do to change it, even if they were. "My God!" she exclaimed as they dropped into another air pocket.

"Nothing to worry about," Dijon called out, smiling at her.

"I sure hope not," she answered, but not loud enough for him to hear.

The turbulence became worse. The small plane was tossed all over the sky.

Several times Lauren felt as if she were going to vomit. But she controlled herself.

She braced herself against the instrument panel and thought about how someday she'd tell her and Doug's children about her wild flight from Mexico City. . . . It was the kind of story out of which could grow a family legend. She smiled.

Crowly stepped off the elevator and into the dimly lit hospital corridor. It was his second visit that night to the Kings County Hospital. The antiseptic smell seemed heavier than it had previously been.

Crowly moved away from the bank of elevators and made his way to the east wing. There were two newly assigned uniformed cops outside Winkler's room. The door was closed.

"Kiern Crowly," he announced, showing his identification. "I'm here to see Lieutenant Fioredeliso."

"He's expecting you," one of the cops said, as he opened the door and announced him.

Crowly entered the room.

Fioredeliso came toward him from the right side. "I'm damn sorry to pull you back here," he said, offering his hand.

"That's the way it goes sometimes," Crowly answered.

They shook hands.

Crowly looked over at the bed. Winkler's body was covered with a sheet.

"Here's what we've been able to put together so far," Fioredeliso said. "A couple of the doctors and nurses in emergency remember a doctor coming in and being helpful. One of the nurses said he told her to get a cardiac patient upstairs. Then he—that is, the doctor—vanished."

"What do you mean, vanished?" Crowly asked, watching two police technicians dust for fingerprints.

"Apparently the doctor in question left the emergency room. He took a stethoscope belonging to another physician with him."

"Then he posed as a doctor to get in here?"

"No," Fioredeliso said. "We checked with the man at the patient information desk. A Dr. Strauss asked where Winkler was."

"How did Strauss—or whoever it was—get past your man?" Crowly asked.

"He said he was you," Fioredeliso answered. "He gave your name. My man admits that he didn't check his identification. . . . What would you say were the chances of someone knowing your name?"

"Damn slim."

"Yes, *damn* slim. But then I remembered I told Winkler's roommate Ziegler to call you. I gave him your name and told him who you were."

"Then you think Ziegler did it?"

Fioredeliso nodded.

"Why did he pose as a doctor?"

"He might have thought it would be easier to gain access to Winkler's room that way. My guess is that he didn't count on finding his friend under guard. And your identity would have more weight with a cop than a doctor."

"Ziegler had the door closed while he was with Winkler?"

"Naturally. He told the man on duty he had some confidential matter to speak to Winkler about."

"How was it done?" Crowly asked.

Fioredeliso moved to the head of the bed.

Crowly followed him.

"Suffocation," Fioredeliso said, pulling back the sheet.

Winkler's face had a bluish tinge. His eyes bulged; they hadn't been closed.

"Was a pillow used?" Crowly asked.

Fioredeliso shook his head. "No. Ziegler used his hands. Probably held one over his friend's mouth and with the other squeezed off his nose. Winkler couldn't put up any fight. It probably took no more than three minutes." He pulled the sheet back over Winkler's head. "I have an APB out for Ziegler."

"You have a description of him?"

"From the nurse, the man at the information desk, and my man. He's a dignified-looking individual, with a mustache and graying sideburns. We have a very good description of him."

The two men walked out into the corridor.

"The question," Fioredeliso said, "is why Ziegler would murder him? What was the motive?"

"To keep Winkler from talking about their real reason for being here," Crowly answered. He didn't bother telling Fioredeliso that he had been banking on Winkler to open the way to other German agents. "But on second thought, I don't think it's as simple as that. . . . Ziegler would have to be a fool not to know that by murdering Winkler, he'd be calling our attention to him. No—there just has to be another reason why Ziegler did it. Something so important that it was worth the risk to do it."

"Any ideas?" Fioredeliso asked.

"None."

"Maybe we'll get lucky and be able to pick up Ziegler," Fioredeliso said.

"I sure as hell hope so," Crowly answered.

"Come on, I'll ride down the elevator with you," Fioredeliso said. "I'm sorry one of my men screwed up."

"Could have happened to anyone here," Crowly answered magnanimously. "But I'm damn sorry that it did happen. Winkler could have been the key to unlocking at least one cell of Nazi spies."

"Even if my man hadn't let Ziegler pass," Fioredeliso said, "if it was that important to kill Winkler, he would have found another way."

"That's for sure," Crowly replied, as they stepped into the elevator. "That's for damn sure!"

Though Ed was several miles from where the plane had crashed, German patrols were close-by. He could hear the men's conversations, and knew they were looking for him, with orders to shoot him on sight.

The storm was his only protection. Twice he had passed within a couple paces of the German patrols. And both times he had been able to elude them. First, by standing absolutely still; the second time, by dropping behind a rock outcrop. Like a phantom, he watched the Germans pass on either side of him.

But the storm was sapping Ed's strength. The wind and sand made him feel as if he were walking against a grindstone. His eyes hurt from squinting and the skin on his face was rubbed raw. He was very thirsty and annoyed with himself for not taking the canteens from the bodies of the Germans.

Ed was forced to make frequent stops for longer periods of time. And when he dropped to the ground, he struggled to remain awake, knowing that should he sleep, the Germans would certainly find and kill him.

"But that's not what's going to happen," Ed told himself over and over again. "I'm going to get back across the border. I'm going to stop those Kraut bastards!" Sometimes he spoke to himself, vocalizing his grim determination to survive and destroy the Germans. His mind wandered, and he remembered what it was like for a sixteen-year-old boy to ride with Pershing; he smiled. He forgot the long hours in the saddle, the flies, the heat, and the bad food. He even forgot the fact that they never made contact with Pancho Villa, that Pershing had gotten them lost. None of that really mattered. . . . What counted was that for the first time in his short life of sixteen years, he was happy. He was with other men who acknowledge his manhood around the campfires after a long day in the saddle. He laughed with them, ate and drank with them, and if the dice went that way, he'd die with them. They were fleeting memories: the lean face of Corporal Reilly caught in a sudden burst of light from a match, or Sergeant Williams, shouting to the men to mount up. But there was something else he remembered as vividly as if it had happened within the past few days: The time he'd had his first woman, in the back of a cantina in a village so small it didn't even have a name, or if it did, he didn't know it. . . .

The woman's name was Juanita. She was more Indian than anything else, with high cheekbones, long black hair, and lovely wide black eyes and a nut-brown skin. She was only a couple months older than he was.

The cantina was made of adobe. It stood on the crown of a low, dun-colored hill. There were four other adobe buildings on the side of the hill. It was late afternoon when he and another trooper rode up to the cantina. They had been riding on the right flank of the main column. . . .

Ed stopped. He needed to rest again. He sank down to the ground where he stood. . . .

The cantina looked yellow in the slant of the sun. He and the other trooper went inside. Juanita was sitting off to one side. And a short time later they wound up in the back room on her bed. Up until then, Ed had never seen a woman naked. It was the most beautiful sight he had ever seen. Her breasts stood straight out and the nipples on them were rose pink. The flare of her hips was—

Ed heard the two Germans before he actually saw them. They were close. He made the mistake of trying to roll onto his stomach.

The Germans stopped in their tracks and began shooting.

The bullets swacked into the earth in front of Gripper and pinged off some nearby rocks. "God-damn!" he swore silently, as he realized they were spraying the area with a Schmeisser machine pistol. They were doing it with Kraut-like efficiency. He was prone now, and pointing the rifle toward the Germans he squeezed off three rounds.

They were still firing.

Ed couldn't manage to get a good sighting. Suddenly a hot flash of pain slashed through his left arm. He had been hit.

The Germans stopped shooting.

Ed was having difficulty holding the rifle steady. The pain came in searing waves, traveling from his elbow to his shoulder. He was bleeding but he couldn't tell how badly. He listened intently, hoping to locate the Krauts from the sound of their voices. But all he could hear was the booming of his own heart and the sound of the wind. The sky in the east was beginning to gray.

Then one of the Germans took a step.

Ed squeezed off two rounds.

One of the Germans screamed and the other struck the ground with a thud.

Ed fired, squeezing off rounds until the clip was empty. Then he dropped the rifle, slipped his .45 from his holster, and bellied his way toward where he thought the Krauts were. He found them not more than six feet from where he had been. One was dead and the other dying. Ed put the .45 to the head of the dying man and squeezed the trigger. Then he picked up one of the machine pistols, several clips of ammunition for it, and took the canteens from the bodies before he took the time to examine his wound. It was superficial. He used his belt to make a tourniquet and staunched the flow of blood.

Suddenly another German called out, "*Felix, was ist los?*"

Ed tried to think of a suitable answer. But the words wouldn't come and he crawled away from the sound of the voice. He moved slowly and began to count. At one hundred, he paused for a few moments to check if the Germans were following him. When he was sure they weren't, he started to crawl and count again.

He forced himself to keep going. The light in the east became much stronger and the pain seemed lessen a bit.

Ed stopped crawling and stood up. He could not allow himself the luxury of a short rest period. The last one had almost cost him his life.

From what Ed recalled of the map he'd been using just before the plane went down, the town of Este Guzman was not more than ten miles in a north-northwesterly direction from the crash site. He guessed he had traveled no more than five miles, but part of that distance—or maybe all of it—could have been on any compass heading, not necessarily the one that would take him to Este Guzman.

His arm hurt and was caked with blood. With any luck, the wound wouldn't become infected. Now and then he loosened his tourniquet and then tightened it again.

If he failed to reach Este Guzman within the next few hours, he was probably wrong about where he thought it was in relationship to where the plane had gone down. And if that proved to be the case, he would probably die in the desert from exhaustion. He couldn't die. He had to make it back to the States in time to warn Hanahan and Fitzhugh about the Krauts.

He paused to drink from one of the canteens. It was light now and the wind had diminished considerably, only carrying a light brown dust that quickly caked on his wet lips. From previous experience, Ed knew that the wind would soon die altogether, and the sky would clear and the sun would shine. Then, his chances of eluding the Krauts would be nil. His only hope lay in the reason for them being there in the first place: namely, that they would want to move north again as quickly as possible after having been delayed by the storm.

After the debacle at the airport—that was the way Krieger described what had happened—Krieger and Walther were detained by Captain Juan Lopez of the Mexican police in his office at the airport.

Lopez was thirty years old. He was a tall man, with a black mustache. He asked Krieger and Zwig to identify themselves, and after they had, he asked for an explanation of what happened.

"You see, Captain," Krieger said, "Señor Zwig's wife was running away with the pilot of the plane."

Lopez nodded sympathetically. "Two men were killed, and— "

"That was not our doing," Krieger told him. "Señor Dijon was responsible for the deaths of two of my men."

"There was an exchange of shots," Lopez said, lighting a cigarette.

"Señor Zwig was defending his honor and his home," Krieger responded. "You understand how much a man's honor and home mean to him. . . . The price, Captain, no matter how much, would be reasonable."

Lopez nodded, leaned forward, and picked up a

pencil. On a piece of white paper he wrote the number *5000* and the words *American dollars*. Then he turned the paper upside down and moved it across the desk.

Krieger glanced at it, nodded, and said, "Why not come by for cocktails this evening, Captain."

"It would be my pleasure," Lopez answered, picking up the paper and tearing it into small pieces, which he threw into a wastepaper basket. "I am sorry for the inconvenience. . . . Señor Zwig, I hope that your difficulty will soon come to an end and you are happily reconciled with your wife."

"That, Captain, is my fondest wish," Walther said, speaking for the first time since he and Krieger had entered the captain's office.

Lopez shook hands with Krieger and Zwig, and escorted them to the door. . . .

Less than an hour later they were back in Krieger's house. Krieger dropped his coat on a chair in the foyer, then went directly to the bar and poured himself a double whiskey, which he drank without offering one to Walther, who stood near the window, still wearing his coat.

"You realize, of course," Krieger said, as he put the glass down, "your wife and Dijon now know—" A knock at the door stopped him from continuing. "Come in," he called out.

"Excuse me, Colonel," the man said, opening the door, "But this just came over from Berlin."

Krieger took the message and read it.

"Will there be a reply?" the man asked.

"No," Krieger answered. He waited until he and Walther were alone again before he said, "You have been ordered back to Germany."

Walther's jaw went slack.

"You will leave tomorrow," Krieger said. "You can fly to Buenos Aires, from there to Lisbon, and then on the

Berlin."

"Would you mind if I poured myself a drink," Walther asked in a tremulous voice.

Krieger gestured toward the bar.

Walther drank two whiskeys in rapid succession. "I haven't been there in twenty-five years," he said in a low, tight voice.

"The message is signed by Canaris," Krieger said.

"If I do . . . "

"My dear Walther, it is not a matter of choice. You will go."

Walther poured another whiskey and drank it. "You know what will happen to me once I am back there?"

Kreiger did not answer. He was almost certain that Walther was being ordered home because Canaris had had to give the Führer an explanation of what happened, and Walther's homosexual proclivity had to be part of it. Knowing the Füher's attitude toward homosexuals, Krieger was not in the least bit surprised by the order.

"I will be imprisoned," Walther said, finding it difficult to stop his hands from trembling.

"Perhaps not. . . . Perhaps your service to the Fatherland will permit—"

"My service to the Fatherland must mean something," Walther said. "I have always served Germany."

"What are you getting at?" Krieger asked.

"I cannot go back, and obviously you cannot allow me to remain here," Walther said.

Krieger nodded. "That's true."

Walther put the whiskey glass down and returned to the window. "It will be better this way," he said, removing his revolver from the right pocket and at the same time facing Krieger.

Krieger started to speak, then stopped himself.

"There is no other way," Walther said.

"Probably not," Krieger nodded.

Walther raised the revolver. "Canaris would never have known, if you hadn't told him."

"My God!" Krieger exclaimed, looking at the revolver. Smiling, Walther squeezed off two rounds. The first caught Krieger in the groin and dropped him to the floor; the second blew away the front of his face. Walther placed the revolver against the right side of his own head. He closed his eyes and squeezed the trigger again.

# 12

General Alt's jeep pulled up in front of the headquarters building just as the base bugler was blowing reveille at 0530 in the morning. With him were his two aides, Colonel Edward Claw and Major Paul Winters.

Alt swung himself out of the front seat of the jeep. "Sergeant," he said to the driver, "the mess hall is in the building directly across the quadrangle. Go on over there and get yourself some chow."

"Yes, sir," the man answered.

Alt turned to his aides and with a nod he said, "Let's find out what has Hanahan in a boil." He walked quickly up the steps and into the hallway. He was a tall, lean man of fifty-five, with a long face, buck teeth, a receding chin, kind brown eyes, and an almost-bald head.

The armed guard outside Fitzhugh's office snapped to attention.

"General Alt and two aides to see General Hanahan," Alt said, exchanging salutes with the man.

The guard knocked at the door.

"Yes . . . yes, open it," Hanahan rumbled from inside the room.

"General Alt—" the guard began.

"Send them in," Hanahan exclaimed, coming out

from behind the desk and crossing the room to greet Alt and his aides. Alt was his main rival for a field command. They had graduated together from the Point in 1906. Both of them had seen action in France under Pershing, but after the war they had gone in different directions. Alt had seen service in China and the Philippines, while Hanahan had remained in Washington.

"I'm starved," Alt said, after the handshaking was over. "We've been on the road since 0300."

Hanahan picked up the phone and ordered breakfast for all of them.

"Where's Charley?" Alt asked.

"In communications. He's been there for the last hour. I'll call him." Hanahan picked up the phone and asked to speak to Fitzhugh. "Harry's here," he said, when the base commander came on the phone.

"I'll be right there," Fitzhugh responded.

"Anything?"

"Negative."

Hanahan put the phone down and helped himself to a fresh cigar. He noticed that Alt was looking at the situation map that displayed the disposition of their forces. "We just might have more trouble than fighting each other, in these war games," Hanahan said, lighting up.

Fitzhugh came into the office.

"Well," Alt said, shaking his hand, "I hope whatever it is isn't as serious as you made it sound over the phone."

"You can judge that for yourself," Fitzhugh said. He shook hands with Alt's aides, then settled into an empty chair facing the desk.

Hanahan was about to speak, but a knock at the door stopped him. "Probably breakfast," he said.

"Breakfast it is!" Major Winter exclaimed, opening

the door and stepping back to allow the orderly to roll in the serving cart.

"Where shall I set it up?" the soldier asked.

"We'll serve ourselves," Hanahan told the orderly.

The man saluted and left the room.

"We can eat and talk at the same time," Hanahan told them, going to the cart to pour himself a cup of coffee. When he sat down again, he said, "I've taken casualties, Harry. Real ones. Ed and a pilot are down somewhere south of here near El Charo, and a mobile scout unit has been destroyed less than fifty miles from the border. That's why I called yesterday and asked you if your men were using live stuff."

Alt put his toast down on the plate he was balancing on his knees. "Bandits?" he asked.

Hanahan glanced at Fitzhugh and shrugged. "I wished the hell I knew."

"Who the hell else could be out there?" Alt asked.

Again Hanahan looked at Fitzhugh. But this time Fitzhugh spoke: "Krauts."

"Come on," Alt responded, "you're pulling my leg."

"No," Fitzhugh said quietly. "We're not."

For several moments no one in the room spoke. Then Colonel Claw said, "Sir, let's assume there are Germans out there, could you tell us what they're doing there?"

"Moving north to attack us," Fitzhugh answered before Hanahan could speak.

"But how would they have gotten there in the first place?" Alt questioned.

Hanahan threw up his hands. "Beats the shit out of me! If I knew, I'd know whether they're Krauts or bandits."

Fitzhugh put his coffee mug down on the floor next to his chair. "We picked up a transmission on the radio, it was in Spanish, but the accents seemed German." He stood up. "I know this sounds crazy, but we heard Rommel congratulating a Colonel Becker for destroying the scout unit."

"Rommel? . . . Irwin Rommel?"

"We're not sure that it was Rommel," Hanahan said.

"Who the hell was doing the translating?" Alt asked. "I know neither of you can speak Spanish."

"Turk, Douglas Turk," Fitzhugh said.

"I didn't know he was back in. I heard he was was—"

"He's not in yet," Hanahan said. "He's still a reporter with I.N.S. He happened to be in the communications room when the transmission came in." He had no intention of giving Alt any more details of what had taken place than was absolutely necessary.

Fitzhugh went to the window. The dawn was coming in, the light easing slowly across the sky. "Turk was very definite," he said.

Alt lit a cigarette. "Okay, just tell me how the Krauts managed to get there?"

Fitzhugh shook his head.

"Unless we can answer that one," Major Winters commented, "then we can eliminate the Krauts."

"Okay, so we have Mex bandits to deal with," Hanahan said, feeling more secure than he had since the transmission had come over the radio.

"Mex bandits who are damn well-armed from what you told me," Alt commented.

"There's no arguing that."

"The question is, What are we going to do about it?" Fitzhugh said. "If they're as well-armed as they appear to be, they might decide to come across the border. Hell, Pancho Villa did it in 1916."

Alt chuckled. "I chased him with Pershing. Ed was just a green trooper in my troop then. He's a hell of a good man. I hope nothing has happened to him."

"We can't go into Mexico to get them," Fitzhugh

said.

"Telling the Federale commander in Juárez about them," Hanahan said, "would be like pissing in the wind."

Alt agreed.

"We can go through channels to the State Department," Colonel Claw said.

Hanahan shook his head vigorously. "If we do that, then I'll have to explain the casualties. We'll be better off if those men are listed as having been killed in accidents related to the exercise."

Fitzhugh raised his eyebrows. He didn't like that suggestion at all, and said as much. Hanahan was going for a whitewash job, not wanting Washington asking questions for which he might not have answers.

"The way I see it," Hanahan said, "mentioning bandits to anyone in the War or State Departments invites all kinds of questions. I'd rather just treat the deaths as accidents.

"But that doesn't solve the problem of the bandits. We have to be sure they don't cross the border, and the only thing we can do is to put some men on the border and if the bandits attempt to come through we'll—"

"Before we do anything," Alt suggested, "why don't we wait to see if they move north? My guess is that they'll fade into the hills. They know what they've done."

"We can't be sure of that," Fitzhugh said. "Even a small, well-armed group could cause a great deal of damage north of the border."

"There's no disagreement on that score," Hanahan said. "But let me offer a suggestion: we wait, say, thirty-six hours, say sometime around 1200, December seventh. If we don't have any more incidents, we'll assume they turned and fled south, or any other direction, except north."

"That's reasonable," Alt responded.

"Fitzhugh?" Hanahan asked.

"I'll go along with it."

Out of courtesy, Hanahan asked Colonel Claw and Major Winters for their opinion.

Both men agreed that it was reasonable to wait the thirty-six hours.

"But what the hell are we going to do about Turk?" Alt asked.

"Know what I'd like to do?" Hanahan commented.

"Let me handle him," Fitzhugh said. "I think I can get him to go along with us for the next thirty-six hours or so."

"Okay, you handle it," Alt replied.

Fitzhugh looked questioningly at Hanahan.

"I'll go along with it," Hanahan said. He was extremely pleased with the outcome of the meeting. Suddenly he was hungry and he began to eat with gusto, even though the food was cold.

Casualties happened during maneuvers. There was no way to avoid them, especially if there was bad weather, or the men were careless around live ammunition. . . .

The phone was ringing. Turk heard it through several layers of sleep and a mélange of dreams, the last of which momentarily thrust him back to Paris to watch the conquering German Army march through the Arc de Triomphe and down the Champs Élysées, which somehow changed into the Main Street of El Paso. . . . The phone was still ringing when Turk opened his eyes, cleared his throat, and picked up the phone.

"Doug, is that you?"

"Lauren?"

"Yes. . . . Yes, my darling, it's me," she answered with a laugh.

Sleep vanished. Turk pulled himself into a sitting position. "Where are you?"

"A place called Persidio," Lauren answered. "We ran into a storm. Dijon said we'd be better off playing safe than risking a crash."

"Are you all right?" Turk asked.

"I'm fine. We should be coming in around two. Can you meet me at the airport?"

Turk was about to answer that he'd be there, but then he remembered Manuel and realized he couldn't make a definite commitment. "Come to the hotel. Tell Dijon there'll be a room waiting for him at the hotel."

"Honey, I don't have any clothes with me, other than those I'm wearing."

"You'll buy some," Turk said.

"How's the boy?" Lauren asked.

After a momentary pause, he answered, "I'll tell you about him when I see you."

"Are you all right? You sound strange."

"I'm fine! You're just hearing my first cigarette of the day," he lied.

"See you soon, my love," she said.

"Yes."

There was a click on the other end and the line went dead. Turk put the phone down. He reached for a cigarette and, lighting it, he looked toward the window. He had forgotten to lower the shade the previous night—not that anyone could look into the room. The window, like the one in the other room, faced the park across the street from the hotel. A pigeon flew onto the window ledge, looked through the glass at him, then took several steps and flew away.

Turk checked his watch. It was eight-thirty in the morning. He looked toward the window again. The sky was a light ashen color, more gray than white. He guessed it was cold outside.

The phone rang again.

Turk picked it up.

Hicks was on the other end. "I had Manuel's body picked up by Gonzales and Sons. They're at two-five-one Rio Piedres. Old man Gonzales said he'd arrange to bury the boy in the Mex cemetery in Juárez. He said it'll cost ya one hundred and twenty-five dollars, and that'll include a wreath of white carnations."

"Thanks," Turk said. "If I can do you a favor. . . . "

"The funeral will be at noon," Hicks told him.

"I'll be there."

"I might show up. . . . That is, if you don't mind?"

"No, I don't mind."

"See ya," Hicks said and put the phone down.

Turk stubbed out the cigarette and swung his feet onto the floor. He shaved, showered, and dressed within twenty minutes. Before he left his room he put through a call to Fitzhugh and was politely told by an aide, "The general is in conference."

"Maybe you might know if Colonel Gripper has been found?" Turk asked.

"Please hold the line," the aide said.

For the better part of two minutes, Turk heard nothing. He was growing impatient, when suddenly Fitzhugh announced himself on the other end.

"Any word about Ed?" Turk asked.

"Nothing."

Turk uttered a deep sigh.

"Can you come out to the fort?"

"Not until sometime this afternoon," Turk answered. "I have something important to do."

"If you intend to file a story about what has been happening in the desert," Fitzhugh said, "as a favor to me, I wish you wouldn't. General Alt came in this morning for a conference with me and Hanahan."

"Tell me about it," Turk said, dropping down on the bed to lean back on the pillows and make himself comfortable. The story he had thought of writing hadn't really taken shape in his mind yet. Manuel's death had gotten in the way.

"It'd be easier if you came out here," Fitzhugh responded.

"I would if I could. But I have several—"

"Okay," Fitzhugh said. "I'll tell it to you straight. We figure that a large group of bandits are operating south of here, and that they ran into Barth and—well, you heard it."

Turk blew a cloud of cigarette smoke into the air. "You figure the same bandits shot down Ed?"

"That's the way I see it," Fitzhugh said. "He probably spotted them at El Charo and . . . "

Turk felt a sense of relief. There wasn't any way for German troops to be transported to Mexico, and unless he could prove there was, then Hanahan and the others were making a logical assumption. "Suppose you're right," he said. "Just what the hell are you going to do about it?"

"Wait until Sunday," Fitzhugh said. "It's our considered opinion that the bandits will have turned away from the border and lost themselves in the desert. They know we can't go after them."

"And after Sunday, then what?"

"If there aren't any more attacks, we'll notify the Department of the Army and let them decide what to do."

After a long pause, Turk said, "It's reasonable, at least from your, Hanahan's, and Alt's points of view. It might cause some waves but nothing that can't be handled."

"I'm sorry about Ed," Fitzhugh said. "He was a damn

good man."

"One of the best," Turk answered. "One of the goddamn best!"

"After Sunday," Fitzhugh said, "you can have the exclusive on the bandits. It would make one hell of a story. . . ."

"Okay," Turk said, "I'll go along with you on this, Fitzhugh. But you owe me one."

"I owe you," Fitzhugh said.

"Do you still want me to come to the fort?" Turk asked, killing his cigarette in the ashtray.

"Sometime later in the evening to have cocktails with me?" Fitzhugh suggested.

"Fine. I'll be there around seven. But I'll have two people with me: The future Mrs. Turk and a friend from Spain."

"It will be a pleasure to have them," Fitzhugh said.

Turk put the phone down, and a short while later bought the local paper in the hotel lobby. The headline story was about the u-boat attack on a U.S. merchantman, the USS *Sagadoc,* which had been torpedoed and sunk in the South Atlantic. All of the crew had not been accounted for, and those that were missing, the story went on to say, had to be presumed dead. The second lead story on the front page was a U.P. report, filed in Moscow, of a Russian counterattack along a broad front to the west of the Russian capital with subsequent German withdrawals from key positions, and heavy losses reported on both sides.

Turk folded the paper under his arm and wondered how the Russians had managed to put fresh troops in the line, when their own losses up until now had been in the hundreds of thousands. To do something like that, Turk guessed, must mean that they had another—or perhaps even several—armies in the east waiting to be committed when the weather would turn against the Germans and favor them. There wasn't any doubt that winter would be Russian's strongest ally.

Turk returned to the luncheonette that he and Manuel had gone to after the incident at the Owl. Feeling hostility on all sides, Turk settled on a stool. But he felt better when he spotted Estaban, the man Manuel knew, through the opening that led to the kitchen.

With a scowl on his face, the counterman came up to Turk and in English asked what he wanted. What the man was really asking, though he didn't use the words, was *What the hell are you doing here, gringo?*

Turk pushed his hat back on his head. In Spanish, he said, "Two eggs, ham, and coffee."

The counterman's jaw went slack.

"Tell Estaban I want to see him," Turk said, still speaking Spanish.

"You police?" the man asked.

Turk shook his head. "I'm a newspaperman."

The man nodded and disappeared behind a swinging door at one end of the counter.

Turk opened the paper and began to read the details of the torpedo attack on the *Sagadoc.* From the corner of his left eye, he saw Estaban look out at him from the opening to the kitchen. A moment later the door swung open and Estaban came out.

"If you are looking for the boy," Estaban said, coming up to Turk, "I don't know where he is. That one is like the wind."

The counterman put a cup of steaming black coffee down in front of Turk.

"Did the boy steal something from you?" Estaban asked.

Turk shook his head. "You know who his mother is?"

"He lives in the streets," Estaban answered. "He pimps for some of the girls."

"Carmen," Turk said, remembering the girl's name. "Carmen. You think I could find her?"

Estaban raised his eyebrows. "The kid could take you to her."

"Manuel is dead," Turk said, looking straight at Estaban. "He was shot last night."

"Holy mother of God!" Estaban exclaimed, crossing himself.

"He took the bullet to save my life," Turk said. "His body is at Gonzales and Sons. The funeral is at noon. I thought maybe Carmen would—"

Estaban waved the suggestion aside. "Even if you could find her, she wouldn't be willing to give up an hour on a Saturday afternoon. Today is the first Saturday of the month. It will be her busiest day. The men from Fort Bliss were paid on the first. Today is the sixth, and unless she's got the rag on she'll be flat on her back working. Besides, the girls and the kids who peddle their asses are used to death."

Turk's order of ham and eggs was brought by the counterman.

"You going to be at the funeral?" Estaban asked.

"Yes, I'll be there—me and a detective named Hicks."

"Why him?" Estaban asked. "I know him. He doesn't seem to be the kind to care about what happens to kids like Manuel."

Turk shrugged. "I don't know. Maybe he thinks Manuel was different from the other kids. Maybe he respects what Manuel did. Anyway, he asked and I said it would be okay. There'll just be the two of us."

"There'll be the three of us," Estaban said, rubbing his grizzled chin.

Turk nodded. "Can you arrange for a priest?"

"Yes," Estaban said, and reaching across the counter he shook Turk's hand. "Any time you eat here, it's on the house."

"There's no need to—"

"Yes," Estaban said, "there is a need between friends to give."

"A great need," Turk responded.

"Now I must go back to the kitchen," Estaban said, letting go of Turk's hand.

Ed came on the town from the southeast, across some low hills of dark red sandstone. The heavy cloud cover was beginning to become ragged, and in the rents were large patches of blue sky.

Ed hoped the town was Este Guzman, or some other place close to the border. He moved slowly. The wound in his arm ached, and the crude bandage he had made was caked with dried blood. Luckily the weather was cold. If it had been summer, the flies would have feasted on his arm.

He paused on the ridge and looked at the town. A main street, several streets leading off it. A few of the buildings, like the town hall, were made of white-washed adobe, but most were dun colored.

There were several smoking chimneys. The darkest smoke came from the center of the town. But Gripper didn't see any people, even though it was late in the morning.

"At least the Krauts didn't burn it," he said aloud, and he began to move down toward the road. The marks made by the armored cars were clearly visible. But there wasn't any way for him to tell how many vehicles the Germans had.

Ed entered the town. The main street was absolutely deserted. The shops were closed. But the door to the blacksmith was open. Keeping close to the buildings, Gripper headed for the cantina. He had the feeling that dozens of pairs of eyes were watching him from behind the shutters.

When he reached the cantina, he eased the machine pistol slightly forward and pushed the door open with his right foot. Inside, the light was dim. He crossed the raw wood floor. The place smelled of sweat, cooking oil, and beer. There were a half a dozen men sitting at four different tables. He quickly scanned them. They were Mexicans, and from the expression on their dark faces, they knew who he was and were frightened.

Ed went directly up to the bar. "I want a tequila," he said in Spanish.

The barkeep, a burly man with a drooping mustache, nodded and moved his eyes to the right side.

Ed whirled to the right and fired. A half-dozen rounds chewed up the door. The noise filled the cantina. A man in a black suit pitched through the splintered opening and another one, similarly dressed, dropped to his knees.

Ed fired another burst at the man on his knees until he fell to one side. A wisp of smoke curled up from the muzzle of the machine pistol. He lowered the weapon and turned back to the bar. His tequila was waiting.

He drank it Mexican style, with salt and lemon. When he was finished, he pushed his glass back to the barkeep and offering his hand, he said, "I'm Major Gripper."

"Louis Borga," the barkeep answered, shaking Gripper's hand.

Then Ed turned to the men in the cantina. Several more had come in. Pointing to the two bodies, he asked, "When did they come here?"

"Early in the morning," Louis answered. "They said they were looking for a gringo army officer."

"They found him," Ed responded, facing the barkeep. He raised his drink to the man and said, "You've got a good way with your eyes."

The man grinned.

"I need a car or truck," Ed said, "and a driver to take me back to the States."

No one in the cantina answered.

"Those men that came through here have already burned El Charo and—"

"They wrecked anything that has wheels," one of the men said.

"And smashed the telephone switchboard," another added.

"They even shot every horse and mule," Louis said.

Suddenly Ed realized that he still didn't know whether or not he was in Este Guzman, so he asked, "What town is this? Esta Guzman?"

"Fiores Magon," Louis answered. "Este Guzman is maybe eighty kilometers north of here." He put several pieces of cornbread on the bar along with a bowl of chili.

Ed nodded and began to eat. He was hungry, and wolfed down the food. Either the storm had blown the plane sufficiently off course to throw his dead reckoning completely out of whack, or he had spent a good part of the night moving south before he turned north when he saw the light come into the eastern sky. Whatever the cause, the result wasn't good. He was further south than he had thought.

He turned back to the men in the room. "I must get back to the States," he said, still chewing the cornbread. "Those Germans will do a lot of damage and kill a great many people if they're not stopped. I must get back to Fort Bliss."

"Maybe by taking parts from one car or truck we could—"

"Yes, that might work!" Ed exclaimed.

"What do we do about tires?" one of the other men

asked. "The Germans slashed all of them."

"I got wagon wheels," a man said. "I take the fenders off and mount wagon wheels." He was standing in front of the door. A chunky, barrel-chested man, with long muscular arms and big hands. He looked more Indian than Mexican.

"That's Pablo, the blacksmith," Louis explained, momentarily leaning toward Gripper.

"Use my truck," another man said. "It's already on the side of Pablo's shop."

"What about gas?" Ed asked.

"I still have two barrels the Germans didn't take," the blacksmith said.

"How long will it take?" Ed asked.

"An hour, maybe two.

Ed looked at his watch; then, remembering it wasn't going, he asked what time it was.

"Maybe close to noon," the barkeep answered. "But not yet noon."

"How far from here to the border?" Ed asked.

The men looked at each other and then Louis said, "It's maybe a half a day's ride from here. Slower, with a truck on wagon wheels."

Ed nodded and searched his pocket for cigarettes. He didn't find any and asked the barkeep for one. Lighting it, he inhaled deeply, enjoying the taste. "Ten hours if everything goes well, but most probably a lot longer," he said, letting the cigarette rest in the corner of his mouth. "It will be too late. By then the Krauts will be across the border, maybe into El Paso itself." He shook his head at the enormity of the possibility. "There's nothing there to stop them from destroying it. Nothing but a few fieldpieces and even fewer armored cars.

Several of the men standing along the opposite wall began whispering to one another. Then one of them said, "Señor Major, there is an airplane on the estancia Montablan and the son, Julio, and the father, Tomas, fly it."

Ed was on his feet. "How far to the estancia?"

"An hour's walk to the southwest."

"Maybe the Krauts didn't touch them," Gripper said, grinding the cigarette into a shallow metal can on the bar top that served as an ashtray. "Maybe I'll get lucky."

"The Montablans do not like gringos," another man in the room said. "I do not think they will help you."

"If I have to, I will fly the plane myself," Ed answered. "But I must beat the Krauts to the border."

"They have four big dogs at the house," Louis said.

"Thank you for your hospitality, Louis," Ed said, shaking hands with the man. Digging into his pocket, he pulled out a five-dollar bill and put it on the counter. "Drinks for everyone."

A murmur of approval came from the men in the cantina.

Ed walked to where the two dead men lay. Each held a Luger. He took a gun from one of them and said to Louis, "You keep the other gun. But when their friends come, say that Major Gripper killed them and took their guns."

"Then more will come here?" Louis asked.

Ed shrugged. "Maybe," he answered. "Maybe. The Krauts probably put men in some of the other nearby towns and villages."

"There aren't any other nearby towns or villages," Louis answered. "The estancia Montablan is the only other place where there are houses and people for maybe two or three hours' ride by car in any direction."

Ed went to the door. "Everyone, thanks again!" he told them.

"Go with God!" Louis answered.

"Yes, go with God," the men in the cantina called

out, in choruses of two or three voices.

Ed opened the door and stepped into the street. The patches of blue sky were larger and more numerous now. He walked to the south end of the town and turned slightly to the west.

# 13

After breakfast, Turk decided to walk around for awhile. It would be better than sitting up in the hotel room waiting until it was time to go to Manuel's funeral. Eventually he found himself in front of a Gothic-looking building made of red sandstone, with heavy oak doors. A badly weathered sign on the lawn told Turk he was looking at the El Paso Lending Library, open on Saturday from 10 a.m. to 12 p.m.

Turk decided it was a place to spend some time. He walked up the path and pushed open the doors. He was in a large room with shelves of books on each of the walls. A librarian was seated at an oak desk in the center of the room. There were several long tables with chairs on either side for the readers. But the room was absolutely empty.

The librarian looked up from the book she was reading and seemed surprised to see someone there. She was a pinched, narrow-faced woman, with thin gray hair and dull black eyes.

"We close at noon," she said perfunctorily, and resumed her reading.

Turk walked past her, his footsteps making the only

sound in the room. He was at the history section when he realized that he had forgotten the details of the Zimmermann telegram, and since reading about it would give him something specific to do, he went directly to the reference section and checked the Britannica index. The explanation of the Zimmermann telegram was in the twenty-third volume.

Turk sat down and began to read. Because Germany was losing the Great War, the article said, the German High command had decided on a course of unrestricted u-boat warfare. But, for this action to be completely successful, the United States had to be kept out of the war. To accomplish this, the Germans tried to embroil Mexico and Japan in a war against the United States.

The German Undersecretary, Arthur Zimmermann, sent a message to Count Johann von Berstoriff that was to be passed on to Eckhart, the Imperial Minister to Mexico. Eckhart was instructed to offer President Carranza of Mexico the return of Texas, New Mexico, and Arizona in return for a Mexican invasion of the United States. It was suggested that Carranza invite Japan to declare war on the United States for which it would be given territorial gains.

The message was intercepted and decoded by the British. A copy of the decoded message was shown to Mr. Edward Bell, a member of the American Embassy . . .

Turk closed the book and leaned back in the chair. What he had just read refreshed his memory about the entire incident. The Japanese had even sent several warships into the Gulf of California, and there had been many German advisors with the Mexican Army, teaching the Mexican troops how to use German tactics and German-made weapons. The exposure of the Zimmermann telegram had done more to put the

United States in the war than the sinking of the *Lusitania*.

Turk reached inside his pocket for a pack of cigarettes, but then, remembering where he was, he replaced it. He returned the volume of the Britannica to the shelf and walked out onto the street.

He lit a cigarette as he thought. . . . An invasion coming from New Mexico now could achieve what the German High Command had hoped for in 1916. America just wasn't ready for war, though it was a clear President Roosevelt, unlike Wilson, understood that sooner or later the United States would have to enter the war. Now most certainly would be the wrong time, however. The country lacked everything from trained men to various kinds of equipment needed to fight a modern war. Still, circumstances were now very different from those that had existed when Zimmermann sent his famous telegram. President Avila Comacho of Mexico was friendly toward the United States and Roosevelt welcomed this friendship, even though there were elements in and out of the Mexican government who were avowed fascists, especially the large landholders in the north. For all their posturing, though, these fascists were not a serious threat.

Turk glanced at his watch. He had time for another cup of coffee before going across the bridge for Manuel's funeral. He stepped into a nearby luncheonette.

He sat on a stool at the counter and lingered over the coffee. After the funeral Turk planned to drive out to Bliss, spend most of the afternoon there, and then return to the hotel. By then he hoped that Lauren and Dijon would have arrived. That he would be making love to Lauren in just a few hours was sufficient to set off a flood of warmth in his groin.

Turk paid for his coffee, and walked out into the street. The wind seemed to have picked up again. He turned up his collar, pulled his hat down over his forehead, and headed toward the Santa Fe Bridg

Canaris stood at the French door and looked through a pane of glass at the Landwehr Canal, which was directly across the street from the Abwehr Headquarters. Despite the deepening twilight, the canal was busy with barge traffic vital to the war effort.

He was a tall, lean white-haired man, simply dressed in the unadorned uniform of a naval officer. There were dark circles under his eyes from lack of sleep. He clasped his hands behind his back and began to pace. He had spent the better part of the last hour at his desk, trying to develop "new intelligence information" that would enable him to issue the order to Colonel Becker delaying Operation Zimmermann until 1200 the following day, December 7. Within the next ten or fifteen hours, Canaris hoped to arrange a meeting with Hitler in an effort to convince him to abandon the operation.

Canaris sat down at his desk. His two dachshunds, Sepple and Sabine, dropped off the nearby cot and trundled to their master. Sepple climbed into his lap, while Sabine settled down next to him with his head resting on the admiral's right foot.

"Not easy," Canaris said, scratching Sepple between his ears, "to come up with just the right fabrication." In the past when particular situations had demanded what to himself he euphemistically referred as "creative intelligence," he had had one of his field men send a message, which he had previously drafted. But none of the previous situations had involved the Führer as directly as Operation Zimmermann did. The other pieces of "creative intelligence" had affected either his own operations, those of the SS, or the Gestapo.

Sometimes the army.

"Think of something," he told himself aloud, "that the Führer and the generals around him will accept without questioning." Canaris was particularly concerned about how Heydrich would react to any delay. Though Operation Zimmermann was Hitler's idea, it was Heydrich, the head of the Gestapo, who had designed and implemented it. Heydrich had conceived of using men from one of the Afrika Korps' discipline battalions; of using Spanish and Argentinian ships to transport the equipment. He had even devised a number of ingenious methods that permitted the men to get to their respective destinations in northern Mexico. Heydrich would be the first to become suspicious of any piece of intelligence that would delay the operation.

Canaris's thoughts were interrupted by a jarring ring of the telephone. He picked it up and identified himself.

"This is Major Klien," the high-pitched voice on the other end said. "Sir, there's a message coming in from our Hamburg radio station headed, 'For Admiral Canaris's eyes only.' "

"Thank you," Canaris replied, trying to remember how Klien looked.

"Sir, then you will decode it yourself?"

"Yes." Canaris left his office and went through a warren of passageways that brought him into another building on the Bendlerstrasse. This portion of the Abwehr headquarters was more heavily guarded than the building from which Canaris came. He walked down two flights of steps into the building's subbasement and was stopped for an identification check. Finally he was admitted to the code room, where Germany maintained a battery of a dozen of its top-secret cipher machines, known as the Enigma.

"The message," Canaris said, going straight to Major Klien, who was seated at the duty officer's desk.

Klien stood up, saluted, and handed the admiral a sheet of paper with columns of numbers and letters.

Canaris looked around for a place to sit and decode the message. All of the cryptographers were busy.

Klien offered his desk and use of the duty officer's Enigma.

"If you're sure it will not interfere with your work. . . ." Canaris said.

"It will not interfere," Klien answered.

Canaris nodded and sat down. He immediately began to decode the message. It came from X24-1, Eugen Ott, the German ambassador in Tokyo. The decoded message read: "Frm extre reli sour. Jap. flt steam tow Pearl H. Att Sun morn loc ti. Att Philips Ilds, sam ti."

Canaris frowned, stuffed the message in his pocket, and handing Klien the original cipher, he said, "Thank you for the use of your desk."

"It was my pleasure," Klien answered, saluting again.

This time Canaris returned the salute and left the code room. He walked quickly back to his office. The message from Ott disturbed him. The Japanese obviously had no intentions of informing Germany of its actions, though war would certainly result from their attacks.

When Canaris reached his office, he was told by one of his secretaries that his wife had called to remind him that they were going to the theater. Canaris responded with a nod, and entering the office he went straight to the desk, sat down, and spread the message out in front of him. War between Japan and the United States would mean war between the United States and Germany. And Germany was already in difficulty in

Russia and in North Africa.

He leaned against the back of his chair and rubbed the corners of his eyes. The Japanese were about to commit a fatal mistake. Their attack on American installations would certainly nullify the desired effect of Operation Zimmermann, which was to demonstrate Germany's ability to wage war even against the continental United States, thereby keeping the Americans from entering the European war. Hitler and Heydrich were convinced that Operation Zimmermann would intensify the antiwar feelings in the country and allow the will of the isolationists to prevail.

Canaris did not think the operation would serve that purpose. All along, his opinion had been that any attack on the country would do the opposite. It would galvanize the people to unity, giving Roosevelt the climate he wanted that would enable him to bring the United States into the war. But now, with Japan poised to attack, there wasn't any way for Germany to avoid a war with the United States.

The phone on Canaris's desk rang. He answered it.

"Wilhelm, I think you should come early tonight so that you'll have enough time to change before we go to the theater," his wife said.

Canaris ground his teeth together. "Erika, I'll be home when I can. If I am not home in time to go to the theater with you, go without me." Going to the theater together was just a part of the charade he and Erika played. Their marriage had been one in name only ever since their youngest daughter, Bridgitte, was conceived in the spring of 1925. He often referred to the marriage itself as the "Canaris front."

"I can see you're in one of your more difficult moods," Erika said and hung up.

"Difficult mood," he repeated aloud, putting the phone down. With a shake of his head, he dismissed

Erika from his thoughts and went to the window where could look out at the canal.

"What I need," Canaris told himself, "is to be able to take advantage of the Japanese attack." He opened the French doors and stepped onto the balcony. A cold, biting wind rushed against him. For several moments, he watched a small, black-smoke-belching tug push a huge coal barge along the canal. Then suddenly he realized that in a perverse way Hitler and Heydrich could be right—right only because of Japan's forthcoming attack. Two blows would stun the American people. Even if Operation Zimmermann had already been compromised, the United States might still prefer to fight the Japanese and stay out of the war in Europe. The American people had a longstanding distrust and fear of the Japanese, though, oddly enough, not of the Germans, though they were enemies during the Great War.

Operation Zimmermann would still serve to put the American people on notice that their war was not with Germany but with Japan. Americans would, Canaris was certain, react more violently to the Japanese attack than the German. And what would make Operation Zimmermann more effective would be to have it cross the border on the same day that the Japanese intended to launch their attack.

The two blows coming within a few hours of each other would make Roosevelt think twice about becoming involved in a European war. His main concern would be the Far East and the possible loss of Australia, to say nothing of the Philippines, the Dutch East Indies, Malaya, and possibly India. Roosevelt couldn't afford to ignore possible losses like those. He'd have to fight Japan. There was the chance that Operation Zimmermann might convince him to leave Germany alone, at least for a while. . . .

Beginning to feel chilled, Canaris stepped back into the office and closed the doors. "There is still something missing," he said aloud. "Something to tie it together." He began to pace. Then suddenly he stopped. By the terms of the treaty Germany had with Japan, Germany would have to declare war against the United States. But if it didn't, if it remained neutral, then the United States could concentrate all its power against Japan and destroy it, which eventually Germany would have to do anyway, since Japan could not be allowed to exist as a world power. Roosevelt would most certainly agree with that!

Canaris went to his desk and sat down. He now had the perfect reason for delaying Operation Zimmermann from crossing the border until 1200 hours, December 7—though the reason for doing it was very different from the original one he had sought.

Canaris rubbed the bridge of his nose. He was certain the Führer would agree to remaining neutral, especially since it would mean the eventual destruction of Japan. And Heydrich, when he learned about it after his return form the east, would not have any objections. But the ultimate success of Operation Zimmermann was predicated on the idea that the American people would be told about the attack. If, for some reason, this did not happen, then the operation would have failed and a battalion of German soldiers would have been wasted. . . .

Canaris shook his head. "I never liked the plan," he told himself. "Never." Then he picked up the phone and asked the operator to connect him to the Führer.

The cemetery was located at the southwest corner of Juárez, off Highway 45. A low wall of stones and adobe enclosed a small area. A deserted church was nearby.

And the dirt road leading to the entrance was packed hard and covered with sand and dust from the previous night's wind.

On some graves there were bouquets of dead flowers. But most had nothing more than simple wooden cross to mark them.

Turk was the first to arrive. He lit a cigarette. In Spain he had seen many cemeteries, some no more than pits gouged savagely out of the earth to hold as many bodies as possible. Friend and foe alike were thrown together for eternity. But there were other burial places, much like the one he was in now. Turk looked around him. The place was even more melancholy than he had thought it would be. Some cemeteries had trees, stone benches, and other things to give them the illusion of peaceful harmony. But this was nothing more than rows of mounds and parched weeds that grew along the wall.

The weather was beginning to change. The wind had picked up in the last few minutes, moving large balls of tumbleweed across the road and over the desert on either side of it. Stratocumulus clouds covered the entire northwestern quadrant of the sky, and it had turned colder.

The change in weather deepened Turk's melancholy feelings. Ed's death, and now Manuel's . . . It was difficult for him to take. Ed had been a good friend. More than likely, the best he'd ever have. And as for Manuel—well, he would have given him a better life. Probably adopted him. . . . In Spain, he had seen many men die, some not much older than Manuel. And though he had grieved over their deaths, he had never felt guilty because he was alive and some man or boy he had known had been killed. But now he was full of guilt and grief. Manuel had seen the gun and had rushed to save his life. . . . Ed had saved his life by getting him out of the French internment camp. . . .

Turk took a deep drag on his cigarette and let the smoke pour from his nostrils. There wasn't any way for him to ever repay either of them. He dropped the cigarette to the ground and crushed it under his heel; then he used a handkerchief to wipe the tears from his eyes.

Suddenly he saw the hearse turn off the highway and come up the dirt road, raising a cloud of dust behind it. Behind the hearse came three cars. Turk could account for two of the cars. One had to be Hicks and the second, Estaban. He had no idea who the third car might belong to.

The hearse stopped in front of the archway. Two men left the front seat and opened the back of it.

By the time Turk walked to the archway, the three cars had arrived. He greeted Estaban and Hicks with a handshake and asked. "Who's in the third car?"

"I asked around," Estaban said, "and I found two old women who will mourn for Manuel."

Turk looked toward the car. The two women were already out of the car and with them were two men. One of them was the driver. Turk asked about the men.

"They'll dig the grave," Estaban answered.

"What about a priest?" Hicks asked.

"Father Domingo said he would be here," Estaban said. "While we wait, the grave might as well be dug."

Turk nodded.

Estaban took charge, and between him and the men from the funeral parlor, the gravediggers took their shovels out of the car's trunk and set to work in an empty space in the lee of the west wall.

"Did you find out anything more about the man who tried to kill me?" Turk asked, looking at Hicks, who wore his Stetson low over his face.

"We're working on it. He's a tough customer."

Turk didn't answer.

"I asked you before," Hicks said. "But I'll ask you again. Do you know anyone who'd want to kill you?"

"I don't know anyone here except the other reporters and some of the officers at Bliss."

"Is there anyone? I mean, even someone who's not here," Hicks said.

Turk raised his eyebrows.

"Well, is there someone?" Hicks pressed. "If one try was made, there's no reason to think that a second attempt won't be made. If someone wants you dead bad enough, there's no way on God's green earth that you can really stop him from killing you."

"You just made my day," Turk responded.

"I just gave you the truth," Hicks said. "Now think hard. Is there anyone—"

"It's crazy, but there's a man in Mexico City. . . ." Turk shook his head.

"What's his name?" Hicks asked.

"Zwig. Walther Zwig."

Hicks nodded with satisfaction. "I've got a few friends down there. I'll wire them and maybe I'll come up with something. By the way, why would he want to have ya killed?"

Turk felt himself flush. "His wife and I—"

Hicks held up his hand. "Say no more. A jealous man is a really dangerous man," he said.

"It was a marriage of convenience," Turk said. "Walther was a homosexual."

Hicks took a cigar out of his breast pocket. "Homosexual or not," Hicks said, biting off the end of the cigar, "he's still our best bet. If he sent that guy to kill ya, we can at least get the Mexican police to arrest him."

"What about the guy you have in custody?"

"He'll probably hang, or at least get life," Hicks

answered, blowing smoke. "Now he's meat for the DA."

"Looks like they're finished digging the grave," Turk commented as he watched the men climb out of it and lay their shovels down on the mound of raw earth.

"I think the priest is coming," Hicks said, gesturing toward the road where a pickup truck was coming toward them.

The truck stopped and a priest, wearing his cassock, got out of the cab while a four-piece mariachi band climbed off the back.

"I'm Father Domingo," he said, approaching Turk and Hicks.

Turk, shaking the priest's hand, introduced himself and Hicks.

"These men agreed to play," the priest said, gesturing toward them. He was a scarecrow of a man, with a long sad face and a long nose, on which were perched a pair of white metal-frame glasses. "José told me the circumstances of Manuel's death," he commented. "One must accept it as God's will."

Turk said nothing.

Estaban returned from the grave, shook hands with Father Domingo, and said, "Everything is ready."

They went to the rear of the hearse, where the two men from the funeral parlor were waiting. They removed a small wooden casket and placed it on Turk's and Estaban's shoulders.

Father Domingo took the lead. He was followed by the mariachi band. Turk and Estaban came next. Hicks followed them, and the two professional mourners brought up the rear.

The mariachis played a sad tone as the procession made its way to the grave. Though the distance between the archway and the grave was short, it took a long time to cover it, or so it seemed to Turk.

When the grave was finally reached, the coffin was

set down on ropes and then lowered into the ground. The mariachis continued to play until Father Domingo signaled them to stop. Speaking in Latin, he performed the burial rite. He made the sign of the cross over the open grave many times. Then in Spanish, he asked everyone to recite the Twenty-third Psalm after him. Then he said, "I personally did not know Manuel, but my good friend José assures me that Manuel was a good boy. . . . perhaps not good in the same way as children who live in a proper house with a loving family to guide and protect them. But Manuel was good in quite another way. He possessed a strong sense of honor and loyalty. José says he always paid his debts, and when it came to standing up for a friend . . ." Father Domingo looked directly at Turk. "He made the supreme sacrifice in the name of friendship." Still looking at Turk, he said, "Most of us will never have our friendship to others tested in that extreme way. But Manuel did and he was not found wanting. The proof of his sense of loyalty is that we are standing at his graveside."

Turk took a deep breath and uttered a ragged sigh.

The priest spoke the final words of the burial service and, reaching down to the mound of earth, he took a handful and let it fall on the coffin. He nodded to the mariachis, who immediately began to play again. The two professional mourners started to wail.

Turk reached down, picked up a shovelful of earth, and dropped it onto the coffin. Estaban did the same and Hicks followed him.

Except for the two women and the gravediggers, everyone else made their way back to the archway.

Turk thanked Father Domingo and gave him a donation for his church. "I'd appreciate it," he told the priest, "if a Mass could be said for Manuel now and then."

"As long as the church stands a perpetual Mass will be said for him," the priest answered, shaking Turk's hand.

"Ya want a ride back to El Paso?" Hicks offered.

"No thanks," Turk answered. "I'd rather walk."

"I'll let ya know if I get anything on Zwig," Hicks called as he slid behind the wheel of his car.

Father Domingo and his mariachis drove off, leaving Estaban and Turk alone. The two men looked at each other and nodded. Estaban went to his car and Turk walked back to the grave. He waited until the gravediggers were almost finished before he asked one of them for his shovel. While the men stood by, Turk put the last three shovels of earth on the mound himself.

# 14

Ed kept off the road, but moved parallel to it, using the massive boulders for cover. It took him less than an hour to reach the estancia Montablan, which consisted of a large Mexican-style ranch house, a stable some distance from it, and a wind-driven pump on a wooden tower, to which a tall radio antenna was attached. He didn't see any signs of the plane. But there were two four-door sedans in front of the stable and a pickup truck. any one of the vehicles would get him back across the border.

Suddenly he saw a large doberman pinscher move out from behind the house. The animal sniffed the air. Gripper was too far away from the dog to hear if it was growling or see if it was baring its teeth, but he had a healthy respect for the dog. If there were any more like the one he was looking at, he'd have to kill them before he'd risk making a move for one of the vehicles or the plane.

Ed started to circle around the house. The dog turned and trotted off. There were three men working on a piece of machinery in the rear yard. Ed could hear their voices but he couldn't make out what they were saying. Just as he started to move away, a German soldier came out from around the other side of the house.

Ed swore under his breath. The chances were slim that the German didn't have some of his friends nearby. Ed hadn't figured on having to deal with German soldiers. "Dogs," he muttered angrily, "and now Krauts!" That Montablan was involved with the Germans didn't surprise him. Many of the ranchers in northern Mexico were Nazi sympathizers. But what did amaze Ed was that the Krauts had managed to put a large mobile strike force into the country. The men could have arrived as terrorists, but the equipment had to have come by ship and then by rail.

Ed shook his head. If he survived, there would be time enough to put all the pieces in place later. But first he had to find a way of getting back to Bliss. He began to move to the far side of the house. He saw a second Kraut and the shed for the plane. But the plane wasn't there. The shed consisted of a roof and several uprights to support it.

The German was sitting on a bench, petting a dog—a big-boned shepherd. Ed weighed the odds: two Krauts, four dogs, and three ranch hands against his machine pistol, a Luger, and two grenades. And the element of surprise. Between him and the house were maybe one hundred to two hundred yards of open space. The dogs would probably be at him before he got halfway across. He'd have to kill them and the Krauts in a matter of seconds. Then he'd have to get the three men in the rear of the house before he could even consider going for one of the cars or the truck. And if there were additional men in the house, he'd have to fight his way past them also.

The two soldiers were walking toward a large open area at the front of the house. The shepherd was with them and then two other dogs, both dobermans, came bounding out from the far side of the house and ran to where the soldiers were.

Ed heard the plane's engine some moments before he saw it. It was coming in from the south.

In a low crouch Ed darted back to the boulders at the rear of the house. One of the three men was pointing at the plane, which had not yet begun its descent.

Ed took a deep breath, held it for a moment, exhaled, and aloud said, "Now!" The next instant he was on his feet and running toward the men in the yard.

One of them saw him, and was just about to shout when Ed squeezed the trigger. The short burst cut down the three men. The roar of the plane overhead drowned out the sound of the shooting.

Suddenly a dog came rushing toward Ed from the side of the house. He squeezed off two rounds. The dog yelped, started to leap, and dropped in its tracks.

Ed was in the yard now.

The plane circled and was coming in for a landing. It took Ed a few seconds to get the keys for one of the vehicles from the pocket of one of the dead men. Then he ran to the water tower next to the house. Pulling the tape from one of the grenades, Ed lobbed it at the tower and he ran for the front of the house.

Ten seconds later the explosion sent several thousands of gallons of water cascading over the house, smashing the roof under the crushing weight.

Ed went for the truck first. The key fit. He switched on the ignition just as the plane touched down. The two Germans were already running back toward the house.

Ed turned toward them. One of the men dropped to his knee and began firing at him. The bullets pinged off the truck's fenders. The second man was still running for the house.

Ed floored the gas pedal and went right over the man

shooting at him. Then he turned and went after the other one. He caught him with the right edge of the bumper and tossed him into the air. The man came down some twenty feet to the right. Ed didn't stop or slow down. He headed for the road.

The plane was back in the air and it was coming after him. It made a pass at him. Someone other than the pilot started shooting.

Ed left the road and drove in a circle.

The plane came roaring down, banked, and made its run toward the truck.

Ed could see the man with the rifle. He was young, had a black mustache, and wore sunglasses. The bullets slammed into the rear of the truck and put two holes in the roof of the cab.

The plane began to climb, made a low turn, and came racing back.

Ed swung directly at the oncoming plane.

The plane was very close. Just a few feet off of the ground and moving fast.

Ed was sweating so profusely he could hardly see out of his eyes. But at the very instant the plane swerved, to avoid a head-on collision, Ed turned toward the aircraft, sideswiping the plane's wing with the truck's cab.

For several moments Ed continued to drive, sure that nothing had happened. But as he eased his foot off the gas and began to turn, he saw the plane dip sharply to the right, strike the ground with its right wing, and cartwheel over. With an enormous roar it burst into flames.

Ed swung back to the road and put his foot down on the gas. He felt very tired, almost limp. Every part of his body ached. But he wasn't going to be able to rest until he reached Fort Bliss, and that was eight or ten hours away.

Turk crossed back to the States from Juárez on the Stanton Street Bridge and walked to the hotel, where he stopped to ask the desk clerk if there were any messages for him.

The clerk glanced over his shoulder at the pigeonhole and shook his head. "Nothing, sir."

Turk thanked him and said, "I'm expecting a—" He paused, not wanting to refer to Lauren as a friend. "My wife is going to join me sometime this afternoon," he continued. "I'd appreciate it if you'd tell her I'll be back about four."

"Certainly."

"And I reserved a room for a Mr. Dijon," Turk said.

"Yes. It's listed here," the clerk answered, checking his reservation file.

"Please bill me for Mr. Dijon's room and for whatever he orders," Turk said.

"I'll make a notation on Mr. Dijon's room card," the clerk answered.

Turk thanked the man and left the room. A few minutes later he was driving along Montana Street toward Bliss. He lit a cigarette and held it between his lips. The only brightness in the dull gray that seemed to fill his brain was Lauren's imminent arrival. If he had ever needed anyone at any time in his life, Turk unabashedly admitted that he needed her. He looked toward the Franklin Mountains. The clouds now seemed to be resting directly on them. He hoped that deteriorating weather would not delay Lauren and Dijon.

By the time Turk eased his car into a parking slot, many of the post soldiers who were not involved in the war games were already lined up for the El Paso bus. Payday had been the previous Monday, and now the men would flock across the border to Juárez for booze and women. Tonight the brothels and gin mills would be busy. Juárez would be a wild town. By reveille tomorrow morning, practically all of the men would be hung over and not worth a damn.

Turk had done exactly the same thing when he was in the army and when he was in Spain. But in Spain, because he was actually fighting, his boozing and whoring were always more intense. Many times he had awakened next to a woman whose name he couldn't remember. And sometimes he'd just drunk alone, or with a few other men like himself who were trying to forget what they had just lived through, or to push from their hearts and minds the fear of what might happen to them during the next battle.

Turk left the car and walked up the steps to the post's headquarters. He went directly into the press room and over to the coffee urn.

Rick Nathan came up to him. "Word is out that there was a big pow-wow here early this morning."

Turk took a sip of the black coffee and made a face. "I think the army is trying to tell us something by serving us this mixture of iodine and water. Know who was at the meeting?"

"Hanahan, Alt, Fitzhugh, and assorted aides," Nathan answered. "Any idea why the brass should be meeting before the rest of the world is up?"

"Come on, Nathan," Turk said with a smile, "would you tell me if you knew?"

"Nope—but I figured you're more altruistic than I am."

"Not when it comes to a news story," Turk answered.

"At least you're honest," Nathan said.

"You didn't happen to see Fitzhugh around?" Turk asked.

Nathan shook his head.

Turk drank the remainder of the black coffee and

dropped the paper cup into a wastepaper basket. "I think I'll see if Fitzhugh is in his office," Turk said, starting toward the door.

One of the phones in the room rang. Owens, of the *Los Angeles Times*, answered and called out, "Hey, is Douglas Turk here?"

"Sure I am," Turk answered.

"Some guy from the police department wants to speak to you," Owens said.

Turk took the phone from Owens. "Hicks?" he asked.

"Right! Say, ya sure do know a lot of dead people," Hicks said.

Turk's first thought was that something had happened to Lauren or Dijon. Perhaps both of them? He was about to ask, when Hicks said, "Your man Zwig in Mexico City shot hisself. But before he did that, he shot a guy by the name of Krieger. Does that name ring a bell?"

"Antique dealer," Turk answered. "But probably working for the Nazis." There wasn't any way that Lauren could know about Zwig, unless it made the Presidio newspaper, and that was unlikely.

"Some time before Zwig killed Krieger and hisself, the two of them were out at the airport tryin' to stop a guy named Dijon from takin' off. There was a lot of shooting. A couple of German nationals got themselves killed. You don't happen to know Dijon, do ya?"

"If you want to meet him, I'll introduce you. He's coming here this afternoon."

"Ya sure do travel wit' some interestin' folks," Hicks commented.

"Did your friend give you any reason why Walther shot Krieger?" Turk asked.

"None. But I got somethin' more fer ya. Ready?"

"Go ahead!" Turk said.

"The guy that tried to kill ya is dead."

"What?" Turk shouted.

"Thought that would grab you," Hicks chuckled. "Waitin' on the coroner's report. My guess is he took cyanide, or it was given to him. Maybe on a cigarette or in his food. I'll know more later."

Turk was speechless.

"Now I got a question for ya," Hicks said.

"Shoot!"

"What's the connection between the corpse here, the two in Mexico City, and you."

Turk took a deep breath, and after he exhaled he said, "I don't know, Hicks. But there sure as hell must be one."

"Yeah, that's the way I see it too," Hicks replied. "Like I said before, ya sure do know a lot of dead people."

"So it seems," Turk answered, managing to fish a cigarette out of his pack while still holding onto the phone.

"If ya come up with any ideas, ya know where ya can reach me," Hicks said.

"I'll give you a call," Turk answered. "And thanks."

"Just doin' my job," Hicks said.

Turk put the phone down, took a deep drag on his cigarette, and let the smoke slowly escape from his nostrils. He went to the window and looked out on the quadrangle. Why was someone sent to kill him? And who'd sent the killer? Walther? Not likely. Then who? Turk couldn't come up with a name. Why had it been so important to stop Lauren from leaving Walther? Surely the marriage couldn't possibly have been of any interest to Krieger. Yet Krieger had been willing to kill Lauren and Dijon to stop them from leaving. Perhaps it was the other way around: he had been trying to stop them in order to kill them. Again, why?

"Something wrong?" Nathan asked, coming alongside Turk.

"I don't know."

"If there's anything I can do . . ."

"Thanks, but it's something I just can't fit together," Turk said.

"I know how that feels," Nathan responded.

Turk nodded and walked out of the press room, turned down the corridor, and headed for Fitzhugh's office. He had almost reached the door, when it opened and Hanahan and Fitzhugh came out.

"Glad to see you, Turk," Hanahan said, shooting out his hand.

Turk shook each of their hands and asked, "Anything more from the south?"

"Everything is very quiet," Hanahan answered. "It looks more and more like the work of bandits. Sometime tomorrow I'm going to send another team to look over the situation. Maybe they'll find Ed."

"His body, you mean," Turk said, instantly angered with Hanahan's stupidity. "If he survived the crash, the bandits, if that's what they are, would have killed him."

"Our feeling," Fitzhugh said, coming into the conversation, "is that the bandits must have moved off. Probably headed into the mountains to the west, or retreated further south."

"What if they didn't?" Turk suggested. "What if they're letting you *think* they took off, and when you send another team down there, they'll jump them just the way they did—"

"I don't anticipate any trouble," Hanahan said sharply. "Besides, the second team will have more men."

"How many more men?" Turk answered.

Hanahan looked at Fitzhugh.

"A full company," Fitzhugh said. "That should be

more than enough to handle any group of bandits."

"Should be," Turk agreed.

"Now, if you'll excuse us . . ." Hanahan said.

Turk stepped aside.

"Remember," Fitzhugh said, "we have a dinner date this evening."

"I haven't forgotten," Turk answered. "I'll be there."

# 15

Freshly showered and wearing Turk's white terry-cloth bathrobe, Lauren stood to the right of the window. A strong wind was blowing, making the people she saw bend their heads into it. The long shadows of twilight were already gathering among the trees in the park across from the hotel.

Lauren moved away from the window. She wished Doug would come back soon. She longed for him. She had so much to tell him, so much. . . .

She saw an open pack of cigarettes on the dresser, took one, and dropped into the chair. That she was finally safe was something of a miracle. Even when she was in the plane, she had half expected to be chased either by the Mexican Air Force, or by Walther's friends.

Lauren blew smoke toward the center of the room. Now that she was back in the United States, she would have to start divorce proceedings against Walther and have her property returned, especially the paintings. There were six or seven of them that a gallery might be interested in showing.

Lauren returned to the window. It was very gray outside now, and sand was rattling against the pane. She braced herself against the window sash. When was Doug coming? When? She dropped her arms and clasped her hands.

Suddenly she remembered that he would soon have to report for active duty, and that would mean another separation until he could find a place for her to live, near wherever his duty station would be.

"I'm going with him, even if I have to sleep in a fleabag motel until I can find something better," she said aloud, stubbing out the cigarette in an ashtray. Because it was getting quite dark in the room, she switched on the nighttable lamp. The very same instant she heard the sound of the key in the lock. Her heart started to race.

Turk stepped into the room, and by the time he pushed the door shut behind him, Lauren was in his arms. He kissed her passionately on the mouth. "I love you, Lauren," he said huskily. "I love you." He kissed her again and moved his hands over her back and down to her buttocks. "You feel good," he whispered.

She pressed herself against him.

"I was so worried about you," he said, "when you called from Mexico City."

"Walther and Krieg tried to—"

"Later," he said. "You'll tell me everything later. Now, the only thing I want is you." And stepping away from her, Turk removed his coat and hat. "Is Dijon all right?"

"He's fine," Lauren answered as she slipped the knot on the bathrobe's belt.

"He's a good man."

Lauren agreed, and opening the robe, she let it drop to the floor.

"You're beautiful!" Turk exclaimed, looking at her naked body.

"If you don't hurry up and undress," she said, "I might have to start without you."

Turk shook his head. "Not on your life!"

She went to the bed, pulled back the cover and blanket, and then lay down on the sheet. "Where's your son?" she asked, smiling at him.

"Nothing now," Turk answered, clearing his throat before he spoke. "Nothing now, except us." He was naked.

Lauren raised her arms to him. "Oh Doug, Doug, I love you."

Turk eased himself down to her. He kissed the side of her neck and then the nipple on each of her breasts.

"These past couple of days," she told him, "I couldn't stop myself from thinking about how it would be between us. . . ."

"I wanted you too," he said, moving his hand between her thighs.

She trembled and then arched to him. "God, that feels good," Lauren sighed. "Come into me, my love." She reached up, placed both her hands on his shoulders and wrapped her bare legs around his back. "Go deep, my love," she said. "Go deep!"

Turk could feel her body tense.

She smiled up at him. "It's like being wound tighter and tighter!" she said in a throaty voice and began to move her hands across his back. "Oh, my love," she exclaimed. "My love!" Then heaving herself against him, she cried out, "Now. . . . Oh *now*!"

Turk's own climax came storming out of the depths

of him, making him oblivious to everything but the exquisite surge of pleasure in his loins. . . .

Afterward, Lauren's head nestled on his arm, Turk said, "A few things have been happening. He paused, deciding where to begin. "My friend Colonel Ed Gripper went down in Mexico."

"Oh no!" Lauren exclaimed.

"Could have been the storm, or it could have been bandits."

"Bandits?"

Turk took several drags on the cigarette before he said, "There are bands of them in northern Mexico. Seems like one of those bands even tangled with our troops. Anyway, Ed may have been shot down. There doesn't seem to be much of a chance for him to have survived."

Lauren reached out and placed her hand on his arm. "I'm really very sorry. I know how much he meant to you."

"If it wasn't for him—" Turk started to say. "But you already know that. Then Manuel—"

"The boy?" she asked.

"The boy, Manuel," Turk said. "I buried him at noon."

"You did what?" she cried, sitting straight up.

Turk explained how he met Manuel and what had happened to him. "He took the bullet meant for me."

"And you think Walther hired someone to kill you?" she asked.

"I can't think of anyone else who'd want me dead," he answered, deciding not to tell her that Walther was dead, at least not at this time. Turk stubbed out the cigarette. "Now you tell me exactly what happened to you."

Lauren said, "As soon as I mentioned the *City of Cadiz*, Walther became furious. He knew I had gotten the name of the ship from you. By the way, who asked you about it?"

"Harris," Turk answered. "You know him. He's with the British embassy."

"Richard Harris?" she asked hesitantly.

"Yes," Turk answered, recognizing the catch in her voice. "Why?"

"Oh, Doug, he was robbed and murdered," she said.

He was going to say, *that's impossible.* But instead he got out of bed and went for the bottle of scotch. He took a long drink before he returned to the bed. "Harris asked me to find out what I could about the ship. He couldn't check on the ship because—" He stopped. "That could have been the way it was done. That could be the answer. Good God, the answer has been in front of me all the time and I didn't see it!" He took another drink from the bottle. "The *City of Cadiz* could have been used to transport men and equipment from Germany. . . ."

"What answer?" she asked.

"I don't think Walther sent someone to kill me," Turk said. "But Krieger probably did."

"Why?"

"For the same reason he wanted to kill you," Turk said. "You and I knew that there was a ship named the *City of Cadiz*."

"Harris did too."

"That's why he was murdered," Turk said. "He was murdered and then, my guess is, robbed to make it look like the robbery was the motive for the murder."

"I still don't understand," Lauren said.

"You will. Listen to what I say to General Fitzhugh,"

Turk said, picking up the phone. "You'll understand everything." He asked the hotel switchboard operator to put him through to Fort Bliss. "I want to speak to General Fitzhugh," he told the duty officer, who identified himself as Lieutenant Chase. "Listen, Lieutenant, this is urgent. Just don't fuck around. Put the goddamn general on the line." He glanced at Lauren. She was sitting on her legs looking at him.

Fitzhugh came on.

"Listen, General," Turk said, "there's a damn good chance those bandits aren't bandits."

"What?"

"They're Germans," Turk said.

"What the hell are you talking about?"

"There was a ship, a Spanish ship named the *City of Cadiz*, that sailed in and out of Tampico. She brought the equipment and probably most of the men."

"How can you be sure?"

"I can't," Turk answered. "But you can have Washington check the ship."

"Hold on a minute," Fitzhugh responded.

Turk looked at Lauren. She had moved back against the pillow. "Fitzhugh is talking to Hanahan," he said, putting his hand over the mouthpiece.

"Who's Hanahan?" she asked.

"Another general at Fort Bliss, Hanahan is—"

"Turk, this is Hanahan. Those are fucking bandits out there. That's what we decided they are, and that's what they are."

"Listen, Hanahan," Turk said, "listen carefully to what I say. . . ." He told him how Walther and Krieger had tried to stop Lauren from leaving Mexico City because they were afraid she knew more about the *City of Cadiz* than just its name. "A British cultural attaché by the name of Richard Harris," Turk explained, "who was also an M.I.6 agent, also knew about the ship. In fact, he was the one who asked me to get a line on it. He was murdered. And last night someone tried to kill me."

"Someone tried to kill you, and you didn't say a word about it when Fitzhugh and I saw you?" Hanahan asked with disbelief.

"Okay, Hanahan, check my story with Detective Hicks of the El Paso police," Turk said, motioning to Lauren to bring him the bottle of scotch from the dresser.

"If you were this fellow Walther, and your wife was going off to be with another man, wouldn't you try to stop her? Hell, the way I see it, he even has a good reason to have you killed?"

"Maybe," Turk said, taking the bottle from Lauren, "but he was a homosexual. Now explain this, Hanahan: the man sent to kill me is dead from what appears to have been cyanide. You can check that with Detective Hicks, too." He took a long drink from the bottle.

"Everything you've said still doesn't say Krauts," Hanahan responded. "Especially Krauts coming up from Mexico."

"Just have Washington run a check on the ship," Turk said.

"And ask for what?" Hanahan growled. "I don't want to start something going when there's no reason to start anything. You know Washington as well as I do."

"It's worth the risk of—"

"Turk, it's fifteen-thirty hours here," Hanahan said. "It's two hours later in Washington. It's Saturday night. Now who the hell would I get to do that check? Everything is buttoned down tight until Monday morning."

"You're a fucking fool, Hanahan," Turk shouted and slammed the phone down. He took another drink from the bottle. "Tomorrow morning," he said, "I'm going to get Dijon to fly me over the area and look around. There are Krauts down there and I'm going to find them."

The phone rang.

Turk answered it.

Fitzhugh was on the other end. "Do we still have a dinner date?" he asked.

"Are you sure you still want us?" Turk asked. He guessed that either Hanahan had left the room, or Fitzhugh was calling from a different office.

"Yes," Fitzhugh answered.

"Then we'll be there," Turk answered. "But make it about twenty-hundred, or even twenty-thirty would be better."

"Twenty-thirty would be fine," Fitzhugh said and hung up.

Turk set the bottle down on the nighttable, next to the phone. "This is not exactly what I planned for us," he said, looking at Lauren.

"It doesn't matter," she answered. "We're together. That's all that really matters." She patted the empty place next to her. "Come back here for a while."

Turk settled down next to her. "If I'm right and the Krauts are moving north, all hell is going to break loose soon," he said.

She held his head against her breasts and stroked the top of it.

"There's something else I have to tell you," Turk said, looking up at her.

"Bad?"

"I guess any man's death is bad. . . . Walther killed himself."

"Oh my God!"

"He killed Krieger before he turned the gun on himself," Turk said.

Lauren shook her head. "I have no tears for him. No tears! Yet if you hadn't come into my life I still would have been living with him. Hold me, Turk."

He took Lauren in his arms.

"Hold me tight," she whispered.

Surrounded by spacious lawns and green shrubbery, General Fitzhugh's ranch-style house was located at the far end of Officer's Row, the area where married officers and their families lived on base.

Turk pulled up in front of the house and parked.

"Generals live damn good in the States," Dijon said with a laugh from the rear of the car.

"Not like in Spain," Turk answered. He walked around to the other side of the car and opened the door for Lauren.

Dijon let himself out. "Are you sure you want me along?" he asked.

"I told Fitzhugh you'd be coming," Turk answered.

At the door they were greeted by a Mexican houseboy, who took their coats and led them into a large Spanish-style living room. "The general will be with you shortly," he said and left.

Turk pointed to the photographs on the wall and said, "Fitzhugh said, "Fitzhugh is an amateur archeologist and a damn good photographer."

"They're beautiful!" Lauren said. "Absolutely beautiful."

The houseboy returned with a tray of hors d'oeuvres and set it down on an end table. Then, going over to the bar cart, he asked them what they would like to drink, and with a smile said, "I make very good martinis."

"I'll take one of those," Dijon answered.

"And so will I," Lauren responded.

"Scotch neat for me," Turk said.

By the time they had the drinks in their hands, Fitzhugh entered. Wearing tan slacks, a Harris tweed sport jacket, a brown shirt, and a tan ascot, he looked very much like a college professor.

Fitzhugh greeted Turk warmly and introduced himself to Dijon and Lauren. After the handshaking, the houseboy handed him a drink. "To health and happiness," Fitzhugh toasted, holding up his glass.

All of them touched glasses and then drank.

Lauren sampled the hors d'oeuvres and commented on how good they tasted.

"José's mother made them," Fitzhugh explained. "She's my cook. Her husband tends the garden and helps with heavy work, and José takes care of things and my guests when I have them."

"Your photographs are stunning," Lauren said.

Fitzhugh beamed. "Are you interested in photography?" he asked.

She nodded. "But my main interest is painting."

"Ah, how wonderful!" Fitzhugh exclaimed. Then turning to Dijon, he asked, "Are you interested in the arts too?"

"Only as an observer," Dijon answered.

"Louis flies," Turk said. "He flew Lauren up from Mexico City."

"You didn't happen to see anything strange on the

flight up here?" Fitzhugh asked.

Dijon shook his head. "We were in storms most of the way."

"I was going to ask Louis to take me up tomorrow and have a look around," Turk said.

Fitzhugh finished his drink and asked José for a refill before he said, "I guess this is as good a time as any to tell you that I'm expecting a call from a friend of mine in military intelligence."

Turk raised his eyebrows.

"After you and Hanahan got finished yelling at each other, I convinced Hanahan to let me call Colonel Clark Gammell and have him check out the *City of Cadiz*. He said he'd get back to me between 2300 and 2400 hours, our time."

"What did you have to do to Hanahan to get him to agree with that?" Turk asked with a broad smile. "Threaten him with—"

Fitzhugh held up his hand. "You just rub him the wrong way. Even at the Point you did."

"Hell," Turk answered, "you have it all wrong. He rubs me the wrong way, ever since the Point."

The four of them began to laugh.

"What do you think Gammell will come up with?" Fitzhugh asked.

Turk shrugged. "I don't know."

"And if we draw a blank," Fitzhugh asked, "will you forget Krauts and accept bandits?"

Turk took a long swallow of scotch. It was obvious that Fitzhugh had traded off with Hanahan and was not seeking a similar trade off with him. "A *B* for a *B*," he said. "I'll accept bandits for a blank."

Fitzhugh offered his hand and Turk shook it.

"Now," Fitzhugh said, "let's have dinner." He gave his

arm to Lauren and escorted her to the table.

The dining room was lovely, with three walls of walnut-stained panels, a fourth with large French doors that opened out on the rear lawn, and low rough-hewed ceiling beams. The table was laid with Mexican-style china and silver. Two tall candles threw their wavering light across the center of the table and a fire was burning in the fireplace.

"It's charming," Lauren commented.

"Thank you," Fitzhugh said, helping her with the chair.

The dinner began with a fruit cup and was followed by rich garlic soup. For the main course there was chili, meat and chicken enchiladas, and Mexican rice. A full-bodied Rioja was served with the food.

Dijon was something of an amateur chef and, to Turk's surprise, so was Fitzhugh. The two of them began to trade recipes for various Mexican dishes from chicken molé to cazuela de mariscos.

"What about you, Doug?" Fitzhugh asked. "What are you interested in besides your work? I mean, what do you do for relaxation?"

"Read. Listen to classical music."

"Don't let him kid you," Dijon said. "Doug is interested in just about everything and anything. You think he wasn't listening to us, but I can tell you from experience that he was. And he'll remember what each of us said better than we ourselves will."

"Hanahan thinks you're a wise-ass," Fitzhugh said.

"And I think he's a jackass," Turk answered.

Suddenly the phone began to ring. Turk glanced at his watch. It was 2215. His heart skipped a beat, then began to race. He lit a cigarette and blew smoke toward the ceiling.

Picking up the phone on the sideboard, José said, "For you, General, from Washington."

Fitzhugh excused himself from the table. "General Fitzhugh here," he said, then listened. "Yes. I understand," he answered. "Yes. Anything else, Clark?" Another few moments of silence. "Thanks, Clark. Keep me posted." He put the phone down and returned to the table. "The *City of Cadiz* sent an SOS message five days ago and nothing has been heard from her since. She never gave her position. She is presumed lost with all hands."

"Holy Christ!" Turk exclaimed, stabbing the cigarette out in an ashtray.

Dijon gave a long, low whistle.

"There's more," Fitzhugh said, wiping his brow with the napkin. "Clark spoke to his British counterpart in London and was bluntly told not to ask any questions about the *City of Cadiz*, or anything connected with it."

"That's goddamn strange," Turk commented.

"That's what Clark thought, which is why he is asking questions. You heard me tell him to keep me posted."

"Well, we didn't draw a blank," Turk said.

Fitzhugh nodded.

"Hanahan is not going to like it," Turk said.

"No, he's not. But he must know."

"Did your friend Clark have any idea about what's going on?"

"None," Fitzhugh answered. "None at all."

At Fitzhugh's suggestion, they left the table and returned to the living room, where José served them strong black coffee, a delicate strawberry flan, followed by a rich homemade chocolate ice cream.

"Does your friend know why you asked him to check

on the ship?" Turk asked, looking across the coffee table at Fitzhugh.

"No. I thought it best to just ask him to do it as a favor for me."

Turk lit a cigarette, stood up, and walked to the hearth. Fresh faggots had been laid across the andirons by José, and they were ringed with yellow flames. "Why the hell would the British respond the way they did?" Turk asked, without looking at anyone. "The *City of Cadiz* was, according to Harris—" He turned around. "They must know more than we do about the ship. They must know it was delivering men and equipment."

"You're jumping to conclusions," Fitzhugh responded.

"What do you say, Dijon?" Turk asked.

"It's not so easy to get rid of a ship, unless you sink it," Dijon said.

"Sink it!" Turk exclaimed. He stepped away from the fireplace. "Just suppose that's what happened."

"Who sunk it?" Lauren asked, entering the conversation.

"The Krauts could have," Turk answered.

"It's a Spanish ship," Lauren reminded him.

"Yes, but—"

The phone rang again.

"I'll get it," Fitzhugh told José, moving toward the end table where the phone sat. "Yes, Clark," he said. "Thanks for getting back to me so soon." He looked toward Turk and nodded. Then he said, "I really do appreciate this. If there's anything I can do for you, please call me. . . . The war games are going well. Thank you and good-bye." He put the phone down and returned to where he had been sitting. "Clark was able to get more information out of the British. The *City of Cadiz* is in some way tied into a German operation in Libya against Auchinleck. He doesn't know why. But the Germans are expected to make a push against the British left flank—that is, coming up from the south."

Turk sat down and lit another cigarette.

"There's more," Fitzhugh said. "Our FBI sent the British a message that they apparently uncovered in, of all places, New York, from a critically injured German national, suspected of being a spy. The message sent to M.I.6 was that 'The Fox' was 'in place'. Obviously, the British have interpreted it to mean that Rommel is ready to launch his counteroffensive against the Eighth Army."

Turk took a long drag on the cigarette. The pieces fit.

"Well, at least we know what we're dealing with," Fitzhugh commented.

"Better bandits than Krauts," Turk said.

"I'll tell Hanahan about it in the morning," Fitzhugh responded. "Now, how about an after-dinner drink of Kahlua?"

"Love it," Lauren answered.

"Something a bit stronger for me," Dijon said. "A Courvoisier, if you have it?"

"What about you, Doug?" Fitzhugh asked.

"A Drambuie."

"You heard the requests, José," Fitzhugh said. "Only Lauren and I are going to enjoy Kahlua. . . ."

During the drive back to the hotel from Fitzhugh's house, Lauren rested her head against Turk's shoulder; Dijon was asleep in the rear of the car.

"You're not very talkative," Lauren commented.

"Not much to say," Turk answered, slipping an arm around Lauren's shoulder. He drew her closer. She smelled good, and for a moment he thought about how he would make love to her when they were back in the hotel room. There were so many pleasurable things he wanted to do with her.

"You really don't accept the idea that bandits killed Ed, do you?"

"That was what the facts indicate," Turk answered.

"But you don't accept them—or rather, you don't accept the conclusion drawn from them?"

Turk shrugged. "As I've already said, I'd rather it be bandits than Krauts. . . . But Fitzhugh's friend still didn't explain why the *City of Cadiz* was in Mexican waters, when supposedly she has something to do with whatever is going on in North Africa, or why she sent an SOS and then vanished with all hands."

"That's what I was thinking," Dijon commented from the rear seat.

"I thought you were asleep," Turk said.

"Just resting," Dijon replied. "Listen, Doug, if you still want to go up and take a look around tomorrow, I'll take you.

"Thanks," Turk answered. "I want to go."

"I never realized you were so tenacious," Lauren said.

"If I weren't," he asked, glancing at her, "would I have gotten you?"

Lauren thought for a few moments before she answered. "Probably not."

Turk nodded and gently squeezed her breast.

"Doug!" she exclaimed.

"I can't see a thing," Dijon said. "I have my eyes

closed." Then, after a momentary pause for dramatic effect, he added, "But I sure as hell am listening to everything."

The three of them laughed.

# 16

*December 7, 1941*

Ed had misjudged the distance to the border, the limits of his own strength, and the effect of the storm on his driving. He was forced to slow down. Even with the headlights on, the blowing sand and dust made it difficult for him to see more than a few feet ahead. His eyes burned from lack of sleep and his wounded arm ached.

To keep awake, Ed talked to himself. "When I get out of this man's army," he said, "I'm going to get me a nice cottage somewhere near the ocean. Somewhere near the ocean and maybe even buy a sailboat. . . ." He searched his pockets for a package of cigarettes, didn't find it, and remembered he had smoked the last one in the cantina.

With the coming of nightfall, it became colder. Ed stopped. "Take ten for piss call," he said aloud. He was back in the truck as soon as he was finished.

"Got to beat those Krauts to the border," Gripper said, beginning to drive again. "But they're not going too much faster than I am—if they're moving at all in this storm." His best guess was that the Germans would be forced to stop until the weather improved.

"I'd call a halt," he said, "if I were their commander." He reasoned it would be almost impossible for the German vehicles to remain in visual contact with each other and radio communication would, at its best, be intermittent. "It'd be different," he said, "if they were using a highway and could move one behind the other. But they're not doing that. They're cutting across open country, following maps, and their visibility for all practical purposes is zero."

Ed ran his hand over his eyes and glanced down at the dashboard to look at the gas gauge. The needle was at the halfway mark. He couldn't remember if it had been there the last time he looked at it.

"Right now," he said, "my problem is sleep." He knew that if he didn't get some sleep, he'd never make it to the border. He most certainly would fall asleep at the wheel and run off the road. "Probably wind up killing myself," he said. "But if I sleep, how the hell will I get up in an hour, or, at the most, two? How will I wake myself?"

Ordinarily, Ed never had a problem of waking up when he wanted to. Some inner mechanism worked and he'd wake at the right time. But nothing about this damn situation was ordinary. He couldn't go on. He had to sleep. "Okay," he said, "now decide where? Do you stay on the road, on its shoulder, or do you pull off it completely?" To stop on the road would be to run the risk of being hit by another driver, especially in a storm. The danger of going too far off the road was that he might wind up in sand and not be able to get out of it.

Ed opted for stopping on the shoulder. He turned the wheel and eased the pickup off the road. He cut the ignition and turned off the headlights. Then he rolled up the windows, locked the doors on either side of the cab, and put the machine pistol within easy reach on the floorboards. With a weary sigh, Ed stretched out on the seat, closed his eyes, and slept.

Ed awoke with a start and a stabbing pain in his wounded arm. It took him two or three seconds to realize three men on foot were looking at him, one at each window and two in front. Another two seconds passed before he saw that they were armed and four more were on horseback, standing off to the side of the roadway.

"Fucking bandits," Ed exclaimed. "Complete with sombreros and bandoliers across their chests."

The one at the side window knocked at it and said in English, "Roll the window down, gringo."

Ed smiled at him, nodded, and eased his hand over the machine pistol. With a quick burst he could get the three on foot, if he moved fast enough. But the four on horseback would be difficult. If they decided to start shooting, he might be hit before he could start the engine and get away. Suddenly Ed realized the storm had stopped, leaving the sky a sullen gray.

"Gringo, open the window," the man outside said, "—or I kill you." His breath steamed in the cold air. He started to raise his rifle.

Ed snapped the machine pistol, pressed its muzzle against the window, and squeezed the trigger.

The glass shattered. The man didn't have time to scream. His face dissolved into a red pulp. He staggered backward and fell.

Ed swung the muzzle toward the bandits in front of him. The windshield shattered and the two men dropped to the ground.

Neighing loudly, the frightened horses reared up.

Ed switched on the ignition and threw the shift into first. He was beginning to move.

The bandits were trying to steady their mounts.

The pickup gained momentum. Ed shifted straight

into third. He was back on the roadway. He glanced up at the rearview mirror. The bandits were turning away, leaving their dead companions where they had fallen.

Ed looked at his watch. It had stopped at ten after one. But he had no way of knowing whether it was 0110 hours or 1310 hours. He would have to wait until he came to a town to find out what the time was. But he did know it was Sunday, December 7. Then he reached out and pulled some of the jagged pieces of glass free and threw them off to the side of the roadway. He wasn't as tired as he had been. But he was hungrier and colder. . . .

Turk put the phone down. "That was Louis," he said. "There's some trouble with the plane. An oil pump isn't working properly and the plane won't be ready to fly for at least four hours."

"What time is it?" Lauren asked, stretching languorously.

Turk picked up his watch from the night table. "Nine-thirty," he answered, turning toward her. She was nude and her body was warm. He put his hand on her breast and felt the nipple rise under his palm.

"Since you're not going to fly away," she said, "what would you like to do?"

"I'm open for suggestions."

"I'd like to put flowers on Manuel's grave," she said.

Turk gently squeezed her breasts. "We'll have breakfast at a place I know and then go there. Okay?"

"Sure," Lauren answered.

Turk let go of her breast and helped himself to a cigarette. "Want one?" he asked, looking at her.

She shook her head.

He lit up and leaned back into the pillow, while Lauren snuggled up to him. "You would have liked him," he told her, knowing she'd understand he was talking about Manuel. "He had some rough edges, but he would have grown into one hell of a man."

"You're one hell of a man," she responded, kissing his chest.

"Listen, if we don't get out of bed," he said, "we're not going to until I make love to you again."

"If you can," Lauren answered, running her hand over his penis, "—and I see that you can—then I most certainly can."

Turk stubbed out his cigarette in the ashtray on the night table; then, taking her in his arms, he kissed her passionately on the lips. "It's nice waking up next to you," he said. . . .

When Turk and Lauren left the hotel it was cold and there was enough wind blowing to make walking uncomfortable. Turk drove to Estaban's luncheonette.

"Are you sure you want to breakfast in there?" Lauren asked, pausing to look at the shabby exterior.

"My friend owns it," Turk said, opening the door.

They sat at the counter. When Estaban came over to shake hands, Turk introduced him to Lauren.

"You have excellent taste in women," Estaban said, looking at Turk while kissing the back of Lauren's hand.

"We're going over to Juárez," Turk explained, "to put flowers on Manuel's grave."

Estaban nodded and gave each of them coffee.

"Ham and eggs for me," Turk said. "Eggs over well and hash-brown potatoes and toast."

"I'll have the same without the potatoes," Lauren said.

Estaban shouted the two orders to the chef in the kitchen and then he said, "Things look bad between this country and Japan."

Turk agreed. He had been so involved in his own problem for the last couple of days that he hadn't followed the international situation in more than a cursory way.

"War would be a bad thing if it comes," Estaban said.

"War is always a bad thing," Turk responded.

"I was a small boy when there was fighting. I remember Zapata and Pancho Villa. . . . Bad, very bad," Estaban said, lapsing into Spanish.

With a nod, Turk agreed.

"Have you ever been in a war?" Estaban asked.

"In China and in Spain," Turk answered.

"Spain?"

"Against Franco," Turk said.

"Mother of God," Estaban exclaimed, reaching across the counter and grabbing hold of Turk's hand, "my brother was there, too. He was killed during the battle for Madrid."

"I was there," Turk told him.

Estaban looked at Lauren. "This one is a man," he said, speaking English again. "This one is truly a man!"

"Yes, I know that," she answered in Spanish, placing one of her hands over Turk's.

Estaban went to the kitchen to pick up the order.

"He's most certainly a fan of yours," Lauren commented. "How did you meet him?"

"Through Manuel," Turk answered, and explained the circumstances of their meeting.

Estaban put their orders down, wished them a hearty appetite, and went off to serve two men who had just come in and sat down at the counter.

"You know," Lauren said, "I'm the only woman here."

Turk looked around. "I guess you are."

After a few moments of silence, Lauren asked, "Do

you really think there'll be a war between us and Japan?"

"There might be, especially if we fight Germany. Japan is part of the Axis. She would have to go to Germany's aid. . . . But alone, I don't know. The only way I could see it happening would be if the Japanese were able to destroy our navy . . . and then, maybe. But if it becomes a long, drawn-out struggle, then Japan has no chance against us."

"Walther was friendly with members of the Japanese embassy," Lauren said. "Some of the things he imported from time to time came from Japan."

"I knew some of their embassy staff too," Turk said. "The Japanese I knew were either educated here in the States, or in England."

They finished their breakfast and each of them drank a second cup of coffee.

When Turk asked for a check, Estaban refused to give him one. "I told you that when you come here to eat, you're my guest."

"Then let me pay for Lauren," Turk said.

"Anyone with you is also my guest," Estaban answered with a smile, "especially a beautiful woman."

Turk nodded, shook Estaban's hand, and thanked him.

"Take care of him," Estaban told Lauren.

"I will," she answered.

They went back to the car and Turk found an open florist across from the Southern Pacific Railroad terminal. He bought a large bouquet of red and yellow roses, purpose and white mums, and blue gladiolas. They drove across the Stanton Street Bridge, and a few minutes later pulled up in front of the cemetery archway.

Turk went around to the other side of the car and helped Lauren out. Hand in hand they walked into the cemetery. Other people were there to either put flowers on a grave, or, in accordance with the Indian tradition—though the cemetery was Christian—leave small bowls of food for the dead. Some just stood at the foot of a grave and meditated in silence or quietly wept.

Turk led her to where Manuel was buried. "You place the flowers," he told her.

She bent down and put the bouquet at the head of the grave and whispered, "Rest in peace." Then she went back to Turk's side.

"Before he died," Turk said, "Manuel asked me if he would go to heaven, despite the sins he had committed. I assured him he would. He was more afraid of going to hell than he was of dying."

"I'm sure God will embrace him," Lauren responded softly. "After all, he did give his life for you. Such a selfless act must loom large in the eyes of the Almighty."

Turk didn't answer, and gently taking Lauren by the arm he started back toward the car.

"You don't believe, do you? In God, I mean?" Lauren asked.

"No," Turk said. "I don't."

"There must be someone who—"

Turk shook his head. "I don't believe there's a God," he said. "But if He does exist, He has a great deal to answer for, a great deal of human suffering in all its forms must be laid to His blindness or egomania. Take your choice."

"You really don't mean that," Lauren answered.

"But I do," Turk said; then, with a wry smile, he added, "For me, God exists in your cunt but nowhere else."

"That's—"

"If you're going to tell me that it's a terrible thing to say, don't. It was meant as a compliment to you and the pleasure you give me."

"And I thought I knew you," she said, going back into the car.

"You do know me," Turk told her, starting the engine. "But what you don't know is that I stopped believing in God a long time ago."

It wasn't until they were almost at the Sante Fe Street Bridge that Lauren said, "I believe, Doug, I really do. I believe in God!"

"That's good," Turk said, putting his hand on her knee and squeezing it. "I won't try to change your mind about it, and don't you try to change mine." He was moving up toward the bridge. There were just three vehicles in front of him: two cars and a beat-up pickup between them. Though it was slightly past noon, Juárez was not yet awake. Here and there a few soldiers were straggling toward the bridge after spending a night at one or another of the town's brothels. Suddenly Turk realized something was wrong. People were running out of shops and shouting. Because the windows were closed, he couldn't make out what they were saying. He was about to roll the window down on his side when he caught sight of Luis Garcia, the man he had argued with in the Tivoli two nights before. Garcia was close to a battered pickup, and there was a gun in his hand.

Turk hit the brake, came to a stop, and shifted into neutral. "Keep your hand on the horn," he said, swinging himself out of the car. At a run, he went for Garcia.

The sound of the horn drew Garcia's attention away from the pickup. He looked over his shoulder and saw Turk coming at him.

People were still running out of the shops.

Garcia stopped, turned, and pointed the revolver at Turk.

The next instant the driver of the pickup was out of

the cab, and with a short burst from a machine pistol, he cut the man down.

It took Turk another moment to realize he was looking at Ed.

By now, people were shouting and running. More horns were blowing. Some of the GI's were running toward the bridge. Others looked stunned.

"I saw him go for you," Ed explained. "The sound of the horn made me look up into the rearview mirror."

"Thought you were dead," Turk said.

"Almost was," Ed answered.

Suddenly Turk realized Lauren was running toward them. "Doug—Doug," she shouted, "the Japanese have bombed Pearl Harbor."

"What did you say?"

"The Japanese have bombed Pearl Harbor," Lauren repeated breathlessly. "That's why the people are running out of the shops."

All at once they were surrounded by a half-dozen Federales.

Turk pointed to the dead man and in Spanish he said, "His name is Luis Garcia."

"I saw him in the rearview mirror," Ed said. "He was going to shoot my friend. You can see the revolver is still in his hand."

The Federale sergeant nodded. "The two of you and the lady will have to come with me."

Ed shook his head and said to Turk, "Better get ready, Doug." Then he pushed the muzzle of the machine pistol against the sergeant's stomach. "You're dead, if you make any attempt to stop me. Turk, you and the woman get in the pickup. Sergeant, tell your men to drop their weapons and climb into the back of the pickup truck, and then you follow them."

Ed clambered onto the rear of the truck. "I'll kill any one of you," he said calmly to the Federales, "who tries to stop us, or attempts to escape." Then he shouted to Turk, "Drive, and don't stop until you reach headquarters."

Turk set the pickup in motion. "I'm going to crash right through the barriers," he told Lauren, "so hold on." And swinging out of the line of vehicles waiting to go onto the bridge, he pressed his foot down on the accelerator. Within moments he smashed through the first barrier on the Mexican side and then a second one on the American side. Almost immediately the Border Patrol and El Paso police were chasing after him.

"Good God," Lauren exclaimed, "they're shooting at us!"

To slow them down, Ed answered with a burst from his machine pistol.

Turk shook his head and continued to drive. He swung off El Paso Street and went east along Fourth Street for several blocks; then turned north until he reached Piasano Drive, where he swung east. His plan was to get out on U.S. 62; then go cross-country, parallel to the railroad tracks leading into the base.

Lauren braced herself against the dashboard with two hands. "What do you suppose happened to Ed?"

"Don't know," Turk answered. He had made several screeching turns and was heading up Pershing Drive. "But whatever it was, he must think it's damn important to be doing this." The pickup was bouncing badly over the open desert.

As soon as they came into the fort, several military police cars joined the chase. One tried to block Turk off, but he managed to swing around it; then he came to an abrupt halt directly in front of headquarters.

Ed was off the rear of the truck before Turk was out of the cab. He raced up the steps.

Turk was directly behind him.

"Where the hell are Hanahan and Fitzhugh?" Gripper shouted. "Get one of them here immediately!"

The Border Patrol people, the cops, and the military police rushed into the lobby.

Ed whirled around. "All of you halt!" he ordered, leveling the machine pistol at them.

The door to the communications room was flung open. Hanahan strode out; Fitzhugh followed. Both were white.

"We've got trouble," Ed said, looking at them.

Hanahan nodded. "MPs, clear the corridor of civilian police and federal Border Patrol officers! And get those damn Federales back across the border!"

The ranking Border Patrol officer started to protest.

"God *damn*," Hanahan shouted. "I gave an order!"

Immediately the military police formed up in front of the other officers and started to ease them toward the door. At the same moment several of the reporters assigned to cover the war games came into the headquarters. All of them wanted a statement from Hanahan and Fitzhugh about the Japanese attack on Pearl Harbor.

"Later," Hanahan said. "We will make a statement later." Then looking at Ed, he said, "Into Fitzhugh's office."

"Turk goes with us," Ed responded.

Hanahan looked balefully at Turk and nodded.

"I don't want Lauren interfered with," Turk said to Hanahan.

Hanahan turned to one of the officers in the corridor. "See that she has an MP escort back to the hotel and assign two MPs to guard her at the hotel."

"Yes, sir!" the officer answered.

"I'll be back at the hotel in a while," Turk said, kissing Lauren on the cheek and followed Ed into Fitzhugh's office.

"The Japs have bombed Pearl," Hanahan said, dropping into the chair behind the desk. "We've taken heavy casualties. The fleet has been badly damaged, and now this."

Ed placed the machine pistol and the dog tags he had taken from the dead Germans on the desk. "There's a Kraut column out there, moving north. I suspect they've already crossed the border."

"Are you absolutely sure?" Hanahan asked, squinting up at Ed.

Ed gave a quick resume of what happened to him and pointing to his wound, he ended by telling them, "I got this from one of the Krauts."

"Better call Alt," Hanahan said to Fitzhugh, "and tell him what the situation is." Then he moved his eyes to Turk. "Guess I owe you an apology."

Turk shook his head. "I'd much prefer that you were right and I was wrong."

"But how the hell did the Krauts put men and machines into Mexico?" Ed asked and then answered his own question. "It had to come by ship."

"It did," Turk said. "One of the ships was the *City of Cadiz*. But we can fit the pieces together later. Now we have to stop them."

Hanahan lifted the phone and said, "This is General Hanahan. Put me through to either General Marshall or Secretary of War Stimpson at the War Department in Washington. This is a high priority phone call, a matter of life and death." He waited for a few moments; then he shouted, "I don't give a flying fuck if the lines are busy. Get me through!" And he slammed the phone down."

"Come in!" Hanahan barked, answering a knock at the door.

The door opened and a corporal from the Communications Room entered, saluted, and handed Hanahan a slip of paper.

"The column has crossed the border," Hanahan shouted. "They've attacked and destroyed a South Pacific freight." He stood up and went to the wall map. "They're moving in this area here," he explained, putting his hand on the map west of El Paso.' He turned toward the corporal. "You tell the officer in charge of the communications room that everything, including the message he just sent me, is now classified as top-secret—and that means no discussions about the material handled in that room by any of the men."

"Yes, sir."

Hanahan returned to the desk and picked up the phone. "Get a doctor over to General Fitzhugh's office immediately."

"General," Ed said, "I think we should start to assemble a deterrent force immediately." The longer we wait, the deeper that Kraut column is going to go and the more damage it's going to cause."

Fitzhugh came back. "The reporters are clamoring for some sort of statement," he said.

"Did you get to Alt?" Hanahan asked, ignoring what Fitzhugh had said.

"Yes. He'll be back shortly."

"Ed says we should go after the Krauts without waiting for a word from Washington," Hanahan said.

"What kind of armor do the Krauts have?" Fitzhugh asked.

"The best I could make out was the heavy scout car, the SDKFZ 233. Better armed than our scout cars and our tanks."

"We can put a total of eleven light tanks into the field from Alt's force and my own. But they have only 37mm cannon, a .30 caliber machine gun, and no armor," Hanahan said.

"We don't even have an observation plane," Fitzhugh commented ruefully. "We could blunder into them and have our force wiped out, just the way Barth was."

"Then you know!" Ed began.

"We thought it was a well-armed group of bandits," Hanahan explained. "We sent out a mobile scout patrol under Captain Barth. He found them but was shot to pieces before he could radio us what he found."

"We have a plane," Turk said. "My friend Louis Dijon flew Lauren up from Mexico City. You could use his plane. He's an experienced flier. He flew against the Krauts in Spain."

Hanahan made a face. "I don't want to use—"

"Listen," Turk told him, "you don't have much choice. Not if you want to know where those Krauts are."

"Doug is right," Ed said.

"I don't have to like it," Hanahan responded sourly.

Fitzhugh went to the map. "I was in the communications room when the message came in about the Southern Pacific train. What we have to know is whether the Krauts are going to strike at Deming, or are they going to continue up this slot and head for Hatch? Between where they hit the train and Hatch is about fifty miles. . . . Doug, how long before your friend is ready to fly?"

Turk looked at his watch. "His plane needed some repairs. But I would guess in about an hour."

A knock at the door brought a quick response from Fitzhugh.

"Captain Roberts, Medical Officer, reporting as ordered, sir," the man said, saluting Fitzhugh.

"That man there," Hanahan said, gesturing toward Gripper.

"Just creased," the doctor announced after examining the wound. "It will hurt for a few days and you'll have a scar."

"Can you dress it here, Doctor?" Ed asked.

"Yes," Roberts answered, opening his medical bag.

Ed winced while Roberts applied mentholate and sulfa powder to the wounds.

While Ed was being bandaged neither Hanahan nor Fitzhugh spoke.

Another noncom came from the communications room and handed Hanahan a message. "All war games are hereby terminated," he read aloud. "Base commander will place all units on stand-by alert. Those units who have completed basic infantry training will be immediately readied for shipment."

"Doctor," Ed said, "what you just heard you didn't hear. Do you understand?"

"Yes, Colonel," Roberts answered.

"What's the real situation at Pearl?" Turk asked.

"Bad," Fitzhugh answered. "Thousands of casualties, most of the fleet sunk or badly damaged, and most of the air force destroyed on the ground."

Turk shook his head. "I didn't think the Japs would attack, and it seems that Washington didn't think they would either. Between the Japs and the Krauts, they put this country between a hammer and a very hard place. There isn't any way we could hold those islands if the Japs invade." Years before, he and Ed had met at Scofield. Pulling Hawaii for a duty station then was considered the best of luck. The islands were beautiful. It was very, very difficult to imagine that paradise being changed to the hell it now was. . . .

"Done," Roberts said, applying the last piece of tape. "Stop by and see me in a couple of days, and I'll change the dressing. . . . I guess even in maneuvers it can get a bit hairy."

"I guess it can," Ed said. "And thanks."

As soon as the doctor was gone, Hanahan went up to the wall map, and without speaking he looked at it for a long time. "As long as we know where they are," he commented, turning toward the others in the room, "we're okay, at least for the next twenty-four hours."

"I don't understand," Ed said.

Hanahan stepped away from the map. "It's about 1400 hours now. By 1530 it will be getting on toward twilight, especially where the Krauts are."

"Okay, so it will be twilight," Turk interjected. "What the hell does that have to do with what we do?"

"It will take us that long—if not longer—to get our six tanks and whatever else we can bring to bear against them ready. By the time we'll be ready to roll it will be nightfall. And the Krauts will have to stop too. Now if Doug's friend can pinpoint their positions, say at 1700 hours we'll know where to find them tomorrow morning."

"What do you want, Hanahan?" Turk asked. "Washington to give you the order so that if there's any flak, you can always say, 'That order came from Marshall,' or 'I was told to do that by the Secretary of War'?"

Hanahan flushed. "I can order you out of here," he said in an angry voice.

"You were wrong before," Turk shot back, "and you're wrong now."

Fitzhugh stepped between them. "Pat," he said, addressing Hanahan by his nickname, "we've got to let the Krauts know we're onto them—at least make them sweat a bit."

"We wait," Hanahan responded. "We wait until word comes from Washington."

Ed threw up his hands. "Okay, I'll go up with Turk's friend and have a look around."

"No," Fitzhugh said, "I'll go up."

"He won't fly unless I go," Turk told them.

"You're not back in the army yet, Turk," Hanahan said, "and you won't be going on any military mission until you are, and if you're in my command, not even then. But now I'll go."

"Dijon won't fly unless—"

"I'll confiscate his plane," Hanahan shouted, losing patience. "I'm not going to fuck around with you and your friend. He'll fly me or I'll take the plane and have one of my own pilots do it. No, you go back to your hotel and wait until Ed calls you. But don't, just don't get in my way!"

"You're making me tremble," Turk answered; then he turned to Ed. "Give me a call. I'm at the Cortés."

Ed nodded.

Turk saluted Fitzhugh and left. Had he stayed a moment longer, he would have slugged Hanahan.

Seated by the window, Lauren listened to the radio. All of the regular programming had been suspended. The news was grim, very grim.

The announcer continued, ". . . Though the reports from Pearl Harbor are still very sketchy, we know that several of our battleships have been hit by Japanese bombs and are on fire . . . Casualties are heavy . . . Many of the sailors aboard the ships were still sleeping when the first wave of Japanese aircraft struck. . . ."

Within the past few minutes Lauren had heard the same words, spoken by the same announcer, in the same choked voice, at least four different times. She suspected that the military authorities had already begun to censor the news emanating from the islands.

She stood up, went into the bathroom, and washed her face. She looked into the mirror. She was pale—pale with fear. She felt it deep in her being. It gripped her vitals. The war had come. It had exploded five thousand miles away and was about to explode here in the States. . . . That Walther had helped make it possible for the Germans to invade the United States was almost too incredible for her to believe, much less understand.

She moved back into the bedroom just in time to hear the announcer say, "Ladies and gentlemen, this has just come in! Japanese planes have bombed Clark Field in the Phillipines. Once again, reports are sketchy. We expect more on this latest surprise attack by the Japanese within the next few minutes." Then he went back to repeating the news he had given so many times about the Japanese attack on Pearl Harbor.

Lauren stood at the window. During the past three days, she had known more fear than ever before in her life. Krieger would have had her killed, if he could. And Walther could have done nothing to stop him.

But now her fear was no longer for herself. She was desperately afraid of what might happen to Doug. Soon—by the first of the year—he'd be back in the army, and with the war on, he might never—

She stopped herself from completing the thought, and stared out the window, vaguely aware of the deepening shadows of the late afternoon. She was filled with dread.

Suddenly the sound of a key in the lock made her turn. "Doug?" she called, leaving the window.

"Yes," Turk answered, opening the door and stepping into the room.

Lauren ran into his arms.

He held her tightly to him. "What's the news?" he asked.

"Word came a few minutes ago that Clark Field was also bombed, and in Pearl Harbor many of our ships are on fire."

"They did what I didn't think they'd do," Turk said, taking off his coat, hat, and jacket and loosening his tie. He dropped down into the chair and lit a cigarette.

"Hanahan refuses to do anything until he gets the word from Washington. But he is going to go up with Dijon and have a look at the Krauts."

"How's Ed?"

"Tired but still filled with enough piss and vinegar to fight," Turk answered, letting the cigarette dangle from his lips. "He was wounded out there."

"Oh!" she exclaimed.

"Just creased, but he'll carry the scar for the rest of his life."

Lauren sat down on the arm of the chair and ran her hand over his head and then gently moved it against her breasts.

"You're going to burn yourself," Turk warned. "Let me get rid of the cigarette." And then he pressed his face to her breasts. "I know you're frightened and so am I. I guess anyone listening to the radio is frightened."

"Could you imagine what would happen in the country if the people knew that the Germans were about to attack us."

"They have already," he said, looking up at her.

"Oh dear God, no!" she exclaimed.

He nodded.

"Where?" she asked.

"The less you know, the better off you'll be."

Lauren leaped off the side of the chair. "For God's sake," she exclaimed, "I'm not a child. I'm a woman. You made love to me in that bed. Doug, I have a right to know what's going on."

"They're no longer in Mexico," he said. "Sooner or later we're going to have to find and destroy them."

"When?"

"It's up to Hanahan," Turk said, suddenly getting to his feet. "He's the senior officer. But it must happen soon. The Krauts must have planned this operation very carefully. They must have stockpiles of water, fuel, food, and ammunition. . . . The longer we wait, the more damage they're going to do and the more difficult it will be to destroy them without causing a nationwide panic."

Suddenly the announcer said, "Ladies and gentlemen, this just in from Pearl Harbor. The following ships are now known to have been badly damaged by the Japanese raid earlier this morning on Pearl Harbor: the battleships *Arizona, California*, and *Oklahoma*. . . ."

"We don't really have much time, do we?" Lauren asked.

"No," Turk answered.

"Do you think you'll be going after the Germans with Ed?"

He nodded. "I'm going to try to go."

"And if I asked you not to go?"

He shook his head. "You know I must."

"Hold me tight, Doug," she whispered, coming close to him. "Hold me tight!"

"I love you, Lauren," he said, undoing the button of her blouse and putting his hand into her bra.

"I'm frightened, so very frightened."

Turk lifted Lauren in his arms and carried her to the bed. "At least we can have some time together."

"Turn off the radio," Lauren said. "I don't want to hear about death and destruction while we're making love."

# 17

Hanahan stormed into Fitzhugh's office, dropped his coat and campaign hat on a chair, and went directly to the map. "Couldn't find the sons of bitches," he said, looking at the map. "Got a good look at the train they shot up. It was made up mainly of gasoline tank cars. The Krauts must have known that." He faced Ed and Fitzhugh. "Couldn't even see any wheel marks because they're moving over a rock surface. But they're in this area, between where we are and Deming."

"Washington still hasn't called back," Fitzhugh told him, turning down the volume of the radio behind him.

Hanahan left the map and sat down on the edge of Fitzhugh's desk.

Ed, who had been standing with his back to the window, now sat down in a chair and bent slightly forward. Fitzhugh remained behind the desk.

"What you're trying to tell me is that the Krauts have a specific objective, and that it's no coincidence they attacked here on the same day the Japanese attacked Pearl. By the way what's the latest from there?"

"Bad," Fitzhugh answered. "Many of our capital ships have been sunk and the casualties are heavy. . . ." He gestured toward the radio. "I have been listening to it. But the information is still incomplete."

Suddenly the door opened and Alt stepped into the room. He was alone.

"Still can't get Washington on the phone?" Hanahan asked.

Alt looked at the machine pistol and the German dog tags on Fitzhugh's desk. "Any idea where the Germans are now?" he asked.

"None," Hanahan said. "I just made an air reconnaissance and saw what was left of the train they hit, but that was it."

Alt dropped his coat and hat on the chair over Hanahan's. "We've got to get through to Washington."

Ed looked at Fitzhugh and hoped he would say something to make Hanahan and Alt take some action against the Germans. But when it was obvious that Fitzhugh intended to remain silent, Ed made the task his. "I think the Krauts have a specific target in mind. If they took either Albuquerque or Santa Fe and held it for even a few hours, there would be absolute panic in the country, especially with what has happened at Pearl."

Hanahan launched himself off the desk and went back to the map. "They couldn't do that!" he exclaimed.

"What's going to stop them?" Ed asked. We don't have anything to put in their way to slow them down, let alone stop them. Hell, we don't even know where the fuck they are!"

"Ed has a point," Alt said. "But that presupposes some sort of supply chain."

"Yes," Ed answered. "But that wouldn't have been too difficult to set up."

"It also presupposes a reason," Hanahan said.

"To keep up out of the war in Europe," Ed said. "It would show Washington just how vulnerable we are to attack and that battles can be fought on American soil. And that American cities can be captured by German troops."

"Those are very big suppositions," Hanahan responded. "It also supposes that the Germans and Japanese coordinated their attacks and were able to keep their plans secret."

"I agree with Patrick," Alt said. "Washington has to know what is going on and give us the necessary direction. We are not at war with Germany yet."

Ed stood up and went to the shelf where the bottle of scotch was sitting. "General," he said to Fitzhugh, "I need a drink."

"Help yourself," Fitzhugh answered.

Roosevelt was seated in a wheelchair at his desk. The drapes on the window behind him were drawn. The air in the Oval Office smelled of cigarette and cigar smoke. On various end tables were cups of cold coffee and half-eaten sandwiches. Roosevelt was in his shirt-sleeves and his collar was open. He put the phone down and said to the other men in the room, "The Japanese have attacked the Malay Straits. Winston will ask the House of Commons for a declaration of war tomorrow morning."

General Marshall, head of the Army Chiefs of Staff, frowned. "England will not be able to hold the straits if the Japanese make a concerted effort to take them." He spoke from the far side of the room, near the fireplace.

Admiral Stark, Chief of Naval Operations, who was seated on a small couch in front of an inlaid coffee table, said, "They have the *Repulse* and *Prince of Wales* out there to stop the Japanese from coming down the Malay Peninsula. Those battleships can lay offshore and with their big guns just fire at anything moving south toward Singapore."

Suddenly the phone on Roosevelt's desk rang.

Harry Hopkins, the president's aide, answered it. He listened for a moment and then said, "Mr. President, the secretary of state says that Herr Hans Thomsen, the German chargé d'affaires, has a very important note from Hitler to deliver to you, which he has been ordered to deliver directly into your hands."

Roosevelt nodded. "Tell Cordell I don't have more than ten minutes to give Thomsen."

Hopkins related what the President said, listened for another few moments, said good-bye, and put the phone down. "They'll be here within the next few minutes," he said.

"I've already issued orders," Marshall said, "to maintain a twenty-four-hour alert at all military installations, so that we can start shipping troops to Hawaii and the Philippines."

Roosevelt nodded. "Harry, run through the list of people who'll be at the legislative conference at nine-thirty tonight."

Hopkins picked up a leather portfolio, opened it, took out a sheet of paper, and began to read: "Vice President Wallace; Speaker Rayburn; John McCormick, Majority Leader; Joseph Martin, Minority Floor Leader; Sol Bloom, Foreign Affairs Chairman; Tom Connally, Foreign Relations Committee; Charles Eaton, Foreign Affairs Committee; Warren Austin, Military Affairs Committee; and Senator Charles McNary."

"That should do it," Roosevelt said.

"Are you still sure you don't want the committee chairman leaders?" Hopkins asked.

"That would mean having Congressman Ham Fish," Roosevelt answered, taking the cigarette holder from between his teeth, "and I don't want that man in the

White House."

While Hopkins was reading the list of people called to the nine-thirty conference, Admiral Stark was on another phone, obtaining an updated report on the situation at Pearl Harbor from the Navy Department. "Mister President," he said, "forty-seven officers and one thousand fifty-six men were killed or counted as missing on the *Arizona*."

"My God!" Roosevelt exclaimed.

"The *West Virginia* is down too," Stark said.

"Just what the hell was Admiral Kummel thinking of when he had those ships set up like ducks in a shooting gallery? Messages were sent to him about a suspected attack."

Stark nodded moved away from the telephone, and sat down on the couch again. "We're just lucky our carriers were not in port."

Roosevelt was about to answer when the phone on his desk rang again.

Hopkins picked it up. "The secretary of state is outside," he said.

"Send him in," Roosevelt said.

The door opened and the German chargé d'affaires, Herr Hans Thomsen, entered the room, immediately followed by Cordell Hull, the secretary of state.

Thomsen and a small staff had represented Germany in Washington ever since Roosevelt had ordered the closing of the German embassy the previous year. Thomsen was a seasoned diplomat who had been a member of the Nazi Party since its inception in the early thirties. He was highly regarded by Hitler.

"Well," Roosevelt said, "I understand you have a message for me."

Thomsen nodded. He was a stiff-backed man with a thick neck and a shaved head. He was dressed in frock coat, pin-striped pants, and he held a top hat in his left hand. "Yes, Mr. President. My Führer has directed me to deliver this message directly to you." Removing a long white envelope from his breast pocket, he handed it to Roosevelt. "I was further instructed to await for your answer."

The envelope bore the German eagle. Roosevelt looked at it for a few moments before using a small, single-blade penknife to open it. He withdrew the sheet of paper, unfolded it, and read to himself.

> *To the President of the United States—At this moment a mobile German strike force has already crossed the Mexican border, and is moving north into the southwest portion of your country.*

Roosevelt's heart raced. This was the second time within seven or eight hours that a foreign dignitary had delivered a message from his government to the United States. The first, which was handed to Cordell Hull by Messrs. Kurusu and Moura, the Japanese emissaries to Washington, had been nothing more than a cover for the attack on Pearl Harbor. And now this one from Hitler was, as he saw it, the German way of trying to bully the United States into a nonbelligerent role with regard to the war in Europe. He glanced up at Thomsen, and clearing his voice, he said, "I assume you know the contents of this message?"

"Yes, Mister President," Thomsen said, "I was made aware of them some time ago."

Roosevelt was tempted to ask what Thomsen meant, "by some time ago." But instead he just accepted the chargé d'affaire's answer with a nod and continued to read:

> *"This entire operation has one purpose and that is to show you, your military advisors, and the American people, that Germany can strike where and when it must with absolute impunity. Your country is no longer safe*

*from the ravages of war. It is my fervent hope that you will see in this incursion into the United States my keen desire to maintain peace between our two countries. War will gain us nothing. Europe belongs to the Third Reich. England will soon surrender and in time Russia will also be beaten. The war in Europe does not concern the United States. It is Germany's destiny to conquer and rule all of Europe. Adolf Hitler."*

Roosevelt placed the letter down on his desk and took time to set another cigarette in his holder. He was just about to light it when the phone on his desk rang.

Hopkins hesitated.

"Answer it, Harry," Roosevelt told him.

"It's for you, George," Hopkins announced. "You can take it on the extension."

"We'll wait, Herr Thomsen, until General Marshall is finished with his call," Roosevelt said.

"General Marshall here." Then he listened to what he was being told. After a few minutes he said, "General Hanahan, I will be back to you shortly." He put the phone down. "General Hanahan reports a German strike force has entered the United States." As he spoke, Marshall's eyes moved from the President to Thomsen.

Instantly, Admiral Stark was on his feet.

Hopkins made an audible sound of dismay, while Hull's jaw went slack.

"Read this," Roosevelt said, handing Hitler's message to Marshall. "Better read it aloud, George, to everyone else. it will save time."

Thomsen stood absolutely motionless.

When Marshall was finished, Roosevelt said, "Does Hitler really think we would ever allow Germany to destroy England?"

"Mister President, you have the Japanese to fight.

Becoming involved in a European war would give you two wars to fight. I am certain the Führer will be reasonable. . . . If you do not become involved in a European war, Germany will not interfere with what you do in the Pacific."

Marshall stepped forward. "Mister President, the strike must have limited men and matériel."

"You are quite right, General," Thomsen said. "Our purpose will be served if every man in that force must die. We do not want you to become involved in a European war."

"The Zimmermann Telegram actually put into action," Hopkins commented dryly, "—a quarter of a century later."

"Yes," Thomsen said, "but this time Germany did not depend on anyone else."

After several moments of silence, Roosevelt said, "Mister Secretary of State, will you please escort the German chargé d'affaires out of this office and deliver him to the two Secret Service men outside the door? Tell them they are to accompany him to his residence on my orders. By Executive Order, he is under house arrest. Tell them to make the necessary arrangements to have a twenty-four-hour guard placed on him and every member of his official staff and household."

"We are not yet at war, Mister President, and I will naturally protest your treatment." Thomsen said.

"You do that," Roosevelt answered. "Now, Mister Secretary, will you please remove the German chargé d'affaires from this office? . . ."

"Just where the hell are they?" Hull asked, when he returned to the Oval Office a few moments later.

"According to Hanahan," Marshall answered, lighting a cigarette, "they're somewhere between El Paso and Deming, New Mexico. He says that Colonel Edward Gripper made contact with them several days ago, when he was shot down while flying a recon mission over El Charo, Mexico."

"Holy good God, why didn't Hanahan get to us then?" Stark asked.

"That doesn't concern us now," Roosevelt commented. "We have to decide what to do."

"I don't think we have any choice," Hull said. "We have to declare war on Germany as well as Japan."

Roosevelt pointed his empty cigarette holder at Marshall. "What do you say, George?"

"They've given us the reason," Marshall answered.

"Okay, we declare war on them," Hopkins said, "and what reason do we give the people? If we tell them a German strike force has come into the United States, the isolationists will begin to shout for our immediate withdrawal of all lend-lease to England and Russia. They will say Germany is punishing us for becoming involved in a war that is not our affair. They will claim that Japan and not Germany is our enemy. They will yell 'yellow peril' and say, 'This is what happens when we don't mind our own business.' " By the time he finished, Hopkins was almost shouting. "Goddamn it," he added, "we can't risk telling the American people about this."

"Then what's the alternative?" Stark asked. "Keep it bottled up? Fine. But how?"

"One question at a time, or, rather, one problem at a time," Roosevelt answered. "Tomorrow I'm going to go before the joint houses of Congress and ask for a declaration of war against the Japanese. Not even the isolationists would dare take issue with that. But I am going to wait until Germany declares war on us—which they must, according to their treaty with the Japanese. We will then declare war on them—though, make no mistake, our major effort will be to destroy Germany. That done, we will turn our entire effort against the Japanese."

"Mister President," Marshall said, "we don't have the men and equipment to deal with the strike force."

"We're going to have to deal with it," Roosevelt replied. "We're going to have to destroy it, and do so under an umbrella of absolute secrecy. First, we need a commander, someone who knows all about German armor."

"Ed Gripper is the man," Marshall answered. "He was going to get his star the first of the new year."

"He'll need more than one star to handle Hanahan and Alt," Roosevelt said. "I know those two."

Marshall couldn't help smiling. "They're good men, but—"

Roosevelt waved him silent. "I'll give Gripper three stars on a temporary basis. I can do that, can't I?"

"Yes. You can give him the brevet rank of lieutenant general."

"Good, have the orders cut and wired tonight," Roosevelt told him. "Gripper has my authority to use whatever he needs to stop and destroy the Germans. But he can't take any troops or equipment from other army areas."

"What about aircraft?" Marshall asked.

"We don't have enough to guard our coasts," Roosevelt said. "But speak to Gripper and see what he asks for. He's going to have to outwit the German commander if he's going to beat him."

Marshall agreed with a nod, and picking up the phone he placed a call to General Hanahan. As soon as Hanahan was on the line, Marshall didn't waste any time. "The President has appointed Ed Gripper overall commander for the operation. Orders are coming through giving him three stars. Everyone there, including you and Alt, are subordinate to him. Is that clear, Hanahan?"

"Yes, sir," Hanahan answered.

"Now put Gripper on the phone," Marshall said.

"Colonel Gripper here."

Marshall repeated what he had just told Hanahan, but he added, "I want you to tell me who else you want with you."

"Douglas Turk," Gripper said without hesitation. "He was coming back into the army after the first of the year. As a brevet lieutenant colonel."

"Where is he now?"

"Here in El Paso, covering the war games for I.N.S."

"Okay," Marshall said, "you've got him. I'll make him a brevet colonel."

"That's fine," Ed answered.

"Now, Ed," Marshall said, "keep the operation as small as possible. Say, something around fifteen hundred men. I'd guess the Germans have no more than a battalion, if that. And Ed, we can't afford the press to get a hold of this. If you have to say something, just have word leaked out that you're after Mexican bandits, who have taken the opportunity to cross over and do some plundering."

"I understand," Ed said.

"What do you need in the way of aircraft?" Marshall asked and quickly added, "We're damn short on them, Ed. Our coasts are wide open. We've got fifty-four operational fighters on the East Coast and forty-five on the West Coast."

"I'm going to use a civilian plane to do our recon," Ed said. "The first few times it won't attract too much attention. But if you could send me two or three Lockheed Hudsons—the kind that we've been ferrying over to England—for a couple of days, I'd appreciate it. I don't want them for the complete operation. Just for a phase of it."

"Have you thought about—"

"General," Ed said. "I've been sitting here in Fitzhugh's office for several hours with nothing to do but look at a map of this area and think about what I'd do if I were the Kraut commander and then what I'd do to stop him. But first I have to find the Krauts; then I'll fight them."

"If you need anything, radio me. It will be a hell of a lot quicker than trying to get me on the phone."

"Yes, sir," Ed answered.

"Ed," Marshall said, "we can't let that column get anywhere near any of our towns or cities."

"I know that, sir."

"Good luck," Marshall said. He put the phone down and said, "Now, Mister President, all we have to do is wait."

Roosevelt nodded. "In some ways that's almost as hard as fighting." Then in a subdued voiced, he said, "No, those who fight are asked to bleed and die."

Lauren opened her eyes. Turk was next to her, sleeping. She could hear his slow, rhythmic breathing. His right hand was on her left breast. The room was filled with darkness. Lauren felt it protected them, almost as if it isolated them from the terrible insanity that had swept over the entire world.

Other than from films, Lauren had no real idea what a war was like. Of course, she had seen newsreels of what was going on in Europe and the Far East. But even if the cameraman happened to photograph a man being shot, it was still an act that she watched without any direct emotional or physical participation.

But now the man who had so passionately invaded her life might, someday soon, run the risk of being killed in front of a photographer's camera. Her throat suddenly tightened. She wanted Doug with her. She wanted him to share her life; it was why she had come to him.

Lauren gently kissed the side of his face.

"I didn't know you were awake," Doug said. "You were so still I thought you were asleep."

"And I thought you were asleep," she told him.

"I must have been for awhile. But—" He didn't want to tell her he had had a nightmare about how Manuel had been killed. "But I decided it would be more enjoyable to squeeze your breasts if I was awake."

She placed her hand over his. "Squeeze, my darling, squeeze!"

Suddenly the phone rang.

Turk bolted up and answered it. He listened for a couple of minutes and then he said, "I'll be there as soon as I can. Yes, I know what it means. Good-bye, General." He put the phone down and switched on the light. "That was Ed. The President just made him a three-star general. We're going to go after the Krauts. Ed is in total command." He began to dress.

She said nothing. He seemed as excited as any schoolboy going off for a day's outing. A new adventure! She didn't understand his attitude. That he could literally go from the warmth of her to the reality of killing was achingly painful. He didn't seem to realize how much she loved him; indeed, how much of herself she had given him.

Turk buckled his belt and was about to go for his jacket when he stopped. "You're awfully quiet," he said, moving closer to the bed.

"And you seem awfully anxious to be on your way," she answered reprovingly.

Turk sat down on the bed and took hold of her hands. "No," he said softly. "I'm only awfully frightened that this may be the last time we'll ever have together."

Lauren said nothing, afraid that if she spoke she'd

weep, or worse, try to convince him not to go. She reached into her pocketbook and took out a small silver figure of a man. "Take it," she told him. "It will bring you luck."

Turk held the figure in his hand. "I won't say good-bye," he told her. He kissed the back of her hands; then, bending over her, he put his lips gently against the bare nipple of each of her breasts. Then he stood up, put his jacket, coat, and hat on.

"Go with God," Lauren said in Spanish.

At the door, Turk looked back at her. "Wait for me, Lauren. Wait for me."

"I will wait, my love," she answered.

By the time Turk reached headquarters, he had managed to put Lauren out of his mind, at least for the time being. Though not a follower of any religion, he knew well the Biblical lines, "A time to love and a time to hate; a time of war and a time of peace." And he knew now was the "time of hate" and the "time of war." There wasn't any other way to keep men and women free. That freedom had to be fought for and won with blood.

Turk entered Fitzhugh's office and found Ed standing in front of the large wall map of the area, studying it.

Hanahan sat off to the side. He was quiet, though attentive. Alt on the other hand stood near the fireplace and nodded to Turk. Fitzhugh was behind his desk.

Without turning to welcome Turk, Ed said, "Colonel, you'll be my operations officer. I don't want to clutter up the mission with a lot of brass. What we're going to need out there are a few good men."

Turk dropped his hat and coat on one of the chairs

and lit a cigarette. He could see the grimace of Hanahan's face caused, no doubt, by Ed's last remark. But everyone was calm. "Any more reports about the column?" he asked.

"Seems to have halted for the night," Ed said. "Now tell me, Harry: What can we put in the field in the way of a mobile force?"

"Some seventy jeeps, mounted with air-cooled .50-caliber machine guns and twelve tanks—all of them light and armed with 37mm antitank guns," Alt said.

"Does anyone know what kind of armor the Krauts have?" Hanahan asked sourly.

Ed turned from the map. "Equal to anything we have, and probably better. But more important is the fact that they're probably experienced troopers and none of our men are." He moved away from the map and sat on the corner of the desk. "We're going to ask for a total of fifteen hundred volunteers from both the red and the blue forces," he said. "And, say, of that number about a hundred officers. None above the rank of captain. As for the enlisted men, I want the meanest, the toughest sons of bitches in the unit. . . . And I don't want fuck-ups. Fuck-ups can't be depended on when the chips are down." He looked at Fitzhugh. "Get on the phone, General, and have those men assembled here within five hours. I want them fully equipped with three days' rations, live ammo, and four grenades per man. Make sure that we're not going to get guys that the company or battalion commanders want to dump."

Fitzhugh immediately picked up the phone.

"I want the area that runs in an arc from El Paso to Deming sealed off. And I mean *seal it off*. Keep that arc parallel to the Southern Pacific tracks. I don't want anyone in the area. I don't want any trains going through it, and I don't want any trucks moving across its highways. Anyone found in that area will immediately be placed in our stockade here."

"You might as well declare martial law," Hanahan said.

"Can't do that," Ed answered, facing Hanahan. "It will tell everyone that something is going on here that shouldn't be. We'll just patrol that area and keep it tight, General," he said, still looking at Hanahan. "That's your responsibility. We've got thousands of horses and mules here and the troops to ride them. I want men in the saddle twenty-four hours a day. No trooper rides alone. Troopers ride in squads of three. You can use half the jeeps and trucks we have to keep the area sealed off. The men involved in your phase of this mission, General, are to be told nothing about the overall objective other than that they are there to protect the area to the north from a large band of Mexican bandits."

"What about the press?" Turk asked. "They're going to know something is up."

"Okay," Ed answered, "you tell me what to do about them. You've been part of them for awhile now."

"Get them the hell out of here!" Hanahan exclaimed.

"Best way to handle them," Turk said, "is to have Hanahan go into the press room and make an announcement that because of the present national emergency the war games have been terminated, and that he is not at liberty to discuss the immediate disposition of any of the troops who were involved in the exercises. Once those last few words are uttered, the reporters will immediately assume that some of the men are going to be shipped to the West Coast, or even to Hawaii. That should help cover any troop movements they might accidentally see."

Ed nodded approvingly.

"What happens when they discover they can't move west or north out of El Paso?" Alt asked.

"Easy," Turk answered. "Get the word on the local radio stations and into the local newspapers that for the next several days all rail traffic west and northbound is being used by the military to transport men and equipment."

"Any other questions about the press?" Ed asked.

Hanahan shook his head.

"I don't have any," Alt said.

Alt put the phone down. "The troops will be here as ordered, General."

Ed nodded and walked back to the map. "According to my rough calculations our area of concentration runs west to Deming and, say, north to Hatch. That's about fourteen hundred square miles. Our first objective is to find the Krauts in that area, contain them there, and then destroy them."

"How long do you think this operation will take?" Alt asked.

"Not more than a day or so," Ed answered. "Anything longer, and the Krauts will have gotten into either Albuquerque or Santa Fe."

"You think that one or both of those cities are its objectives?" Turk asked.

"I'm not sure. But it's an assumption worth making because it enables us to develop a plan of action to stop them."

"Maybe their purpose would be better served by random-hit tactics," Turk countered. "But if we can contain them in that fourteen-hundred-square-mile rectangle, I guess it won't matter what their objective is."

"We're going to put a defense perimeter around Deming and Hatch. All road approaches will be covered by .75's. We've got enough of them for that, and I want those roads mined. That goes for every road leading in and out of those two towns, including the dirt ones. All citizens are to be kept within the town limits. They'll be told that a military exercise is in progress, and that until it's over their movements will be restricted. Alt, you're in command of the defensive operation."

To Turk and others in the room it was obvious that Ed had at least thought out the defensive portions of the operation. Now they were anxious to hear how he intended to stop and destroy the German column.

"Now we get down to where the action will be," Ed said. "First, I'm going to use Turk's friend to do our scouting. He'll be in the air at dawn tomorrow and we'll be ready to move. I'm going to commit what armor we have only when I'm sure we have them. In the meantime, jeeps and mounted troopers and infantry will begin to move out into that rectangle tonight. When we finally make contact with the Krauts, they're going to fight. I don't think they'll take any prisoners and neither will we."

Alt was about to object, but changed his mind and kept silent.

"I'll tell the men I command about that," Ed said. "It's not going to be easy for them out there. But the Krauts must be destroyed. We don't want any of them to get away."

"What are you going to do about rations?" Fitzhugh asked.

"If we need food brought up," Ed answered, "I'll radio and tell you where to bring it. Two more very important points: The Krauts are no doubt going to be monitoring our radio transmissions. I don't want it done in Morse, or any of the other standard codes. I want voice transmissions only, and I want two Indians from the same tribe on a hookup."

"Where the fuck are we going to get Indians?" Hanahan asked.

"Put out a call for them. We've got a few dozen in the ranks. They don't have to work the damn radios, they just have to use the mikes. The Krauts won't be able to understand our transmissions."

Turk smiled. The idea of using Indians on a radio network seemed to come straight out of a Saturday-afternoon Western serial. But in this situation it would work—it was a stroke of genius, he thought.

"The Krauts have to have supplies," Ed went on, "and those supplies—food, water, and fuel—have to be cached somewhere. We've got to find some of them, especially those where the fuel is stored, and destroy them."

"That's going to be tougher than finding the column," Fitzhugh commented.

Ed nodded. "If we get their fuel, we'll force them to stand and fight. We want them to fight. We don't want them to keep moving."

"Finding their supplies will be like looking for that needle in the haystack," Hanahan commented.

Ed agreed. "But Dijon will be able to help out. From the air he'll be able to tell those patterns of rocks or mounds that are out of joint with the general topography of the land. He'll be in direct communication with me, and I will dispatch the troops necessary."

Then with a wry smile, he added, "Of course, an Indian will be flying with Dijon."

The last comment brought a chuckle from everyone in the room.

The phone on the desk rang. Fitzhugh looked up at Gripper.

"Go ahead, answer it," Gripper said.

Fitzhugh picked up the phone and identified himself. He listened for several minutes and then said, "Thanks, Clark. I've got the picture." Then he put the phone down. "That was Major General Gammel," he said. "I've been in touch with him trying to find out about the *City of Cadiz*."

Ed glanced at Turk.

"Clark says that word has come through from his British counterpart that everything is quiet on Auchinleck's southern flank, and M.I.6 is beginning to consider the possibility that Jerry is trying to pull off a ruse, so that he can attack somewhere else. Rommel is now certainly pinpointed in Africa, and any lookalike is being used to bolster the morale of the local troops somewhere else."

"Well, at least we now know that the real Rommel is not going to bother us," Turk commented. "We only have to deal with his lookalike and a Colonel Becker."

"It's not the Rommel lookalike that we have to worry about," Ed said. "It's Colonel Becker. You can bet that he's going to give us one hell of a fight."

"There was a Becker in Spain. Only it was Captain Becker. If it's the same Becker, I don't have to bet," Turk answered. "I know. He was with the Condor division. He's tough and he's an excellent field commander."

"I think we should all chow up now," Ed said. "We've got a long night ahead of us. And Doug, better get yourself some field clothes from the QM. After we eat, I'll go with you and get you to look like a real soldier again."

Turk nodded. He wanted to say something witty but couldn't think of anything that would fit the situation. There was nothing humorous about it that he could think of.

By 1930 hours, enough of a wind was blowing to move the small balls of tumbleweed across the flats. A full, very white moon showed intermittently through the ragged openings in the clouds to the east, over

Greenwood Mountain, silvering the top of it. But when the moon was covered by the clouds they were filled with an eerie light. The Franklin Mountains, black and foreboding, were on the west side of the valley. And it was so cold that everyone's breath steamed in the night air.

Colonel Turk was standing off to General Gripper's right. In front of them were the fifteen hundred officers and men Gripper had ordered assembled. Before he said a word to them, he had ordered them into trucks and had them driven five miles away from the headquarters area—and now they were lined up in ranks, waiting for someone to explain why they were there.

The troops were dressed for combat, complete with World War I metal helmets and knapsacks, and half of them were armed with 1903 bolt-action Springfield rifles, while the other half carried the newer-issued M-1. All had bayonets, extra ammunition, and the four grenades Gripper had ordered.

Gripper climbed up onto the hood of a jeep. "Can everyone see me?" he called out.

Everyone could.

"Can everyone hear me?" he asked.

A few men raised their hands and complained that they couldn't hear him too clearly.

"Okay, move in closer and form a semicircle around the front of the jeep," Gripper told them.

Turk took his position at the left side of the vehicle. Just before Gripper had started to address the men, he was thinking about Lauren. After he had gotten his clothing from the quartermaster, he had gone back to Fitzhugh's office and had phoned to warn her to say nothing about the German column to anyone, especially not to any of the reporters who might ask where he had gone.

"I love you," she's said.

"I love you too."

"Take care of yourself."

He had promised her he would.

It occurred to Turk that if he should not come back, Lauren would most certainly begin to ask questions. She would want to know what happened to him. She might even want to claim his body. Then what? She most certainly would have to tell someone about the Germans and that—

The sound of Ed's voice burst in on Turk's thoughts. "Now listen up," Ed said. "I'm not going to repeat what I'm about to say. You've been assembled here for a particular mission. You are soon going to be fighting for real. You'll be fighting Krauts. That's right, men, the war games have been terminated."

The men began to murmur amongst themselves.

"Better quiet down and listen," Ed said. A Kraut column has come north out of Mexico and it's bivouacked for the night somewhere not too far from here. It has already destroyed a Southern Pacific train. Mainly, it seems, to get fuel. We're assuming the Krauts are going to try to capture and hold Albuquerque or maybe even Santa Fe. But the truth is that we don't know where it is or where it's going. We're going to have to find the Krauts first and then destroy them." Ed paused and took a deep breath before he continued. "We don't know its strength. But we know it's mobile and it's equipped with the best Kraut scout cars made. Eight-wheel jobs that mount anything from 20mm cannons to three-inch pieces and the usual Kraut heavy machine gun. I don't know how many men are in the column. There could be some infantry to ride along with them. But usually there are four men to a scout car. So far, any questions?"

"Yeah," one of the troopers called out. "How the fuck did the Krauts get here?"

"Don't have time to tell you men that now," Ed answered. "They're here and we're going to get them before they do too much damage."

"Why the hell can't the Air Force just bomb the shit out of them?" another man asked.

"Because every plane we have is needed on either the West or East Coast."

"Do we take any prisoners?" one of the officers asked.

"No," Gripper answered. "And don't think that the Krauts will take any, either."

Again there was a murmuring among the men, but this time it sounded more agitated to Turk.

"There's no sense bullshitting you men," Ed said. "The Krauts are here on a suicide mission. They know they can't go anywhere."

"Then why the fuck are they here?" a trooper shouted.

Ed looked down at Turk. "You better come here with me," he said in a lower voice, "and tell these men what the score is—at least how you see it."

Turk clambered up alongside Ed.

"I'll let Colonel Turk answer the question," Ed said.

"It's my guess," Turk said, "the Krauts are trying to scare us out of the war in Europe. They figure that if they can show us how strong they are by making an incursion into our country, we'll stay out of the war in Europe and let them knock over England and Russia."

"Shit," a trooper yelled, "they sure took the short odds."

The men agreed with that.

"Okay," Ed said, "we fight to kill and we don't surrender. We fight to kill," he repeated, "and no surrender! Now let me hear that loud and clear."

Shouting, the troopers repeated Ed's words.

"Now listen up," he told them, "—we don't have time for elaborate organization. Except for the scout teams, who'll go out looking for where the Kraut supplies are stored, the rest of us will close on the Kraut column once we locate it. We're going to fight them our style. We're going to beat the shit out of them—isn't that right, men?"

The troopers roared back their assent.

"Okay," Ed told them, "better spread out, get some rest. Because in less than an hour, you'll be moving out. There's one other thing: Radio communication not carried on by Indians will be in pig Latin. Most of you guys know some variation of it. Use it, along with as much slang as you can mix in. I don't want the Krauts to know what we're saying." He wished them good luck, then called all the officers forward and jumped down from the jeep's hood.

Ed didn't waste any words. Hunkering next to the jeep, he used his trench knife to draw a rough map of the area from El Paso north to Hatch. "I don't have a specific plan of action," he told the assembled officers. "We want to get at the Krauts as quickly as possible. Maybe we can just beat them in an old-fashioned shoot-out, but I doubt it. They're experienced. They know how to move and when to stand and fight. We're going to have to improvise as we go along.

"Okay, I want a force of one hundred and forty men to leave immediately and go straight north. But stay to the east of the highway. About ten miles below Hatch, swing west across the highway and establish positions on the high ground overlooking the valley. Set up a battery of .75's with a field of fire that won't let anything pass."

"I'll get on that," a captain volunteered.

"Take a radio with you," Ed said.

Within a matter of minutes, Ed had made his assignments. He had units of approximately one hundred and forty men covering every sector of the valley between El Paso and Hatch. Some were equipped with machine guns in addition to the .75's. He formed two units consisting of jeeps, which were further divided into groups of twos and threes to search for the German supply caches. The larger units were assigned letters A through J. Ed took A company for himself. The smaller units used the letter of the larger unit they belonged to and a number.

"I'll hold the tanks under my command," Ed told the officers. "Once we locate the Krauts I'll converge on them. All previous positions will be abandoned and all troops committed to the one engagement."

"You think there will only be one big fight?" a lieutenant asked.

"Yes," Ed answered. "Only one. Neither the Krauts nor we can afford a couple of slugfests. But I wouldn't rule out a few skirmishes before the big one."

"Maybe once they know we're after them, they'll try to get back to Mexico," a captain suggested.

"They might try," Ed said fiercely, "but we're not going to let them. They came here to die, and by the living God, die they will. Any more questions?" he asked, looking at the men.

There weren't any.

"Then saddle up," Ed said, standing erect, "and let's get going!" The officers saluted and he returned the courtesy. When he and Turk were finally alone, Gripper commented, "A couple of bombers would make a hell of a difference."

"That's like saying if we had a fully trained armored division we could take the Krauts hands-down."

Ed nodded. "Doug, we're going to have to take them. The President wants them wiped out."

"It's going to cost," Turk said. "Most of those guys have no idea what the real thing is like, what it's like to fight men who from the time they were children have been trained to fight for and, if the situation demands, die for the Fatherland."

Ed pulled out a pack of cigarettes, offered it to Turk, and took one for himself. "This is the last place I figured I'd be fighting Krauts," he said, blowing smoke through his nose.

"I wouldn't have figured this place either," Turk answered. "Not in a million years."

# 18

*December 8, 1941*

The dawn came gray and ugly, with clouds resting on the tops of the mountains on either side of the valley. Turk had managed to get a few hours' sleep. Not since his internment in France had he slept out of doors and it was even more unpleasant than he remembered, especially since it was very cold and he had had nothing more than an army blanket with which to cover himself. He had slept sitting up, with his back resting against the tank that served as Gripper's command post. Every one of Turk's joints was stiff. Though he was trim, he wasn't used to roughing it anymore. He was grossly out of condition. But that would change if he managed to survive the coming battle.

Turk pulled himself up to a standing position, but kept the blanket around his shoulders as he walked a few paces to the radio-equipped jeep where Ed was standing.

"How does it feel to be a general?" Turk asked.

"Might as well ask a boy how it feels to be a man," Ed answered. "He sure as hell doesn't know until he is one, and I sure as hell won't know until I fight this battle. The three fucking stars don't make me a general. You know that and I know that." Then he added with a wry smile, "But let's hope these men don't know that. They have to believe I'm the best fucking general that this man's army ever had."

"It's cold as a witch's twat," Turk commented, rubbing his hands.

"Got some reports in from a few of the units," Ed said. "The Krauts tore up a lot of railroad track north of here. They killed everyone at the Tobin ranch and burned the buildings. Killed most of the cattle too. And blew a bridge over the Little Yellow Creek." As he spoke, he pointed to each of the places on a large map tacked onto a piece of plywood. "They didn't have to kill the Tobins."

Turk shrugged. "They did worse in Spain."

"The telephone lines have been cut between El Paso and Las Cruces. But I've ordered crews out from Bliss to repair them."

"Dijon in the air?"

Ed nodded. "But he won't be for long," he added. "Another bad weather system is closing in fast. Dijon says it's already snowing at the two-thousand-foot level."

Turk shook his head. "Not much luck," he commented.

"We're going to have to find the Krauts ourselves," Ed said, starting to walk back toward the tank. "The only thing worth talking about is that all our units are in position."

Suddenly a voice came over the radio.

Ed did an immediate about-face and returned to the jeep. He looked at the man, who was standing by to translate.

"Pueblo," the man said. "First jeep unit, squad C, found a supply dump."

"Where?" Ed asked.

"Coordinate Jack fiver."

"That puts it here," Gripper said, making an X on the map. "That's in the middle of nowhere."

"They're destroying it," the translator said. "It's food and water."

"Good work!" Ed exclaimed. "Tell them damn good work!" Then, pointing to the X said, "That's up by Gold Springs. Near the Duddly Ranch, according to the map." He asked the operator to get him Dijon. "Listen," Gripper said, "one of my units just knocked out a food-and-water supply cache at Jack fiver. Are you anywhere near it?"

The Indian translated as fast as Ed spoke.

"It's off to my right," Dijon answered. "I can see your men. You have two jeeps. Hey, they're going to come head-on with a Kraut scout car."

"Warn squad C that a Kraut scout car is coming up in front of them," Ed ordered.

The radio operator immediately switched frequencies and the translator got on the mike.

"The rest of the column has to be close by," Ed said, looking at Turk.

"One jeep has been knocked out," the translator said.

"Switch back to Dijon," Ed said.

The translator with Ed came back on. "One jeep is burning," he said. "Second one is heading east. The scout car isn't following. It has stopped where the supply cache was. Two Krauts are looking it over. Can't hang around here; strong winds and snow have come off the mountains. Heading back to Biggs. Over."

Ed unwrapped a cigar and began to chew on it. "There must be more than one food-and-water cache," he said. "Besides, if forced to, they could live off the land for a few days. The real question is whether or not the rest of the column is close-by. So far they've maintained radio silence. I'd do the same thing. Once they begin to broadcast we can get a fix on them." He looked at the map again. "Once that scout car gets back to the main column, Colonel Becker is going to know we're on to him. He's going to figure that we're going to be looking for his supply caches and will probably find a few more. Now Turk, tell me what you would try to do if you were a Kraut colonel?"

Turk stepped closer to the map. He didn't feel very clever. He thought a minute and said, "I'd either make a run back to the border, or I'd go where I'd be least expected to go."

"Going where you'd least be expected is something I'd like to hear more about.

"It would have to be Las Cruces or El Paso," Turk said, surprised at his own words.

"That's exactly right," Ed responded. "That's where he could do the most damage and give Hitler something to crow about in Berlin. Becker has probably guessed that we fortified Hatch and Deming and that we figured he'd make a run north for Albuquerque or Santa Fe if everything went his way. But now he doesn't know what we have to throw against him, and he can do more damage by doubling back toward Las Cruces and El Paso. Let's hope we can cut him off before he gets near one or the other place."

Ed ordered all units to converge on coordinate Able ten, which would put them twenty miles to the west of Las Cruces. "All radio transmission will, as of now, be carried on in English."

Almost immediately Hanahan was on the radio, demanding, "What the hell is going on?"

"Just sit tight," Ed answered. "And tell Harry to do the same." Then turning to Turk, he said, "Better get these tanks cranked up. We're going to have to do some fast moving in the next few hours."

Turk issued the necessary orders to put the tank unit

into motion.

Ed took the lead. Turk was in the second tank. Because of the rough terrain, they couldn't do more than fifteen miles an hour. Going at that speed put them a good four or five hours away from the coordinates Ed had given to the other units.

Turk rode with the hatch cover open. The sky was still gray, but the snow hadn't come. The combination of wind and movement made it seem colder than it was. Turk's eyes teared and he had to wipe them frequently.

Ed got on the radio and said, "Listen up, all units: I want those .75's available for use as soon as I arrive."

Turk guessed that Ed was purposefully broadcasting to worry Becker. There was no way those mule-packed .75's would be ready for use before late afternoon, or maybe not even by sundown. The possibility of having to fight a night battle against experienced troops worried Turk.

Ed came on the radio again. "Have one squadron of dive bombers stand by at Biggs," he said. "Load with two-hundred-and-fifty-pound bombs."

Turk hoped that Hanahan and Alt wouldn't suddenly come on the air and ask Ed if he had lost his mind, or worse, tell him flat out than there wasn't one serviceable plane at Briggs, let alone a squadron of dive bombers.

An hour after Ed's force got under way, two tank commanders reported mechanical trouble and were forced to drop out. That lessened their firepower by almost twenty percent. There wasn't any way that they could be repaired in time for the coming battle. Figuring they'd need every man when they met the Krauts, Turk ordered their crews aboard the other tanks.

The combination of wind and stinging cold was too

much for Turk; he dropped back inside the tank and closed the hatch cover. The noise inside was worse that the din in any metal-working factory he had ever visited. Everything inside the metal shell either squeaked, groaned, or banged. To communicate with the driver, he used a series of taps with his hands and feet. When the time came, he'd do the same to the gunner. He himself would fire the machine gun. Each tank carried twenty rounds for the 37mm cannon and a thousand rounds for the .50-caliber mounted directly in front of him inside the turret.

Turk was worried about the tank's high silhouette. The Italians had used similar tanks in Spain. They were easy to spot and if the artillery was within range, they made good targets. But German tanks were designed to give a minimum silhouette, and even if they were in range of the artillery they were hard to knock out.

Using pig Latin, Ed was on the radio again. This time he was attempting to pinpoint the position of several of the other units, especially the two groups of jeeps. He was beginning to use them for reconnaissance, and activity for which they were ideally suited.

Turk was frightened; his throat was dry and his stomach growled. He didn't know how he'd come out of the coming fight—or if he'd come out of it at all. He took several deep breaths. All the other times he had been under fire, he had had no one to come back to. But this time was different. There was Lauren. He wanted to come back to her a whole man. The possibility of losing an arm or a leg made him sweat. He'd never want himself to be a burden to her. . . .

The tank suddenly dropped into a gully and clawed its way out.

With the back of his hand, Turk wiped the sweat out of his eyes. He wasn't the least bit ashamed of being frightened. He had been under fire too many times not to know that only the true killers weren't afraid.

Turk found himself wondering if Lauren realized how important she was to him. Though he had told her many, many times how much he loved her, he still wasn't sure she realized how deeply committed to her he was, especially now that she had taken such a risk to come to him. He fished out the small silver charm Lauren had given him. It was shaped like a man, with eyes, mouth, and nose formed by cutouts in the metal.

Ed came on the radio again. "Recon units, keep a sharp lookout. Don't close with the enemy. I repeat, Don't make any attempt to engage the enemy."

Ed was becoming edgy. Turk couldn't blame him. He was throwing dice in a big roll. If he crapped out, either Las Cruces or El Paso would be in flames in a matter of hours. Maybe both, if Becker could break through the defense line Gripper was attempting to throw up between the Krauts and these two cities.

Ed was forced to call for a fuel stop at 1100 hours. Despite the wind and the cold the men left the tanks to stretch their cramped limbs.

Turk used his hands to shield a match from the wind and light a cigarette; then he walked over to Gripper. "You think the Krauts are refueled by now?" he asked.

"Probably," Ed answered, taking Turk's cigarette to light one of his own. "Too bad we can't carry a fifty-five-gallon drum with us. But one shot from a Kraut rifle and the fucking tank would go up like a torch."

Turk agreed and said, "I'll see what I can do to get this refueling over as quickly as possible."

Suddenly Ed's tank driver popped his head out of the turret. "General, got a recon unit on the air. They've spotted the Kraut column."

Ed climbed aboard, while Turk followed halfway into the turret.

"Say again," Ed said. "Say again position." He waited a moment. "Harry—four, got it! How fast are they moving?" He looked up at Turk. "Slow. Not more than ten miles an hour."

"Why that slow?" Turk asked.

Ed asked the same question. Again he looked up at Turk, and in a tight voice he said, "The trucks are hauling antitank guns. Maybe Becker is trying to conserve fuel."

"Maybe, and maybe he's playing fox with us."

"Can you see how many armored cars are in the column?" Ed asked.

"Count—"

The transmission ended abruptly. Ed tried to raise the recon unit on alternate frequencies. "No dice," he said, shaking his head. "The Krauts probably got them." He motioned Turk to get out of the tank, and then he came out of the turret with his map. "Okay, the Krauts are here." He made a penciled X on the map. "That puts them two miles west of the town of Dona Ana—and we're six miles southwest of where they are. There's no way we're going to save that town. No way on God's green earth!"

Turk remained silent.

"Unless Becker turns his column south and runs it down along Highway 85, he's not going to go for Las Cruces," Ed said.

"He could come at it from the east," Turk said. "He might try that, thinking that we wouldn't be prepared for that kind of movement."

"Christ, we're not prepared for anything!" Ed exclaimed. He threw away his cigarette, and pulled out another cigar and began to chew on it.

"We should be ready to roll in about ten minutes,"

Turk said.

For several minutes Ed studied the map; then he said, "I'm going to order our recon units to attack the column." He took the unlit cigar out of his mouth and used it as a pointer. "Becker is here."

The low rumble of thunder suddenly came down on them from the northeast.

Ed winced.

Four more booms of thunder sounded over the valley and a large black column of smoke erupted toward the low clouds.

"That's got to be seen in Las Cruces and El Paso. Maybe even in Hatch," Turk said.

Ed nodded. "As soon as I'm finished here I'll get on the radio and order Alt and Hanahan to pull back to Bliss and tell the local press that—"

"Tell them that two bombers collided over Dona Ana and caused heavy damage and casualties," Turk said. "Tell them that for security reasons civilians aren't allowed to go there for the present time."

"You transmit that to Hanahan and Alt," Ed said. "but let's go back to what I was saying." His cigar was still pointed at the map. "I'm going to order the recon units to make hit-and-run attacks at the column. I want to keep Becker from swinging back toward Las Cruces and to draw him toward the San Andres Mountains, here to the east. I want to put those mountains at Becker's back and come at him from three sides, or in an arc."

"There won't be too many jeeps left, if any, once Becker begins to suspect what they're doing."

"Don't suppose there will be," Ed said. "But can you think of a better way to herd the Krauts where we'll be able to fight them?"

Turk shook his head.

"I want it over before nightfall," Ed said. "Come

darkness and they might slip by us, or worse, abandon their equipment and try to get over the mountains."

Turk looked down the line of tanks. They were all gassed up and ready to roll.

"Okay," Ed said, "let's move out!"

The sound of gun firing started to come from the northeast.

Turk's radio was tuned to the assigned recon frequency. More and more jeeps were reporting contact with the enemy.

Becker broke radio silence. German crackled on all frequencies, the Spanish now dropped as the soldiers reverted to their native tongue.

"Doug, can you make it out?" Ed asked.

"Something about changing direction," Turk answered.

"I got that too," Ed said.

"They must be transmitting to a station in Mexico," Turk responded.

Ed didn't answer.

"Those fuckers have big stuff mounted on them," one of the men reported. "Gon' shoot us to pieces!"

Even over the radio Turk was able to hear the staccato bark of U.S. .50-caliber machine guns, quickly followed by the sharp snap of a German shell falling somewhere near the jeep.

Turk recognized the sound of German fire. It hadn't the explosive boom of other artillery. Even the Kraut small-arms fire had a snap to it.

Sometimes, after the fighting was over in Spain, those sounds would become part of a nightmare. Part of what it had been like to fight from building to building, from floor to floor, in the woods and in the open fields. And now he was doing it again.

Suddenly Ed came on the radio. "Becker is turning toward Las Cruces," he shouted. Then he rattled off the numbers of three of the recon units closest to the German column. "Turn the Krauts east again," he yelled. "Turn those bastards east."

"General," Turk said, "we're close enough to make an intercept."

"No way," Ed answered. "That's what Becker would like. No way!"

By 1300 hours several of the mounted units began to come into view. They were still a few miles away to the north, but the dust they raised was clearly visible.

"The Krauts are swinging east," one of the recon units reported.

"Where are the other two jeeps?" Ed asked.

"Shot up," came the laconic answer.

Turk had already seen the wreckage of a half-dozen jeeps. Most of them had taken direct hits and had been turned into careening masses of flames before any of the men in them knew what had happened. But the driver of one of them had purposely crashed into one of the Kraut trucks, turning it into a torch also. The truck was over on its side and still burning.

Ed asked for any one of the recon units to give him a fix on the Germans.

"This is Dog six," one of them answered. "Krauts are headin' east northeast. Say, about Peter twelve."

Ed came on the radio. "That's going to put them into Flint Canyon."

Turk flicked the mike on. "General, my guess is that Becker doesn't know the country. I don't think he has maps for it."

"Could be," Ed answered.

Several more jeeps were shot up.

Ed began to press his mounted troops more. "I'm going to need every goddamn gun I can get my hands on," he told Turk. "Start swinging toward Peter twelve."

Turk first caught sight of the German column on a low ridgeline. It was moving vertically across the front of him. The light behind the Germans was beginning to gray and the mountains, normally ochre or red sandstone in the bright sunlight, were shading into blackness.

"Krauts dead ahead!" Ed shouted.

"See them," Turk answered, suddenly aware that the terrain had become rougher. He was bouncing around more than he had been.

"Don't think they've spotted us yet," Ed said.

Suddenly three of the armored cars swung away from the column, increased their speed, and headed toward the mounted troops.

"Warn them," Turk yelled into the mike. "Give those poor bastards some time to make a run for it."

"Units two through eleven. . . . All units two through eleven. This is Mustang. . . . Listen up! Krauts heading your way. Three armored cars heading your way fast." He repeated the message three times.

Turk looked at his watch. It was 1515 hours. He figured the Krauts would close with Ed's men by 1545 if they were lucky enough to find them quickly. A half-hour should give them some time to get a few .75's set up and the rest of the troopers scattered.

"We're going to go after Becker now," Ed said. "Right front interline, march." The column fanned out in a horizontal line.

The heavy boom of a .75 thundered against the mountains. Another explosion followed by the sudden eruption of a plume of smoke. Instantly the snaplike sounds of German fire followed. Machine guns on both sides opened up.

"At least we got one of those bastards," Turk said into the mike.

"Listen up," Ed said. "We've got to make every round count."

Suddenly the German column slowed down and the armored cars began to change positions on the ridgeline.

"Good God," Ed said. "Becker's going to try and fight us from that ridgeline!"

"He sure as hell is," Turk answered. He could see the German antitank guns being wheeled into position.

"Here it comes!" Ed exclaimed.

The first shells from the antitank guns landed short and blew up portions of the rock surface, splattering it over Gripper's and Turk's tanks.

"Break formation," Ed ordered. "Keep changing course!"

Turk was sweating now. He signaled his driver to swing to the right and give him maximum speed. Within two minutes he changed course. The other tanks were doing the same.

Becker's guns were laying down a pattern of fire, sweeping from left to right.

"Can't keep pushing this baby like this," the driver shouted up at Turk. "We'll burn the fuckin' engine out, and if we don't do that, we'll run out of gas."

"General," Turk said, "suggest we pull back and refuel."

"Affirmative," Ed answered. "Unit one . . . Withdraw unit one. Withdraw!"

The tanks lumbered back in the direction from which they had come.

The German firing ceased. Not one tank in Gripper's force had gotten close enough to the Germans to fire a round.

Even before Turk and Ed could scramble out of their tanks, a recon jeep reported two German armored cars coming down at them from the northwest.

Ed ordered the tanks to scatter toward the southwest.

"Just those two could pick us off one by one," Turk called to Gripper.

"We've got to get those Kraut cars before they get us, Ed said. "The following four tanks will go after them. I want two on a Kraut car: One to draw fire and the other to go after their wheels. Hit their fucking wheels, or if you're lucky get around in their rear, where their gas tank is." He called off the names of four tank commanders and gave them the task of destroying the German armored cars.

Suddenly a jeep reported it was close-by.

"Follow the tanks in," Ed said. "Keep that fifty of yours going."

Turk and the other tankers swung around toward the northeast again and ground to a halt. They watched the four tanks and the jeep move toward the German cars.

The two German vehicles were moving almost parallel to one another, with about twenty yards between them.

"If you can," Ed told his tankers, "one of you get yourself between the Kraut's lines of fire."

"You tankers keep that big gun busy for a bit," the man in the recon jeep said, "and I'll do some fancy driving." He swung around in a circle.

The rough terrain protected the tanks from the German gunners. Whenever the Germans got off a round at a tank, one of the other tanks clanked down at them and fired its 37mm. But the shells bounced off the front and side armor.

Suddenly the jeep was coming in from behind the armored cars. The machine gunner in the jeep fired at the wheels of one car and then at the other. As he passed between them the two vehicles went out of control, veering toward one another, and they trapped the jeep between them. Two tanks went in for the kill. They fired point-blank into the gas tanks. Before the sound of the explosion died, a huge ball of fire burst over the three vehicles. Several more explosions followed, and the fire sent billows of black smoke into the wind.

"General, south of you to the west and east," someone shouted on the radio. "Kraut cars coming up fast."

Turk swung his body around in the turret just as one of the armored cars dipped below a low hill to the west. He got on the radio. "Mustang, we better get the hell out of here!"

Ed gave the order to move. "We'll head northwest."

"No way, Mustang," Turk said. "Becker is sending four more cars against us."

As they closed, the armored cars to the west and east took advantage of every piece of level ground, firing with deadly accuracy.

Two tanks were hit. One burst into flames instantly, and the other spun around on its one good tread until the driver was able to cut the engine. The men scrambled out of the disabled tank only to be cut down by German machine guns.

"If we can't get any more speed out of these steel traps," a tank commander shouted over the phone, "we'll all be shot to pieces."

Ed didn't answer.

The four armored cars coming at them from the north would soon be in range of the tanks.

"Turk," Ed said, "those fucking cars are going to cut in front of us."

"We're getting low on fuel," Turk's driver shouted up.

The armored cars closing from the east and west had stopped firing, but were moving in closer and closer.

Turk guessed they were, at the very most, a mile away. With their heavier weapons they could fire from that range and make a kill. But it would be a much surer kill if they could cut that range in half. And with the kind of armament the tanks carried, they didn't have any chance of stopping the Germans.

The firing began again—this time from the armored cars swinging in front of the tanks.

"We're like fucking ducks in a pond!" Turk shouted.

A tank on the far left took a hit, went over on its right side, and burst into flame.

"We've got to try to double back around them," Ed said.

A German round landed just to the right of Turk's tank. The force of the explosion popped several rivets and they whipped around like pieces of shrapnel until their energy was spent.

"Anyone hit?" Turk asked.

The driver and gunner reported minor grazes.

"We got plating loose," the driver added. "It's banging like a son of a bitch."

"Turk, you okay?" Ed asked.

"Okay," Turk answered.

Then suddenly there were three explosions in front of them, just short of where the armored cars were.

The German commanders were on the radio again.

"There's a couple of our .75's out there," Turk said.

Another round from a .75 came. It was a direct hit on one of the four armored cars. It burst into flame and kept moving with the other cars. Then several secondary explosions wrecked it.

"The other fuckers are turning away!" Ed shouted.

"We still got those guys behind us," Turk said.

"Let's see if we can bring them into the field of fire of the .75's" Gripper answered.

The Germans fired from behind again.

A tank on the other side of Gripper came to an abrupt halt. A plume of flames, like a long, vertical tail, leaped out of its rear. The turret cover was thrown open; the commander and the driver scrambled out and leaped to the ground.

One of the German machine gunners began firing at them.

"I'm going to try for them," Turk said into the mike. Before Ed could answer he signaled the driver to make a right turn. "Fire at the tires," he ordered the gunner. "Just keep firing!"

Turk's sudden change of direction confused the Germans. The machine gun stopped firing.

Turk threw open the turret cover, pushed his head out, and shouted to the men from the destroyed tank to climb aboard. His gunner continued to fire. A round caught the right front tire of the armored car bearing down from the west. The car heeled over to one side and came to a halt.

"Good work," Turk shouted down to his gunner.

The men ran alongside the tank, grabbed hold of anything they could, put their hands on and came aboard.

"You're going to have to hang on," Turk shouted. "There's no room inside for you."

"Thanks!" the commander yelled back. "Better to hang on than to be chewed up back there by a Kraut machine gun."

Ed moved in the direction of the burning armored car.

Suddenly there was a burst of German on the radio.

"I got that," Turk said. "Becker is ordering the other car to return to the ridge. But first it's going back to pick up the men from the car my gunner hit and then blow it up."

"Kraut thoroughness," Ed answered; then he added, "Let's go find that .75 and see what we have left." On the way he called for another rendezvous with fuel trucks.

The .75, it turned out, had been taken off a dead mule by the men from a jeep recon vehicle. They had found about ten rounds and were coming up to join Gripper when they saw the Kraut armored cars.

"We just decided to cream them" the driver, a sergeant, said with a flat voice. "They really did a job on our guys some miles back toward the northwest. There's dead all over the place. Men, horses, and mules."

"How many men, do you figure?" Ed asked.

"Two maybe three hundred men."

"No wounded?"

The man shook his head. "The Krauts worked them over with machine guns."

"Thanks for saving us," Ed said, offering the man his hand.

"General," the sergeant asked, "we gonna take them or they gonna take us?"

"We're going to take them, sergeant," Ed answered. "But it's going to cost."

Ed put his hand on the sergeant's shoulder and squeezed it. Then he turned to Turk and said, "We're not going to have much more daylight. We better get all of our men in front of that Kraut-held ridge."

"I'll set it up," Turk said.

"Picking up those men was a damn brave thing to do," Ed commented.

He pointed to the sergeant and his men. "They did the brave thing," Turk said. "It took guts to take on four armored cars with one damn .75. They could have made a run for it, and no one would have been the wiser."

"They sure did save our ass," Ed agreed, going back to his tank.

He got on the radio, trying to put together a status

situation. There were six tanks left and ten recon jeeps, and about six hundred mounted and unmounted troopers.

The Germans outgunned them, even though they had lost five of their armored cars. And Becker probably had just as many men capable of fighting.

Hanahan suddenly came on the radio, shouting for information on what was happening. "People in Las Cruces are complaining about hearing gunfire and seeing many columns of black smoke."

"Tell them we're using live ammo," Ed said.

"What the hell *is* going on?" Hanahan asked.

"You just try to get me some planes from Marshall," Gripper answered. "I'll take anything I can get. Over."

Lauren had slept very little the night before, and now in the late afternoon she was standing at the window looking down on a small park.

The news coming over the radio was grim. The Japanese had bombed Clark Field in the Philippines and had succeeded in destroying half of the Army Air Corps assigned to the Far East. And Lieutenant General John L. De Witt, head of the Western Defense Command, was quoted as having said about San Francisco, "Death and destruction are likely to come to this city at any moment. These planes were over our community for a definite period. They were enemy planes. I mean Japanese planes. They were tracked out sea. Why bombs were not dropped I do not know." There were also reports of huge sea battles raging somewhere southeast of the Hawaiian Islands.

Just once the newscaster mentioned something about military units holding extensive maneuvers in an area around Las Cruces—and Lauren had trembled.

A sudden knock startled Lauren. Her first thought

was that Walther's colleagues had caught up with her.

There was another knock.

"Who is it?" she called out.

"Turk's friends," a man answered.

Afraid that something had happened to Doug, Lauren ran to the door, unlocked it, and swung it open. "Is he all right?" she cried. "Is Doug all right?"

"Mrs. Zwig," the taller of the two men said, "we're federal agents. Will you please come with us?"

"What? Why?" she asked. "I've done nothing wrong." She began to back into the room.

"Mrs. Zwig," the other agent said. "This can be as easy or as difficult as you wish. We are fully prepared, if necessary, to handcuff and take you by force."

From the tone of the man's voice, she knew he meant it.

"That won't be necessary," she said, picking up her coat, hat, and bag. "But could you tell me where I'm being taken to?"

"No," the same man answered. "We can't."

Lauren left the room, walked between the two federal agents. In the lobby they were joined by the two agents escorting Dijon.

Ed's force dug in behind a low hill facing the German-held ridgeline. To prevent the Germans from slipping past them, he spread observation posts, at intervals of two hundred yards, halfway between his position and Becker's, along their entire front. The men manning the OPs were ordered to fire signal flares if they saw or heard anything suspicious.

Ed also dug in his remaining .75 directly behind the hill, giving it an effective field of fire that just fell short of the German-held ridge. He placed all of his .50-caliber machine guns in positions to cover the distance between the OPs and the ridge with intersecting fields of fire.

"Neither one of us can make a move tonight," Ed told Turk and the rest of his commanders. "Tomorrow morning will spell it all out for us and the Krauts." Then he suggested that everyone get some sleep.

Most of the men had already stretched out against their tanks, or jeeps. All of the mounted troopers remained with their horses, who were in need of food and water.

Turk lit a cigarette and handed it to Gripper.

"Thanks," Ed said. "But what I could really use is a good bolt of bourbon."

"Right now I'd settle for hot coffee," Turk answered, rubbing his hands.

"Don't think the Krauts are faring any better," Ed answered.

"Probably not," Turk suggested.

"Here we are engaged with the Krauts," Ed commented, blowing smoke into the cold night air, "and some four thousand miles from here the Japs are kicking the shit out of us."

It was the first time either one of them had mentioned the war that had come so suddenly.

"This is the only war around, at least the only one that's real to us," Turk answered.

"It's real enough," Ed said with a weary sigh. "I'm going to visit our guys out there. Care to come along?"

"Sure," Turk answered.

The two of them crushed their cigarettes under their heels and started up the hill.

For the better part of an hour Ed and Turk went from post to post. None of the men had seen or heard anything from the German position.

"It's almost like they're not there," one man said. "Can't see much 'cause of the clouds, and I don't hear anything. But I sure as hell do smell food. The Krauts must be cooking some kind of meat and I know I smelled coffee. But the wind has got to be right to pick up the smells."

"There'll be hot chow for all of us," Ed told the man, "once this is over. We'll all go down to Juárez and drink up a storm."

"Sure enough, General?"

"Trooper," Ed said, "you have my word."

When Turk and Ed were just about to go over the crest of the hill, Turk stopped and looked toward the German position. "Either that man was imagining, or he has a very keen sense of smell," Turk said. "But if it's the latter, then it explains why Becker headed for this place."

"A supply cache!" Ed exclaimed.

Turk nodded. "Maybe something more. I'm just guessing, but suppose there was a cave on the other side of that ridge?"

"A cave?"

"A large one that could hold a great many men. They could cook in there and the smells wouldn't be obvious to anyone, unless the wind was just right and the person had one hell of a good nose. The wind seems right, and that soldier seemed pretty sure of himself. . . ."

"With enough money and ammo," Ed said, "they could put up a hell of a fight."

"Absolutely."

"Becker and the generals in Berlin know that we have to keep this whole thing quiet. Make believe it never happened. The longer Becker is able to prolong the fight, the harder it will be for us—for Washington—to pretend that the Germans haven't invaded the United States.

Before Ed spoke again, they moved off the crest and

back to where Gripper's tank was parked. "Becker knows we're going to have to try and blow him off that ridge come morning. And he knows we can't do it with what we have. We've already done more damage to him that I thought we could without any air support."

"Ed," Turk said, "twenty men on top of Angel Mountain could make one hell of a difference. We could set up a couple of machine guns, throw grenades, and do some real damage with satchel charges. You come at them from the front. That's where they'll be expecting to be hit. But we'll be above them."

Ed rubbed his grizzled chin. "You know you'll have even less of a chance then of ever coming out of this alive from up there. Once Becker realizes he's taking fire from behind, he'll send men after you."

"We've got to knock the Krauts out," Turk said. "We've got to do it before it becomes too much for Washington to deal with."

"Okay," Ed said. "Do it! Ask for volunteers."

"I want all of them with BARs," Turk said. "And I'll take a satchel charge and rope for each of us. We'll use horses to get us around to the other end."

Gripper nodded.

"After I pick the men, I want to take a good look at the map. As far as I remember, Angel Mountain is just a high point along a block fault."

"That's what it is," Ed said. "You'll have to go about ten miles around to get to the opposite side. The tricky bit will be getting into a position above the Krauts."

"We'll do it," Turk answered.

"Okay, choose your men," Ed told him.

Within a half-hour, Turk had the twenty men assembled and ready to move out. His driver and gunner wanted to go with him, but he convinced them to stay with Gripper.

"Looks to me like your best bet for getting on top

would be from the north," Ed said, pointing to the map with an unlit cigar. "The gradient isn't as steep that way as it is from the east or south."

Turk agreed and pointed to a group of contour lines squeezed together, resembling a finger with the ball ending on the top of the rock fault. "That'll be steeper but quicker," he said. "I want to be up on top to give the men some rest before the fighting begins."

"I'm going to hit them before dawn," Ed told him. "I don't want the sun—assuming there will be sun tomorrow—in my eyes when I attack."

"Sunrise will be about 0700," Turk commented. "It will take another thirty minutes or so before the sun will come up over the mountain."

"I'll begin the attack at 0630," Ed said.

The two of them synchronized their watches.

"Good luck." Ed shook Turk's hand.

"We're all going to need luck," Turk answered, and swinging into the saddle, he led his men west, away from the bivouac area.

The ride around to the other side of the mountain took five hours, and it was another hour before Turk was able to find the narrow, steep arroyo that would lead them to the top.

"We're going to rope ourselves together," Turk said, "with about ten feet of line between a man. I don't want anyone slipping down and breaking his leg or ankle. We've got about two thousand feet before we get to the top. We're all carrying the same weight, so it won't be easy for one man to carry another man's gear. We'll go slow, with a ten-minute rest whenever I think it's necessary. Okay, men, let's get that rope on us and begin to climb." Turk glanced at his watch. It was 2200 hours.

The first few hundred feet weren't at all difficult. There was even some soft sand underfoot amidst the rocks. But then the gradient became steeper, and they were soon climbing hand over hand, grabbing hold of whatever they could to pull themselves up.

Their hands were raw and bleeding by the time Turk called for the first ten-minute break. Each man wiped the sweat from his brow and lay back against the face of the mountain.

"I feel like a goddamn ant trying to make my way up a slippery wall," one of the men commented.

They began to climb again.

Turk forced himself not to think about the pain in his hands, or the ache in his muscles. He thought about Lauren. He also thought about Manuel, and told himself that he'd go back to the grave and put fresh flowers on it. Then all he thought about was reaching the top of the mountain.

Foot by foot the men moved upward. But it was slow going. So slow that it almost seemed to Turk as if he weren't getting any closer to it. His pants and jacket were now torn in several places, and both of his boots were cut along the leg.

"Maybe another hundred feet," he called back to the men.

"A breeze!" answered a trooper facetiously.

Then suddenly one of the men screamed as he slipped and began to fall, dragging the men behind and two men in front of him down until the rest of them, Turk included, grabbed hold of the line, bracing their feet against the rock on which they stood.

Turk nodded wearily, the near disaster averted.

"Any broken bones?" he asked.

Only some bad scrapes and bangs were reported.

"Okay, let's try for the top now," Turk told them. "We can rest once we're up there."

The last thirty or forty feet were straight up. Each man pushed himself upward between two vertical walls.

Turk wiggled his back up one side of the wall and pushing his feet against the other, climbed it as if he were sitting down. "If I ever meet the son of a bitch who drew the map," he told himself, "I'm going to deck the bastard!"

Finally Turk lifted himself onto the top of Angel Mountain. The wind slammed into him, almost bowling him over. But he reached down and pulled the next man up. And that man in turn gave his hand to the man behind him. It took thirty minutes for all of the men to gain the top of the mountain. They were too exhausted to speak and afraid to stand up lest the wind blow them off the mountain. For warmth, they huddled together.

# 19

*December 9, 1941*

Turk needed the rest as much as the other men. Every part of his body ached, and he found it painful to move his hand. He let an hour pass before he spoke to the men in low tones. "We can't stay here," he said. "We're going to have to move out and be ready to hit the Krauts when the general launches his attack at 0630. Between now and then, we have to get into position."

After a long silence, a trooper asked, "Just what position will we have?"

"Anyplace on the west face of the mountain where we can fire from and drop our satchel charges on the Krauts. My guess is that there's a cave in this damn mountain, or the Krauts wouldn't have picked it to make their stand."

The men said nothing.

"Time to move," Turk said. "Let's go." He pulled himself to his feet, picked up his BAR, the satchel charge, and a coil of rope. "C'm'on men."

The men responded by slowly untangling themselves. There was a lot of cursing, but Turk would rather have them mouthing off than silent and angry.

He knew they were aware it might well be the last night of their lives. Even he had difficulty looking squarely at that possibility.

He wanted to go back to Lauren, to know the warmth of her body again, to hear her voice and laughter, just to be with her.

The knifelike wind cut into Turk's thoughts. He bent his body into it and motioned to the men to follow him across the narrow spine of the mountain.

"We're goin' ta be in real trouble," a trooper commented, "if'n we get some clouds comin' our way." And he pointed to the northwest, where the clouds seemed to be lower than across the rest of the sky.

"Clouds or no clouds," Turk said, "we've got to get down, close to where the Krauts are."

"We sure could use some moonlight," another trooper said.

"It's tougher this way, but a hell of a lot safer," Turk answered. "This time of night the moon would be a big round spotlight."

They moved down swiftly. In less than an hour, they had descended more than three quarters of the way down, to where the gradient was so steep it was almost vertical. The only way for them to continue was by rappelling.

"There's enough rope to put each of you about a hundred feet above the Krauts," Turk said. "When we're there, most of us will be dangling from the end of our ropes, but some of you might find a niche in the rock face that'll hold you. Get into it and use it for cover. The rest of you will have to take your chances. Once the shooting begins, go for the rear of those scout cars. They'll go up like torches if you can put a few rounds into their gas tanks." He paused. "If there's a cave, we'll try to blow it. The reason we're here, the only reason, is to knock out their armor and to kill as many Krauts as we can. Any questions?"

"What the fuck is going to happen once the Krauts realize where we are?" a trooper asked.

"They'll try to blow us off the mountain," Turk answered, getting his rope ready for the descent. He put the rope between his legs and brought it back over the left buttock, then in front of him; over and across his chest, and finally over his right shoulder. "You men do what I'm doing with my rope," he said, adjusting the line carefully on his body.

"Don't seem like we're goin' ta have much chance of getting down alive," another man commented.

"Not much," Turk agreed. "Okay, men, spread out and secure your lines to boulders, or whatever else will hold your weight and let's start down." He tied one end of his line to the large mass of rock, and eased himself over the ledge. Working the rope bruised his hands even more than they had already been. He walked carefully down the vertical face. It was slow, arduous work.

He paused to catch his breath and look at the other men. Luckily, all of them were descending at approximately the same rate.

By 300 hours, they were still moving toward the Germans. Turk stopped and looked down. The scout cars were clearly visible; so were the antitank guns and the guards around the perimeter of the position. But the rest of the soldiers weren't anywhere in sight. Turk caught the smell of meat and coffee. There *was* a cave, and the scent of the food was either coming out of its mouth or escaping up through fissures in the rocks.

He started to move again, when suddenly one of the men exclaimed "Ah, fuck it!" Turk stopped. The man had accidentally dropped something.

The next instant the Germans began to shout.

Turk understood what they were saying. "They're

onto us," he yelled. "Let's get down closer, if we can."

A flashlight went on and began to work up the face of the cliff.

"Get that light!" Turk shouted.

A BAR opened up. The light fell to the ground.

Turk was down to the end of the line. He hoped Gripper wouldn't wait, that he'd hit the Germans now.

The Germans began firing at the cliff, but they couldn't see what they were shooting at.

Some of Turk's men fired back.

"Okay," Turk shouted, "let's give them a few grenades." He pulled the pin and threw the grenade down. Several others exploded simultaneously.

"Fire at the scout cars," Turk yelled.

Several bursts slammed into the rear of the cars, but ricocheted off the armor plate with high-pitched *pings*.

Suddenly Turk saw he was less than three feet above a ledge that went for some distance across the face of the cliff. He took a deep breath and let himself fall. His feet struck the ledge. He almost fell over, but managed to throw the weight of his body back and strike the rock wall behind him.

Gripper's machine guns opened up. Moments later the .75 began lobbing shells. They were falling short of the ridge but they frightened the Germans into trying to pull back their armored cars.

Several of Turk's men opened up with their BARs.

One of the armored cars managed to turn around and play its lights on the rock wall. A burst from a BAR killed the lens.

A German machine gun opened up, spraying the rock face. Several men were hit and dropped from their lines.

Turk tossed a grenade at the scout car, but it fell short. He worked his way along the ledge until it was too narrow for him to move any further.

"Get those satchel charges down there," he shouted. Moments later there were several thunderous explosions that sent huge plumes of earth and rock fragments into the air. Turk guessed that a good many of the Germans were still in the cave, afraid to run the risk of being fired upon from the wall.

Gripper had moved his .75 up, and its shells were bursting alone the ridgeline.

Turk could hear the tanks coming toward the German position. "We've got to get those armored cars," he shouted when there was a momentary lull in the firing.

The scout cars were rolling back. They were now close enough to the rock face to come under fire from Turk and his men. A burst for a BAR slashed into the gas tank of one of the armored cars. The explosion brought a sudden rush of heat to where Turk's men were, and the flames cast a reddish light.

The illumination improved, German guns caught some of the men at the end of the ropes and shot them down.

Turk hurried back along the ledge. Bullets bit into the rock above and below him. He glanced down: a group of four men were firing at him. Without pausing, he pulled the pin of a grenade and dropped it on them. The explosion lifted them off the ground and threw their bodies in different directions.

One of the men dangling from the end of a rope managed to get a grenade on top of a scout car. The vehicle burst into flames, turned, and slammed into another armored car, causing that one to explode.

The flames from the burning cars now illuminated the entire area.

Gripper's .75 scored two direct hits, but another armored car turned its cannon and machine gun toward the wall and methodically began to fire.

Turk continued moving along the ledge. A few feet

past the place where he had come down on it, there were two other men. One had been hit in the stomach and was bleeding profusely. The other, a tall, thin, rawboned sergeant, was firing down at the Germans whenever one or more of them tried to run out of the cave.

"The general's tanks are comin' to the ridge," the sergeant said.

Another round from the .75 demolished an armored car.

"I wish to fuck they'd get the bastard that's firing at this wall!" the sergeant exclaimed.

"Maybe they will," Turk answered. "But we sure as hell better not wait around to find out."

"What are we going to do about him?" the sergeant asked, gesturing with his head toward the wounded man.

"No choice," Turk said. "We leave him."

The sergeant nodded, pointed the BAR at the wounded man's head. "Better this way than slow and painful." He squeezed the trigger.

For a few moments neither of them moved; then the sergeant said, "He was a buddy . . . . He'd have done the same for me."

Turk took a deep breath. "Do it for me if I get hit and can't make it out of here."

The sergeant nodded. "We better haul ass, Colonel."

"The ledge seems to slope downward," Turk said, starting off.

"Yeah," the sergeant answered. "Let's hope it goes down close enough for us to make a jump for it, Colonel."

Four jeeps suddenly came over the ridgeline. Their .50's were firing at the wheels of the scout cars.

The Germans in the cars shot back.

One jeep went out of control and turned over. A

second burst into flame and came to a halt. A third crashed into an armored car, burst into flames, and then was rolled on its side by the scout car. But one jeep managed to blow away the tires of two of the armored cars before it disintegrated in a burst of cannon fire from a third car.

"What's your name, Sergeant?" Turk asked without looking back. They were still moving along the ledger.

"Calvin Day. But mostly I'm called Cal."

"Did you see any of our other men, Cal?" Turk asked.

"Two. One guy was in a crevasse, way off to the right of where I was," Cal answered. "I only saw him because he had to stick his head out whenever he fired. And the other guy was beyond him. But he was dead. I saw him fall when he got hit."

"The Krauts have been hurt," Turk said. "Most of their armor is wrecked."

"Maybe," Cal answered, "but the Krauts still have a lot of fight in them."

"That's for sure, but so do we," Turk said.

Gripper's tanks went into action, but within minutes the German antitank guns knocked out four of them.

In the wavering light of the flames, Turk could see that the ledge ended about ten feet from the ground. He and Cal had just about reached it when they were spotted by a gunner on one of the armored cars. They were under fire when the ledge gave way under then and they fell.

Dazed, Turk started to stand, but Cal grabbed hold of him. "Play dead, or that cocksucker will open up again."

Neither one moved.

After a couple of minutes, the armored car started to turn around.

"Let's get the fucker now!" Turk said.

"With you," Cal answered. The two of them dashed forward. From a distance of ten feet, each threw a grenade under the vehicle. The force of the explosion turned the car on its side. But it did not explode. The top hatch door opened and the first man bolted out.

Turk waited until all four men were free of the car, then he cut them down with a burst from the BAR.

The area between the rock wall and ridge was strewn with wrecked and burning vehicles, dead and wounded men.

Gripper's .75 finally knocked out the antitank guns but not before they had destroyed all but two of Gripper's tanks.

Most of the fighting now was between the men.

Suddenly one of the remaining tanks blew up and the second lost a tread, forcing it to come to a stop and be abandoned.

None of the German armored cars were able to move, though some of them could still fire their guns.

The .75 was brought onto the ridge, to the west of the cave. Before it could fire, a German grenade killed its crew.

Covering each other, Turk and Cal fought their way to where they thought some troopers were. When they found the troopers, all of them were dead.

A sudden burst of fire caused Turk and Cal to bellyflop. Eight German soldiers were bearing down on them.

Cal opened fire. His burst killed two and drove the others back.

Turk threw a grenade. Then he and Cal rushed them. Firing in short bursts, they killed the remainder of the small group.

Despite the wind, the air was now filled with the stench of burning flesh and rubber.

The volume of small-arms fire diminished. From the

sound, the fighting had moved off to the far right, and Turk and Cal headed that way.

They passed the mouth of the cave. "Better make sure," Turk said.

"I only got two grenades left," Cal said.

"Same," Turk answered. He was almost too weary to speak. His throat was dry and the smoke made his eyes tear. "Let's each use one of them."

They pulled the pins together. Cal let his grenade fly first; Turk's immediately followed. The two explosions came within moments of each other. Then there was a huge secondary explosion from inside the cave that lit it up with a white incandescence. A powerful blast of hot air knocked them off their feet.

The mouth of the cave collapsed as a large portion of the rock face came crashing down. Rocks rained down around them and a large cloud of dust caused the two men to break into spasms of coughing. When they could, they scrambled to their feet and ran.

The firing was random now. Then it ceased altogether.

Turk looked up. Against the lightened sky, the empty ropes were clearly visible.

"A graveyard," Turk said in a whisper. "A fucking graveyard." He paused to take a swig of water from his canteen and spit it out.

"Company!" Cal said, leveling his weapon toward the two men emerging from behind a burning armored car. "I got a few rounds left."

Turk reached out and pushed the barrel of Cal's BAR down toward the ground. "The hell with orders. No need to kill them, even if they're Krauts. The fight is over." Then he called out, "Halt and identify yourself!" He was about to repeat the words in German, when one of the men answered. "I'm General Edward Gripper. With me is Lieutenant John Hawkins. Who are you?"

"Doug!" Turk shouted. "The man with me is Sergeant Calvin Day."

The four men ran toward each other.

"We heard that tremendous explosion," Gripper said, "and figured it was either the work of one of our guys, or a Kraut."

"My guess," Turk answered, "is that Becker had enough ammo there to hold out for a least a week."

They spoke in low tones. As they made their way to the ridgeline, the sun was just coming up over Angel Mountain. Most of the sky in the east was clear of clouds, but in the west, running north and south, there were still dark-gray clouds.

Turk looked back over the battlefield. Practically all of the vehicles were still burning, and there were bodies everywhere, many twisted into obscene positions by the sudden death visited upon them.

"Didn't think I'd even see you alive again," Gripper told Turk. "What caused you to start shooting early?"

"One of the men dropped his satchel charge, and that tipped the Germans off to what was happening."

"If I had been in Becker's place," Gripper commented, "I wouldn't have figured on getting hit from above."

Turk was too tired to reply.

"I left the communications jeep back where we were bivouacked," Gripper said, gesturing out in front of them. "It's behind the hill."

The four of them walked slowly. Turk slipped his hand into his pocket and closed it around the silver medallion Lauren had given him.

"Thank God the wind died down," Cal remarked. "When the sun moves higher, it will warm up. We could use some warmth."

When they reached the jeep, Hawkins and Cal dropped down on the ground and stretched out.

"Better stand by," Ed told Turk as he switched on the radio and called Hanahan.

"What the fuck is going on out there?" Hanahan shouted.

"Patch me through to General Marshall," Ed said in a harsh, precise voice.

"Goddamn it, Gripper. . . ."

"General," Ed said, keeping his voice steady, "I want to speak to General Marshall now!"

"Hold on," Hanahan said with an audible sigh of disgust.

Several minutes passed before Marshall came on.

"It's over," Ed said. "The operation is over."

"That's damn good news," Marshall answered. "Damn good, General."

"Request permission to return to Fort Bliss," Gripper said.

"How many casualties?" Marshall asked.

"Including myself," Gripper answered, "there are only four survivors."

"Good God, you mean we lost the entire force?"

"Yes."

Marshall cleared his throat. "I want you to move a few miles from your present position. Give me a set of coordinates, and before nightfall a light plane will come in for you and the others."

"Hold a few moments, General," Ed said. He asked Turk to pick out a set of coordinates for him.

"Dog eight," Turk said. "Tell Marshall we're using a geological survey map of the area dated January 7, 1929.

Gripper relayed the information.

"Any of the men with you wounded?" Marshall

asked.

"Negative. We have some bad bruises, but no bullet or shrapnel wounds."

"Ed, you and your men did a one hell of a job," Marshall said.

"Thank you, sir," Ed answered, "but the men who deserve your thanks are dead. They stopped the Krauts. I'm honored to have been with them." His throat tightened, and unable to speak, he handed the mike to Turk.

"General," Turk said, "this is Colonel Douglas Turk. General Gripper is unable—"

"I understand," Marshall told him. "Over."

"Roger," Turk said, and put the mike down.

Ed used the back of his hands to wipe away the tears. "The only damn thing I can think of are those words in the Gettysburg Address, . . . 'they gave the last full measure of devotion.' They did, Doug. They sure as hell did!"

Neither Turk nor Ed realized that Hawkins and Cal were on their feet until Hawkins commented. "If this is what the war is going to be like, it's going to be hell from start to finish."

"It's going to be hell all right," Turk said, "because we can't afford to lose. No matter what it costs, the Germans must be beaten. If they're not, if we lose and they become our masters, then civilization as we know it will no longer exist. We'll be plunged into a dark age from which mankind may never again have the chance to emerge." It wasn't exactly what Turk had intended to say, but once he had started to speak the words had come tumbling out. His experience had shown him what the Germans were capable of doing: He had seen them do it in Spain, in Poland, and in France. "I'm sorry," he apologized. "I didn't mean to make a speech."

"It's the truth," Ed said. "It's the goddamn truth."

Cal pointed toward the ridge. "Those fuckin' buzzards are already there."

A large flock of them were flying in a wide circle above the ridge.

Hawkins raised his rifle and squeezed off several shots. Two birds fell.

"Waste of good ammo," Turk said.

"I hate those fucking birds," Hawkins answered.

Turk nodded, put his hand on the lieutenant's shoulder. "The buzzards didn't kill the men. They're just doing what buzzards do. We did the killing. We and the Krauts."

Hawkins nodded.

"Let's saddle up," Ed said. "We have a ten-mile walk to the pick-up area, and it's going to be a long ten miles.

"A very long ten miles," Turk added, aware of his own exhaustion.

## 20

The President, the Chiefs of Staff, Secretary of State Cordell Hull, Secretary of War Henry L. Stimson, Presidential aide Harry Hopkins, and an officer from the Army and Navy Intelligence units were assembled around the large, elliptical, highly polished mahogany table in the situation room. On the table, within easy reach of the President, were several newly installed phones that could put him in communication with anyone he chose to speak to in this country or abroad.

The table was covered with several large maps of the Hawaiian Islands, the Philippines, and Southeast Asia. But directly in front of the President was a detailed topographical map of the area of southeast Texas and southeast New Mexico.

For several minutes Roosevelt studied the map in silence. Then, removing his glasses, he rubbed the bridge of his nose as he looked up. "Gentlemen," he said in a quiet voice, "I summoned you here this morning to inform you that the German strike force has been completely destroyed."

A burst of applause came from the men around the table.

Roosevelt let a few moments lapse; then he raised his right hand. "Out of the original American force of fifteen hundred men, there are only four survivors. Think about that, gentlemen. Four survivors!"

The men at the table remained silent.

"Marshall has put together the facts for me about how it was possible for the Germans to assemble the men and equipment to do what they did. Believe me, gentlemen, those facts are beyond belief. Our British allies unwittingly helped the Germans by not sharing certain information with us, part of which oddly enough went to them from our own FBI via a New York City police detective."

"Excuse me, Mr. President," Marshall said pointedly. "If the FBI had shared that information with military intelligence, we might have been able to determine what the Germans were up to and notify them that we were ready for them."

"But we weren't ready, George," Roosevelt said. "We couldn't have been ready unless we had taken those sixty thousand troops involved in the war games down there and placed them squarely in front of the German column." Roosevelt paused to fit a cigarette into the black holder, and when he finished lighting up, he continued. "We must develop an intelligence network second to none, and we must convince our allies to share their intelligence with us."

There were a number of verbal approvals from the men at the table.

"But my reason for summoning you here has to do with a more immediate problem, which, gentlemen, simply stated, is: What are we going to do with the four survivors?"

"Pardon me, Mr. President," Hull said, "but I don't understand the question."

"Harry," Roosevelt said, "will you clarify it?"

Hopkins leaned forward. "What the President means," Hopkins told them, "is that we cannot afford to let any word about this battle come out. We must cover it up completely. As far as we are concerned, it never happened."

"But how can we do that?" Admiral King asked. "Too many men were involved."

Captain Grimes from Naval Intelligence raised his hand.

"Go ahead, Captain," Roosevelt said, then added, "I want a freewheeling discussion here. Please don't wait to be recognized by me or anyone else at this table. I will make my decision after hearing all of you."

"In my considered opinion," Captain Grimes said in a marked Southern accent, "it would be impossible to keep the men silent. It is our recommendation to the President they be killed."

"Are you insane?" Marshall shouted.

"I, for one," Stimson said, "prefer not to continue this discussion, if certain individuals—"

"Mr. Secretary," Captain Grimes interrupted, "we are in a life-and-death struggle with the enemy. We are convinced that within days Germany will declare war on us, and we will answer that with a declaration of war against them. If by sacrificing four men to prevent our people from panicking—and they are close to panic now over what happened at Pearl Harbor and what is happening in the Philippines—then I suggest that the sacrifice is well worth it.

"We cannot allow Germany to capitalize on the fact they were able to invade the United States. They were willing to sacrifice a thousand men to prove their point. Another four men added to the losses we have already sustained is not such a high price to pay to keep this whole episode buried."

"What's going to stop the Germans from telling the world about their incursion?" Hull asked.

"Their force was destroyed," Colonel Gammell of

Army Intelligence said, "and we're not crowing about its destruction. Now, it seems to me that they have nothing to gain by telling anyone about it. They achieved nothing. They were defeated. They wouldn't want their people to know that—not with their reversals in Russia and Africa."

Roosevelt looked toward Marshall. "What security measures have you taken thus far to keep this matter under wraps?"

"A woman by the name of Lauren Zwig and a man named Louis Dijon have been taken into custody and are being held at the William Beaumont Army Hospital. They are being kept under sedation."

"How could two civilians have any knowledge of the matter?" Hopkins asked.

Marshall explained the relation of Lauren and Louis to Colonel Douglas Turk. "And," he said, "Mrs. Zwig was married to a German agent working out of Mexico City. The agent has subsequently killed himself."

"Would you recommend that Mrs. Zwig and Mr. Dijon also be killed?" Hopkins asked, fixing his gaze on Captain Grimes.

"Yes," the captain answered.

"Mr. President," Marshall said, ignoring the exchange that had just taken place, "I have issued the following orders: All personnel, with the exception of Generals Hanahan, Fitzhugh, and Alt, who have direct knowledge of the action have had orders cut transferring them to our units in the Philippines, or to temporary duty with British units in Africa and Southeast Asia. These transfers are effective immediately and without leave in the States. I have also ordered Generals Hanahan, Fitzhugh, and Alt to treat the entire matter as top-secret, and I have ordered them back to Washington. I have ordered General Gripper, Colonel Turk, Lieutenant Hawkins, and Sergeant Day disarmed, to be taken by plane to Biggs Air Force Base, then by ambulance under armed guard to the psychiatric section of the William Beaumont Hospital—where they will be kept until it is decided what to do with them."

Roosevelt placed his cigarette holder in the groove of a nearby ashtray. "I agree," he said, after a long silence. "We can't have any information about this—this action get out to the public. And I also agree that the Germans will remain silent about it because they can't call it a victory. In no small way, it's a defeat. It will not keep us out of the war in Europe. It has made it clearer than ever where our effort must be concentrated. We must destroy Germany. But as to the question at hand, I disagree about what we should do with the survivors."

"So do I," Marshall commented. "They deserve more from us than their deaths."

"Do you want to handle it?" Roosevelt asked.

"Yes, Mr. President," Marshall answered. "I'd much prefer to handle it myself."

Roosevelt smiled. "It's yours," he said. "Including Mrs. Zwig and Dijon. You know what the stakes are and what could happen if something goes wrong?"

Marshall nodded.

"The subject is closed," Roosevelt said. "Now, gentlemen, let's get on to other business. We've got a war to win."

Admiral Canaris was physically and emotionally exhausted, but he couldn't sleep. He listened to the wind-driven rain beat against the window of the room he occupied on the upper story of the German embassy in Madrid. His mission to enlist Franco's active participation in the war had failed. But Canaris had know it would, even before he had left Berlin. He had even told

Hitler that the Spanish Army lacked guns, tanks, and planes, and that it, like the rest of the country, was exhausted from the civil war and needed years to recover. Hitler had wanted Franco to attack and capture Gibraltar, for if Spain held Gibraltar, then all of the Mediterranean would be sealed off.

Canaris got out of bed and went into the adjoining bathroom to get a pill to help him sleep. It was the second pill he had taken in the last three hours. The doctor had warned him that three were the absolute limit within the space of eight hours.

A soft knock at the bedroom door brought his attention to it. "Yes," he answered. "What is it?"

"A message from Hamburg, sir," the man on the other side of the door answered.

Canaris turned on the light and opened the door. He was handed a sheet of paper folded three times. He nodded and stepped back into the room, closing the door behind him.

He put on his glasses, unfolded the paper, and began to read:

*For Admiral Canaris from Ziegler, Mexico City—ZIMMERMANN IS DEAD. NO DETAILS AVAILABLE.*

Canaris folded the piece of paper; then began to tear it into very small pieces He crossed the room to the fireplace and dropped them onto the red, glowing log. They instantly burst into flame.

# 21

*December 10, 1941*

After they arrived at the William Beaumont Army Hospital and went through a physical examination, they showered, shaved, and were given clean uniforms, It wasn't until the four of them were escorted by half a dozen armed guards to the room they were going to occupy that they realized something was wrong.

Turk make an attempt to speak to the guards, but none of the six men escorting them would answer him.

Suddenly stopping, Cal said, "I'm not going anywhere until I'm told what the fuck is going on!"

That brought a quick answer from the sergeant in charge of the guard detail. "You go, soldier, or we make you go. You can walk on your own two feet or be carried in."

"Better walk," Ed said.

"General—"

"Forget the rank," Ed answered. "My name is Edward. But guys like Doug call me Ed."

"Okay, Ed, why can't you speak to the commandant of the hospital," Cal suggested, "and find out what the hell is going on?"

"It wouldn't do any good," Ed answered. "The orders

to do this to us come from somewhere near the top. Maybe even from the top."

The four of them were placed in a large room with barred windows overlooking a green slope of grass that ended where the slope steepened and became brown rock.

There were four hospital beds, two on each wall. Next to each bed was a night table with a lamp and a radio, an ashtray, and a pack of cigarettes with a book of matches.

"I guess if we have to take a piss or a crap," John said, "we knock on the door and get a guard to escort us."

Turk pointed to a door. "That's probably the bathroom."

Ed opened it. "That's what it is, all right," he said.

Turk went over to one of the radios and switched it on. "Might as well find out what's happening in the rest of the world."

"Right now," Cal said, "I honestly don't give a damn about the rest of the world. I want to know what the fuck is happening here to us."

Turk turned the dial. None of the stations were playing anything other than music. He looked at his watch. "Probably get the news on the hour or half-hour," he commented.

The door to the room swung open and a cart with hot food was wheeled in by a male orderly. Two of the armed guards accompanied him.

"Every knife and fork has been counted," one of the guards said. "If the same number are not returned, the room will be searched and then each man will be individually searched."

Cal was going to say something but Turk waved him silent. When the four of them were alone again, Turk said, "Not worth your time or effort to blow off at him or any of the guards. They're just carrying out their orders. My guess is that they don't even know who the hell we are, and most assuredly they don't know why we're here." He gestured to the food. "Let's chow up and relax!"

"There's not a fuck of a lot else we can do," Hawkins commented.

After they ate, they slept. In the late afternoon, they were brought newspapers and magazines, and were told they could have whatever books they wanted if they were in the hospital library.

"But how are we supposed to know what books are there?" Turk asked.

"If it's there, you'll get it. If it's not, you won't get it," the orderly said and left.

The newspaper carried a story about an Army pilot named Colin P. Kelly who had dove his plane into a Japanese battleship after being hit by antiaircraft fire from the ship.

At five o'clock Ed turned on his radio. The men gathered close-by.

The war news was extremely grim. The Philippines had been invaded and the Japanese were forcing the American forces back on all fronts.

After the newscast, there wasn't anything for them to say to one another.

# 22

*December 11, 1941*

The following morning they slept late, and the day passed very slowly. The news that Germany had officially declared war on the United States didn't mean much to Turk or the other men. They had already been blooded by the Germans.

Turk's own anger was building up and it was obvious to him that so was everyone else's.

"This shouldn't be happening to us," Hawkins said. "For the love of God we fought a damn good fight!"

"We did," Turk commented. "We sure as hell did!"

During the afternoon, Ed came over to Turk and said, "I never did have the opportunity to tell you how much spunk I think Lauren has. She's okay. Hell, more than okay, in my book."

"In mine, too," Turk answered. He was trying not to think about her until he knew more about what was going to happen to him. He didn't want to make himself more miserable.

"If you don't have anyone else, I'd be proud to stand as best man," Ed said.

"I was going to ask you to," Turk replied. "And I'll have John and Cal stand as witnesses. . . . Either of

you guys have girls?"
"Sure," Hawkins answered. "Back home in Pittsburgh."
"What about you, Cal? Have you got a girl?" Ed asked.
Cal laughed and said, "I got several in Juárez—black-eyed, black-haired señoritas, who give the best lays and blow-jobs in the damn world."
The other men laughed.
"Listen, I've—"
The door suddenly opened and one of the guards called out, "A'ten-'hut!"
The men in the room bounded to attention.
"At ease, men," General Marshall. "At ease." He turned toward the open door. "Please, Mrs. Zwig and Mr. Dijon, will you come in?"
Lauren stepped into the room, saw Turk, uttered a small cry of surprise, and ran into his outstretched arms. "Oh, thank God," she whispered. "Thank God you're alive!"
Marshall told the guard to close the door; then he took off his coat and cap and threw them across Turk's bed. "I would have been here earlier today," he explained, "but because we are now officially at war with Germany, I was detained in Washington an hour longer than I expected. Then on the flight down here we encountered bad weather over Dallas." He asked all of them to sit down in a semicircle around him. "First, I want to tell each of you men that you did a magnificent job out there. You too, Mr. Dijon, I was told you flew a recon mission for us."
Dijon nodded. "But it came up negative."
Marshall smiled. "Thanks just the same." Then he took a few moments to light a cigarette and suggested, "Anyone else who wants to smoke, please do."
Turk and Hawkins lit up.

"Let's get down to business," Marshall said. "First, I didn't come here to glad-hand you men. I came here to tell you that you have an important choice to make."

"We're listening," Ed responded.

Marshall explained the state of the country. ". . . and we don't have anything to fight back with at this time. We have men, but not enough of them are trained. You know better than anyone else that what we can put into the field isn't equal to what the Germans have. If word about the German invasion becomes common knowledge, the people will panic. They won't be able to take it, not after the catastrophe at Pearl Harbor."

None of them took issue with that.

"You men were in the desert fighting the Germans. All the other men who fought them are dead. Everyone—with the exception of Generals Hanahan, Fitzhugh and Alt—who had any knowledge of what was happening has been reassigned. And just to be on the safe side, I issued several bulletins that will be released tomorrow saying that we have been conducting maneuvers down here with real German equipment that was captured and sent here by the British, and that German was spoken by the bogus enemy force to allow the men in the units fighting them to hear the sound of the language. As of eight hours ago the two areas where you sustained your heaviest casualties have been sealed off. They will, as soon as possible, be heavily bombed. Nothing, but absolutely nothing, will remain out there. Our casualties will be reported from the Philippines, making it seem that they died fighting the Japanese."

"Are there any questions?" Marshall asked after he had taken a deep drag on the cigarette.

"Where do we fit into all of this?" Turk asked.

"I need your word that for the rest of your lives none of you will say anything about what happened here. If you can't give it to me, well . . ." He glanced around the room. "You will be well-treated here. But you have my word that none of you will ever get out, at least not alive."

"Not much of a choice, is there, General?" Ed responded.

"Even less than is immediately apparent," Marshall answered. "I must have a guarantee from each of you, or none of you will get out."

"What will happen to us if we get out?" Dijon asked.

"Ed, Doug, Cal, and Hawkins are in the Army; they'll continue to be in the Army. As for Louis—"

"I was thinking of joining the American Air Force," Dijon said.

"I can easily arrange that," Marshall told him. "Probably get you commissioned a captain."

"What about me?" Lauren asked.

Marshall's eyes twinkled. "You'll be Mrs. Douglas Turk, won't you?"

"Yes," Lauren answered. "And I'll be with him as long as I'm able."

"Is there anything else we should know?" Turk asked.

Marshall nodded. "You'll be watched. Should you suddenly feel the need to tell someone about the Germans you fought in the Southwest, you will be killed, either outright—by that I mean gunned down—or you will have a fatal accident. Whichever way is more expeditious at the particular time."

Lauren gasped.

"You sure gave it to us," Hawkins said.

"There are those who would have killed you by now," Marshall answered. "But you didn't survive fighting the Germans to be killed by your own people. That's not what this war is all about, at least in my opinion. But we are at war and the American people are frightened, so frightened that they see a Japanese invasion fleet where there are only our fishing boats. Should they find out about the German incursion—well, the panic it would cause would give the Japanese an excellent reason for putting men ashore on the West Coast. That's something that we can't risk, even if it means killing the six of you."

"You have my word, General," Gripper said.

"And mine, too," Hawkins added.

"And mine," Turk said.

"Mine," Cal responded.

"Mine, too," Lauren told him.

"And mine," Dejon said.

"Thank you," Marshall responded. "Thank you for what you have done and for what you have just given me. Now, if you will follow me, we'll spend an hour or two over an early dinner. There are some things I can do for each of you to show this country's gratitude and, you have my word, I will do them."

"An early dinner sounds fine to me," Gripper said.

"Damn good!" Cal exclaimed.

"Dinner is a hell of a lot better when you're a free man," Turk commented as he stood up and took hold of Lauren's hand.

"That, gentlemen," Marshall said, "is what we're fighting for: to remain free men and women!"

# Epilogue

*August, 1985*

A large mahogany conference table in the center of the room was littered with containers of coffee and several ashtrays filled with stubbed-out cigarettes. Despite the air-conditioner, the room smelled of smoke. Directly in back of the chief's desk the large window was painted gray with twilight. And the white fluorescent ceiling light was already on.

Turk leaned forward and rested his hands on the table. "That's what happened," he said, looking at Mr. John Gillin, chief of the southwest district of the NSA.

"That's it," Gripper said from across the table, where Estaban was also seated.

Estaban and Lauren had been picked up by two other agents, and were in the office by the time Turk and Gripper had arrived.

Turk turned to Lauren and took hold of her hand. "Can you remember anything else?" he asked gently.

She shook her head.

Gillin, an owlish-looking man of medium height, with gray hair and a gray mustache, removed his glasses and rubbed the top of his nose. "Twenty years ago there was a fire in one of our national record vaults," he said. "Very little that was in the vault was saved. Perhaps a dozen folders at the very most. In one of them we found information about the 'Zimmermann Plot.' We didn't have any idea what the hell it was all about until recently, when some government people went out into the desert to survey a site for a new missile installation and found a German helmet and several other things that shouldn't have been there." He paused and picked up the container of tepid coffee in front of him. After a few sips, he put the container down and said, "We reported the find to the President, who directed me to find out why those German artifacts were there."

"You mean no one in the government knew?" Gripper asked.

"No one," Gillin said. "We were able to identify the markings on the helmet, and discovered the unit had seen action in North Africa. There were also several references in the German files that it had been sent to Mexico. But these were at best ambiguous."

"I'm surprised there were even those," Turk said. "My guess is that only two or three people at the very most in the German High Command had any knowledge of the operation."

Gillin nodded.

"Where does Pike come in?" Turk asked.

"He's one of ours," Gillin answered.

"So we were told when your men arrested us," Turk said.

"He was just doing his job," Gillin answered.

"We didn't kill him," Turk said. "I came here to buy the helmet, and the general joined me because he was curious."

"And what did you intend to do with the helmet?" Gillin questioned.

"Photograph it and use it in an article I was going to write about the—"

"You can't do that!" Gillin exclaimed.

Turk took a deep breath and slowly exhaled. According to the clock on the wall, he had been in custody for four hours and had been talking for at least three of them. He was very tired, and Lauren and Gripper looked even more tired than he felt.

"Look," Turk said, "we can discuss that later. What I want now is to know exactly what is going to happen to us."

Gillin picked up the phone, struck three numbers with his forefinger, and said, "It's time." Then he put the phone down and took several more sips of coffee.

The door opened.

Turk turned. "Pike!" he exclaimed. He turned toward Gillin. "What the hell is going on?"

"Agent Pike was just doing his job," Gillin said.

"Then all of this—"

"We had to find out what had happened out there, and now we know."

"So the advertisement was just bait!" Gripper exclaimed.

"Bait," Gillin agreed. "We figured that someone who knew what the markings on the helmet meant would answer the ad. You, Turk, seemed more intensely interested than anyone else who answered. You were so interested that you were willing to come down to El Paso and see the other things that Pike said he had found in the desert."

"You're telling me I was suckered in?"

Gillin nodded.

Turk looked at Gripper, then at Lauren and Estaban. "I'm sorry," he said. "I'm sorry I—"

"There wasn't any way for you to know that you were

being set up," Gillin said.

"But why couldn't you come directly to me or Gripper and ask us about it?" Turk questioned. "It would have been a lot simpler than doing it the way you did."

"Simpler, yes," Gillin answered. "But this way we're sure we have the right information. Until Pike walked in, you had no idea whether or not you would be charged for his murder. Given that kind of sword over your head, I was sure you'd tell us what we wanted to know."

Turk pursed his lips. "Then there's no charge against us?" he asked.

"None. You're free to go," Gillin answered.

Turk was angry. He put his hands on the table. "I am going to write about it," he said.

"Leave well enough alone," Lauren cautioned.

Turk shook his head. "I don't like what has happened to us today. I don't like being threatened. I don't like being accused of a staged murder. And most of all, I don't like the fact that you brought my wife and friend here, when neither of them had anything to do with—"

Gillin help up his hand. "Whatever I did, was done in the interest of national security."

"Bullshit!" Turk exclaimed.

"I can only warn you," Gillin said, "that the NSA would not appreciate seeing anything print about the German attack or the events of this afternoon."

Turk smiled. "Whatever I will write," Turk said, "I will write in the interest of keeping the first amendment of the Constitution alive." He stood up. "Come," he said, motioning to Lauren. "They got what they wanted; now it's time to let the American people know what really happened down here."

Lauren, Estaban, and Gripper stood up.

"No one will believe you," Gillin said.

"Maybe not," Turk answered. "But at least the story will be known. I can't make anyone believe it; I can only write it." Then turning to the others, he said, "Let's get out of here and go someplace where we can drink, eat, and celebrate our freedom."

**THE SURVIVALIST SERIES**
by Jerry Ahern

| | |
|---|---|
| #1: TOTAL WAR | (0960, $2.50) |
| #2: THE NIGHTMARE BEGINS | (0810, $2.50) |
| #3: THE QUEST | (0851, $2.50) |
| #4: THE DOOMSAYER | (0893, $2.50) |
| #5: THE WEB | (1145, $2.50) |
| #6: THE SAVAGE HORDE | (1232, $2.50) |
| #7: THE PROPHET | (1339, $2.50) |
| #8: THE END IS COMING | (1374, $2.50) |
| #9: EARTH FIRE | (1405, $2.50) |
| #10: THE AWAKENING | (1478, $2.50) |
| #11: THE REPRISAL | (1590, $2.50) |
| #12: THE REBELLION | (1676, $2.50) |